e

Matt Beaumont

HarperCollins*Publishers*

HarperCollins*Publishers*
77–85 Fulham Palace Road,
Hammersmith, London W6 8JB

www.**fire**and**water**.com

A Paperback Original 2000
1 3 5 7 9 8 6 4 2

A catalogue record for this book
is available from the British Library

ISBN 0 00 710068 X

Set in PostScript Linotype Minion by
Rowland Phototypesetting Ltd,
Bury St Edmunds, Suffolk

Printed and bound in Great Britain by
Clays Ltd, St Ives plc

Ave Maria

Monday
3 January
2000

David Crutton – 3/1/00, 8.13am
to... Fiona Craigie
cc...
re... your butt

Take that fucking Walkman off, get your arse in here and show me how I do an all-staff e-mail. Every time I click 'ok' on the address it copies it to Miller Shanks Helsinki.

David Crutton – 3/1/00, 8.27am
to... All Departments
cc... james_f_weissmuller@millershanks-ny.co.usa
re... NEW MILLENNIUM – NEW HEIGHTS

First, a happy new Millennium to each and every one of you. Thank you also for sacrificing your bank holidays today to come in and begin the bid for the Coca-Cola business. As you know, in two weeks we pitch for this most prestigious advertising account. To win it we must all perform out of our skins.

Daunting as it may seem, I know we can scale this peak. Those in doubt should take a look at what we have achieved in the last twelve months. When I joined you at the beginning of '99 we were in the doldrums and Jim Weissmuller in New York gave me a mountain to climb.

He said 'make Miller Shanks London big again'. Pitch wins for Freedom Catalogues, the LOVE Channel and the £11m Mako Cars account have catapulted us back into the *Campaign* top twenty for the first time in eight years.

He said 'make Miller Shanks respected'. In the *Marketing Week* survey that asked clients which advertising agency they would most like to work with, we rocketed from 45th to 33rd.

He said 'win awards'. I brought in Simon Horne to shake up the creative department and to do just that. His efforts are already paying off, with Pinki and Liam's fabulous ads for Kimbelle Sanpro scooping bronze at Creative Circle.

We can all be extremely proud of our efforts. We are still a long way from the summit, but base camp has been established and the final assault beckons!

Let's break camp, attach our lines and get off to a flier in 2000 by adding an $84 billion brand to our client list.

Go, go, go!

David Crutton
CEO

pertti_vanhelden@millershanks-helsinki.co.fin
3/1/00, 8.46am (10.46am local)
to... david_crutton@millershanks-london.co.uk
cc...
re... NEW MILLENNIUM – NEW HEIGHTS

Your e-mail I think is coming to me in Helsinki by mistake, but it's notwithstanding fun to be reading about my chums in London. I was not realising that mountaineering was possible in Old London Town. Most fascinating!

By the way, is there any help we give you with the Coca-Cola pitch? It is a very popular drink here in icy cold Finland, especially with our many 'groovy' young folk. As fellow CEO, I am asking my red-hot creativity department to have lots of brilliant ideas for you.

While I am on cyberspacenet, can please you get me tickets for *Great Balls of Grease?* Mrs van Helden and my good self will be visiting in London at 12 February. We will be packing our crampons.

Your pal, ~~Pertti~~

David Crutton – 3/1/00, 8.49am
to... Fiona Craigie
cc...
re... your fat butt

Get your fucking nose out of *Ms London* and explain why, despite your best efforts, my last e-mail went to that pathetic twat, van Helden. And get me two tickets for *Great Balls of Fire* or *Grease* on 12 Feb. I don't think the gobshite Finn knows the difference.

Daniel Westbrooke – 3/1/00, 9.17am
to... All Departments
cc...
re... a new face

I would like you all to join me in welcoming Katie Philpott, who joins us today as a trainee account executive. Katie will be working in Harriet Greenbaum's group on Mako. She will add her spark and vivacity to an already lively team. Please give her the warmest of Miller Shanks welcomes.

Daniel Westbrooke
Head of Client Services

Rachel Stevenson – 3/1/00, 10.10am

to... All Departments
cc...
re... changes

Sadly, Fiona Craigie has decided to leave us and is no longer David Crutton's PA. I am sure you will join me in wishing her well for the future. Lorraine Pallister will be temping until a permanent replacement arrives. Please make her welcome.

Rachel Stevenson
Personnel

Simon Horne – 3/1/00, 10.14am

to... Creative Department
cc... David Crutton; Daniel Westbrooke
re... arses in gear

You will need no reminding of the Coke pitch. This is the big one.

Excalibur.

The Holy Grail.

Eldorado.

The Most Famous Brand in the World.

David Crutton and Dan Westbrooke will brief us at noon in the boardroom.

Be keen.

Be sharp.

Be clever.

Above all, be there.

Si

Daniel Westbrooke – 3/1/00, 10.18am
to... Simon Horne
cc...
re... arses in gear

Simon, I know this might be a silly little thing, so excuse my pedantry. I do not mind you calling me Dan in private, but to the great unwashed, please refer to me as Daniel. The diminutive sounds far too familiar and, as Head of Client Services, I find it pays to remain a little aloof from the rabble! See you at 12.00.

Daniel Westbrooke – 3/1/00, 10.22 am
to... James Gregory
cc...
re... Katie Philpott

James, my duties as Head of Client Services mean that I am far too busy to bestow upon young Katie my traditional welcome of tea and muffins. Since you are the account manager with whom she will be working most closely, may I request that you take her under your wing and make sure that she is familiar with our ways? Suffice it to say that I would not wish a repeat of what happened with the last trainee.

Simon Horne – 3/1/00, 10.30 am
to... Susi Judge-Davis
cc...
re... Coke

Susi, darling, be an absolute treasure and make sure all the creative teams are aware of the Coke briefing at 12.00. And get me a pot of decaffeinated and some of those itty-bitty cinnamon biscuits they have in the kitchen.

Susi Judge-Davis – 3/1/00, 10.31 am
to... Simon Horne
cc...
re... Coke

Doing it right now, darling ... Sx

pertti_vanhelden@millershanks-helsinki.co.fin
3/1/00, 10.32 am (12.32 pm local)
to... david_crutton@millershanks-london.co.uk
cc...
re... your butt

We are loving your ironicalism. 'Pathetic twat, van Helden'! There is nothing to beat English humours. *Robin's Nest, Love Thy Neighbour, Are You Being Severed?*. We see them all on Satellite Golden Hits Station. However, we are not comprehending 'gobshite'. It is in not one of our excellent dictionaries.

'I'm free!' – Pertti

Daniel Westbrooke – 3/1/00, 10.35am
to... Katie Philpott
cc...
re... bienvenue

Katie, profound apologies that I will be unable to sit down with you this morning. You have joined our happy family at the busiest time and I find myself caught up in getting the Coke pitch off to a roaring start. I am sure that you must feel a little dazzled by the glamour of it all, but you will find your feet in no time. I have attached a crib sheet that sets out the key roles in our agency. Previous neophytes have found it to be indispensable. Any questions, ask James Gregory, whom I have appointed your 'big brother'.

 Attachment ...

CHIEF EXECUTIVE OFFICER – *il maestro, le chef de cuisine*, the head honcho and the person with whom the buck most certainly stops.

HEADS OF CLIENT SERVICES – the power behind the throne, if you will. Custodian of all the agency's clients and responsible for the performance of everybody in the Account Management Department. A crucial part of his job is to approve every CREATIVE BRIEF before it goes to the Creative Department. These unassuming A4 sheets are the 'sacred texts' without which no piece of advertising can be conceived. It is fair to say that with such a spectrum of responsibilities, a head of client services must possess both fierce drive and a passionate vision.

ACCOUNT DIRECTOR – In charge of day-to-day running of one or more accounts; runs a team of account managers and executives; in turn reports to the Head of Client Services.

EXECUTIVE CREATIVE DIRECTOR – if the Head of Client Services supplies the client with an expansive blank canvas, then the Creative Director applies those vivid splashes of cobalt, verditer and vermilion that bring his humdrum products so gloriously to life in the nation's parlours.

THE CREATIVE TEAM – each comprises of a COPYWRITER and an ART DIRECTOR. The Creative Director allocates creative briefs to teams, and then nurtures from them their finest work.

James Gregory – 3/1/00, 10.36am
to... Katie Philpott
cc...
re... hello, new girl

Hi Katie. I'm James and I'll be your account manager on Mako. Dan Westbrooke has asked me to keep a close eye on you. I'm up to my neck organising this afternoon's Mako meeting (usual bloody panic), but I'll clock in with you later. In the meantime, enjoy reading the attached. It was penned by some anon. copywriter and has been handed down through generations of trainees. It tells you all you need to know about how your typical agency works (or rather, doesn't).

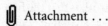 Attachment ...

CHIEF EXECUTIVE OFFICER – some CEOs have been known to have a brass sign on their desks that reads THE BUCK STOPS HERE. This is either a misprint or a bare-faced lie. It should say THE BUCK *STARTS* HERE. The CEO is in the highly responsible position of having to designate the mug who will officially carry the can for whatever mire the agency has landed itself in. All he/she needs for this are a comfy and ergonomically designed swivel chair, an internal phone list and a nice, shiny pin. Decisions, decisions . . .

HEAD OF CLIENT SERVICES – sounds grand, and so it should because this title was invented as compensation for those witless account directors who will never, ever make CEO. They have no power whatsoever, but if they begin sentences with 'as Head of Client Services . . .' often enough, it will make them think that they do. This title also impresses at cocktail parties where no advertising people are present.

ACCOUNT DIRECTORS – Light bulb joke #1:
Q – How many account directors does it take to change a light bulb?
A – 'How many would the client like it to take?'
This tells you all you need to know about account directors.

CREATIVE DIRECTORS – All creative directors are Useless Tossers. This fact has been established in a number of clinical trials. It doesn't matter how good they were *before* they were creative directors (and, no kidding, some of them were certifiably brilliant), the moment they settle into that palatial corner office with the wide-screen TV and Bauhaus furniture, they assume the mantle of Useless Tosser. This phenomenon has baffled the few scientists who give a shit, which to be frank, isn't many.

CREATIVE TEAMS – Legend has it that the modern copywriter/ art director creative team was invented in the sixties by the advertising luminary Bill Bernbach. This is bollocks. In fact it couldn't be more bollocks if it were wrapped in a soft leather scrotal sac and suspended between the hind legs of a bull. The truth is that the first team actually paired up after seeing the notorious David Bailey shot of the Brothers Kray. Upon inspection, this visionary twosome figured that if they, too, dressed in black and looked well 'ard, it would serve to scare anyone from account management off, who had the temerity to suggest 'a few little tweaks' to their work.

Lightbulb Joke #2:
Q – How many art directors does it take to change a light bulb?
A – 'Fuck off, I'm not changing a thing.'

Pinki Fallon – 3/1/00, 10.39am
to... Simon Horne
cc... David Crutton; Daniel Westbrooke
re... arses in gear

Sorry guys, but can you excuse me from Coke? They represent all that is wrong with the Western capitalist socio-economic model and my yoga teacher would never forgive me. In any case, Liam and I are up to our necks on the Kimbelle Super Dri launch, which should keep us v.v.v. busy for the next couple of weeks. Sorry, etc ... ☺

Katie Philpott – 3/1/00, 10.42am
to... James Gregory
cc...
re... HI YOURSELF!

Thanks for the e. Didn't understand most of it, but guffaw, guffaw anyway! Haven't the foggiest what I'm supposed to do yet, but if I can help with your Mako meeting – pens, pads, that sort of thing – give me a shout. By the way, what happened to the last trainee? I've heard some rumours, but no one will tell. Katie P

Liam O'Keefe – 3/1/00, 10.45am
to... Vince Douglas; Brett Topowlski
cc...
re... NEW MILLENNIUM, OLD BOLLOCKS

There goes another thousand years. How was it for you? I boy-cotted it – well, the whole fucking thing was a marketing con by the Christians to get us to buy Cliff Richard's piece of shit. I stayed in with a Tesco korma, Jose Cuervo, my new Sony Vega and a hard-on for Gaby Roslyn – I recommend it if you're around for the next one. Don't know if I'll see you at the Coke briefing.

Pinki's just e'd Horne with another moral stand. Wonder how the sad old git will talk her round this time – watch this space.

James Gregory – 3/1/00, 10.50am
to... Katie Philpott
cc...
re... HI YOURSELF!

The story is that the last trainee spent his first month sitting by the fire escape waiting for a proper desk. He got hypothermia and sued. Don't worry, things have changed. That's why they stuck you by the big copier on the 3rd – you'll overheat rather than freeze.

Nigel Godley – 3/1/00, 10.54am
to... All Departments
cc...
re... room to let

Room to let in cosy central Balham flat.
• Near shops, buses and Jet filling station
• Hygena kitchen w/ ceramic hob
• Neighbourhood Watch area
• Non-smoker preferred
• Must like cats
• And gerbils
• £380 PCM
• First to see will move in!
Call x4667 – Nige.

Brett Topowlski – 3/1/00, 10.59am
to... Liam O'Keefe
cc...
re... NEW MILLENNIUM, OLD BOLLOCKS

Unbelievable – the first bank holiday of the year and I'm sitting in the Miller Shanks creative department staring at Vin and trying to come up with a campaign for Freedom Catalogues. Told him we need a visual idea. He's the art director, so it's his problem now.

Our Millenniums in brief. Mine's a total blank – woke up in a skip in Poplar at five am, 1 Jan, but had a spectacular view of the Dome as I leaned over the edge to puke. Vin was in Berlin and was so depraved he can't bring himself to tell me what he got up to. On the way back he was gutted that the Y2K bug didn't kick in and make the Airbus drop from sky – figures the adrenaline rush would've worked wonders for his hangover.

Don't bother e-mailing him. He made a New-Year res' to get computer literate. First thing this morning he got me to fire up his Mac and log him onto Notes. He had 4,735 unread e's. He freaked and made me switch it off. Hasn't said a word since. I gave him some Crayolas and a pad and he's started to recover.

David Crutton – 3/1/00, 11.04am
to... Simon Horne
cc...
re... hippie dipstick

Is there anything the dizzy cow Pinki *will* work on? She won't do Embassy Regal for obvious reasons; Army Recruitment because she's anti-military; Action Man, ditto; Floréal Haircare because they torture kittens. For Christ's sake, she won't even work on Everest because they screwed up her mother's replacement windows. You keep saying she and Liam are the best creative team we've got, but have you thought that her delicate political sensibilities might be better suited to a different business? (VSO comes to mind.) Look into it, because if we don't win Coke and she hasn't lifted a bloody finger, I'll have her on the next flight to Somalia.

Simon Horne – 3/1/00, 11.24am
to... David Crutton
cc...
re... hippie dipstick

Leave it to me. I'll have a word in her shell-like.

Simon Horne – 3/1/00, 11.33am
to... Pinki Fallon
cc... Liam O'Keefe
bcc...David Crutton
re... Coke

Pinki, I respect your principles, but we really need you and Liam playing ball with *l'equipe 'A'* on this one. Can I say a couple of things before you make up your mind?

Naturellement, we share your concerns *vis-à-vis* the Coke/Mammon scenario. It is a vexing state of affairs.

David promises to register forcefully our feelings when next he meets their people.

Secondly, if we do not win it, people will lose their jobs.

I am certain you would not want additions to the unemployment statistics to prey on your mind.

I hope we will see you at the 12.00.

Si

Pinki Fallon – 3/1/00, 11.39am
to... Simon Horne
cc... Liam O'Keefe; David Crutton
re... Coke

I phoned Master Shenkar and he's cool. I know this account is worth more than the GNP of Guatemala, but David won't accept the business unless we can present them with a more holistic alternative to capitalist imperialism, will he? ☺

David Crutton – 3/1/00, 11.41am
to... Pinki Fallon
cc...
re... Coke

Trust me, I'm an adman. See you at the meeting.

Susi Judge-Davis – 3/1/00, 11.56am
to... Creative Department
cc...
re... Coke

Please make your way to the Coke briefing in the boardroom.
Simon asks you to bring pads and *not* to be late.

Zoë Clarke – 3/1/00, 12.30pm
to... Carla Browne
cc...
re... that bastard!!!

Un-fucking-believable!!!!! Have you heard what the bastard, Crett-
tin, did to Fi? She's gone!!!!! He made her clear her desk that
minute. She didn't even have time to meet me in the loo for a
good cry!!!!!! Can't believe he fired her on a bank holiday!!!!! We
shouldn't even be here!!!!! The story is he did it 'cos she couldn't
make his stupid e-mail work!! Incredible!!!! I've been trying to
get her on her mobile all morning. She must be able to do him
for wrongful something or other. Let's talk at lunch!!!!!!! See you
in Bar Zero? Zxxx

Carla Browne – 3/1/00, 12.35pm
to... Zoë Clarke
cc...
re... that bastard!!!

I heard, poor cow!! Doesn't that shit know this is a bad time for
her – did you see how much she put on over Christmas? And,
apart from her weight, she was a fucking brilliant PA. Anyway,
no chance of me coming to lunch. I've still got the hangover
from hell – glad these bloody millennium thingys only come
once every ten years. And I've got to start Desperate Dan's Coke
presentation. God, you should see this document. Bloody sodding
pie charts everywhere!!!!!!!! Who reads this bollocks? Looks like
I'll be in all night – bang goes step. If you get hold of Fi, e me
back with details!!!! I feel so sorry for her!! Cxxx

Liam O'Keefe – 3/1/00, 12.42pm
to... Brett Topowlski
cc...
re... tossers

Is the Coke brief the biggest wank-off yet, or what? Do Crutton
and Westbrooke really think we can write decent ads on a strategy
like that? 'Coke: lifeblood' – what the fuck does it mean? And
what's a 'carbonated lifestyle delivery system' when it's at home?
Even Pinki says it stinks. Major worry – I rely on her magic touch
with shit briefs. See you in BZ in fifteen and we'll talk tits: i.e.
how the fuck I can get Joanne Guest's award winning baps into
a Kimbelle Super Dri ad without Pinki having me up for Grievous
Political Incorrectness.

Simon Horne – 3/1/00, 12.45pm
to... Creative Department
cc... David Crutton; Daniel Westbrooke
re... arses in gear 2

I am sure you will join me in thanking David and Daniel for a
staggeringly inspirational briefing.

'Coke: lifeblood' is a truly incisive strategy – one that gives you
the chance to do some really famous work.

No doubt your creative juices will be flowing like the Ganges in
flood.

I would like to see first thoughts early next week.

Let us get out there and grab the advertising Rottweiler by its
hairy testes.

Si

Brett Topowlski – 3/1/00, 12.49pm
to... Liam O'Keefe
cc...
re... tossers

BZ at 1.00. By the way, you got any idea what creative juices look like? Vin just blew his nose and I think his are now in a Kleenex.

David Crutton – 3/1/00, 12.59pm
to... Chandra Kapoor
cc...
re... e-mail

When the Microsoft ads ask me, 'Where do you want to go today?', I do not reply with 'Finland' – after Latvia, the dullest country in Europe.

As Head of IT, surely you can answer this simple question. Why is it that every time I send a bloody internal e-mail it ends up in Helsinki? One member of staff has already lost her job today because of this. Sort it out now.

NB: do not blame this on the Millennium Bug. This is the sorriest excuse since 'the dog ate my homework'.

Zoë Clarke – 3/1/00, 2.10pm
to... Carla Browne
cc...
re... the dirt!!!

Boy, oh boy!!!! Finally got Fi on her mobile and we went for a quick one at Bar Zero. Just got back!! Un-fucking-believable!!!!! She's in such a state, poor thing!!!!! Gotta go. Stupid Pinki's yelling at me to book her shiatsu and that bitch, Susi, won't lift a finger!! Who the fuck does she think she is, stuck up cow?!!!! Zxxx

Carla Browne – 3/1/00, 3.00pm
to... Zoe Clarke
cc...
re... the dirt!!!

God, poor Fi!!!! But what about me?!!!! Don't tell a soul, but

Rachel whatsit called me down and says the bloody Crettin wants me to work for him!!!! No one lasts five minutes with him (Fi broke the record at four months!) and 'cos I've been here the longest, they think I stand a chance of sticking it out. Bloody hell! !!! What do I do now!!!!? Desperate Dan will have a fit if he loses me, but Rachel did a good sell on it. It's 5k more!!!!! Cxxx

Zoë Clarke – 3/1/00, 3.03pm
to... Carla Browne
cc...
re... the dirt!!!

Can't believe it! Fi was on 5k more than us? That bitch. She was shit anyway and she's got a right mouth on her. She deserved everything she got!!! Do you know she told me about you and Brett T. at the Christmas party? Wasn't going to say, but you deserve some honesty! Anyway, do you really want to work for the Crettin? Money isn't everything!!!!!!!!! Zxxx

Carla Browne – 3/1/00, 3.07pm
to... Rachel Stevenson
cc...
re... our meeting

Rachel, thanks everso for the offer. I'm thrilled that Mr Crutton suggested me for the job. Obviously it involves a huge amount of responsibility, with plenty of room for personal growth, so it's not a hard decision to make. I'd love to accept – Carla

**james_f_weissmuller@millershanks-ny.co.usa
3/1/00, 3.15pm (10.15am local)**
to... all_departments@millershanks-london.co.uk
cc...
re... NEW MILLENNIUM – NEW HEIGHTS

I write to endorse wholeheartedly the sentiments contained in David Crutton's stirring all-staff note earlier in your day.

The Executive Board in New York are unanimous in their delight at the efforts you put in last year to push the peanut forward and keep us on our toes in the Big Apple.

Under David's outstanding leadership, Miller Shanks London is well on the way to reclaiming its rightful place as lead office in our European network. I look forward to seeing the evidence with my own eyes when I visit to lend my support to the Coca-Cola pitch.

Winning that one really would be a feather in our caps. Keep up the tremendous work!

Jim Weissmuller
President, Miller Shanks Worldwide

Zoë Clarke – 3/1/00, 3.21pm
to... Rachel Stevenson
cc...
re... hooray!

I'm so pleased for Carla that she's been offered the chance to work for David! She really, really deserves it and I hope she says yes. I think it's brilliant that we work for a company that's prepared to give second chances. That embarrassing thing with the Arabian Airways client wouldn't have been treated nearly so sympathetically by a lot of agencies – Zoe

PS I know you swore her to secrecy, but I hope you don't mind her telling me – I am her best, best friend in the world!!!!!!!!

pertti_vanhelden@millershanks-helsinki.co.fin
3/1/00, 4.13pm (6.13pm local)
to... david_crutton@millershanks-london.co.uk
cc...
re... FASCINATING FINLAND

Oh, how your last e-mail has ignited a debating! 'The dullest country in Europe'? We are compiling a small list of 'Finnish Delights' to provide you with foodstuff for thinking.
• The noble reindeer.

- 397 different flavours of vodka.
- A thriving dancing scene inspired very much by your own Pan's People.
- The Autumn Skate-a-thon in Räahe, which is lasting for four days and nights!
- Reindeer à la Grêcque, the speciality of the head chef at the Helsinki Holiday Inn.
- The annual clubbing of the pilot whales on Björkoby Island.
- The National Museum of the Herring in Väasa.

I will be making sure to send to you a copy of the Finnish Board of Tourism and Fisheries' illuminating booklet, *Finland: the Culture, the History and the Fish*. I think you will be finding it most stimulatory!

Tally-ho! P̶e̶r̶t̶t̶i̶

PS: My own creativity boffins are now working out their first 'well-wicked' Coca-Cola concepts. You are baiting your breath, yes?

Daniel Westbrooke – 3/1/00, 4.16pm
to... Rachel Stevenson
cc...
re... Carla Browne

Carla tells me that she has been offered the job of Personal Assistant to David. Pardon my French, but I am getting really bloody hacked off with this place. Why am I the last person to find anything out? I would stand more chance of knowing what is going on here if I went to the Groucho and heard it from the chaps at Saatchi and Bartle Bogle.

This is bloody awful timing. I am in sole charge of the most important pitch in this agency's history. How am I supposed to manage without adequate secretarial support?

I have been at Miller Shanks for fifteen years and it would be nice just for once to be treated with the respect due to the Head of Client Services.

Daniel Westbrooke – 3/1/00, 4.24pm
to... David Crutton
cc...
re... Carla Browne

I am *so* chuffed for Carla that she has decided to take you up on
your fantastic offer. She is a cracking girl and her time in the
exacting role of PA to Head of Client Services has prepared her
well. Much as I will miss her, I am certain you will be brilliant
for each other. If there is anything, anything at all, that I can do
to help her make the transition to the seat outside the Big Office,
please do not hesitate to ask. Superb choice!

Brett Topowlski – 3/1/00, 4.43pm
to... Liam O'Keefe
cc...
re... PHWOOOAR!

Seen that temp who's in for Crutton? Vin picked up her phero-
mones in no time – I swear that boy's dick is a divining rod
when it comes to muff. Find an excuse to use the copier by her
desk, then look at the bird on p46 of *Razzle* (36DD/aerosol of
Anchor Cream/torque wrench). It's her twin!

Zoe Clarke – 3/1/00, 4.59pm
to... Carla Browne
cc...
re... SLAPPER!!!!!!!!!!!!

Have you seen the Crettin's temp yet? Talk about cheap!!!! Just
saw Vince Douglas dribbling all over her cleavage!!!!!!!!!!!! Can
you believe I used to think he was cute? Zxxx

Ken Perry – 3/1/00, 5.08pm
to... All Departments
cc...
re... carpeting

You may have noticed that new carpet tiles went down in reception during the Christmas break. To ensure even wear and tear across the full width of the carpeted area, could employees below the level of group account director please make the short journey from front door to lifts by stepping round the perimeter of the foyer? This will leave the all-important central tread zone for senior management, clients and other visitors.

Thank you for your co-operation.

Ken Perry
Office Administrator

Liam O'Keefe – 3/1/00, 5.36pm
to... Brett Topowlski
cc...
re... PHWOOOAR!

Just clocked her. Registered 9.6 on the Totty Scale. And when she opens her gob she sounds like a Boddington's bird. Brace yourselves – I happened to get chatting to her – like you do – and she's coming to BZ with us. Be there in fifteen. Her name's Lorraine – Lol to her close mates.

David Crutton – 3/1/00, 6.09pm
to... Simon Horne
cc...
re... fucking ghost ship

I just walked our Freedom Catalogues client through our 'energetic, buzzy creative department' and it's like the *Mary Celeste* down there. Even your hot-shot, Pinki, was rushing out – late for Zen aerobics apparently. I caught that dozy secretary, Zoë, putting on her eyelashes. She said they were all in a research debrief. Bullshit! More likely in Bar Zero researching the tits on my temp.

This is the first working day of a new century. If this carries on, I'll be more than happy to live up to my trigger-happy reputation.

I operate on the tried-and-trusted principle of 'last in, first out' (which would put you at number five on the list).

Simon Horne – 3/1/00, 6.42 pm
to... David Crutton
cc...
re... fucking ghost ship

I have only this minute stepped out of a heavy meeting with Mako. You are right, this situation is quite untenable.

It is time to apply Timberlands *à derrières*. Leave it to me.

By the way, Mako is turning into the proverbial smelly one.

Apparently, they bombed our campaign out before Christmas, but even though she is supposed to be running the business, Harriet 'forgot' to mention it.

We have already booked Little and Large to appear in the TV spots.

We are up a creek by the name of *merde*.

Sans paddle.

As if trying to make a car assembled by the Filipino peasantry seem alluring is not sufficiently *difficile* in the first place.

Si

Simon Horne – 3/1/00, 6.44pm
to... Susi Judge-Davis
cc...
re... teams

Susi, darling, do me a teeny-weeny favourette: have a look-see round the department and tell me if any of my bloody teams are still here?

Harriet Greenbaum – 3/1/00, 6.48pm
to... David Crutton
cc...
re... Mako

Just to keep you in the loop, we're running into trouble on Mako. Before Christmas, I made Simon aware that our clients would never approve Little and Large, but he remained committed to them. As Creative Director this is his right. However, at today's meeting they were surprised and disappointed that we were re-presenting the same work.

Time is not on our side. The launch date for their new model is fixed, and we have to present them with a new campaign on Friday.

Susi Judge-Davis – 3/1/00, 6.50pm
to... Simon Horne
cc...
re... teams

Not a soul in sight, I'm afraid, darling . . . Sx

Harriet Greenbaum – 3/1/00, 6.59pm
to... James Gregory
cc...
re... Mako

You were at the meeting so no need to tell you how deep we're in it. I suggest you join me for a post-mortem. Grab Katie. She might as well be introduced to the unpleasant realities of advertising.

Simon Horne – 3/1/00, 7.28pm
to... Creative Department
cc...
bcc...David Crutton
re... your careers

A nightmare is developing on Mako.

We have yet to crack Kimbelle Super Dri.

And we are about to embark on the biggest pitch any of us will ever work on.

Why, then, is my department deserted? Am I the only one who gives a tuppenny damn?

Starting tomorrow, I expect to hear the ear-piercing squeak of permanent marker pen on paper as the precious ideas lodged in your crania tumble forth onto layout pads.

And before you bring me the fruits of your labours, ask yourselves just one question:

'Is it a gold?'

Si

Nigel Godley – 3/1/00, 11.34pm
to... All Departments
cc...
re... anybody out there?

It's 11.30 and I'm still here, collating timesheets. E me back if you, too, are still 'at the coal face'!

Nige

Carla Browne – 3/1/00, 11.36pm
to... Nigel Godley
cc...
re... anybody out there?

Yes, I am!!!!!!!!! Who are you? What floor are you on? And can you make those stupid wedge shapes in pie charts on PowerPoint? If you can help, e me immediately – I want to go home!!!!!! Carla on the 4th.

Tuesday
4 January
2000

David Crutton – 4/1/00, 7.57 am
to... Harriet Greenbaum; Simon Horne
cc...
re... Mako

Last night the entire dress circle at the Royal Opera House was disturbed by my mobile phone. The MD of Mako UK wished to know how many times he has to tell us he doesn't like Little and Large before we get the message. What were his precise words? 'Putting those end-of-pier excuses for comedians behind the wheel of my brand new, £22,000 executive saloon is not my fucking idea of sexy car advertising.' I think he made his point.

I'd like the pair of you in my office in thirty minutes and perhaps we can work out how not to lose this account before we've made a single ad for them.

pertti_vanhelden@millershanks-helsinki.co.fin
4/1/00, 8.02am (10.02am local)
to... david_crutton@millershanks-london.co.uk
cc...
re... Mako

It's good to see you starting off your day with the early worm, too! How we are loving your Little and Large here in Finland. All of their *Seaside Specials* are on Satellite Golden Hits Station. Such a pity Mr Mako isn't sharing your cutting-edge excellent good taste. Oh, well, clients like these are the crutches that we who are choosing advertising must be bearing.

Pip pip! Pertti

David Crutton – 4/1/00, 8.09am
to... Chandra Kapoor
cc...
re... P45s

Yesterday lunchtime I informed you that my e-mails were mis-routing to Finland. I expected an immediate response. So far, sweet fuck-all. I've met plumbers more reliable than your depart-ment. Do you actually want to end up outside Mile End tube flogging the *Big Issue*?

David Crutton – 4/1/00, 8.17am
to... Rachel Stevenson
cc...
re... IT

In the midst of some grief I'm having with my e-mail, I had a brainwave. During WW2, when the Nazis were having difficulties with the French Resistance, they'd round up the population of an entire village. Then, for every hour that the partisans didn't give themselves up, they'd shoot a villager in the head.

I'd like to do something similar with IT. I suspect that shooting them is out of the question, but how about firing one of them for each hour they don't sort out my problem?

I'd be obliged if you could check out the legality of this under current employment legislation.

Rachel Stevenson – 4/1/00, 8.32am
to... David Crutton
cc...
re... IT

David, I'm so sorry. I just got Chandra on the phone. He was unaware of your trouble. If you've been trying to reach him by e-mail, he hasn't been getting them. He says IT is extremely busy but he'll get straight onto it.

Nigel Godley – 4/1/00, 8.43am
to... All Departments
cc...
re... for sale

BREVILLE WAFFLE IRON
• Jasmine yellow finish
• Nearly new
• Includes adapter to make perfect toastie sarnies!
• The perfect way to 'toast' the new Millennium!!
• First to see will buy
• £12 o.n.o.
Call x4667 – Nige

Harriet Greenbaum – 4/1/00, 9.04am
to... Simon Horne
cc...
re... Mako

For the record, Simon, I didn't forget to tell you about Mako's dislike of Little and Large. There was no need. You were at the client meeting before Christmas to hear it for yourself. If you're going to tell lies to David about what I have or haven't done, I'd prefer you didn't do it when I'm in the room. It insults my intelligence.

Simon Horne – 4/1/00, 9.10am
to... Harriet Greenbaum
cc...
re... Mako

Do you realise the pressure I am under?

I am expected to manage and inspire a department of twelve creative teams.

I am required to represent the agency's creative product to our clients – Philistines the lot.

On top of that I have somehow to find the time to deliver creative *coups de grâce* of my own.

If occasionally I forget some little thing a client says in a meeting, well, I am only human.

Si

Simon Horne – 4/1/00, 9.11am
to... Susi Judge-Davis
cc...
re... stress

Migraine, migraine!

Susi Judge-Davis – 4/1/00, 9.12am
to... Simon Horne
cc...
re... stress

Coffee and Migraleve on the way, darling ... Sx

Harriet Greenbaum – 4/1/00, 9.16am
to... Simon Horne
cc...
re... Mako

I'm sorry to split hairs, but I wouldn't have defined the client saying he not only hates Little and Large, but thinks them totally wrong for his brand as a 'little thing'. All this, though, is academic. I suggest we now co-operate on finding a new campaign. Friday feels horribly close.

Brett Topowlski – 4/1/00, 9.35am
to... Liam O'Keefe
cc...
re... no-go zone

If you and Space Cadet First Class Pinki are planning to show Horne any ideas today, don't. He's in a right fucking mood. Vin and me took him our Reeves and Mortimer scripts for Freedom. He pissed all over them – said it was hardly the first time they'd been used. Vin pointed out that this was *the first time* anyone had used them in a mail-order shopping ad, but it didn't wash. Who the fuck does he think he is, going on about originality? Poxy Little and fucking Large? Tosser. You know Barry Clement used to be his art director? My mate Nick is in his group at Abbott Mead now and apparently Clement claims Horne didn't have one original thought in the four years they were together. Clement used to come up with all the ideas and all Horne ever said was, 'Yes, love, but is it a gold?' They haven't spoken since they split up and Clement nearly lamped him at D&AD last year.

Anyway, what happened to you after BZ last night? You were all over that temp like chicken pox. Vin's well pissed with you. Says he saw her first.

Susi Judge-Davis, 4/1/00, 9.39am
to... Creative Department
cc...
re... Simon's diary

Si's having a terribly stressful morning, so if you have work you need to see him with, could you keep it till later, please. If it's frightfully urgent, give it to me and I'll try to get it in front of him. Thx ... Susi.

Melinda Sheridan, 4/1/00, 9.39am
to... Harriet Greenbaum; James Gregory
cc...
re... bat suits

A dickie bird tells me that we are no longer to produce three forty-second commercials for Mako featuring Messrs Little and Large.

Why are us mugs in the TV production department always the last to hear information of crucial relevance to us?

Simon assured me that the scripts were as good as signed off by the client and you must be aware that we have contracts with these gentlemen of mirth. They will expect money. They have also been to four wardrobe sessions, so I now have a pair of made-to-measure bat suits with pink Lycra capes in my possession, as well as an invoice for £16,000.

It never rains, darlings . . .

Nigel Godley – 4/1/00, 9.39am
to... Carla Browne
cc...
re... helpmate

Top o' the morning! It was so nice to be able to help you with your document last night. Remember that creating presentable charts on PowerPoint is easy-peasy so long as you remember Nige's Handy Hints! Any time I can be of service, look me up in my little cubby in accounts – Nige

PS: want bags-first option on the waffle iron?

Carla Browne – 4/1/00, 9.52am
to... Zoe Clarke
cc...
re... fuck, fuck, bloody fuck!!!!!

Fucking hell!!!! I've done the stupidest thing!!!!!!! I only got that

dick, Nigel, who does the timesheets to help me with the Coke
document last night. I'm a fucking idiot, I know – but it was
nearly midnight and I just wanted to go home!!!! Now I can't
get rid of him!!!!!!!! Think he fancies me!!!!!! What am I gonna
do?!!!!!! He wears grey slip-ons and he's into the Shopping Channel!!!!!!!!!!!!!!!!!!!!!!!!!!!!!!!!!!!!! Cxxx

James Gregory – 4/1/00, 9.54am
to... Harriet Greenbaum
cc...
re... it wasn't me!

Harriet, I know what you're going to say, but it wasn't me. I
swear I never told Melinda or anyone else in TV that the client
had signed off approvals on L&L. I don't know how this could
have happened. Can we hide the 16k on another job?

Harriet Greenbaum – 4/1/00, 10.16am
to... James Gregory
cc...
re... it wasn't me!

I know it wasn't you. This account has been going rat-shit since
a certain senior member of the creative department took up
permanent residence in Teletubby Land. Don't worry, I'll handle
it.

Ken Perry – 4/1/00, 10.24am
to... All Departments
cc...
re... 0898

As from today you will no longer be able to dial the premium-rate
numbers prefixed by 0898. These form a significant portion of
our monthly telecom overhead.

I appreciate that many of you find the business and traffic bul-
letins available on these lines invaluable. I apologise for the incon-

venience, but ask you to find alternative sources for the
information thus obtained.

Thank you for your co-operation.

Ken Perry
Office Administrator

Harriet Greenbaum – 4/1/00, 10.33am
to... Simon Horne
cc...
re... Mako

I've had an alarming e-mail from Melinda regarding an obligation
to L&L. I've tried to come to talk to you about it, but Susi
wouldn't let me anywhere near you. I am quite certain that
no-one on my team authorised you to run up pre-production
costs on Little and Large.

It beats me how this has happened. Perhaps you can apply your
legendary creativity to helping us recover the 16k Melinda says
we've spent.

Liam O'Keefe – 4/1/00, 10.58am
to... Brett Topowlski
cc...
re... need aspirin

Just got in. Read your e. Fuck, that was some night. Lol? My lips
are sealed. Will Vin ever talk to me again? Hope so – got to tell
the poor geezer what he missed out on.

No more 0898? How the fuck am I supposed to talk to Trixi on
Ripe 'n' Raw 1–2–1 now? She's the only bird I know who truly
understands a bloke's deep-rooted need to talk about massive tits
and impractical lingerie.

Head needs Bloody Mary. BZ at lunch, or will you be at your
desk making squeaky with your markers?

Simon Horne – 4/1/00, 11.15am
to... Harriet Greenbaum
cc...
re... Mako

So, on top of everything else I am expected to fret about the purse strings?

I believed that once the client saw Little and Large standing before him in bat suits, even a Neanderthal like him would no longer deny the self-evident merit of the idea.

Was I so wrong to think £16,000 a small price to pay in defence of our art?

Clearly I was naïve to assume I would have your support.

But I am a professional, and not in the business of pointing fingers.

I will pick myself up, dust myself down and move on from here.

Simon Horne – 4/1/00, 11.23am
to... David Crutton
cc...
re... Harriet Greenbaum

Believe me, David, I do not wish to drop anyone in the brown and gooey. You know that is not my *modus operandi*.

But I must make it clear that I had numerous verbal assurances from Harriet that the costs we were running up on Mako were authorised.

I am not having a go at her.

I have the utmost respect for her both as a human being and as an advertising practitioner. However, she has been under a great deal of stress lately.

There is a feeling about the office that James Gregory has been carrying her since her divorce. The unauthorised £16,000 may not be the only over-run on her business.

She needs our support at this difficult time.

Perhaps an audit of her other accounts would be helpful.

Si

Brett Topowlski – 4/1/00, 11.33am
to... Liam O'Keefe
cc...
re... need aspirin

Think you've got it bad? Vin and me have just been put on Kimbelle because you two useless gits can't crack it. What we know about 'the curse' could be written on a very small Rizla. I don't know how we'll fit it in before *we fly off to the sun-kissed island of Mauritius at the weekend for our LOVE Channel shoot, accompanied by top topless totty (over-endowed, over-eager and all over me).* Don't like to rub it in, but them's the breaks. Vin's getting over you and Lol the only way he knows. He's got a spotty trainee from IT to help him surf the net for farmyard porn and it seems to be taking his mind off Miss Manchester. It's quite touching how a pretty Danish dairy maid frolicking with a couple of Dobermans and a pig can restore a man's spirits. BZ at 1.00.

Rachel Stevenson – 4/1/00, 11.45am
to... Carla Browne
cc...
re... job changes

Carla – I have an urgent issue to discuss. I have tried to call you about it, but you have been engaged for over thirty minutes.

I'm afraid there's been a change of plan on the David Crutton front. He reviewed your file and felt he'd been wrong to overlook the Stringfellows matter with the marketing delegation from Arabian Airways. He regretfully feels that, given the minor diplomatic incident that ensued, a job with such a strong element of client and public interface would be inappropriate for you at this time.

We both feel very sorry to let you down like this, but want to reassure you that your future is bright, and, in Dan Westbrooke, you are working for one of the most respected executives in the agency.

If you'd like to discuss this further, please call me.

David Crutton – 4/1/00, 11.57am
to... Daniel Westbrooke
cc...
re... Coke

I believe I asked you to have a draft of the Coke presentation on my desk first thing this morning. Where the fuck is it? When I joined this company I only agreed to keep you on because you let Weissmuller use your house in Tuscany. If you can't deliver a few simple pie charts on time, why am I bothering?

By the way, you can keep your secretary. I was reminded that the silly tart's antics with a tequila bottle last year nearly started Gulf War II.

Brett Topowlski – 4/1/00, 11.59am
to... All Departments
cc...
re... IT'S A RECORD BREAKER

If you happen to go into trap 2 in the gents on the creative floor, please *do not* flush. The *Guinness Book of Records* has been informed.

Daniel Westbrooke – 4/1/00, 12.02pm
to... Carla Browne
cc...
re... Coke

Please can you get a bloody move on with the Coke presentation. I would like to remind you that it was only my pleadings that saved your job last year after the Arabian Airways débâcle. If a few simple pie charts are causing so much trouble, I am not sure why I bothered.

Carla Browne – 4/1/00, 12.09pm
to... Zoë Clarke
cc...
re... fuck, fuck, fuck, fucking shit, fuck!!!

God, you won't fucking believe what's happening!!! Just got an e from stupid bloody Rachel telling me I'm not being offered the job with Crettin any more!!!!! Just because of that stupid thing with the Arabs!!!! It wasn't my fault – those tequilas were spiked. I honestly thought it was forgotten. Can you believe it?!!!! I feel so humiliated!!!! It's not that I was going to take the stupid job – who'd want to work for that git anyway?!!!!! It's the bloody principle!!!! Do you think I can get them for false mis-representation? Can we go to Bar Zero for lunch? I really need your support right now!!! Cxxx

Rachel Stevenson – 4/1/00, 12.11pm
to... Zoë Clarke
cc...
re... job changes

Unfortunately Carla Browne's move to David Crutton's office didn't pan out as we'd hoped. However, David would very much like you to consider the position yourself. Obviously it would represent a big change for you and I'm sure you'd like to talk about it. Perhaps you could give me a call and we can find a time.

Zoë Clarke – 4/1/00, 12.13pm
to... Rachel Stevenson
cc...
re... job changes

On my way!!!!!!!!!!!!!!!!!!!!!!!!!

Zoë Clarke – 4/1/00, 12.14pm

to...   Carla Browne

cc...

re...   fuck, fuck, fuck, fucking shit, fuck!!!

God, you poor fucking cow!!! This place doesn't deserve you!!!!!! Got to do some urgent copying now!!!!! The stupid hippie is screaming for it!!!! I'd ask Susi to help, if she wasn't such a bitch!!!!! See you at lunch – you need a friend right now!!!!!!!!!!!!!! Zxxx

pertti_vanhelden@millershanks-helsinki.co.fin
4/1/00, 12.30pm (2.30pm local)

to...   david_crutton@millershanks-london.co.uk

cc...

re...   Coke

So, you await for your Coca-Cola documentation? Oh, how I sympathise with your plight! Before Christmas already I am asking for new light bulbs in the executive toilet, and still I am dangling. Both cubicles one and two are in gloomiest black pitchness and it is only because I did so much night training during my national service that I am able to avoid brown-staining embarrassment!

Perhaps we should place the issue of staff respondingness at the top of the agenda at the forthcoming Miller Shanks CEO Conference in Waikiki.

Aloha! **Pertti**

Zoë Clarke – 4/1/00, 2.23pm

to...   Carla Browne

cc...

re...   this shit hole!!!!

God, it was good to get out of here at lunch!! Hope you feel better!!!!!! Remember what I said – I think you should definitely, definitely leave!!!!! You're my best friend in the world and I don't know how I could work here without you!!!!! But you've got to think of yourself, and you're better than this place!!!!! Zxxx

Zoë Clarke – 4/1/00, 2.27 pm
to... Rachel Stevenson
cc...
re... job changes

Rachel, thanks so much for the offer. I'm so excited that Mr
Crutton suggested me for the position. Obviously it entails extra
responsibility and is a big step up. As I said I would, I've given
it a lot of thought over lunch. In the end, though, it's an easy
decision to make. I'd be thrilled to accept – Zoë

Carla Browne – 4/1/00, 2.29pm
to... Zoë Clarke
cc...
re... this shit hole!!!!

I don't know what I'd do without you, Zoë!!!!!! You're the only
one in this stupid bloody place that stops me from going
mad!!!!!!!!!! I do feel better, and I've decided that I'm *not* going
to resign!!!!!!!!! I can't let those bastards win!!!!!!!!!!!!!!!!!!!!!!!!! Cxxx

Zoë Clarke – 4/1/00, 2.41 pm
to... Carla Browne
cc...
re... fuck, fuck, fuck, fuck, fuck, fuck, fuck, fuck, fuck, fuck,
fuck, fuck!!!!!!!!!!!!!!!

In-fucking-credible!!!!!!! That two-faced, lying cow, Rachel, has
only gone and offered me the Crettin job!!!!!!!!! I mean, doesn't
she know we're best friends in the world?!!! The thing is, though,
I think I've got to say yes. Before you go mad, I don't want to,
but I don't really have a choice! It *is* 5k more and I've got a
massive Barclaycard bill to pay off and my gas is about to be *cut
off*!!!!! And you *really, really didn't want it*, did you?!!!!!! Oh, God,
what am I gonna do?!!!!!!!!! . . . Zxxx

Pinki Fallon – 4/1/00, 2.52pm
to... Ken Perry
cc...
re... emergency!

I think we need some of your maintenance guys to help us out here. There's been a bit of an incident between Zoë Clarke and one of the other girls. Zoë'll need a new desk lamp and PC, unless you can get the potting compost from the yucca out of her floppy drive. Also, there's a bit of blood on one of the carpet tiles. It's only a small cut, so no need for first-aid. Ta . . . ☺

Simon Horne – 4/100, 2.55pm
to... Susi Judge-Davis
cc...
re... hormonal women

Darling, have those dreadful girls finished their caterwauling yet? What was that commotion? I have to see David with a Mako idea and I would like to make it to his office with life and limb intact.

Susi Judge-Davis – 4/1/00, 2.56pm
to... Simon Horne
cc...
re... hormonal women

The coast is clear, sweetie . . . Sx

Carla Browne – 4/1/00, 3.05pm
to... All Departments
cc... james_f_weissmuller@millershanks-ny.co.usa
re... fuck the fucking lot of you!!!!!!!

I'm leaving now, but before I go there's some things you should know!!!!!!!
• Zoë Clarke is a lying slag and she gave Simon Horne a BJ at last year's D&AD.
• She swallowed.

- Daniel Westbrooke keeps tarts' phone cards in his desk drawer.
- David Crutton buys his coke off Vince Douglas.
- Crutton also spent £3,500 in one night at a table-dancing club and put it through on his expenses as 'qualitative research fees'.
- You can all fuck off and die!!!!!!!!!!!!!!!!!!

Rachel Stevenson – 4/1/00, 3.09pm
to... Chandra Kapoor
cc... David Crutton
re... urgent

Please delete Carla Browne's User ID from e-mail with immediate effect.

Thank you.

Rachel Stevenson
Personnel

David Crutton – 4/1/00, 3.20pm
to... Harriet Greenbaum
cc...
re... cracked

It would appear Simon has saved your arses on Mako. He has shown me his new idea and it is a very clever way out. Come see.

james_f_weissmuller@millershanks-ny.co.usa
4/1/00, 3.21pm (10.21am local)
to... david_crutton@millershanks-london.co.uk
cc...
re... Carla Browne

I'm concerned, David, very concerned. Is this Carla Browne the same individual who led us a merry dance with our Middle-Eastern friends? Is there truth in her ranting?

I am particularly troubled by her claims about narcotics. You will be acutely aware of corporate policy on this issue.

Reassure me that you haven't a Monica Lewinsky on your reservation.

Jim

david_crutton@millershanks-london.co.uk
4/1/00, 3.27pm
to... james_f_weissmuller@millershanks-ny.co.usa
cc...
re... Carla Browne

Jim – worry not. The Carla Browne situation has been dealt with. We were certain that, after the Arabian Airways incident, her wilder personality traits had been subdued. Rest assured, she has now been marched off the premises, and will not return.

We reminded her that in the UK, we have some very tough slander laws and that if she repeats a word of her fantastical claims, we will bear down on her with the full weight of the legal establishment.

Of course, there is not one iota of truth in her bizarre allegations. Let me put your mind at rest completely on the drugs matter. All employees here know my strict views on this, and no transgression will be tolerated.

I'm sorry that this storm in a teacup has intruded on your busy day.

By the way, Coke is proceeding splendidly and we already have some very exciting thoughts on the table. I look forward to your coming over to this side of the pond to head up the pitch.

Please pass on my regards to your beautiful wife and lovely children.

David

David Crutton – 4/1/00, 3.31pm
to... Simon Horne
cc...
re... Coke

I've just had occasion to e-mail Weissmuller and I mentioned that we had some cracking Coke work in development. I trust you won't let him down.

Simon Horne – 4/1/00, 3.46pm
to...   Creative Department
cc...
bcc...David Crutton
re...   one down . . .

. . . two to go. You now only have Coke and Kimbelle to crack. I have spent all morning and my lunch hour in the company of a layout pad. As a result I have solved the Mako problem.

I suggest you take a leaf out of my book.

If Susi tells me she has seen any of you idling by the coffee machine, I will want to know why.

If she mentions she has seen you slouching over the pool table, I will be livid.

You will remain at your desks wearing your pencils to stubs.

You will not show your sorry faces until you happen to be clutching ideas of astonishing brilliance.

Si

pertti_vanhelden@millershanks-helsinki.co.fin
4/1/00, 3.47pm (5.47pm local)
to...   david_crutton@millershanks-london.co.uk
cc...
re...   Carla Browne

Thanks for holding me in the loop-the-loop on matters of staff discipline and morale that you are touching on in your e-mailing to Jim.

It is fascinating me that you, too, have troubles with work hands going off the straight and perpendicular. Perhaps it is our sunless winters or our proximity to the vodka distilleries of the former Soviet Union, but we in Finland are having a similar problem with many company members becoming 'one picnic hamper short of a luncheon box'!

I have a tip for you. I am employing the revolutionary techniques pioneered by Dr Jari Nepstad at the Nordic Institute of Animal Husbandry. These are involving giving staff a daily tonic concocted of the extracts of lemming spleen and reindeer urine. As a result I am seeing insanity rates falling by 18%. I mail the recipe to you, though maybe you find lemming spleen in short supply at your otherwise excellent Asian corner shops.

Keep your pecker firm and erect – Pertti

Rachel Stevenson – 4/1/00, 3.48pm
to... Lorraine Pallister
cc...
re... job changes

Lorraine, I know you've only been here five minutes, but I wonder if we can tempt you with a permanent position.

Zoë Clarke, one of the creative secretaries, will shortly be taking over as David's PA, which would leave an opening in that department. It's a really lively group of people on the 2nd floor, and Simon Horne, the Creative Director, is a lovely, charming man. This is a fantastic opportunity. If you're interested, call me and we'll discuss.

Harriet Greenbaum – 4/1/00, 3.49pm
to... James Gregory; Katie Philpott
cc...
re... woe is us

I've been looking everywhere for you both. As soon as you're back at your desks, I need you in my office. I've just come back from a meeting with David. Things, I'm afraid, are going from worse to abysmal.

Simon has 'cracked' Mako. This is his idea: Reeves and Mortimer in bat suits. He believes it to be so brilliant that they'll have to invent a new category of award to honour it. When I pointed out that he'd simply replaced Britain's most unfashionable comedians with its most over-exposed, he wouldn't have any of it.

The final nail in the coffin is that David not only loves it, he wants to build a church in which to worship it.

I don't have much room to argue. The entire blame for the L&L disaster has been laid at our feet and our credibility is less than zero. To beat this one we must not only come up with a very convincing case against Simon's new idea, but also a demonstrably better alternative. Let's see what we can do. We still have three days.

Katie Philpott – 4/1/00, 3.53pm
to... Harriet Greenbaum
cc...
re... woe is us

Golly, what a pickle! Still, I'm up for a challenge. I'll grab James as soon as he's back from the loo and we'll pop in – Katie P

Brett Topowlski – 4/1/00, 4.00pm
to... Liam O'Keefe
cc...
re... rumble in the jungle

While you were poncing around at some photographer's studio shooting panty liners, you missed a top ruck. Carla vs Zoë, armed only with Rexel staplers and *rouge noir* nail extensions. They were tearing lumps out of each other when Pinki the Pacifist steamed in like a UN delegation and broke it up – crying bloody shame. I tell you, if boxing were only half as horny, it wouldn't be going through a crisis right now. Picture Iron Mike in basque and fishnets. (Go on, I dare you.)

So Carla walks and Zoë's going to work for Crutton? How the

fuck did she swing it? Mind you, I'm not sure he'll want her
when he sees her shiner. And your babe Lol's got the creative
job. Compensation for when *we jet off to the Indian Ocean
paradise of Mauritius for the LOVE shoot to enjoy the shimmer
of factor 2 on surgically enhanced tits* – shame you won't be
there.

Wonder what Horne's Mako idea is. Couldn't be worse than
Little and Large, could it? No, don't answer that.

Susi Judge-Davis, – 4/1/00, 4.10pm
to... Zoë Clarke
cc... Rachel Stevenson
re... behaviour unbecoming of a professional establishment

I have just come out of a meeting with Simon, who is quite upset
by this afternoon's events. He has asked me to have a serious
word with you.

He does not feel that fistfights on the creative floor are a thing
to be tolerated and has asked me to have you relocated. I informed
him that you are to work for David Crutton and, to be honest,
he is worried. He is not sure that you are suitable and is going
to ask David to review his offer.

Let me know if you'd like to talk, though I may be in conference
with Simon as we have much to catch up on. Your antics have
thrown out the whole day's timing.

I try so hard to defend you, Zoë, but this time you have really
let yourself down.

Susi

Liam O'Keefe – 4/1/00, 4.10pm
to... Brett Topowlski
cc...
re... rumble in the jungle

Q1: Did you video the punch-up? Mel's got a Digicam in her

desk – tailor-made for this type of blue-riband sporting event.

Q2: Is our little Vinnie Douglas really Crutton's Colombian connection? If so, tell him to cut it with some Vim next time.

Q3: Do you really think that going on about your poxy shoot in Mauritius is getting to me?

Got to go. Harriet is lurking outside our office and she's wearing the sauciest Chanel knock-off. I could be up for this older-woman gig.

Pinki Fallon – 4/1/00, 4.15pm
to... Liam O'Keefe
cc...
re... stop it!

Do me a favour and stop trying to see down Harriet's cleavage. I'm watching you do it now. Transparent? I could glaze a greenhouse with you . . . ☺

Harriet Greenbaum – 4/1/00, 4.50pm
to... Simon Horne
cc...
re... Mako

Susi tells me that, having cleared shelf space for all the awards you are going to win for Mako, you are de-stressing at the Groucho. Whilst you unwind after your triumph, you should know that my team and I are not happy. I don't see our client buying into Reeves and Mortimer any more than they did Little and Large. We're disappointed that you've taken the rest of the department off the brief.

I would love to debate this with you, but as you are not here I've taken the liberty of talking to Pinki and Liam. I've asked them to carry on working on the project. Pinki believes in Mako. Its low emissions make it the sort of car she'd drive herself, if only she could drive. Liam believes in it because of the 0–60 figures, brightly coloured rear spoiler and beverage holder on the dashboard.

This commitment on their part will lead, I hope, to a very strong idea.

Before you blow a fuse, David is aware of all this. Whilst he still likes your work, he is never averse to covering all the bases and presenting more than one route. He is happy for Pinki and Liam to continue.

I have asked Susi to set up a review for late tomorrow. Given the fix we're in, I think we should all be there.

I'm sure you will make your thoughts on this clear to me upon your return.

Rachel Stevenson – 4/1/00, 5.05pm
to... Susi Judge-Davis
cc...
re... behaviour unbecoming of a professional establishment

Susi, I've spoken to Zoë. She's very upset, obviously by Carla's attack, but also by your e-mail. In future, I'd prefer you not to take these matters up without first speaking with me.

Zoë assures me that Carla's outburst was completely unprovoked, and eyewitnesses bear this out. Given that Carla has now left and that Zoë is extremely traumatised, I think it best that we allow things to settle and try to forget the whole incident. Zoë will take up the position of David's PA as of Monday.

Liam O'Keefe – 4/1/00, 5.15pm
to... Brett Topowlski
cc...
re... steaming pile of shit!!!!

Harriet briefed us to carry on with Mako, and while she was at it she showed us Horne's latest. All he's done is take his L&L stuff and re-write it for ... drum roll ... R&M. (Recognize the casting?) The scripts are as amusing as William Hague's sock drawer. Wake Vin and come and see them in five. Pinki's going to see Perky (her clairvoyant).

Daniel Westbrooke – 4/1/00, 5.33pm
to... Simon Horne
cc...
bcc...David Crutton
re... concerns

Simon, I have to say I am a little worried. I know you have been preoccupied with Mako of late, but I hope your department is not neglecting Coca-Cola. I am sure you appreciate that the eyes of the network are upon us, and winning this pitch would make Mako seem very small beer indeed.

Simon Horne – 4/1/00, 5.52pm
to... David Crutton
cc...
re... needless hassle

I have come back from a very delicate meeting at the Groucho with Quentin Tarantino's British agent.

I feel Tarantino is very close to agreeing to shoot our Kimbelle commercials provided we have a sufficiently high body count.

The kudos we would reap from this is incalculable.

I should be returning to a well-earned pat on the back. Instead I find demented e-mails from both Harriet and Daniel on my laptop.

My loyalty to Harriet is wearing thin. Why should I defend her increasingly flaky behaviour if she deals behind my back in this way?

Her sniping at my new Mako work does, of course, gall.

But this *must* be our recommendation to the client. We cannot risk making ourselves look weak and uncertain by presenting more than one campaign.

Having said that, I can live with another team continuing to look at the brief. It is pretty unlikely that they will best my campaign.

If they do, you know that I will be the first out of my seat to lead the ovation.

As for Daniel, his fears that we will not deliver on Coke are, frankly, hysterical.

Perhaps you should remind him that I was in the same room as the legendary John Webster when he came up with the 'lipsmackin, thirstquenchin . . .' ad for Pepsi.

Furthermore, was it not I who created 'Mr Ffffizzzzzy', the zany animated bubble, for Fun Pops in 1982?

What I do not know about advertising carbonated drinks to British teenagers is not worth knowing.

Si

Simon Horne – 4/1/00, 6.02pm
to... Susi Judge-Davis
cc...
re... tense, nervous headache

What a day, darling! Be an angel and book me a cab to Bibendum in thirty minutes.

Then a couple of Nurofen and a shoulder-rub would not go amiss.

Susi Judge-Davis – 4/1/00, 6.04pm
to... Simon Horne
cc...
re... tense, nervous headache

Cab's ordered, darling, and I'm warming up my hands. Sparkling or still with the tablets? Sx

Melinda Sheridan – 4/1/00, 6.23pm
to... Simon Horne
cc...
re... Worried of Television

I've just bumped into David in the corridor and he congratulated me on being so close to finalising a deal with Quentin T. for Kimbelle. When I pleaded ignorance, he told me there was no need to be so coy, and that he knew negotiations were at an advanced stage.

Alarm bells are ring-a-ding-dinging. While I must say that '*Reservoir Dogs* meets the super-absorbent panty pad' is an intriguing notion, I was not aware that any scripts were written yet. Are we not placing cart before horse? If we commit to QT and can't deliver, I shudder to think . . .

Si, sweetheart, I know the strain on your shoulders has been immense lately, but I do hope we're not digging ourselves into another hole, *à la* Little and Large. My contacts in 90210 tell me that a Tarantino spurned is a far more frightening prospect. Unlike them, he carries a Magnum and he knows how to use it. I feel a meeting is in order.

Simon Horne – 4/1/00, 6.27pm
to... Melinda Sheridan
cc...
re... Worried of Television

Mel darling, it is nothing. I just happened to bump into Quentin's agent in the Groucho.

I mentioned Kimbelle, purely *en passant*.

As usual, David's blown it all way out of proportion.

Besides, you must know that, as Head of TV, I would consult you first on such a radical move.

Must dash, but if you are in *les environs* of Bibendum tonight, pop in for a quick one. I will be there with Al Parker and Ridley.

Si

Liam O'Keefe – 4/1/00, 6.31pm
to... Brett Topowlski
cc...
re... coast clear

I've just seen Horne get into his taxi. Quit pretending to work
and get your arses to BZ. See you there in ten – Pinki's back
from Gypsy Rose Lee and we need to catch up. Look after Lol
till I get there. And if you notice that she's not suffering from
VPL, it's because the saucy minx ain't wearing any.

David Crutton – 4/1/00, 7.33pm
to... Simon Horne
cc...
re... needless hassles

Stop flapping and please humour Harriet's desire to see more
work. I'm sure nothing will be produced that betters your own
stonking efforts, but it's no skin off any noses if it is. And fuck
Daniel. He flies into a panic if the 6.53 to Godalming is thirty
seconds late. I have every faith that you'll deliver a world-beating
Coke campaign. Of course, if you let me down, the consequences
for you scare even me.

Wednesday
5 January
2000

pertti_vanhelden@millershanks-helsinki.co.fin
5/1/00, 8.06am (10.06 am local)
to... david_crutton@millershanks-london.co.uk
cc...
re... be happy!

You are indeed 110% correct to tell your Created Director not to flap! For here is the astonishing Coca-Cola work I have been promising. It is, I think you will be agreeing, mole-breaking stuff. I waste no further ado and reveal all!

Our first commercial is opening on a grey scene of down-in-mouth teenagers sadly missing Coke refreshingness. This is quickly changing to technicolours as Europe's premier pop group, Aqua, appear and are singing their own brand of uplifting, happy music:

> We make fizzy pop,
> And Coke make fizzy pop,
> Put the two together,
> And the fun, it never stop!

Fizzy whizzy pop,
That take you to the top,
It make you oh-so-happy,
And give the blues the chop!

As they sing, dance and lark about in a clean-cut, teenager way,
the with-it youngsters are drinking Coca-Cola and their mood is
transforming to beaming happiness.

And this is just the first TV script! I fax the other five to you
now. Your reaction will be like mine when my top-gun team
bring me this outrageous concept. WOW and DOUBLE WOW!!
I know it will be a brave client to buy an idea of such power,
but with your famous 'ball of steel', I am knowing you can do
it.

Perhaps my overhead projections and me come over for the pitch
to lend mortal support? I take already the liberty to put this
thinking to Jim Weissmuller and he is most enthusing.

As soon as you are getting over the excitement, let me know what
you think.

Toodle-pip – ~~Pertti~~

David Crutton – 5/1/00, 8.10am
to... Chandra Kapoor
cc...
re... COMPETITION TIME

Complete the following sentence:

If my fucking e-mail is not fixed by tomorrow morning...

Ken Perry – 5/1/00, 8.15am
to... All Departments
cc...
re... FIRE DRILL

I would like to remind you of prescribed practice in the event of fire, terrorist alert or other unspecified emergency. All departments have a designated fire officer. This person is responsible for the orderly evacuation of the premises.

If you are unaware of who your fire officer is, you will find a list on the noticeboard at the end of your floor. If you are a fire officer and are unsure of your duties, please see Shanice, my secretary, who will book you onto a short refresher course.

There will be a fire drill today at precisely 11.30am. Please treat it as REAL and stick to the evacuation procedure as outlined in the staff handbook.

And remember, *drills save lives*.

Thank you for your co-operation.

Ken Perry
Office Administrator

David Crutton – 5/1/00, 8.22am
to... Simon Horne
cc...
re... Coke

Last night I believe I sent you an e-mail telling you not to worry. Well, once in a while even I am wrong.

For reasons too ridiculous to go into, our colleagues in Finland have taken it upon themselves to work on the Coke pitch. In their enthusiasm, they have also chosen to inform Weissmuller of their efforts.

I don't have to tell you how we'll look if we're trashed by a bunch of humourless, elk-shagging Scandinavians, but I will, anyway. We'll look like total bloody cunts.

So let me apply a little pressure. I know the pitch is over a week away, but I want to review all work this morning. I have had a preview of the Finnish campaign, and it is unmitigated shite.

Nevertheless, I want to make absolutely sure that there is no opportunity for us to be outdone.

We'll review at 11.30, and I fully expect to be dazzled.

Susi Judge-Davis – 5/1/00, 9.01am
to... Simon Horne
cc...
re... morning!

Good night at Bib's? Did you try the scallops with squid ink risotto? To die for! Anyway, your door is closed so I won't disturb, but when you're off the phone, please can you call David? He's been trying to reach you since I got in, but I did what I'm paid for, darling, and stalled him. Harriet is after you as well. She wants to confirm the Mako review for the end of today. I told her not to get her hopes up! I'm going for a Pret's latte. Do you want a choccy croissant while I'm there? Sx

Zoë Clarke – 5/1/00, 9.09am
to... Lorraine Pallister
cc...
re... welcome!!!!

Hi, we met really briefly in Bar Zero the other night!!!! I'm the girl you're taking over from in the creative dept!!! Give me a shout and I'll show you round and tell you what the job's all about. Don't worry about a thing, 'cos I'm sure you'll fit in really, really well!!!!! Simon Horne's PA, Susi, is an absolute love and she'll make you feel right at home!!!! Zxxx

lorraine_pallister@millershanks-london.co.uk
5/1/00, 9.15am
to... debbie_wright@littlewoods/manchester.co.uk
cc...
re... London calling

Two days in London and I'm in advertising. I went to a temp agency last week and they got me into this place called Miller

Shanks. They did those shite ads for Kimbelle – you know, the Artist Formerly Known as Ginger Spice bunjee-jumping, looking like someone shoved a high voltage cable up her arse. I'm working for the CEO (posh for managing director) who spends his whole time staring at my nipples like I just invented the things. It was only supposed to be for a couple of weeks but it's turned permanent. Next week I start as a PA in the creative department. That's the bit that has the ideas, but all I've seen them do so far is fifty grams of charlie. Some of the lads are a laugh though. One of them thinks he's on for a shag, but he looks too much like Bart Simpson (overbite, spiky hair and slightly jaundiced). Mind you, after a few Stellas he starts looking like Brad Pitt, so who knows? Anyway, it's fucking la-la land here. No one does any work. They just talk about it. Yesterday two secretaries beat ten shades of shit out of each other. Think that's why I ended up getting offered the permanent job. How's Salford since I left? Seen that sad twat, Terry? Tell him if he comes anywhere near London I'll break his other thumb as well. Write/call when you can. Miss you – Lolx

Daniel Westbrooke – 5/1/00, 9.24am

to... Susi Judge-Davis
cc... Simon Horne
re... Coke

Morning, Susi. I trust you are well. I have been trying you and Simon but keep getting voicemail. I know you are both awfully busy, so I thought I would send you a quick e. David wants to review the creative work for Coke at 11.30. I know it is a pain, giving us all such short notice, so let me know if there's anything my temp can do to help set it up.

Daniel Westbrooke – 5/1/00, 9.32am

to... David Crutton
cc...
re... an early review is a good review!

My temp passed on the message about the Coke review. Excellent!

I agree, we should have the work on the table ASAP. I hope our creative *wunderkinder* do not let us down. I do not think any of them are in yet – knowing them, they will have been toiling away until the cock crowed. Let me know when we are on. I am ready and waiting.

debbie_wright@littlewoods/manchester.co.uk
5/1/00, 9.45am
to... lorraine_pallister@millershanks-london.co.uk
cc...
re... Salford replying

We have contact! Well done, girl! They pay a ton in advertising, don't they? What you on – twenty grand? Higher? Salford's the same old, but you've only been gone a week, so it's hardly going to change. Did see Terry at Pizza Hut looking wounded/pissed – couldn't tell really. Got to go. This isn't like your new job – we actually have to work. Call soon. Love, Debs.

David Crutton – 5/1/00, 10.04am
to... Daniel Westbrooke
cc...
re... an early review is a good review!

I was informing you that I wanted to review the work. I wasn't asking you to be there. Please pay attention.

David Crutton – 5/1/00, 10.09am
to... Simon Horne
cc... Susi Judge-Davis
re... are you alive?

I've e-mailed you once already this morning without response. In fact, it seems my entire workforce has tried to make contact with you, with no success. I don't expect any trouble today, Simon. You and I are going to review Coke at 11.30 on the dot.

Brett Topowlski – 5/1/00, 10.20am
to... Liam O'Keefe
cc...
re... Shit, meet Fan

Susi says Crutton has gone fucking apeshit. She doesn't know why, but he wants a Coke review. *11.30 TODAY!* Shit! Got anything? Me and Vin have sweet FA. We were slaughtered last night. Where the fuck were you? You were spot on, Lol wasn't wearing knickers – had to drop my lighter half a dozen times to be certain. Anyway, only just got in, and the one line we had on Coke went up Vin's nose last night. I have a bad feeling.

Liam O'Keefe – 5/1/00, 10.27am
to... Brett Topowlski
cc...
re... Neck, meet Noose

Coke, today? What the fuck is going down? Sorry I didn't make it last night, but Pinki flew back in from her clairvoyant with one of her creative auras, so we did a late one. Reminded me why I put up with her and her Nick Drake albums. She was brilliant and came up with a blinder for Mako.

And stuff your problems. Think about me. I'm a fucking fire officer!

Nigel Godley – 5/1/00, 10.50am
to... Accounts Department
cc...
re... let's make this the best fire drill ever!

As your designated fire officer, I'd like to draw your attention to the diagrams I circulated to all of you. These set out your starting positions for the drill. Can you log off your PCs at 11.23 hrs and take your marks at precisely 11.25 hrs? This will ensure that when the alarm sounds at 11.30 hrs, you will be in the optimum state of readiness to make a safe and rapid evacuation.

And perhaps this time we will beat our previous best of 3 minutes and 21 seconds. Good luck, Team Finance!

Nige

David Crutton – 5/1/00, 10.52am
to... Susi Judge-Davis
cc...
re... sort it

I've e-mailed your lord and master twice this morning, to no avail. You have also fobbed me off on the phone. You'll know me well enough by now to appreciate that patience doesn't figure in my genetic make-up. So let's keep this simple. The Coke review *will* happen at 11.30. If it doesn't, I'll fuck your boss so badly, he'll never get another job in advertising. In fact, he'll be so shafted, he wouldn't get work if he dressed up as a cub scout and did bob-a-job. I trust you'll pass on the message.

Susi Judge-Davis – 5/1/00, 10.54am
to... Simon Horne
cc...
re... PANIC STATIONS!

Darling, your door's locked, and you won't answer your phone or e's. I'm sure you're only having one of your 'can't-be-disturbed-creative-inspiration-moments', but you should know that David is going mental and is saying some beastly things. He's insisting that the Coke 11.30 happens. You are OK for that, aren't you? I'm going to tell him you are anyway, before he explodes . . . Sx

Susi Judge-Davis – 5/1/00, 10.57am
to... David Crutton
cc...
re... sort it

David, ever so sorry for the delay in getting back to you, but it's been a madhouse with work down here. I've just spoken to Simon. He says 11.30 is fine and he's really looking forward to it!

Brett Topowlski – 5/1/00, 11.09am
to... Liam O'Keefe
cc...
re... Balls, meet Vice

Susi's just been in to tell us to get our stuff ready for the 11.30. Didn't tell her we haven't got any. We need this job – Vin still owes four grand on his Fireblade and I just got the insurance through for my R1 – £1,500! We're fucked!

Liam O'Keefe – 5/1/00, 11.11am
to... Brett Topowlski
cc...
re... relief is at hand

I have a plan.

Liam O'Keefe – 5/1/00, 11.16am
to... Creative Department
cc...
re... FIRE DRILL

The fire drill that will take place in a few minutes is very important. As the fire officer for this floor, I have been informed that the London Fire Brigade will be observing and the renewal of our fire certificate depends on it. Stop whatever you're doing when the alarm sounds and clear the building calmly and quickly. Ken Perry stresses that this drill takes precedence over any meetings or reviews that are scheduled for that time.

Liam
Designated Fire Officer

Susi Judge-Davis – 5/1/00, 11.29am
to... Simon Horne
cc...
re... EMERGENCY!!

Simon, unlock your door now. David's on his way down!!

Nigel Godley – 5/1/00, 12.07pm
to... Accounts Department
cc... David Crutton
re... good, but not good enough

Our evacuation time of 3 minutes, 17 seconds was quite outstanding and does the accounts department credit. I am proud to call
myself your fire officer. However, we were beaten by an adversary
from a most surprising quarter. The creative department cleared
their work stations and were out of the building in under two
minutes.

Isn't it great that another department has decided to take up the
challenge of achieving fire drill excellence? It can only push us
to raise our own standards. I propose weekly training sessions.
Then next time those creative johnnies will have a contest on
their hands – Nige

Liam O'Keefe – 5/1/00, 12.15pm
to... Brett Topowlski
cc...
re... Naga-fucking-saki!

You and Vin shouldn't have buggered off to the pub straight
after the drill because you missed a grade-A spectacle. When the
alarm rang Crutton went straight to Horne's pad. It was locked
so he collared one of the firemen and made him pulp it with his
axe! Horne was inside comatose and semi-naked – totally fucked
from some celebrity piss-up last night. Hadn't heard a thing.
Didn't know about the drill, the review, nothing. I've seen Crutton lose it before, but this was breathtaking. Horne's a gibbering
wreck now. Susi's feeding him Valium like they're M&Ms. And
Ken Perry just got the elbow for having the front to hold a drill
at the same time as Crutton wanted to look at some creative
work. The way it's shaping up, we'll all be out of work by the
end of the day – worth it just to witness Armageddon. Only a
few days behind schedule, too.

David Crutton – 5/1/00, 12.21pm
to... Simon Horne
cc...
re... deathwish . . .

. . . do you have one, and have you the faintest idea how close
you are to realising it? The only reason you still have a job is
that at this moment I have no choice but to keep you on. With
business at the critical stage it is right now, even a creative director
of stupefying incompetence must be marginally better than none
at all. I'm going to lunch. When I return at 3.30 we *will* hold the
Coke review.

David Crutton – 5/1/00, 12.42pm
to... Lorraine Pallister
cc...
re... crap

To add to the metaphorical shit that's been swilling around this
office today, we have a surfeit of the real thing in the executive
washroom. The toilets are blocked and overflowing. Get maintenance to fix it while I'm at lunch. Failing that, do it yourself.

Lorraine Pallister – 5/1/00, 12.54pm
to... David Crutton
cc...
re... crap

That may be a problem. Since you let Ken Perry go, no-one
seems to know where the rods and plungers are kept. As for
doing it myself, I only deal with the metaphorical stuff. Sorry.

Simon Horne – 5/1/00, 12.59pm
to... Susi Judge-Davis
cc...
re... thank you

Darling, you have been an absolute lifesaver this morning.

You seem to be the only person who truly understands the pressure cooker in which I operate. Thank you for your empathy.

Could you do me a couple of favours before you pop out for lunch?

First, let my department know that the Coke review will now take place at 3.30, and I expect no tardiness.

Then have someone from maintenance replace my door. I cannot possibly be expected to do my best work without some sort of protective barrier from the ignorant hordes.

And when you are out could you nip to Dickens and Jones and get me something smelly for Celine? – You know what she wears.

For some unfathomable reason she would not let me in the house last night.

lorraine_pallister@millershanks-london.co.uk
5/1/00, 1.05pm
to... debbie_wright@littlewoods/manchester.co.uk
cc...
re... London calling again

Where the fuck do I start, girl? There was a fire practice this morning and it turned into WW3 with jokes. Next time I see you, have a bottle of Bacardi handy and I'll take you through it.

Then Boss told me to clean out the bogs. He's a scary fucker but if he thinks I'm dealing with his floaters he'll have to pay me a lot more than £8 an hour. Told him to shove his bog brush up his hairy arse. Not those words exactly, but you get the idea. He's gone to lunch and I reckon I'll be out of a job when he gets back. Don't e me here just in case. I'll let you know.

Remember, however dull processing mail order gets, at least it's not a bloody loony bin – Lol

Susi Judge-Davis – 5/1/00, 1.07pm
to... Creative Department
cc...
re... Coke review

This is to inform you that the Coke review due to take place this morning will now happen at 3.30 in Simon's office. Simon has also asked me to point out that after you let him down so appallingly this morning, he will tolerate no absenteeism.

Susi Judge-Davis – 5/1/00, 1.09pm
to... Simon Horne
cc...
re... thank you

Si, darling, you're so sweet, but please don't thank me. After all, if it wasn't for your strength and wisdom under impossible strain, I wouldn't be half the person I am. You've taught me so much.

I've let the department know about the review. I know you're too nice to say so yourself, so I've also told them you'll brook no silliness this time. I talked to Ken Perry's Shanice about the door and she's trying to order a new one. There may be a problem hanging it, though. Since Ken was sacked no-one has the foggiest where the key to the tool locker is . . . Sx

Daniel Westbrooke – 5/1/00, 1.50pm
to... Shanice Duff
cc...
re... front doors

I have a delegation of clients from the LOVE Channel waiting in the street. They are very cold and extremely wet – especially the two charming topless pool players. The automatic doors are refusing to open. I hazard it is some sort of electrical failure, though since I am not mechanically minded, who knows?

You must be aware that we are about to shoot a *very expensive* television commercial for LOVE, and this is hardly the way to imbue them with confidence in our abilities.

I suppose that in the unforeseen absence of Ken Perry, this falls to you to deal with. I would be very much obliged if this embarrassing situation could be remedied PDQ.

Daniel Westbrooke
Head of Client Services

Liam O'Keefe – 5/1/00, 1.53pm
to... Brett Topowlski
cc...
re... welcome back

If you and Vin managed to get past your two LOVE birds (Patsi and Despina – as a major pool fan I'd recognise those cueing arms anywhere), and then make it through the faulty doors, this will be the 2nd e-mail you read, after Susi's, about the 3.30. Well, it had to happen but at least I bought you an extra four hours. The Pink Buddha and me have just resurrected that campaign we did for the John Smith's pitch last year. Horne will never remember it – off his face when he rejected it. I'm changing the pack shots on the storyboards from beer to Coke. Pinki's got a problem with the line. 'BITTER, MOI?' doesn't readily translate to cola.

Brett Topowlski – 5/1/00, 2.17pm
to... Liam O'Keefe
cc...
re... welcome back

We only just got in. Some geezer in a boiler suit had lifted an entire sheet of plate glass from reception and was helping the LOVE babes *(who, you will be aware, are only in the agency for a wardrobe session for our exciting TV ad which is about to shoot on the idyllic beaches of Mauritius)* totter up a step-ladder and through the gap ... welcome to Miller Shanks, at the cutting edge of modern technology.

Just done five Becks each but even so had a blinder on Coke. Surrender to it.

Nigel Godley – 5/1/00, 2.24pm
to... All Departments
cc...
re... stationery requisites

Anyone who has been having trouble gaining access to the stationery cupboard since the departure of Ken Perry might be interested to know that I have a supply of paper clips in assorted colours and staples in two sizes. Although these are my personal property, I would be glad to help the company through this period of shortage. This is a limited supply, so only the genuinely needy, please.

Nige

Simon Horne – 5/1/00, 2.33pm
to... David Crutton
cc...
re... deathwish . . .

David, I must apologise for the way things looked this morning. With the kerfuffle of the drill, I can appreciate how my karmic state of creativity could so easily have been misread for something less productive.

Bizarre as it might appear, flat on my back in my underpants is invariably the repose in which my finest ideas arrive.

The artistic process defies rationalisation.

Legend has it that a personal hero of mine, Bernie Taupin, has reconstructed his father's potting shed at the end of his garden in Beverly Hills.

It is in there that he writes all his lyrics.

When the result is something as ethereally wondrous as *Candle in the Wind* it seems churlish to mock his eccentricity.

But I digress. I write with the news that the answer to the Coke challenge came to me during my reverie. The indefatigable Susi is printing off the scripts as I type.

I would love you to have a preview in advance of the 3.30.

You may, of course, disagree, but I believe it is the advertising idea that the ladies and gentlemen from Atlanta have always deserved but, until now, have never had.

Si

David Crutton – 5/1/00, 2.38pm
to... Simon Horne
cc...
re... deathwish . . .

Bring the work up. I sincerely hope it's as grand as you make out.

Simon Horne – 5/1/00, 2.39pm
to... Susi Judge-Davis
cc...
re... trousers

Have you managed to get my trousers dry yet, darling? Sneak them in here, because I need to see David immediately.

Susi Judge-Davis – 5/1/00, 2.40pm
to... Simon Horne
cc...
re... trousers

They're still a little moist in the crutch, sweetie, but I think they'll get you by. I'll just pop them under the hot-air drier in the ladies . . . Sx

Nigel Godley – 5/1/00, 2.41pm
to... All Departments
cc...
re... stationery requisites

I'm out of blue and yellow but I still have plenty of paper clips in other colours. Come and get them! Nige

Shanice Duff – 5/1/00, 2.45pm
to... Rachel Stevenson
cc...
re... HELP!

Hi, Rachel. I'm desperate to talk to you, but no-one's answering your phone. I've just got back from a late lunch and found a billion rude messages on my voice and e-mail. As you know, they made Ken leave immediately and now everything's going wrong. I haven't a clue what to do and is it true that David's going to fire me, too, if I don't fix his toilet personally? Please call me. I've got one of my heads coming on.

lorraine_pallister@millershanks-london.co.uk
5/1/00, 2.55pm
to... debbie_wright@littlewoods/manchester.co.uk
cc...
re... still here

Debbie, feel free to e me back. Boss loves me – didn't actually say 'sorry' but came close (read attached e – shows you what I've got to deal with). Got to tell you what just happened. There's a ponce called Horne in charge of the creative department. He just came up with these TV scripts for Coke. He swans in and reads his ideas out to Boss. He'd done these cartoon bubbles and they're all singing, 'If you pop, you won't stop' – thinks it's the fucking dog's. Boss points out that it's a rip-off of Pringles Crisps mixed up with something Horne did fifty years ago for Fun Pops or something. Even if it wasn't, it'd still be shite. Horne gets precious, then Boss goes green – he can't breathe and he's gripping the table. I thought he was having a fucking heart attack and I'm trying to remember first aid from Girl Guides, but apparently this is what he always does when he loses it. Horne bursts into tears. If he didn't earn £300,000 I might feel sorry for the git. This is like a normal meeting in Boss's office. Can't wait to start on the creative floor. Horne might be a tosser but at least his department are a laugh. I might shag that Bart/Brad guy (real name's Liam). He's sending me these horny e-mails and I'm a sucker for luurve letters . . . Lolx

 Attachment . . .

David Crutton – 5/1/00, 3.05pm
to... Lorraine Pallister
cc...
re... sorry seems to be the hardest word . . .

. . . so I won't say it. However, you may not have had the stiffest of competition, but you remain the most efficient PA I've had in some time. My previous e-mail about the washroom was supposed to be ironic – do they have that in Manchester? I just want it fixed. I'm sure a girl as obviously intelligent as yourself will find a way. And bring me tea.

Rachel Stevenson – 5/1/00, 3.10pm
to... All Departments
cc...
re... maintenance matters

As you may be aware, Ken Perry's unexpected departure has coincided with a number of maintenance problems. I appreciate that it's like a sauna on the 1st floor, and freezing cold on the 4th, but we are sorting things out as quickly as we can. In the meantime, it's worth remembering there are people in the world with greater hardships than faulty air con and low toner supplies. A little more common sense and a little less hysteria, please.

Rachel Stevenson
Personnel

Harriet Greenbaum – 5/1/00, 3.13pm
to... Simon Horne
cc... David Crutton
re... Mako

Just a gentle nudge. Don't forget we're committed to a Mako review today. You didn't give me a time and Susi refuses to even pencil anything in your diary. I understand you're Coking at the moment. (I mean that in the non class-A sense of course.) I'm sure you'll call me as soon as you're done.

David Crutton – 5/1/00, 3.25pm
to... Simon Horne
cc...
re... earlier

I have gone over and over your work for Coke and still fail to see the difference between your line and Pringles'. I could analyse it at length but, take it from me, it's utter fucking cack. Besides, even the YTS retards in despatch would notice the uncanny resemblance between today's offering and the Fun Pops nonsense you inflicted on them when they were in pre-school.

I've been summoned to a conference call with Weissmuller, so I won't be attending the 3.30 review. I hope that in my absence you'll unearth a diamond for my amazement.

And just to show you I'm not a total cunt, I still like your Mako work. Maybe you aren't completely useless.

Susi Judge-Davis – 5/1/00, 3.26pm
to... Creative Department
cc...
re... REVIEW TIME
Single file outside Simon's office. Now, please.

**pertti_vanhelden@millershanks-helsinki.co.fin
5/1/00, 3.33pm (5.33pm local)**
to... david_crutton@millershanks-london.co.uk
cc...
re... earlier

I am just completed reading your e-mail to your Creating Director.

How I am empathising with your predicament. You see, once you are laying eyes on geniusness, as you are with our Coca-Cola idea, then everything else must pale into nothingness. And I must be saying that on a normal day you would surely be loving an idea so brilliant that it is reminding you of the amazing Pringles advertisements. Still, my friend, if all this falling out is making you glum, then why not sing:

> We make fizzy pop,
> And Coke make fizzy pop,
> Put the two together,
> And the fun, it never stop!

Think happy things – Pertti

Pinki Fallon – 5/1/00, 4.18pm
to... Harriet Greenbaum
cc...
re... free?

Liam and I have a Mako idea to show you which we think is dead right. We should take it to Simon first, but we've just reviewed Coke with him and he's in a destructive mood, so it probably wouldn't be useful. We know you're under heavy pressure, so come down and we'll put you out of your misery . . . ☺

David Crutton – 5/1/00, 4.19pm
to... Simon Horne
cc...
re... bated breath

By now you will have finished reviewing Coke and must have sorted the wheat from the bollocks. I'd like to see the winning ideas, given that I've just spent the best part of thirty minutes on the phone to NY reassuring them that we're well on course to bagging this one.

Simon Horne – 5/1/00, 4.24pm
to... David Crutton
cc...
re... bated breath

I apologise on behalf of my charges.

They let me down with some shoddy and poorly conceived work. I am about to order another review for the same time tomorrow.

I think that, once the pitch is behind us, a major clear-out of this department is warranted.

I know I have been too soft on them to date.

Finally, though I hesitate to say so at this juncture, maybe in the calm light of tomorrow morning the merits of the Coke campaign I showed you earlier will be more apparent.

Si

David Crutton – 5/1/00, 4.26pm
to... Simon Horne
cc...
re... bated breath

No they bloody won't.

Liam O'Keefe – 5/1/00, 4.27pm
to... Vince Douglas; Brett Topowlski
cc...
re... arsehole

For what it's worth, I reckon your Coke idea was twenty-four carat – 'cOKe'! It was staring me in the face – the two most universal words on the planet right there on the bloody can. Horne's a bigger arse than I thought for dumping it. Mind you, he crapped on everything he saw. Either he wants to lose this pitch or he has an amazing idea of his own – no, forget that last thought (airborne pigs etc). Got to go. Harriet's just walked in and she's smuggling melons. Later.

Simon Horne – 5/1/00, 4.30pm
to... Creative Department
cc...
bcc...David Crutton
re... what have I done to deserve you?

I feel very badly let down by each and every one of you.

No, worse than let down.

Wounded.

I seem to spend my life defending your hides.

You repay me with the saddest parade of ideas passing off as advertising that it has been my misfortune to see.

At 3.30 tomorrow we will review Coca-Cola once again.

This is the saloon named Last Chance.

I kid you not.

Si

Nigel Godley – 5/1/00, 4.31pm
to... All Departments
cc...
re... going, going . . .

I'm right out of staples and paper clips but I still have pads (lined and plain) and green Bics – Nige

Simon Horne – 5/1/00, 4.36pm
to... Vince Douglas; Brett Topowlski
cc...
bcc...David Crutton
re... FINAL WARNING

Gentlemen, I held back from singling you out in my note to the department to spare your embarrassment.

However, I would like you to know that your Coke idea was the worst of a lamentable bunch.

If you believe you can convince me that taking the brand name and highlighting the letters 'OK' is *l'idée grande*, one that will win us a multi-million pound account, then you must think I have been in this business five minutes.

It was worse than pathetic.

For too long I have harboured the fond hope that your banal profanities and shabby appearance masked the quick wits of true creative practitioners.

Sadly not.

Maybe you are simply demob happy at the prospect of winging your way to Mauritius next week to shoot LOVE. I would be more than happy to lift that heavy burden from your shoulders and cover the job myself if it would mean your rapt attention on Coke.

And when you have a moment, Vince, you might care to jot down on a scrap of paper exactly how you think that wearing a T-shirt that bears the legend, 'TITS OUT FOR THE ART DIREC-TOR' could possibly be seen as suitable wear on a highly paid professional. I would love to know.

Si

Harriet Greenbaum – 5/1/00, 4.43pm
to... James Gregory; Katie Philpott
cc...
re... phew!

Pinki and Liam have given me some Mako scripts and posters that have put a grin on my face for the first time in weeks. Come and inspect them immediately and tell me that the pressure to salvage this account hasn't totally screwed my judgement.

debbie_wright@littlewoods/manchester.co.uk
5/1/00, 4.45pm
to... lorraine_pallister@millershanks-london.co.uk
cc...
re... still here

Glad you're still in employment, doll. Just one word of warning
on the Bart/Brad/Liam thing: just remember what happened when
you shagged that bloke in the Hacienda cos you thought he
looked like Goldie ... Debs

Katie Philpott – 3/1/00, 4.58pm
to... Liam O'Keefe
cc...
re... genius!

Harriet has just shown James and me your idea for Mako and I
think it's absolutely, totally brill! Well done! I don't know how you
creative chaps come up with it. Me, I haven't got a creative bone in
my bod – totally hopeless! See you later, clever clogs – Katie P

Harriet Greenbaum – 5/1/00, 4.59pm
to... Lorraine Pallister
cc... David Crutton
re... urgent

Lorraine, could I see David as soon as he's out of his meeting
on a very urgent matter? It regards Mako and an excellent idea
that he *must* look at.

Rachel Stevenson – 5/1/00, 5.00pm
to... Nigel Godley
cc...
re... going, going . . .

Nigel, I don't wish to be rude as I value your commitment to
the company tremendously. However, IT tells me your e-mails
are clogging the already over-burdened server. I've also had a
number of complaints from people tired of wasting time on trivial

memos. As I said, your hard work is appreciated. Please keep it up. Just go easy on the all-staffers.

Harriet Greenbaum – 5/1/00, 5.02pm
to... James Gregory; Katie Philpott
cc...
re... drop everything

David wants to see us right away. His office, two minutes.

Brett Topowlski – 5/1/00, 5.04pm
to... Liam O'Keefe
cc...
re... arsehole

Complimenting our work? It must be fucking brilliant. Horne shat on us big time. Had a go at everything, including Vin's T-shirt. Even threatened to take us off LOVE – twat. I've been on the phone to the headhunter. Vin called his mum. Apparently, she once went to his school and kicked the living shit out of his maths teacher when he got a bad mark. Said teacher needed reconstructive surgery on his ear. Letitia the fluffy headhunter had fuck-all in the way of jobs, so I reckon we'll call in Mrs Douglas and her big baseball bat. We're off to BZ – no point hanging round where we're not wanted. See you there.

Nigel Godley – 5/1/00, 5.07pm
All Departments
cc...
re... censorship

Godley's Office Supplies is no longer open for business. It seems that *certain people* in this company do not wish to see initiative in the ranks. I fully expect to join Ken and Carla on the streets for writing this e-mail, but I've always believed in speaking my mind. I'll be at the Earl of Wessex at six should anyone wish to share an ale and a fare-thee-well with me.

Nige

PS: I would also like to point out that, unlike the so-called 'trendy' Bar Zero, the Wessex is very reasonably priced and serves an excellent pint of Poacher's Snaffle, not to mention pork scratchings.

David Crutton – 5/1/00, 5.17pm
to... Pinki Fallon
cc...
re... Mako

Harriet has shown me your Mako idea and I have to say it's pretty bloody good. See me at 5.30 and we'll discuss. Until then, perhaps you and your scruffy partner can give some thought as to how you'd like to break the news to your boss that you've been sneaking work around behind his back.

David Crutton – 5/1/00, 5.19pm
to... Rachel Stevenson
cc...
re... who?

I pride myself on being a caring chief exec who's at one with his staff, but please answer me this. Who the hell is 'Nige', what is he going on about and should I give a toss?

Liam O'Keefe – 5/1/00, 5.20pm
to... Vince Douglas; Brett Topowlski
cc...
re... arsehole

Boys, my thoughts are with you at this difficult time. Crutton wants to see Pinki and me on Mako. Haven't shown Horne the work yet, so it could be fun when this gets out. I'll be at BZ after that. Lol's coming. By the way, I'm getting fan mail from the new girl, Katie. She fancies me. Have you seen the arse on it though? Mad eyes too. Definite bunny-boiler.

pertti_vanhelden@millershanks-helsinki.co.fin
5/1/00, 5.32pm (7.32pm local)
to... david_crutton@millershanks-london.co.uk
cc...
re... who?

You must be more pressured with work than I am realising to
not know about Nige Godley. He is indeed a Pillar of Hercules
inside the Miller Shanks network. For much time now your Nige
and Matti Littmanen of our own accountings department have
been sharing productive e-mailings which result in a super-
dooper efficient computer system to control our inventory of
stationeries. This has made a major contributing factor to our
becoming the 11th most profitable office in the European organ-
isation.

He is not all work, work, working either. He is being an enthusi-
astic partner in a cultural exchange with our *Blake's 7* fan club
here in Helsinki. I am already recommending Nige to Jimmy
Weissmuller for a senior network position. He is exactly the type
of far-sighting personality we need to meet the challenges of the
next 2000 millenniums.

May the Force be with you – Pertti

David Crutton – 5/1/00, 5.38pm
to... Chandra Kapoor
cc... Rachel Stevenson
re... come in, Kapoor, your time is up

What exactly do you get up to in your den in the basement?
Macramé? Tai chi? Or do you just sit on your arse and watch
daytime TV? Because whatever the fuck it is, it's not fixing the
fault on my e-mail. You have until the morning.

Letitia Hegg / letitia@tavistockhegg.aol.com.uk
5/1/00, 5.44pm
to... simon_horne@millershanks-london.co.uk
cc...
re... new stars in the firmament

Si, darling, thx for Xmas cocktails at la casa Horne. Always a pleasure, and I've yet to meet a living soul who knows his way round the Spanish wine regions as well as *el Horneo*.

On to business. I have a team that you will simply want to eat for brekky. Charming, talented and multi-multi-award winning, they are the toast of Italian advertising. Now they are dying to try their hands in the toughest arena of all. Their English is a bit flaky, but these days it's all about the big visual, isn't it? Words are so 20th century. At this mo they're my little secret, but that won't last. Trevor Beattie is already sniffing and soon it will be flies round shit. If you're interested they'd come in at under 150k the pair. Shall I fax you their CVs?

Let me know pronto, and kisses to gorgeous, scrumptious Celine – Letty xxx

PS: It wasn't me who told you, but your two likely lads, Vince and Brett, are putting out feelers.

Nigel Godley – 5/1/00, 5.59pm
to... All Departments
cc...
re... DRINKS

Just to let you know that I'll be departing for the Wessex in a moment, if anyone would like to join me in reception for the short walk there. And to *they who must be obeyed*, I will not be silenced and I leave with my head held high.

Nige

David Crutton – 5/1/00, 6.01pm
to... Simon Horne
cc...
re... Mako

Don't ask me how it ended up here but I have some new Mako work on my coffee table. I think it's rather good. Would you like

to see what your department gets up to when you're butt-naked
and barely conscious on your sofa?

Rachel Stevenson – 5/1/00, 6.03pm
to... Nigel Godley
cc...
re... DRINKS

Nigel, this is probably too late to catch you at your PC, but I
must stress that nobody is firing you, or even contemplating
doing so. My earlier e-mail was merely a gentle hint to go easy
on the system. It seems to have had the opposite effect of making
your 'send' button busier than ever. I'll keep quiet in future. In
the meantime, I trust you'll be at your desk in the morning.

Simon Horne – 5/1/00, 6.22pm
to... Pinki Fallon
cc... Harriet Greenbaum
bcc...David Crutton
re... Mako

I have just seen your sidekick, O'Keefe, sneak out of the building
like the weasel he is, but perhaps you could grace me with your
presence.

I would like an explanation as to why a campaign for Mako has
made it all the way to the Chief Executive's office without passing
even vaguely close to the quality control system.

Namely me.

Clearly the account director has a case to answer and I will be
taking up the matter with her in due course.

However, Pinki, I find your part in this grubby business a far
more personal betrayal.

It was I who hired you.

It is I who has stood by you despite numerous office-hours visits
to London's ragbag collection of quacks.

One thing I will expand on in the conversation we are about to have is how I can just as easily end our working relationship.

Si

Harriet Greenbaum – 5/1/00, 6.26pm
to... Simon Horne
cc... David Crutton
bcc...Pinki Fallon; Liam O'Keefe
re... hold your horses

Simon, before you do something regrettable with the best asset in your department, can I try to straighten this out? If you recall, we were promised a review with you on Mako this afternoon. When I tried to pin you down, you weren't available. I appreciate that you have been snowed under with Coke, but it isn't the only brief on your desk with a heavy priority on it. Unlike Coke, Mako is a real client paying real salaries and we are under severe pressure to deliver. Given your inaccessibility, I took it upon myself to look at Pinki and Liam's work and then take it on to David. If you have a problem, have it out with me.

However, I believe our time would be better spent discussing the comparative merits of the Reeves and Mortimer campaign and the new work, which both David and I feel is very strong indeed.

Pinki Fallon – 5/1/00, 6.58pm
to... Harriet Greenbaum
cc...
re... hold your horses

Harriet, I just read your e. Thanks for sticking up for us, but it's too late. Simon was a pig just now. When he used the 'c' word I couldn't take any more and resigned. I've had enough of trying to be helpful and being treated like shit in return – excuse my language. I'm going to see if Liam is in Bar Zero now. Call me at home tomorrow. I'll miss you ... ☺

Simon Horne – 5/1/00, 6.59pm
to... David Crutton
cc...
re... small problem

David, if you're still here I need to see you urgently.

I have just had to fire Pinki.

As I will explain, her outrageous behaviour gave me no option.

I am on my way up to you now.

Si

Nigel Godley – 5/1/00, 11.36pm
to... All Departments
cc...
re... still here!!!!

I popped back to clear the knick-knacks from my desk and it seems I still have a job. Just goes to show that when you display a bit of good old British pluck *the powers that be* back down, eh? So I may as well stick around for a bit – these invoices won't file themselves. Any other workers still around, join me for a cuppa.

Nige

PS: On my return I found some lady's underthings by the lift door in reception. They're size 12, emerald green, 100% polyester with a lacy panel at the front, slightly soiled. If they belong to anyone, they're tucked safely in my drawer. Please feel free to collect.

Thursday
6 January
2000

Simon Horne – 6/1/00, 8.31am
to... Creative Department
cc... Rachel Stevenson
bcc...David Crutton
re... personnel changes

I am sad to report that I had to terminate Pinki Fallon's contract of employment last night.

No doubt this will come as a shock to you all.

Decency prevents me from going into the details, but please be assured that I had no choice.

Obviously, this has come at a very difficult time. The pressure we were under yesterday has now increased tenfold.

But I know that each and every one of you will want to pull together for the company.

If we roll up our sleeves and apply a sprinkling of magic fairy dust we can win the Coca-Cola pitch.

Let us prove the critics wrong.

We review at 3.30.

Amaze me.

Si

David Crutton – 6/1/00, 8.45am
to... Simon Horne
cc...
re... personnel changes

Well, isn't this fascinating? Pinki leaves and we have not one but two riveting versions of the circumstances.

Version 1: last night you told me you fired her. You claim she gave you no choice when she called you 'a fucking cunting cunt who couldn't write the tie-break slogan in a Kellogg's Cornflakes competition, let alone a decent ad.' Such words may not trip off the tongue of the Pinki I know, but you're the boss and I was prepared to stand by your decision.

Then this morning Harriet tells me it would be in my interests to speak to Pinki myself. Which leads us to . . .

Version 2: Pinki claims, with some conviction, that she wasn't fired, but resigned the instant you called her (and I quote) 'a fucking cunting cunt who couldn't write the tie-break slogan in a Kellogg's Cornflakes competition, let alone a decent ad.' Uncanny similarity except in the trivial matter of who spoke the offending words. She says that there is a cleaner who can corroborate her story and she wants to sue the arse off you (i.e. the company).

Our only hope is that this cleaner is one of the Portuguese contingent and her English is so piss-poor that a decent silk can discredit her with some ruggedly British cross-examination.

I wish that were our only problem. We are staring at a life-or-death Mako meeting for which we have one campaign (yours) that Harriet claims is unsaleable, and another now without its creator around to carry out the necessary development.

And then there is Coke . . .

This is *your* mess, Simon. If you don't phone me with a simple and elegant solution the second you click 'close' on this e-mail, you will wish you had begged your careers master for a moped and an application form for Domino Pizza.

Rachel Stevenson – 6/1/00, 8.59am
to... Simon Horne
cc... David Crutton
re... personnel changes

Simon, we need to go over the details of Pinki Fallon's departure yesterday. I've heard it was acrimonious and I need, for the record, your version of events should this return to haunt the company at some stage. I thank you for your earliest response.

Shanice Duff – 6/1/00, 9.19am
to... Rachel Stevenson
cc...
re... Ken's replacement

Rachel, I've just had the contractors on the phone and they say they can't get a temp office manager in for at least another week! I really don't think I can cope with people being rude to me again today. I've already had tons of messages about loos, photo-copiers, and broken this and broken that and it's not even 9.30. I can't fix things myself, you know! Please, please sort this out. Can't Ken come back?

Melinda Sheridan – 6/1/00, 9.23am
to... Vince Douglas; Brett Topowlski
cc...
re... nasty medicine

Just a reminder that your appointment for your jabs is at 10.30 this morning. Please be there. I'd hate to fly you all the way to Mauritius only to have you wilt mid-take from an attack of malaria. And if either of you little angels is scared of horrid needles, Dr Chen has a delightful Hungarian nurse to kiss it better. Run along now.

Letitia Hegg / letitia@tavistockhegg.aol.com.uk
6/1/00, 9.24am
to... simon_horne@millershanks-london.co.uk
cc...
re... have you been a naughty boy?

Simon, dear, your ears must have been burning last night! What did you do to that young woman with the open-toe sandals and Demis Roussos kaftan? She came into Bar Zero in absolute floods. I'd hate to be accused of tittle-tattling, but I couldn't help over-hearing your name mentioned several times in conjunction with *that* hand gesture. I take it she's gone and if that is the case, you simply must call me re the most fabulously creative portfolio that has just come my way. The mighty Pallant at Saatchi is keen and I didn't want to leave you out. You are, after all, one of the great talent-spotters of this darling little industry of ours. Call me, do
– Lettyxxx

pertti_vanhelden@millershanks-helsinki.co.fin
6/1/00, 9.33am (11.33 am local)
to... david_crutton@millershanks-london.co.uk
cc...
re... personnel changes

I am most distressing to hear that the 'hippie dipstick' (quoting of you, 3/1/00) has walkabouted out. And how dare she be disre-spectful of your talented and esteemed Creation Director? But do not be a worrier. I am having my dear friend Benni Hakkinen looking into it. He is a keen student of the veneratable British justice system and has referred to various video tapings of *Rum-pole of the Bailey* and *Crown Court*. He is assuring me that indeed, if the cleaning person was of listening to this conversation, it is inadmissible in a court of laws as it comes up under hearingsay. So, not to fear.

Let us just be getting on with the job in the hand, which is cracking the Mako presentation on Monday. I am very interesting in hearing your work for this. I am sure I can be providing a fair and objectionable view.

Go for Gold – ~~Pertti~~

Nigel Godley – 6/1/00, 9.36am
to... Liam O'Keefe
cc...
re... Pinki Fallon

Hi, Liam, just a little thing. I lent my Garfield Sellotape dispenser to your colleague, Ms Pinki Fallon, and I understand that she walked out last night. This business can be cruel. Something awful happened to me yesterday too, so I know how it feels to be on the receiving end. Anyway, if you find my dispenser, please can I have it back? It does have sentimental value – office-warming gift from my nan. And maybe you'd like to go for an ale and a moan some time, all chaps together if you know what I mean – Nige

Harriet Greenbaum – 6/1/00, 9.38am
to... Simon Horne
cc... David Crutton
re... what have you done?

I told you the blame for the Mako situation must be laid solely at my feet. Given that I'm normally your pet scapegoat, it amazes me that for once you choose to overlook me. The abusive way you dealt with Pinki is a matter for a separate conversation. Of immediate concern, however, is where her departure leaves us with Mako. You know my feelings on the work you have proposed. Like it or not, we need her campaign, as well as her presence to give it the necessary gloss for presentation. For what it's worth, I suggest you find some grovelling words of contrition that will bring her back to the office before the end of the day. Friday looms.

Chandra Kapoor – 6/1/00, 9.41am
to... David Crutton
cc... Rachel Stevenson
re... e-mail

I'm sorry about the delay in repairing e-mail but we've been up to our necks in virus checks. Then we were waiting for some new diagnostic equipment. We're shutting down the server today and hopefully then the problem will be solved. Thanks for your patience.

David Crutton – 6/1/00, 9.42am
to... Chandra Kapoor
cc...
re... e-mail

'Hopefully' doesn't cut it with me.

Susi Judge-Davis – 6/1/00, 9.43am
to... Simon Horne
cc...
re... are you in there?

Simon, darling, the temporary polythene sheet is pulled over your doorway and I can't work out if you are in or not. I thought I saw movement but I'm not sure. If you are, please can I speak to you? Pinki wants to come in and clear her desk tonight – is this OK and should I have security escort her? David needs to talk to you. So does Harriet. So does Rachel. So does Melinda. And Liam is demanding to see you and he's being very uncouth about it ... Sx

David Crutton – 6/1/00, 9.50am
to... Simon Horne
cc...
bcc...Harriet Greenbaum
re... Pinki

I happen to agree with Harriet. While I couldn't really give a fuck about our (ex-?) copywriter's trampled pride, an obsequious apology is the only practical course of action. Harriet merely suggested this. I am mandating it.

Susi Judge-Davis – 6/1/00, 9.53am
to... Zoë Clarke
cc...
bcc...Rachel Stevenson
re... today

Since you left early yesterday with a 'headache', it has been chaos and I have had to cope alone. I hope you are better this morning. When you finally arrive, see me as I have lots I need to delegate – I have to be here for Simon right now.

Incidentally, when you start with David on Monday, perhaps you should warn him that you are prone to 'headaches'. Have you thought about glasses? I'm just looking out for you, Zoë. I want you to succeed in your new position. And maybe you and I should have a chat about the wardrobe of an executive PA? I don't mind at all – Susi.

David Crutton – 6/1/00, 9.56am
to... Rachel Stevenson
cc...
re... problems

- The executive washroom remains an open sewer.
- My air conditioning has broken and my office is an igloo.
- The new carpet tiles in reception are lifting.
- The automatic doors nearly ripped the back out of my jacket when I arrived today.
- My temp has spent thirty minutes searching the building for a working fax machine.
Don't we have a man who deals with these things?

Melinda Sheridan – 6/1/00, 10.03am
to... Simon Horne
cc...
re... Very Worried of Television

At the Atlantic last night my friend congratulated me on clinching Quentin T. for Kimbelle – she goes out with a producer from Miramax so she should know. Why won't this go away? Do tell your Auntie Melinda.

James Gregory – 6/1/00, 10.07am
to... Daniel Westbrooke
cc...
re... early warning

I think we're running into trouble on Kimbelle. As you know, I don't think the client was happy with me caretaking this account until you appoint a new senior account director. Now she's going mad because we're behind schedule on presenting the new Super Dri work – she was expecting it before Christmas. I've talked to Pinki and Liam and they're up to their necks on Mako. They reckon they're at least a week away from cracking it. Brett and Vince are on the brief as well, but have only had it a couple of days and they fly off to shoot LOVE at the weekend. I'm sorry to bother you with this but our client might need some soothing from the senior end of account management. What do you think?

Daniel Westbrooke – 6/1/00, 10.12am
to... James Gregory
cc...
re... early warning

If you had the faintest idea just how busy I am with both Coca-Cola and preparations for the LOVE shoot then surely you would not bother me with this. At your last assessment I distinctly remember you assuring me that you were more than ready to seize responsibility. I venture that if you cannot field the routine threats of your client then you are less equipped for seniority than you would have me believe. Now, if you don't mind, I have work to do.

Daniel Westbrooke – 6/1/00, 10.15am
to... Rachel Stevenson
cc...
re... problem areas

Rachel, the very high standards of which this company is rightly proud have taken a tumble. From the front door to the gate in the basement car park, the place seems to be falling apart. I am not one to throw around my title willy-nilly, but if we do not knuckle down and sort out this mess, then rank will have to be pulled.

On a more personal note, I know you are recruiting a permanent replacement for Carla, but can I inject a sense of urgency into the process? The temp you have given me is way below the quality that a head of client services has a right to expect.

Simon Horne – 6/1/00, 10.20am
to... Susi Judge-Davis
cc...
re... I am here

I have been at my desk for nigh on two hours trying to sort things out in my mind.

I am quite happy to solve all of Miller Shanks's problems.

I do, though, require a little space.

Please keep everyone away from me. And bring decaff and Valium.

Liam O'Keefe – 6/1/00, 10.27am
to... Brett Topowlski
cc...
re... bloody ada

Where the hell are you? Susi the Stick Insect says you're getting your jabs but this is the day you and Vin *absolutely-fucking-positively* have to be here. Something happened last night. Not Pinki being fired/resigning. Much bigger.

I'll take you through it slowly. After Pinki left BZ and you guys fucked off to score, Lol told me her fantasy. I'll spare you the pervier details but it involved a pair of sturdy bulldog clips, my head between her legs and the two acres of Malaysian teak forest that is Crutton's desk.

The Best Bit: By 11 I had her splayed out on DC's desk and she was well up for it (I'm a bloody animal, I tell you). We reached a natural break, so I suggested a quick toot and popped down to the 2nd to get my emergency stash of Medellin's Finest.

The Even Better Best Bit: I passed Horne's office and I heard him in there. I thought I should have a blast at him on Pinki's behalf – I owe her that much, and anyway it was a chance to increase my recovery time between shags. I stuck my head in and saw him bent over his coffee table. He was humping away at a tiny Asian chick. She was biting down hard on his Mulberry blotter (so would you if you had him up your shitter).

The Mother Of All Best Bits: I'm looking at her trying to work out where I've seen her and then it hits me. Her card's in phone boxes all over W1. The one that says 'NEW ARRIVAL ... GENU-INE THAI LADYBOY'. Asian Babe is hung like a horse – well, more like a dinky Shetland pony. I scarpered before he spotted me but only to grab Mel's Digicam.

Our glorious leader, revered throughout the advertising village, devoted husband and doting father, is now the subject of a fly-on-the-wall doc. It premiers in my office the moment you get in. If you're nice about it I'll tell you where Lol's tattoo is and the noise she makes when she comes.

Liam O'Keefe
Sleaze Correspondent

PS: Got any magic fairy dust? I'm fresh out.

Rachel Stevenson – 6/1/00, 10.33am
to... Daniel Westbrooke
cc...
bcc...Shanice Duff
re... problem areas

Daniel, thank you for highlighting the current admin problems. You are right to be concerned. Since Ken Perry's unplanned departure the situation has become intolerable, and finding a temporary office manager to take over his responsibilities is proving impossible.

I believe I have a solution. I think I could persuade Ken to return to his job provided someone could coax David into allowing him back.

If you agree with my suggestion, you might want to have a quiet word with him. It would be worth pointing out that in twenty-two years of service Ken had an unblemished record. His only mistake was to hold a legally required fire drill at a time inconvenient to David's schedule – more misjudgement than hanging offence.

I appreciate you are not one to flaunt your status. But I do think that only someone of your seniority and with your obvious diplomatic skills could have this delicate conversation. What do you think?

Of course, as soon as we solve this I can devote all my time to finding you a new PA of the appropriate quality and stature.

Liam O'Keefe – 6/1/00, 10.36am
to... Lorraine Pallister
cc...
re... knickers, emerald green, size 12

If I can discreetly retrieve them from accounts, fancy losing them again tonight?

David Crutton – 6/1/00, 10.46am
to... Daniel Westbrooke
cc...
re... gold star

You earn a brownie point for the suggestion you left on my voice-mail regarding Perry. Reinstate him with my blessing.

Which wanker fired him anyway? I dare you to answer that
correctly.

Daniel Westbrooke – 6/1/00, 10.48am
to... Rachel Stevenson
cc...
bcc...David Crutton
re... Ken Perry

Rachel, thank you for pointing out Ken Perry's impeccable work
record to me earlier. It is something that was overlooked completely when he was de-hired yesterday. I must accept full responsibility for this careless administrative error.

Could you please see to it that Ken is offered his old job back
immediately with an apology made on behalf of the company. A
small pay-rise (say 3k?) may also be in order. Please take this
from my departmental budget.

Daniel Westbrooke
Head of Client Services

Rachel Stevenson – 6/1/00, 10.59am
to... Daniel Westbrooke
cc...
re... Ken Perry

He says make it 5k and a parking space and he'll be at his desk
tomorrow.

Daniel Westbrooke – 6/1/00, 11.08am
to... Rachel Stevenson
cc...
re... Ken Perry

If that is the price for an office that functions, so be it. Can I
take it that my reward will appear in the form of a high-quality
permanent secretary to greet me upon my return from babysitting
my client in Mauritius?

Simon Horne – 6/1/00, 11.14am
to... Susi Judge-Davis
cc...
re... refreshment

Could you be a darling and fetch a large pot of *caffeinated* coffee right away. I am now ready to deal with the hordes.

Then get Pinki on the phone.

And have Liam see me in fifteen minutes. He is due a severe dressing-down apropos Mako.

You are a treasure.

Simon Horne – 6/1/00, 11.18am
to... David Crutton
cc...
re... a good day's work.

I am happy to report that my morning has been spent most constructively.

Firstly, you should not be surprised that a grovelling Pinki has phoned repeatedly.

I have given much thought as to the effect that her reappointment might have on the morale of my department.

I have also considered her slanderous accusations.

In the spirit of forgiveness, I have decided to grant her one more chance.

I believe she will return chastened and with a more corporate *esprit*.

Secondly, my mind has been focussed on the kind of problem you brought me here to solve – namely Coca-Cola.

I am making serious inroads.

By early tomorrow, if not the end of today, I will be in a position to show you work which will rewrite the advertising lexicon.

Of course, you must decide for yourself whether I have succeeded, but I have every confidence.

Si

Simon Horne – 6/1/00, 11.20am
to... Rachel Stevenson
cc...
re... Pinki Fallon

Please be informed that Pinki will return to work this afternoon.

Could you make a note for your own records, as well as instruct the necessary people in accounts, that her salary will increase by £20,000.

Back-dated to October last.

Si

simon_horne@millershanks-london.co.uk
6/1/00, 11.23am
to... letitia@tavistockhegg.aol.com.uk
cc...
re... a storm in a cup of Darjeeling.

Letty, darling, you were so right to let me know of last night's shenanigans. Thank you for guarding my back as ever. However, it was no more than tears before bedtime.

Pinki is here this morning and is the proverbial busy bee in my creative hive.

Nevertheless, rosy as the garden undoubtedly is, I feel an injection of fresh blooms is called for.

I would love to pop along to your nook in the mews to peruse that Italian folio you praise so highly as well as any others you think might charm.

Perhaps you have some unexposed young buds of talent, fresh from college and eager to be propagated by my green fingers?

And since there is no time like the present, may I suggest you uncork a bottle of that luscious Merlot.

I will materialise at the lunching hour.

Your dearest friend,

Si

Simon Horne – 6/1/00, 11.28am
to... Harriet Greenbaum
cc...
re... our mutual friend

Whatever Pinki has told you about the events of yesterday, I would like you to know that I was fully prepared to give her Mako work a fair hearing. And, despite her unbecoming shrewishness, my magnanimity has, as usual, got the better of me.

She will be returning to work this afternoon.

As for Mako, it comes down to a shoot-out between mine and Pinki's ideas.

I am confident that personal feeling will not interfere and the best will win.

Si

Susi Judge-Davis – 6/1/00, 11.31am
to... Simon Horne
cc...
re... Liam

He's on his way now.

Susi Judge-Davis – 6/1/00, 11.35am
to... Zoë Clarke
cc...
bcc...Rachel Stevenson
re... YOU ARE VERY, VERY LATE

What time do you call this? We will have that chat at lunchtime.

Simon Horne – 6/1/00, 11.43am
to...   Rachel Stevenson
cc...
re...   Liam O'Keefe

Please be informed that in recognition of his unstinting efforts of late I have decided to award Liam a lump sum bonus of £15,000.

Could you please note this in your own records and instruct the appropriate parties in accounts.

Si

Simon Horne – 6/1/00, 11.49am
to...   Melinda Sheridan
cc...
re...   Tarantino

Melinda, precious, I am flattered that my name should be linked with his.

I am sure Quentin feels likewise.

But for the life of me I do not know from where this talk springs.

Rest assured that talk is all it is.

On a separate point, you would be advised to keep your department's Sony Digicam under lock and key.

This is a valuable piece of agency equipment.

It must be kept out of irresponsible hands.

Si

Liam O'Keefe – 6/1/00, 11.50am
to...   Lorraine Pallister
cc...
re...   pay dirt

Sold movie rights. Lunch. Think big (three courses *and* coffee).

Rachel Stevenson – 6/1/00, 11.51am

to... Susi Judge-Davis

cc...

re... you and Zoë

I would prefer you stopped copying me on your rebukes to Zoë. If the pair of you are having personal problems, please sort them out between yourselves. If they persist, speak to me direct. Thank you.

Letitia Hegg / letitia@tavistockhegg.aol.com.uk 6/1/00, 12.00pm

to... simon_horne@millershanks-london.co.uk

cc...

re... Letty awaits

Darling, the '95 is rooming and your favourite crab cakes are *en route* from Silk and Spice. I am slavering!

Rachel Stevenson – 6/1/00, 12.03pm

to... David Crutton

cc...

re... Pinki and Liam

Simon informs me that he has re-instated Pinki Fallon, but I am not clear as to whether she was fired or resigned. From a legal standpoint this is a crucial distinction. There is another rather confusing issue. Have you sanctioned Pinki's 20k rise and Liam's 15k bonus? If the answer is yes, I will put the paperwork in hand. Can we talk, please? Thanks.

David Crutton – 6/1/00, 12.10pm

to... Simon Horne

cc... Lorraine Pallister

re... crunch time

I will return from lunch at 15.30hrs. Then I'll probably go for a piss, call my lovely wife, and then no doubt I'll have my daily video-conference with our American cousins. So at 16.45hrs I should be free to see this amazing Coke campaign. You can also entertain me with the story of Pinki, Liam and thirty-five grand.

Lorraine, make sure he turns up.

Lorraine Pallister – 6/1/00, 12.26pm
to... Liam O'Keefe
cc...
re... nosebag

Well done on your windfall. I've booked a cab to l'Odeon on Boss Man's account. Fuck knows if it's any good, but when I was doing his ex's it looked bloody pricey. If we get a quiet table with an overhanging cloth, I'll show you how a northern girl says congrats to her boy. See you in reception in fifteen. And get my knickers back – they cost me £25.

pertti_vanhelden@millershanks-helsinki.co.fin
6/1/00, 12.33pm (2.33pm local)
to... david_crutton@millershanks-london.co.uk
cc...
re... crunch time

How like the peas in the pods are we! I, too, am evacuating my bladder before I am speaking to my dear wife!

Your twin, Pertti

Liam O'Keefe – 6/1/00, 12.36pm
to... Nigel Godley
cc...
bcc...Lorraine Pallister
re... Victoria's Secret

Nige, discretion on this appreciated, but the scanties in your drawer are mine. Pop them in a brown bag and hand them over when we have a beer. When are you free? Tonight? Can't wait, pal.

Nigel Godley – 6/1/00, 12.54pm
to... Liam O'Keefe
cc...
re... Victoria's Secret

I've put them in the internal post. Sorry, but can't go for that
drink now. The end-of-year reports are in hand. April may seem
an age away, but in terms of workload versus time given, I'm
snowed under. When they're finished I'm off on hols. In Jun/Jul
we're switching to a new payroll system. Then, Aug/Sept are
always busy and before you know it, Christmas will be upon us
and you know what Christmas is like. Oh, well, never mind. Got
to go now, invoices don't reconcile themselves, you know – Nige

Shanice Duff – 6/1/00, 12.57pm
to... Rachel Stevenson
cc...
re... p spaces

Rachel, thank heaven Ken is back tomorrow. Maybe now we can
all get back to normal. He told me to tell you he'd take the parking
space normally reserved for Dan Westbrooke – Ken didn't think
he'd mind.

Susi Judge-Davis – 6/1/00, 12.59pm
to... Simon Horne
cc...
re... lunchy-poos . . .

. . . and your cab's here. Give Letitia a big Teletubby hug from
me . . . Sx

Susi Judge-Davis – 6/1/00, 1.00pm
to... Zoë Clarke
cc...
re... lunch

It's time for our talk.

James Gregory – 6/1/00, 1.02pm

to...   Daniel Westbrooke

cc...

re...   Kimbelle

Just got off the phone to client. I really think we should talk.

Daniel Westbrooke – 6/1/00, 1.03pm

to...   James Gregory

cc...

re...   Kimbelle

James, I have a company to run. This will have to wait. Put some time in my diary for tomorrow afternoon.

Daniel Westbrooke – 6/1/00, 1.06pm

to...   Rachel Stevenson

cc...

re...   Ken Perry

Rachel, I have had Ken's Shanice wittering on the phone. She tells me that you have authorized him to have my parking space and that I am to have one by the rubbish skips. You do realize that this current space is mine by virtue of seniority? I am sure that there has been some mistake. Please confirm.

Zoë Clarke – 6/1/00, 1.07pm

to...   Susi Judge-Davis

cc...

re...   lunch

Sorry, can't do it now. Going for full wax, then need to buy something black – remember I told you it's my next door neighbour's funeral tomorrow and I won't be here. And since I start with David on Monday, there's not much point in chatting, is there? See ya!!!!!!

David Crutton – 6/1/00, 1.08pm
to... Chandra Kapoor
cc... Rachel Stevenson
re... balls on the line

I am about to go to lunch. If I return to find another unsolicited e-mail from Pertti van Helden, Yogi Bear, Deputy Dawg or any other fuckwit masquerading as a lynchpin of the Miller Shanks network, you will find my patience has snapped once and for all.

Susi Judge-Davis – 6/1/00, 1.11pm
to... Rachel Stevenson
cc...
re... Zoë Clarke

I have had enough of her. She is lazy, rude and incompetent. If you want my opinion, she is quite unsuitable for the most senior secretarial job in the agency.

pertti_vanhelden@millershanks-helsinki.co.fin
6/1/00, 1.13pm (3.13 pm local)
to... david_crutton@millershanks-london.co.uk
cc...
re... balls on the line

To be mentioned in the same breathings as Deputy Dawg and Yogi Bear is an honour of which I feel most unworthy of deserving.

You are a true friend – Pertti

Rachel Stevenson – 6/1/00, 1.16pm
to... Susi Judge-Davis
cc...
re... Zoë Clarke

Seems I got your opinion whether I wanted it or not. You had better see me.

Chandra Kapoor – 6/1/00, 1.18pm
to... All Departments
cc...
re... e-mail

We need to carry out urgent maintenance on Lotus Notes and the server will shut down for approximately two hours. This will take place at 1.30 today, so everyone should log off the system before then. We apologize for the inconvenience, but once we are up and running again we will have seen the last of e-mails that end up in the wrong hands.

Chandra Kapoor
Head of IT

Brett Topowlski – 6/1/00, 1.29pm
to... Liam O'Keefe
cc...
re... bloody ada

Just back from doc's. Can't believe what we missed. Vin is catatonic. Does this mea

Chandra Kapoor – 6/1/00, 3.15pm
to... All Departments
cc...
re... e-mail

I'm happy to report that e-mail is online again. Thank you for your patience.

Zoë Clarke – 6/1/00, 3.16pm
to... Susi Judge-Davis
cc...
re... working relationships

What have you been saying to Rachel? She's just had me down there for half an hour, talking to me about the importance of the job of PA to a CEO! What am I? An idiot? I know how important this job is and I can do it standing on my head which is more than can be said of you!!!!!!!!!! I'm more professional, discreet and trustworthy than you'll ever be in a million years!!! And you know I've got a funeral tomorrow. This is a really bad time for me and I'm really upset and have only stayed on at work today because of my professional attitude!!! And don't try and deny that you've been slagging me off! She wouldn't't've known about me being off tomorrow if you hadn't told her!!! As for people slagging people off behind their backs, I wouldn't be so high-and-sodding mighty if I was you!!! Simon thinks you're useless and I know that 'cos he told someone who told me. Given how discreet I am, don't bother to ask me who it was either. You're just jealous 'cos I'm working for David and I'll be more important than you!!

Zoë Clarke – 6/1/00, 3.19pm
to... Lorraine Pallister
cc...
re... Susi

Mate, from one un-stuck-up chick to another, this is a warning. As of Monday, you are going to be working with the bitch from hell!!! She's a fucking little Hitler!!!! She Immacs her top lip!!!!! Anyway, any tips you wanna give about working for David, pass them on. You scratch my back, I'll scratch yours!!! I'm going now. I've got a really traumatising bereavement to cope with, but I'll be in on Monday – in my new job!!!! We'll go for a JD & Coke then! Loveya . . . Zxxx

Susi Judge-Davis – 6/1/00, 3.20pm
to... Rachel Stevenson
cc...
bcc...David Crutton; Simon Horne
re... Zoë Clarke

Rachel, I'm forwarding an e-mail I just received from Zoë. This is the kind of behaviour I have to put up with on a daily basis. I've emboldened the parts that I find the most offensive. This isn't a formal complaint – strictly FYI.

 Attachment . . .

Zoe Clarke – 6/1/00, 3.16pm
to... Susi Judge-Davis
cc...
re... you two-faced bitch!!!!!!

What the **fuck** have you been saying to Rachel? She's just had me down there for **fucking** half an hour, talking to me about the importance of the job of PA to a CEO! What am I? A **fucking** idiot? I know how important this job is and I can do it standing on my **fucking** head which is more than can be said of you, **you fucking self-important, precious bitch!!!!!!!!!** I'm more professional, discreet and trustworthy than you'll ever be in a million years!!! And you know I've got a funeral tomorrow. This is a really bad time for me and I'm really upset and have only stayed on at work today because of my professional attitude!!! And don't try and deny that you've been slagging me off! She wouldn't've known about me being off tomorrow if you hadn't told her!!! As for people slagging people off behind their backs, I wouldn't be so **high-and-sodding mighty** if I was you!!! **Simon thinks you're a useless twat and I know that 'cos he told someone who told me.** Given how discreet I am, don't bother to ask me who it was either. You're just **a jealous bitch** 'cos I'm working for David and I'll be more important than you!! **Shove it up your arse Susi, you vicious fucking cow.**

Simon Horne – 6/1/00, 3.26pm
to... Susi Judge-Davis
cc...
re... review

Be so kind as to let my department know that the Coke review scheduled for 3.30 today is no longer required.

If the wastrels wish to know why, tell them this.

I have once again saved them.

I have come up with *the* Coke campaign and will be visiting it upon David post-haste.

Simon Horne – 6/1/00, 3.31pm
to... David Crutton
cc...
re... creative juices

David, I have just returned from a working lunch where my mind was in creative hyperdrive.

I have a compelling new idea on Coke that demands your immediate attention.

Are you free?

Si

David Crutton – 6/1/00, 3.37pm
to... Simon Horne
cc...
re... creative juices

My video-conference with Weissmuller has been cancelled, so you're in luck. Come up in thirty minutes. Before you do, though, tell your PA that I do not get involved in malicious inter-secretarial squabbles. If she blind copies me on another vicious e-mail, it will be the last thing she does at Miller Shanks.

David Crutton – 6/1/00, 3.40pm
to... Chandra Kapoor
cc...
re... back to normal?

I trust I can send e-mails with impunity once again. For instance, if I choose to write that Pertti van Helden is a Grade-A cunt, I can rest assured that he won't be reading it a couple of cyber-seconds after I click 'send'?

simon_horne@millershanks-london.co.uk
6/1/00, 3.43pm
to... letitia@tavistockhegg.aol.com.uk
cc...
re... eternal thanks

My thanks for a wondrous hour-and-a-half of ravishing cuisine and company.

You also have my gratitude for showing me the portfolios in your tender care. The youngsters you represent demonstrate fresh thinking aplenty.

As I promised, I have given them serious thought. However, upon reflection I feel their ideas lack the killer punch. The one that leaps off the layout and lands a crunching left to the jaw.

So whilst it was illuminating, I shall not be bringing any of your little flock into my fold for the time being.

Never mind, time spent in your delightful company is never wasted.

True friendship, such as we share, is the single thing that keeps one sane in this shallow and Machiavellian business.

Lunch soon? My shout. Give me a call and we will find a window.

Si

David Crutton – 6/1/00, 3.47pm
to... Rachel Stevenson
cc...
re... Zoë Clarke

I enjoyed her outburst at Horne's breadstick of a secretary. It looks like you've finally supplied me with a PA with the balls for the job. Congratulations.

Letitia Hegg / letitia@tavistockhegg.aol.com.uk
6/1/00, 3.50pm
to... simon_horne@millershanks-london.co.uk
cc...
re... eternal thanks

Darling, I am mortified. And you seemed so smitten while you were here. Did you not even like Kitty and Jane, my two starlets from Watford College? I think their campaigns for Blockbuster and 7UP are little wonders. Aah, well, I suppose I should be used to your unflinching perfectionism by now.

And yes, lunch would be heaven. I'll have my Girl Friday speak to yours.

Letty

pertti_vanhelden@millershanks-helsinki.co.fin
6/1/00, 3.55pm (5.55pm local)
to... david_crutton@millershanks-london.co.uk
cc...
re... jokings aside

I must say that your e-mailing is taking lighthearted bantering too far. In my country Künt is a leading brand of fertiliser deriving from the faecal leavings of chickens and other domestic fowls. Even in its premium Grade-A variant, to be likening to Künt is underneath the waistband. I must be asking you in future to be turning down the ratchet a notch or two on the friendly joshing.

What-ho, Jeeves – Pertti

David Crutton – 6/1/00, 3.57pm
to... Rachel Stevenson
cc...
re... Kapoor

No arguments, Rachel, fire Chandra Kapoor immediately and recruit a new head of IT. I don't care if you hire a dimmer-than-average rhesus monkey to do the job. Just make sure he/she/it can fix my fucking e-mail.

simon_horne@millershanks-london.co.uk
6/1/00, 4.01pm
to... letitia@tavistockhegg.aol.com.uk
cc...
re... eternal thanks

Letitia, my sweet, of course you are a headhunter and sounding the fanfare for your young charges is your job.

But your promotion of those Watford girls surprises me.

Their Blockbuster work beggars description; their 'It's in the Can' campaign for 7UP is a self-conscious attempt at fashionability.

Excuse my bluntness, but you risk harm to your credibility by pushing them at the better agencies.

I must hasten away now.

David demands to be dazzled.

Si

Brett Topowlski – 6/1/00, 4.03pm
to... Liam O'Keefe
cc...
re... as I was saying . . .

. . . before I was so rudely interrupted by IT. Me and Vin couldn't wait for you to get back from banging Lol so we dug through your desk and found your copy of the movie. It makes *Blair Witch* look mega-budget slick but it's a fucking stonker. Loved the money shot – Horne excelled himself. I nipped to TV and ran off a copy for a couple of mates at Grey. They used to work in Horne's group at O&M and they'll be gagging to see it. Don't mind, do you?

Simon Horne, 6/1/00 – 4.32pm
to... Susi Judge-Davis
cc...
re... bubbly

Come hither and pop open a bottle now. I think you and I should drink to Polyhymnia, my muse. David is besotted with my Coke idea!

Liam O'Keefe – 6/1/00, 4.37pm
to... Brett Topowlski
cc...
re... as I was saying . . .

The more copies the merrier. Hate to think the best bit of film I've shot in three years wasn't going to be enjoyed by a wide and discerning audience. Just back from lunch. That girl's amazing – what a pedicured size five can do under an overhanging tablecloth doesn't bear repeating. She's getting her mate down at the weekend. I'll give them a guided tour of our great city (I'll start with my bedroom then). So while you're stuck on a poxy longhaul to some crappy tourist trap, guess what I'll be doing. Ain't life a bitch?

Melinda Sheridan – 6/1/00, 4.40pm
to... Daniel Westbrooke; Vince Douglas; Brett Topowlski
cc...
re... LOVE PPM

Right, dearies, the pre-production meeting for LOVE is at 5.00 and here are a few dos and don'ts from She Who Has Been There, Done it and Got the T-Shirt.

Dan – *Do* encourage your client to refrain from suggestions apropos film crew when he clearly doesn't know his grip from his gaffer. *Don't* let him drag us into the usual endless debate on wardrobe – since all we're taking are six lamé thongs and nothing else, I don't see that particular item on the agenda taxing us for long. *Do* coax him into nodding vigorously and enthusiastically during the 'Director's Interpretation'. *Don't* allow him to raise his hand to suggest, for instance, a *crane* rather than a *tracking* shot on the opening. Our director believes his own billing as 'the most dynamic new talent in commercials' (*Campaign* passim) and will not take kindly to tips on camera craft from a marketing executive in an M&S suit.

Brett and Vincent – *Don't* snigger like schoolboys at the back of the bus when we play the casting tape. We've all seen breasts before – maybe not this big nor quite this numerous, but we've seen them, nevertheless. *Do* keep your hands on the table, where I can keep my eyes on them. *Do* pay attention when the discussion reaches the boring matter of schedules – you have a plane to catch on Saturday, and I'd very much like you to be on it. *Don't* address the client directly at any time. In fact, *don't* utter a squeak unless I speak to you first.

Now, boys, come show me the professionalism that is the Miller Shanks way. Actually, scrub that. Just BEHAVE YOURSELVES and pray that by the end of our week in the sun we have a correctly exposed film in the can, a fee well earned and a nicely tanned client. Buddha help us, as Pinki the Divine would say.

Harriet Greenbaum, 6/1/00 – 4.42pm
to... David Crutton; Simon Horne
cc...
re... Mako

I hate to pressurise, but Mako are in tomorrow at 9.30. It is time
we made a decision.

To recap, there are two campaigns on the table. We must now
decide which to present. My thoughts on the matter? No disrespect, Simon, but he will piss all over us if we push Reeves and
Mortimer – he will see it for what it is: Little and Large trying
to look trendy.

My money is on Pinki and Liam's GIVE YOURSELF A LIFT
campaign. It is intelligent, witty and absolutely right for this
client. I've spoken to Pinki and Liam and they can have everything
ready in time. All I need now is the go-ahead. What do you say?

David Crutton, 6/1/00 – 4.49pm
to... Harriet Greenbaum; Simon Horne
cc...
re... Horne 0, Greenbaum 1

The final word: present LIFT, bin R&M. Simon, let the fact that
I like your new Coke idea salve your wounds.

lorraine_pallister@millershanks-london.co.uk
6/1/00, 4.52pm
to... debbie_wright@littlewoods/manchester.co.uk
cc...
re... pack your bags

Oh, my! Just done a major number on my boy, Liam. I did the
under-the-table foot thing as I told him my best mate Debbie
was in London at the weekend and would he like to come and
join us. He exploded in his khakis, poor lad. So it looks like your
weekend's booked. Train leaves Piccadilly at six tomorrow night.
Meet you at Euston. Before you get mad, we'll have a laugh.

Liam's cute and he loves you already – told him you looked just like Lara Croft, only bigger. Go on, girl, don't let me down. Gotta go. Boss is screaming – can't find his TV remote. The psycho bastard will give himself a heart attack. I'll undo another button before I go in and help it along. Get straight back about the weekend. Can't wait – Lolx

Daniel Westbrooke – 6/1/00, 4.53pm
to... Melinda Sheridan
cc...
re... LOVE PPM

Melinda, I do not appreciate your tone of voice. It may do for the likes of Vince and Brett, but do not forget who I am. As you know, I am not one to bandy my title around, but as Head of Client Services, I am not short of experience. I do not need to be told how to behave in a pre-production meeting. And please do not refer to me as 'Dan' in front of junior personnel.

Daniel

Simon Horne – 6/1/00, 4.55pm
to... Harriet Greenbaum
cc...
re... dirty tricks

It seems I have once again worked my heart out.

For nothing.

As you well know, David was ecstatic about Reeves and Mortimer until you meddled.

What is this hold you have over him?

If I were not such a gentleman I might suspect something tawdry.

For the record, I believe GIVE YOURSELF A LIFT is weak.

It is also hugely derivative – of what, I cannot recall, but I am sure it will come to me.

It will not impress our client. I will permit myself a brief moment of *schadenfreude* when he throws it out of court, as he inevitably will.

I know I am down to attend tomorrow's presentation but I feel it would be dishonest of me to turn up and feign enthusiasm for work I have no belief in.

But then, as you seem to be making such an excellent fist of taking the Executive Creative Director's job away from me, you hardly need me there.

I will not forget this, Harriet. My memory is elephantine.

Si

David Crutton – 6/1/00, 4.57pm
to... Simon Horne
cc...
re... well done

I'm looking again at your Coke idea and I'll use a word I save for special occasions. *Genius.* IT'S IN THE CAN is a brilliant concept. It feels as if it's been done by hip teenagers. I really didn't think a fart like you would still have it in you. I love the salesman/beekeeper script. More like that and we're well on the way.

Shit, look at me. I'm gushing.

Simon Horne – 6/1/00, 5.03pm
to... Melinda Sheridan
cc...
re... LOVE

Melinda, darling, I have been thinking about Brett and Vince, and what lies ahead for them. I have tried to tell myself that they are ready for a shoot this big.

Unfortunately, I remain unconvinced.

The LOVE client is spending 650k on this film and it would be irresponsible of me to entrust the custody of such a huge budget to a callow team.

I feel, therefore, it is incumbent upon me to come to the shoot.

It is an extremely inconvenient time, given, *inter alia*, the mammoth task we have on Coke.

But I have just delivered to David a pitch-winning campaign. I feel I can now step back from that and perform another key aspect of my job. Namely, guiding an eager yet inexperienced team through the rocky shoals of the foreign-location shoot.

So, Melinda, one plane ticket on my desk tomorrow and I am all yours.

Spare me the embarrassment of thanking me. You can do that as we applaud Brett and Vince upon receipt of their gongs for 'Best Commercial'.

Si

Simon Horne – 6/1/00, 5.06pm
to...   David Crutton
cc...
re...   well done

I am thrilled that you like 'IT'S IN THE CAN'. I too think it is *le Poisson d'Or* for which we have been angling.

I intend to work on it through the night and by mid-morrow will have a fully-fledged campaign for your delectation.

And Mako is *l'eau sous le pont*. While I still have misgivings about 'Lift', I am prepared, as ever, to bow to the consensus.

Si

Simon Horne – 6/1/00, 5.09pm
to...   Susi Judge-Davis
cc...
re...   last chores of the day

Susi, be an angel – run along to Mel's office and grab the schedule for the LOVE shoot.

Next, type up the other six Coke scripts that are on my Dictaphone.

Finally, order me a cab for the Groucho ASAP.

Oh, and have them pop a bottle of Dom Perignon in a bucket.

Harriet Greenbaum – 6/1/00, 5.11pm
to... Simon Horne
cc...
re... dirty tricks

Simon, I am sorry you feel betrayed. That was not my intention and there has been no dirty tricks campaign.

Pinki and Liam are lined up to present tomorrow morning. If you have a change of heart I would love you to attend the meeting to lend your stature and support. Despite what you clearly think, I am not a person to bear grudges. I hope that neither are you.

Simon Horne – 6/1/00, 5.15pm
to... Harriet Greenbaum
cc...
re... dirty tricks

Harriet, as potatoes go, Mako is the babiest of baby new.

I am immersed in Coke.

Kindly get your priorities in order and desist from pestering me with politically loaded e-mails.

Simon Horne – 6/1/00 – 5.19pm
to... Melinda Sheridan
cc...
re... LOVE

I have just had Susi pop to your office to grab a call-sheet for our shoot. I am looking at it and a couple of things strike me immediately.

I notice we are booked into the Paradise Bay. I have been and, to be candid, I would not send my pool cleaner there.

The *only* place to stay is le Touessrok.

It is a quite superb hotel – a little pricey perhaps, but if we are expected to arise refreshed for the rigours of a dawn call, then nothing less will suffice. I would get on the phone when you are out of your pre-prod and change the booking *tout de suite*.

I also gather that we are booked to fly Club. That may well be fine for the oily rags of the film crew. But First is essential for client, director and senior agency personnel. After all, Mauritius is eleven hours away.

I understand we are to convene at Heathrow at 9.00am. Can you have a car pick me up at 6.30am, no later. I would not want to hold everything up, now, would I?!

If you are in the neighbourhood of the Groucho *ce soir*, do join me and we will have a little pre-shoot *tête à tête*.

Si

debbie_wright@littlewoods/manchester.co.uk
6/1/00, 5.22pm
to... lorraine_pallister@millershanks-london.co.uk
cc...
re... pack your bags

I can't fucking believe you. If you think you're gonna get me in another dodgy situation like we had with the Sedgewick twins at Sandra's 18th, you can fuck right off. Tell Liam that we may be best mates but we don't share *everything*. And tell him to bring a friend – flat stomach/fat wallet. A return to London will clean me out – you're buying the drinks. Gotta go. If I'm supposed to be larging it with you this weekend I need to do my bikini line. See you tomorrow . . . Debs

Susi Judge-Davis – 6/1/00, 5.28pm
to... Simon Horne
cc...
re... job done

Cab's arrived, sweetie. Coke scripts will be on your desk first
thing. Want me to call Celine and tell her you're 'working late'?
Sx

Pinki Fallon – 6/1/00, 5.49pm
to... Susi Judge-Davis
cc...
re... food

We're on a late one with Mako, so can you order some pizzas
for about 8.00 before you disappear? Six large Meat Feasts with
extra ham and pepperoni for Liam and the studio boys. Anything
without meat and cheese for me. Ta mucho ... ☺

Susi Judge-Davis – 6/1/00, 5.55pm
to... Pinki Fallon
cc...
re... food

I work for Simon and Simon alone. I will not order your pizzas.
That would be Zoë's job, though she departed long ago.

Rachel Stevenson – 6/1/00, 6.00pm
to... David Crutton
cc...
re... Chandra

A severance letter has been drafted for Chandra and is with
Lorraine for your signature. The deed will be done tomorrow.
As far as e-mail is concerned, from what I can gather the problem
is inherent in the software. Chandra has already arranged for a
Lotus Notes expert to take a look.

Melinda Sheridan – 6/1/00, 7.31pm
to... Daniel Westbrooke; Vince Douglas; Brett Topowlski
cc...
re... PPM

Well, boys, (apologies, Daniel, *gentlemen*) wasn't that the pre-prod from Shitsville? Daniel, I sincerely hope you'll make a better job of shepherding your client once we hit those beaches. Nathan Zapruder did not leave the building a happy director. I suggest that, when cameras are rolling, we follow the firework code and stand well back.

But if you feel your stress levels bubbling up already, Danny Boy, fret not. Help is at hand. Our creative beacon, Simon Horne, has decided that we cannot possibly cope without him and will be joining our merry band. You will be further gladdened to hear that even before departure, he has had a marked influence. He has demanded we change the hotel booking to le Touessrok. Vincent and Brett, you will have hours of fun soiling sheets that have been rumpled by the regal arse of the Duchess of York.

And, Daniel, you will cherish the expression on your client's face as you hand him the invoice for (ooh, bit of mental arithmetic: thirty-two crew, six cast, half-a-dozen assorted hangers on, plus Simon's mini-bar bill) an extra forty-plus grand. Roll on next week. I can't wait. Can you?

Daniel Westbrooke – 6/1/00, 7.44pm
to... Melinda Sheridan
cc...
re... LOVE

This is quite appalling. Does Simon not appreciate the fact that I have risen to Head of Client Services precisely because I am perfectly capable of nursemaiding a jittery client and a boisterous creative team? You can be assured that I will be taking up the matter with him forthwith.

Brett Topowlski – 6/1/00, 7.49pm
to... Liam O'Keefe
cc...
re... pear-shaped

Fucking disaster. Mel just told us Horne's coming on the fucking shoot. He can't, can he? I mean he's got the biggest fucking pitch of his life in just over a week. Crutton wouldn't let him. Would he?

It's not even as if he likes the script. It only got presented because we'd run out of time and he'd already bombed everything else. This was supposed to be Vin and me on a beach. Alone. With just twelve perfectly spherical examples of the plastic surgeon's art for company (all right, a film crew would be there, but you know what I mean). Why's it all going so wrong? And why are you banged up in the studio *working* when we need you to help us drown in a vat of Absolut? Call yourself a mate?

Daniel Westbrooke – 6/1/00, 7.51pm
to... Simon Horne
cc...
re... LOVE

Simon, I am delighted that you have decided to accompany us to Mauritius on our little jaunt. Naturally, I am thankful that I will have some erudite company to help while away the tropical sunsets. I am more impressed, however, that you are prepared to pass on your Solomonian wisdom to our young creatives. I hope for their sakes that they will see the sacrifice you are making.

Incidentally, I am pleased that you have moved us to le Touessrok. Try hard as she does, I must admit to doubts about Melinda's abilities, particularly given the fleapit she had booked us into. And do not worry about the additional expense. I did not become Head of Client Services by not knowing how to 'lose' unwanted costs in the hurly-burly of billing.

Daniel Westbrooke – 6/1/00, 7.57pm

to... David Crutton

cc...

re... LOVE

Delighted as I am that Simon will be adding his steady hand to the tiller on our LOVE shoot, I must say that I am a little surprised that you have decided to let him accompany us with the Coca-Cola about to go 'warp factor'. I would never doubt your reasons, David, and clearly you are confident enough in the direction the pitch is taking to feel the agency does not need his creative scholarship.

David Crutton – 6/1/00, 8.04pm

to... Daniel Westbrooke

cc...

re... LOVE

News to me. For once you've told me something I don't already know. Bear one thing in mind. If I ultimately choose to let Simon go on your junket, it can only be that I deem his presence at the Coke pitch as inessential as that of the Head of Client Services.

David Crutton – 6/1/00, 8.10pm

to... Simon Horne

cc...

re... LOVE

So when were you planning to tell me that you're swanning off to the Indian Ocean? Perhaps you were going to send me a fax from your hotel. But even *you* couldn't be fuckwitted enough to think that the other side of the world would be out of harm's way when I found out. The only reason I'm not tearing you limb from limb is that you have given me some very good work today. An explanation wouldn't go amiss.

Pinki Fallon – 6/1/00, 8.38pm
to... Studio
cc...
re... Pizzas

Hi, Mac boys. Six lovely, hot pizzas ☺ ☺ ☺ ☺ ☺ ☺. Come and get ... ☺

Liam O'Keefe – 6/1/00, 11.32pm
to... All Departments
cc...
re... reference

Anyone still here got a picture of Left-Eye from TLC? I need it desperately for a Mako ad. I think there was one in last month's *FHM*, but the pages of the only copy on my floor are stuck together. Ta.

Nigel Godley – 6/1/00, 11.35pm
to... Liam O'Keefe
cc...
re... reference

I'm here! Sorry, but I've never heard of TLC. I do have an excellent shot of Cheryl Baker (from her heyday with Bucks Fizz!) if you can live with the drawing-pin marks – Nige

david_crutton@millershanks-london.co.uk
6/1/00, 11.49pm
to... jesus_dasilva@aol.co.port
cc...
re... HELLO FROM YOU MOTHER

JESUS MY DEER SON. GREETING TO YOU AND TO ALL FAMMILY IN LISBOA. WHAT YOU THINK OF YOU OLD MAMA ON COMUTER E-MAIL HEY? I AM START AT BIG ADVERT CUMPANY AND AM CLEAN THE BIG BOSS OFFIS. I SEE HIS COMUTER MACHINE ON SO I THINK TO PRACTIS ENGLISH AND COMUTER CORSE SKILLS

IN ONE GOING. HOW IS YOU STUDYS AND YOU LOOK
AFTER YOU LITTLE SISTER SARA LIKE I ASKING? THIS
PLACE IS DISGUST. THIS NIGHT LAST I SEE MAN
MAKE GIRL WORKER LOOS JOB AND THEN TO SHOW
HOW HE DO NOT CARE HE MAKE SEX WITH MAN
DRESS AS WOMAN ON OFFIS TABLE. I HAVE TO MAKE
CLEAN AFTER. I PRAY TO SANTA MARIA FOR THE
SOLE OF THIS PEOPLE. I SAY TO POOR GIRL WHO
LOOS JOB I GO TO CORT FOR HER AND BE WITNIS. I
GO NOW AND CLEAN BIG BOSS TOILET. IT HAVE
GOLD TAPS AND PERFUME THAT SMELL LIKE YOU
AUNT THERESA MAY GOD FORGIVE HER. MY LOVE
TO YOU AND I MISSING YOU. MAMA

Friday
7 January
2000

Harriet Greenbaum – 7/1/00, 8.02am
to... James Gregory; Katie Philpott; Liam O'Keefe; Pinki Fallon
cc...
re... Mako

Morning all. Mako run-through in the boardroom in ten. See you there.

Pinki Fallon – 7/1/00, 8.06am
to... Harriet Greenbaum
cc...
re... Mako

I'll be a few minutes late. I'm re-writing one of the headlines to refer to Bucks Fizz rather than TLC. Liam apologises. Says it was late and doesn't know what came over him ... ☺

Simon Horne – 7/1/00, 8.35am
to... David Crutton
cc...
re... LOVE

David, I have just arrived to apply the final coat of lacquer to 'IT'S IN THE CAN' and I have read your e-mail.

I am wounded that you think I would abandon ship in our hour of need. I have agonised deeply over this decision.

Let me, if I may, set out my reasons.

You have said yourself that my *idée grande* solves the Coke problem.

This morning I have new scripts to show you which will provide the creative heart of our pitch. The donkey work, I leave for my department of willing and able bodies.

Mauritius may be the other side of the world but it is only a double click's distance via mouse. My laptop flies with me and I have had Melinda upgrade our hotel simply to obtain me a suite equipped with videophone and facsimile.

This will form Mission Control for the assault on Coke.

I have also had Melinda book me onto *every* return flight to Britain. In the event that you need me in the flesh, shout and I will be straight back.

If you think I am going for the 'jollies' you are mistaken. Mauritius was deleted from my wish list of destinations when Celine was attacked there by a Chinese croupier with a blackjack paddle.

She is still unable to talk about it.

I am going simply out of duty.

Vince and Brett are too grass-green to carry the weight of this shoot on their shoulders.

Besides which, while I would hate to steal their thunder, it was my inspiration that led to their LOVE script. I worry that they could not interpret my vision alone.

I hope this allays your suspicion that I have somehow been

derelict in my responsibilities. Naturally, if you still feel I should be here, I will amend my plans in a jiffy.

Si

Simon Horne – 7/1/00, 8.46am
to...   Melinda Sheridan
cc...
re...   LOVE

Mel, upgrade me immediately to a suite at le Touessrok. And make sure it is replete with videophone, fax and PC modem.

Then book me a seat on *every* flight back to the UK.

Should David ask, tell *une petite mensonge blanche* and mention that I requested said items yesterday.

David Crutton – 7/1/00, 8.58am
to...   All Departments
cc...
re...   Dagenham crap

Would someone, anyone, like to tell me why there's a Ford Mondeo in reception. I nearly broke my leg on it. And, should our Mako client see it, he will surely fire us. Whoever is responsible, have it removed. You have half an hour before our client arrives.

David Crutton
CEO

Harriet Greenbaum – 7/1/00, 9.03am
to...   David Crutton
cc...
re...   Dagenham crap

David, you may recall phoning me at 11.00 last night with the quite brilliant suggestion that we put a Mondeo in reception to confront the Mako client with the serious competition he faces when he launches his new car. As a result James and Katie busted guts through the early hours to locate a cherry red car (you were most specific about the colour) and have it placed in reception for this morning's presentation. Have you any idea how difficult it is to find specialists in the removal of plate glass at 3.30am? However, you were calling from what sounded like a very noisy bar, so perhaps I misheard you. Would you still like the vehicle removed?

Ken Perry – 7/1/00, 9.06am
to... All Departments
cc...
re... the car in reception

I have to endorse David Crutton's remarks concerning the car in the reception area. If I may refer you to my all staff e-mail of 3/1/00 re new carpet tiles, it is a good example of the type of load that Dudley Kositredd was not designed to carry. As such it invalidates the extended warranty obtained from the fitters.

Thank you for your co-operation, and it is good to be back amongst you.

Ken Perry
Office Administrator

Brett Topowlski – 7/1/00, 9.09am
to... All Departments
cc...
re... the car in reception

Ken should also have mentioned that for anyone who drives to work, there is a perfectly adequate car park in the basement.

Thank you for your co-operation.

Brett Topowlski
Office Smartarse

Melinda Sheridan – 7/1/00, 9.11am
to... Simon Horne
cc...
re... LOVE

Hate to be a follicle-splitter, luvvie, but it's *un petit mensonge blanc* (*mensonge* being appropriately masculine). On a French-speaking island like Mauritius such a *faux pas* can make all the difference between a table with an ocean view and one by the kitchen slop bins. *À bientôt.*

David Crutton – 7/1/00, 9.12am
to... Harriet Greenbaum
cc...
re... Dagenham crap

Of course I remember calling you. Do you think I'm senile? I was simply testing the knee-jerk response of the freshly returned Ken Perry. He passed with flying colours. Congratulate James and Katie on their ingenuity.

David Crutton – 7/1/00, 9.14am
to... Simon Horne
cc...
re... LOVE

Your attendance in Mauritius is conditional upon the following:

1. You leave your new Coke scripts with Lorraine for my approval, which you will pray to God, Krishna and the fucking Tooth Fairy that I grant.

2. You then put on a clean shirt and tie and proceed to the Mako meeting, where you will smile politely and make suitably positive noises as Pinki and Liam present their work. You will not once bring up Little and Large, Sooty and Sweep or any other alleged comic double acts.

Simon Horne – 7/1/00, 9.17am
to... Susi Judge-Davis
cc...
re... shopping

Well, sweetie, it looks like I have to go to Mauritius after all. It is a ghastly pain, but David is most insistent.

By the time you get to work I will have stepped into the Mako meeting.

Would you pop out and buy me a couple of essentials?

1. Hawaiian Tropic, factors 10, 6 and 2.
2. Mosquito repellant. Boots own label is excellent and odour-free too.
3. A nose protector. Boots again.
4. A pair of black Speedo trunks, 38 waist (their sizes come up frightfully small).
5. Copies of *Captain Corelli's Mandolin* and the French translation of anything by Will Self.
6. Polo Sport shower gel.
7. Repeat prescriptions for Valium, Prozac and Mogadon. (You have my doctor's number, don't you?)
8. Crabtree & Evelyn smellies for my valise.
9. A couple or three XL T-shirts from Virgin or HMV bearing logos for whomever the *zeitgeist* bands are. Genesis? Supertramp? You probably know better than I.

Order me £5,000 of traveller's cheques ($US) and £500 of local currency from Accounts.

And book Celine in for a long weekend at Champney's (use my corporate Amex).

It will soften the blow when I tell her tonight we will not be flying to Vienna and her beloved Lippizaners.

Simon Horne – 7/1/00, 9.23am
to... Harriet Greenbaum
cc...
re... Mako

We can ill afford another setback on this account.

So I have decided to join your Mako meeting after all.

Frankly, if you are to stand any chance of selling this work, you will need my rapport with the client.

If there is a seating plan, place me at the head of the table and Pinki and Liam near the coffee trolley.

They might as well serve some useful purpose.

Si

Brett Topowlski – 7/1/00, 9.33am
to... All Departments
cc...
re... pussy

Me and Vince are away for a week (Mauritius, shoot, topless models, beer, yawn) and he needs somebody to feed his cat. Anyone live in Tooting who'd like to volunteer? Reward: duty-frees of your choice and first dibs on exclusive Polaroids of totty removing kit in name of Art.

Brett (for Vince)

PS He'd e himself if his Mac wasn't still in its bubble wrap.

Nigel Godley – 7/1/00, 9.37am
to... Brett Topowlski
cc...
re... pussy

I'm just down the road in sunny Balham, so happy to oblige. Any particular brand? My own moggy is partial to Gourmet Gold

Duck & Goose and won't be fobbed off with inferior own labels.
Cats, eh? Let me know – Nige

Brett Topowlski – 7/1/00, 9.45am
to... Nigel Godley
cc...
re... pussy

He was hoping for a bird who'd fall hopelessly in love with him
on the strength of his sensitive taste in CDs (Mariah, Whitney,
Britney), but he says you'll do. Ta. Cat's called Bruno (big, black,
crap in a fight). He'll drop his keys down later.

Susi Judge-Davis – 7/1/00, 9.51am
to... Creative Department
cc...
re... there's only so much I can do

As you may know Zoë is 'at a funeral' (!!!) today. While I would
normally cover for her, I am up to my eyeballs organising Si for
his trip to Mauritius. Perhaps for once you can fend for yourselves, secretarially speaking.

David Crutton – 7/1/00, 10.01am
to... Daniel Westbrooke
cc...
re... Kimbelle

You owe me an explanation – a fucking good one. I've just got
off the phone to the Marketing Director at Kimbelle, who's fired
us. She claims she's waited eight weeks for us to schedule a
presentation on Super Dri. I suggested we would be delighted to
show her work this very afternoon (do we even have any?) but
she's already seeing presentations from other agencies. Why
wasn't I aware of this problem? And if your answer is that neither
were you, why the fuck not? You are in charge of *Client Services*.
Do I have to show you a dictionary to explain what that means?
This account represented a substantial 250k of revenue, much of

which went towards your bonus last year. You'd better cancel the swimming pool you're having built because you won't receive a brass farthing at the end of this fiscal. My office, now.

David Crutton – 7/1/00, 10.20am
to... All Departments
cc... james_f_weissmuller@millershanks-ny.co.usa
re... Kimbelle

After a great deal of agonising we have decided to resign the Kimbelle Sanpro business due to irreconcilable creative differences. Over the last few weeks we have presented them with a number of groundbreaking campaigns, to no avail. It has become increasingly apparent that we would not be able to agree without compromising our creativity. In consequence we have decided that it would be against the founding principles of Miller Shanks to give this client creative product in which we did not wholeheartedly believe. A parting of the ways was therefore inevitable. We wish them well in their search for a new agency.

I would like to take this opportunity to thank everyone who worked so hard on this difficult account to produce so much excellent work.

The good news is that there are a number of sanpro brands out there begging for the unique Miller Shanks approach. Now we are free of Kimbelle, let's go to it and win one!

David Crutton
CEO

Brett Topowlski – 7/1/00, 10.27am
to... Liam O'Keefe
cc...
re... off the rag!

Whoopee! We don't have to sort out your dog's mess on Kimbelle after all. And to think I was going to haul pad and pen all the way to Mauritius to wrestle with that one. How am I going to fill the time now? Can't imagine. I did mention that we were going to *Mauritius*, didn't I?

Daniel Westbrooke – 7/1/00, 10.35am
to... David Crutton
cc...
re... Kimbelle

David, your anger over this fiasco is totally justified. As I told you, I was as surprised as you to learn we had difficulties on this. Rest assured that the guilty party has been identified and a severe reprimand is on its way.

James Gregory will not be so cocksure in future.

I promise that, so long as I remain in a senior position at Miller Shanks, this will not happen again. Perhaps in my capacity as Head of Client Services I could instigate a working party to look into 'early warning systems' to prevent a reoccurrence.

If you are agreeable I shall make this a priority the instant I return from Mauritius.

Rachel Stevenson – 7/1/00, 10.40am
to... All Departments
cc...
re... Chandra Kapoor

After ten years with the company Chandra has decided to leave to spend more time with his family. Chandra was our first Head of IT and can take credit for making Miller Shanks a part of the digital revolution.

We will miss him and wish him well in the future.

Until a permanent replacement is appointed, Peter Renquist will take over as Acting Head of IT. Please support him in this challenging role.

Rachel Stevenson
Personnel

Katie Philpott – 7/1/00, 11.07am
to... Liam O'Keefe
cc...
re... awesome!!!

Wow, you were brill in that presentation! Still got goosebumps
– Katie P

Harriet Greenbaum – 7/1/00, 11.10am
to... David Crutton
cc...
re... Mako

Sorry to hear about Kimbelle, but here's some good news. Mako
went very well. Top line: client extremely happy; bought all work
without change; Pinki and Liam excellent; Simon quiet throughout. I'll debrief you fully later.

Simon Horne – 7/1/00, 11.12am
to... David Crutton
cc...
re... Mako

Well, I think I managed to save us on this one.

The work was going down like a plumbeous inflatable for all the
reasons I had outlined. Basically the client spotted the flaws.

Despite finding myself agreeing with him, I stepped in to bring
him round.

He is not convinced of the work, but because he trusts my judgement, he is prepared to go along with our recommendation.

At least I have kept our account losses down to one today.

Si

Harriet Greenbaum – 7/1/00, 11.14am
to... Pinki Fallon; Liam O'Keefe
cc... Simon Horne; David Crutton
re... Mako

I just want to say thank you. Thank you for dropping everything to dig us out of the mire. Thank you for producing a superlative campaign at such short notice. And thank you for presenting with such panache. I owe you.

James Gregory – 7/1/00, 11.16am
to... Harriet Greenbaum
cc...
re... back down to earth

After the triumph of Mako I've just been bollocked by Dan over the Kimbelle cock-up (read attached). Can we talk about this later?

 Attachment ...

Daniel Westbrooke – 7/1/00, 10.42am
to... James Gregory
cc...
re... Kimbelle

James, as far as I can see this mess is entirely of your making. If you were out of your depth, why in heaven's name did you not ask for help? Clearly I was wrong to think that you were ready to handle responsibility. I will do what I can to protect you from the wrath of David. When I return from Mauritius we must have a frank talk about your future. Until then I suggest a low profile be maintained.

David Crutton – 7/1/00, 11.20am
to... Harriet Greenbaum; Pinki Fallon
cc...
re... lunch

I'm sure that you have much to tell me about Mako. I have matters to discuss with you as well. With both Simon and Daniel out of the country next week, we have something of a vacuum at the top. Let's talk at lunch. My car leaves for la Mirabelle at 12.50. See you on board.

Simon Horne – 7/1/00, 11.23am
to... David Crutton
cc...
re... lunch

Since I am away next week we should spend some time going over Coke.

Are you free for lunch?

David Crutton – 7/1/00, 11.25am
to... Simon Horne
cc...
re... lunch

No.

Simon Horne – 7/1/00, 11.28am
to... Harriet Greenbaum
cc...
re... lunch

We seem to have had our fair share of misunderstandings these past few days.

I suggest we spend some time doing a little bridge-building.

Luncheon?

My treat.

Si

Harriet Greenbaum – 7/1/00, 11.31am
to... Simon Horne
cc...
re... lunch

No can do, Simon, I'm booked.

Simon Horne – 7/1/00, 11.34am
to... Pinki Fallon
cc...
re... lunch

I realise that we have not enjoyed the best of weeks.

But you must know that I still have the utmost respect for you.

Why not break some bread and perhaps patch up our differences?

Si

Pinki Fallon – 7/1/00, 11.39am
to... Simon Horne
cc...
re... lunch

Sorry, Simon, but I've made other arrangements. Catch me this afternoon sometime . . . ☺

Liam O'Keefe – 7/1/00, 11.53am
to... Lorraine Pallister
cc...
re... lunch

I was fucking amazing this morning. Mako love me. Worship me at lunch.

Lorraine Pallister – 7/1/00, 11.58am
to... Liam O'Keefe
cc...
re... lunch

Can't. Shopping. You keep losing my knickers. Need more.

Liam O'Keefe – 7/1/00, 12.03pm
to... Katie Philpott
cc...
re... lunch

Fancy lunch then? You can take me through those goosebumps one by one.

Katie Philpott – 7/1/00, 12.06pm
to... Liam O'Keefe
cc...
re... lunch

Gosh, what an honour! Love to – Katie P

Simon Horne – 7/1/00, 12.10pm
to... Katie Philpott
cc...
re... lunch

It was invigorating to make your acquaintance in the Mako meeting today.

You are a breath of fresh air of the Alpine variety.

Your positivity and enthusiasm are just what this jaded old company needs.

Perhaps we can do a little inter-departmental bonding.

Why not start with lunch?

Si

Katie Philpott – 7/1/00, 12.13pm
to... Simon Horne
cc...
re... lunch

Wow, little old me invited to lunch by one of advertising's 'living legends'! I'd really, really love to, but I'm afraid I'm busy. Maybe some other time? Katie P

Simon Horne – 7/1/00, 12.19pm
to... Susi Judge-Davis
cc...
re... lunch

I am snowed under here. There is no way I will be able to escape for lunch.

Could you be a treasure and pop out for a sandwich around 1.00?

Parma Ham, Mozzarella and a drizzle of olive oil on Focaccia would be perfect.

pertti_vanhelden@millershanks-helsinki.co.fin.
7/1/00, 12.26pm (2.26pm local)
to... david_crutton@millershanks-london.co.uk
cc...
re... catchings up

I am sorry to be all quiet on the e-mailing front today but Friday morning is our weekly Reaching Out session. This is where we are gathering in circles, holding of hands and discussing frankly our 'issues'. No holds are barring and everyone from the little post-room girl to Top Cheese like me is speaking of their minds. Today we are overrunning because Astrid, our little post-room girl is bringing in her puppies for us all to be sharing.

Now I am back in the land of cybernetspace and I am sorry you are losing Kimbelle. Maybe you will find that every clod has silvery linings!

You are remaining eerie silent on the Coke matter. I am appreciating that you are treading delicately with your own Creation Director and are not wishing to be hurting his feelings, but I am needing you to press 'THUNDERBIRDS ARE GO!' on 'Fizzy Whizzy Pop' soon. There are many grounds to be preparing!

Ee-aye-adios – **Pertti**

Daniel Westbrooke – 7/1/00, 12.33pm
to... Simon Horne
cc...
re... lunch

Simon, congratulations on your splendid Mako presentation. I just bumped into young Katie and she was thrilled by it all. Perhaps I could buy you lunch to celebrate your triumph. We have much to discuss. As well as the shoot there is the matter of delegating our responsibilities while we are *ex patria*. As respective heads of the client service and creative functions we must not leave any bases uncovered. Let me know if you are free.

Simon Horne – 7/1/00, 12.36pm
to... Daniel Westbrooke
cc...
re... lunch

I am up to my neck clearing the decks before departure.

I could manage a speedy main course, however. The Ivy suit?

Brett Topowlski – 7/1/00, 12.41pm
to... Liam O'Keefe
cc...
re... lunch

Fancy spending your lunch hour at Mambo in Carnaby St, helping Vin and me pick out some babe-licious beachwear?* Go on, you know you want to.

*For our trip to Mauritius, in case you were wondering.

Liam O'Keefe – 7/1/00, 12.47pm
to... Brett Topowlski
cc...
re... lunch

Piss off, I'm busy.*

*Preparing myself mentally for an arduous three-in-a-bed scenario, in case you were wondering.

Simon Horne – 7/1/00, 12.50pm
to... Susi Judge-Davis
cc...
re... lunch

Where the hell are you? I have 1,000,001 things I need you to
sort out.

Anyway, you can forget the sandwich. I am going to have to get
my own lunch.

Before I starve to death.

Nigel Godley – 7/1/00, 1.06pm
to... All Departments
cc...
re... lunch

It seems that the agency has emptied. But if anyone is working
through, I've made too many cheese and Branston sarnies
(again!). Feel free to join me for a nibble – Nige

Susi Judge-Davis – 7/1/00, 3.21pm
to... Simon Horne
cc...
re... lunch

Darling, sorry I wasn't around earlier but I've been out all morning shopping for your trip. Got everything. And I found a to-die-
for pair of Versace shades at D&J! They're so *you* and they were
only £269. I bought them with your card. Hope you don't mind
– you won't when you see them. I also got you T-shirts – Rage
Against the Machine and Megadeth. I've never heard of them
but the man in the Megastore assured me they were very 'in'. I
also got you a 'Tommy Boy' baseball cap. You'll look so with-it!
I guess you're still out to lunch. If you get back in the next few
mins, I've just nipped to the bank to pick up your currency . . .
Sx

Katie Philpott – 7/1/00, 3.41pm
to... Liam O'Keefe
cc...
re... thanks a mill'

Ta for lunch. It was brill! And yes, I'd love to go out on Tues.
Golly, never been to a 'rave' before!!! I'd better find something
really jazzy to wear – Katie P

David Crutton – 7/1/00, 4.03pm
to... All Departments
cc...
re... responsibilities

As most of you will know Simon Horne and Daniel Westbrooke
are both out of the office next week looking after the very important LOVE shoot. After discussion with me they have decided
to delegate their responsibilities to Pinki Fallon and Harriet
Greenbaum. All creative work will go to Pinki for approval and
she will deal with any related problems that arise.

Issues on account management will be handled by Harriet. In
Daniel's absence Harriet will also take over the running of the
Coke pitch. Please give them your full support, as Simon, Daniel
and myself will.

I would like to end the week on a happy note, by mentioning
this morning's Mako meeting. The client has just this minute
phoned me to thank us and to say that it was the most professional
presentation he'd ever seen. Well done to all concerned, but
particularly to Harriet, Pinki and Liam O'Keefe.

Have a good weekend. Especially as, with the Coke pitch on
Monday week, next weekend is cancelled.

David Crutton
CEO

David Crutton – 7/1/00, 4.07pm
to... Simon Horne; Daniel Westbrooke
cc...
re... responsibilities

By now you will have read my previous e-mail and you will not
be best pleased. I would have liked to discuss these matters with
you but you are nowhere to be found. (Feeding your faces or
dusting off your Louis Vuittons?) If you don't like it, tough. The
Mauritian sun will ease the pain.

Melinda Sheridan – 7/1/00, 4.10pm
to... Simon Horne; Daniel Westbrooke; Vince Douglas; Brett
Topowlski
cc...
re... ready, steady, go . . .

We should take some time to ensure that all our little duckies
are in a neat row before our ordeal commences tomorrow. My
boudoir at 5.30? Daniel and Simon, the Sancerre is chilling. Brett
and Vincent, I have Tennents Super.

Daniel Westbrooke – 7/1/00, 4.29pm
to... Simon Horne
cc...
re... the nightmare scenario

If you are reading this then you are back at your desk and you
have seen David's e-mails. It seems that exactly what we both
feared has come to pass. I think the best thing we can both do
now is to greet this *fait accompli* with good grace and spend our
time in Mauritius planning a counterattack.

Simon Horne – 7/1/00, 4.32pm
to... Daniel Westbrooke
cc...
re... the nightmare scenario

Agreed.

Let us assume a united front.

Brett Topowlski – 7/1/00, 4.35pm
to... Liam O'Keefe
cc...
re... Surfin' Safari

You back from lunch? Where the fuck were you? You weren't with Lol because we bumped into her in Soho. Been a naughty boy? And if Pinki is Creative Director, are you deputy? Do we call you sir? Anyway, come and see what we bought. Vin's got one of those cut-off surfer wetsuits. The dozy twat can't even swim.

Simon Horne – 7/1/00, 4.37pm
to... Harriet Greenbaum
cc...
re... congrat's due

Well done, Harriet. Now is your chance to step out of Daniel's somewhat stifling shadow and shine.

I always knew you had it in you.

I have been a little hard on you recently.

It is merely because I know that you and I both share the same exemplary high standards.

Now rise to the challenge by taking my campaign and winning Coca-Cola.

Si

Daniel Westbrooke – 7/1/00, 4.38pm
to... David Crutton
cc...
re... responsibilities

You took the words right out of my mouth. I had pencilled time in your diary this afternoon to recommend that Harriet run things while I am unavoidably detained. I can think of no abler deputy. As for the re-ordering of the Creative Department, I believe that, too, is an excellent move. Lately, Simon has seemed a little run down and below his best. I think that putting Pinki in charge could give our creative resource just the injection of pep that it needs. I will now spend some quality time with Harriet and make sure that she is thoroughly briefed on what lies ahead.

Daniel Westbrooke – 7/1/00, 4.42pm
to... Harriet Greenbaum
cc...
re... thin ice

I am impressed, Harriet. I must say that I admire your stealth. I would like to offer you a friendly word of advice, however. I did not rise to become Head of Creative Services of a top-twenty agency by not knowing how to defend my interests. You are playing with the big boys now. Are you quite certain you are ready?

David Crutton – 7/1/00, 4.43pm
to... Daniel Westbrooke
cc...
re... responsibilities

Thank you so much for endorsing my actions. It feels reassuring to know that you are right behind me. In fact, as I write this, it strikes me that I have not once made a decision with which you did not totally and unreservedly agree. Quite remarkable.

Harriet Greenbaum – 7/1/00, 4.44pm
to... Daniel Westbrooke
cc...
re... thin ice

Thank you for the advice. Next week is looking difficult so any tips on how to cope are useful. Have an excellent trip, Daniel.

Liam O'Keefe – 7/1/00, 4.45pm
to... Lorraine Pallister
cc...
re... *Joy of Sex*, pp 13,48,97,122 . . .

I'm horny. What you doing tonight?

Simon Horne – 7/1/00, 4.47pm
to... Pinki Fallon
cc...
re... conduct unbecoming

Well thank you so, so much. After the way I overlooked your conniving behaviour with the Mako brief and gave you a second chance, this is how you repay me. Still, it is not the first time my good nature has been exploited and I do not suppose it will be the last.

Enjoy it for the short time it endures, Pinki. A week hence, I will be back. And, once again, you will be just a humble copywriter.

Si

Simon Horne – 7/1/00, 4.51pm
to... David Crutton
cc...
re... hand-over

I still believe that I could have acquitted myself as Creative Director from my 'office away from the office' in Mauritius.

However, you have made your decision.

So be it.

Perhaps then Pinki and I should join you before the end of the day and we could brief her fully on what we require for 'IT'S IN THE CAN'.

Si

Lorraine Pallister – 7/1/00, 4.52pm
to... Liam O'Keefe
cc...
re... Joy of Sex, pp 13,48,97,122 ...

Can't tonight. Picking up Debbie then we're going to do girly stuff – washing hair, swapping underwear and make-up tips, you

know the kind of thing. Save yourself. Call me in the morning.
Not early.

David Crutton – 7/1/00, 4.56pm
to... Simon Horne
cc...
re... hand-over

That won't be necessary. I have taken her through your work
and she has a good grasp of it. In fact, she has a few thoughts
on how to improve it. I suggest that you take yourself home and
prepare for your well-earned rest.

Simon Horne – 7/1/00, 4.59 pm
to... Susi Judge-Davis
cc...
re... analgesics

Migraine, migraine . . .

Liam O'Keefe – 7/1/00, 5.06pm
to... Katie Philpott
cc...
re... plans

Tonight?

Katie Philpott – 7/1/00, 5.12pm
to... Liam O'Keefe
cc...
re... plans

Phew, twice in one day!!! But can't. I'm taking Mummy to *Cats*.
It's her Chrissy pressie so can't let her down. Have a fab weekend
– Katie P

Liam O'Keefe – 7/1/00, 5.17 pm
to... Brett Topowlski
cc...
re... plans

What are you and Vin doing? Start off at BZ? Seen Horne in

those ridiculous sunglasses? Claims they help his migraine. Sad cunt's lost the plot. Thinks he's a Backstreet Boy.

Brett Topowlski – 7/1/00, 5.20pm
to... Liam O'Keefe
cc...
re... plans

Can't do a session tonight. Got to go home and pack, find my passport and get a very early night because as you may know *we're flying to Mauritius, Playground of the Naked and the Dead Rich first thing tomorrow.* . . oh fuck all that. We're doing beers in Mel's office in five. See you there and then we'll move on. Fancy a club? And enough of Horne's shades. I've got a whole week to enjoy those. I don't need reminding.

Simon Horne – 7/1/00, 5.23 pm
to... Brett Topowlski; Vince Douglas
cc...
re... be prepared

If you think that next week will involve lounging on a beach, your heads awash with onanistic fantasies, think again.

You will have a lot of work to do.

Vince, take markers and plenty of layout paper.

Brett, pack your laptop and make sure IT furnish you with a modem so you can e-mail the office.

I will not suffer the flaccid excuse that you cannot do your job because you are out of touch.

Simon Horne – 7/1/00, 5.29pm
to... Creative Department
cc...
re... in my absence . . .

I would not have left Pinki in charge if I did not have total respect for her judgement.

I expect you to show it too.

And while I may be thousands of miles away, out of sight will not be out of mind.

I demand to be kept abreast of every development. I will phone both Pinki and Susi on a daily basis for full reports on progress.

And progress is precisely what I require.

Problems, you can reach me at any time. Susi has my phone and fax numbers.

Then there is e-mail.

There is much to do, ladies and gentlemen. While the cat is away, the mice will work their little paws to the bone.

Si

Simon Horne – 7/1/00, 5.36pm
to... Melinda Sheridan
cc...
re... apologies

Melinda, I am afraid I will not be able to attend your little *soirée*.

I have too much to do to make certain this place doesn't fall apart the second I step onto the plane.

I will see you at the airport.

Si

Simon Horne – 7/1/00, 5.42pm
to... Susi Judge-Davis
cc...
re... taxi!

You have been my guardian angel this week. Thank you, precious girl.

One more job before I bid *adieu*.

Two cabs please. One to take my bits and pieces home. The other to carry me to the Groucho. I am in dire need of a correctly served Martini and some civilised company.

And call Celine to tell her I'll be a little late – a meeting with David, you know the drill. Ask her to lay out my standard business trip requisites along with the leather suit bag and the smaller Mulberry case.

That is it, you are free of me. Try your best to relax next week.

Susi Judge-Davis – 7/1/00, 5.53pm
to... Simon Horne
cc...
re... taxi!

Cabs will be ten mins. Celine is briefed (I should warn you she sounded a tad frosty). And thank you, I'd love to relax next week, but I'll be keeping my eye on this lot. I'd so hate them to let you down. I'll miss you so ... Sx

Sunday
9 January
2000

Nigel Godley – 9/1/00, 2.21pm
to... All Departments
cc...
re... have a break!

At last, I've finally capped my Bic for the weekend. Now I'm going to put my feet up in the boardroom to watch the *Eastenders* omnibus. Will poor Ian ever get over being ditched by Mel? If you're in today, I'll see you there – Nige

Monday
10 January
2000

brett_topowlski@millershanks-london.co.uk
10/1/00, 4.20am (8.20am local)
to... liam_okeefe@millershanks-london.co.uk
cc...
re... DATELINE MAURITIUS: DAY 1

There we were descending into Bahrain for our stopover when I heard this pop from 16F. It was LOVEbird Linzi in a lot of pain. One of her implants had ruptured. Something to do with the air pressure. The captain had to do 'is there a doctor on the flight' – there were four and then there was a shit fight to be first to write it up for the *Lancet*. When we landed she was rushed to hospital. Vin was well gutted. He'd earmarked her to provide executive stress relief. Now our cast is down to five.

Got to Mauritius and things started looking up. Vin tipped off customs about Horne's personal pharmacy and they pulled him in. He turned up at the hotel six hours later, bandy as a man who'd just been strip-searched. He went straight to his suite and we haven't seen him since. Hopefully he'll stay there for the duration – wanker.

This place is fucking amazing, no word of a lie. Martine McCutcheon is here – you should see her in a thong bikini – scary. Better
still that French bird who was in *Betty Blue* and the old one2one
ads is staying. Vin hit on her at the bar last night and she told
him 'go fuck yourself' with the sexiest accent you ever heard.
Never seen the brush-off give a bloke a hard-on.

Vin, Mel and Nathan have buggered off in a Mini Moke to look
at locations. I've just had breakfast on my verandah (can you
believe it, this place has five stars and they've never heard of
HP Sauce). I can hear Mandi (38DD-25-36. Hobbies: aerobics,
dancing, tractor pulls – no, honestly) waking up. She's still upset
about Linzi's incredible performing breast and she'll need some
comforting. In the words of the awesome Jay-z, it's a hard-knock
life.

What happened to you Friday night? Did you get off with that
Bosnian barmaid? Vin was so wasted he nearly didn't make the
flight. Had to put him through crash detox in the Heathrow Club
lounge.

simon_horne@millershanks-london.co.uk
10/1/00, 4.48am (8.48am local)
to... susi_judgedavis@millershanks-london.co.uk
cc...
re... jobs

1. Phone my doctor the moment you arrive and order more
drugs. DHL them to me ASAP. The illiterate peasants they have
for Customs here have apparently never heard of Prozac and
have confiscated the lot.
2. When Pinki deigns to come in, tell her to fax over whatever
she has on Coke. No excuses.
3. If David shows any interest at all tell him I am having a bloody
nightmare.

David Crutton – 10/1/00, 8.22am
to... Zoë Clarke
cc...
re... great start

Where in fuck's name are you? Didn't Rachel make it clear that now you work for me your start time is 8.00am? You are no longer part of the please-yourself hippie commune they call the Creative Department. I'm going to a meeting with our bankers now. When you finally arrive I'd advise you to spend time reflecting on your new responsibilities.

Pinki Fallon – 10/1/00, 8.45am
to... Creative Department
cc...
re... new system

I'd like to try a new way of working this week. I propose a daily get-together where we review work-in-progress in a more constructive, less confrontational way. This might lead to a greater sense of collective ownership of our ideas. The first session is at 12.30 in the boardroom. See you there. And give our new girl, Lorraine, a big smile. She's sitting where Zoë used to be . . . ☺

susi_judgedavis@millershanks-london.co.uk
10/1/00, 9.01am
to... simon_horne@millershanks-london.co.uk
cc...
re... jobs

You poor, poor darling! The doctor is issuing new prescriptions and the pills should be with you tomorrow first thing.

Now, I don't want to tell tales but there are some things you should know about. Pinki has just sent round an e about a new review system. It doesn't make a bit of sense to me but I'm sure you wouldn't like it. She's also lit some really smelly incense sticks by the lift. Ken Perry has already been up and said they'll set off the sprinklers. And she says you can't have any Coke stuff until David has seen it. But don't worry, I'm sure it's all nothing, really . . . Sx

Susi Judge-Davis – 10/1/00, 9.12am
to... Lorraine Pallister
cc...
re... pointers

I'd hate us to get off on the wrong foot on your first morning, but there are a couple of things you should know about Simon and the kind of department he likes to run.

TIMEKEEPING: He is terribly strict about starting on time (8.45) so that there is always someone here to 'person' the phones. I noticed you were a couple of minutes late this morning.

DRESS: Although the creative department is traditionally casual, Simon prefers the PAs to be a little smarter. Maybe you could drop the hemlines a tad. And I think you'll find a pair of 'flatties' more comfy with the amount of dashing around you'll be doing.

KNICK-KNACKS: Simon prefers us to keep the personal effects on and around our workstations to an absolute min'. He will allow a couple of photos of mummy/boyfriend, but don't stick them on the wall, pop them in a nice silver frame.

TEA/COFFEE RUN: First job every morning is to pop up to the kitchen and get a couple of pots of tea (Darjeeling for Simon, Earl Grey for me) and a flask of coffee for visitors. It's not compulsory, but Simon really adores those little cinnamon bickies they have.

FRATERNISATION: Simon really hates it when creatives hang around the PAs' desks. He likes to see them in their offices slaving away I'm afraid. I can see Liam by your PC as I type. It's only a little thing but I wouldn't encourage him.

I know I've made him sound like an absolute monster but honestly he's not. If you stick to the rules he's a total, utter sweetie! I know that you and I are going to get along really well. Maybe we can nip out for a quick bite at lunch and get to know each other.

Susi Judge-Davis
Executive Assistant to the Creative Director

Ken Perry – 10/1/00, 9.23am
to... All Departments
cc...
re... 'joss sticks'

I am obliged to point out that the igniting of scent-impregnated candles, incense and other aromatic paraphernalia is prohibited under the terms of our insurance agreement. They are defined in the policy as 'incendiary devices' and, as such, represent a fire hazard. I will send Shanice round the building this morning to gather up all such materials.

Thank you for your co-operation.

Ken Perry
Office Administrator

Susi Judge-Davis – 10/1/00, 9.25am
to... Lorraine Pallister
cc...
re... pollen alert

Hate to be a spoilsport but that gorgeous bouquet you've just had delivered will have to go. Simon is incredibly sensitive to pollen. I know that he's not back for a week but it lingers even with the air con. Sorry.

Lorraine Pallister – 10/1/00, 9.30am
to... Liam O'Keefe
cc...
re... Susi Judge-Dredd

I'm off to a flier with Ally McBeal's even thinner sister. She just went through Simon's dos and don'ts. Apparently I'm unsuitably

dressed, have to get rid of my Leftfield poster and I'm not allowed
to let you dribble on my keyboard. And you'll have to dump the
flowers you sent me. Simon's allergic (would be, wouldn't he?).
But thanks – they're beautiful. Didn't have you down as a soppy
git.

liam_okeefe@millershanks-london.co.uk
10/1/00, 9.33am
to... brett_topowlski@millershanks-london.co.uk
cc...
re... greetings from cloud 9

While you're busy porking Mandi, Candi, Randi or Sandi, some
of us are actually earning money. Pinki's had me knocking out
Coke posters since the crack of dawn. They're the dog's bollocks
as well. They're on the line Horne came up with 'IT'S IN THE
CAN' which I must admit ain't bad for a sad old tosser. He's
done some half-decent scripts too. One of them uses that Air
track, 'Sexy Boy', which is pretty cool. And if you bear in mind
Horne's tastes in Asian 'ladies' it takes on exciting new meanings.

Blinding weekend. It wasn't quite what I had in mind. Lol's mate
Debbie is a horny little minx but she didn't come through on
the O'Keefe sandwich front. She got off with some scruffy little
bloke who deals at Sound Republic and disappeared for the duration. Saw Zoë there too, giving it rock-all with a big black guy
(I'm talking Barry White big).

Lol just gets saucier. I'm a new man. I actually went out to the
deli yesterday to get us croissants and freshly squeezed orange
juice for breakfast. And this morning I experienced an urge to
send her flowers. I tried but I couldn't fight it off. White lilies –
thirty-five sodding quid.

Pinki is trying to turn the place into Haight Ashbury 1969 but
she's managed to get the department working their nuts off. It's
weird. You can tell Susi doesn't approve. Lol came up with Susi
Judge-Dredd. I like that. She could be a copywriter yet. Watch
your arse, matey.

Susi Judge-Davis – 10/1/00, 9.38pm
to... Zoë Clarke
cc...
bcc...Rachel Stevenson
re... my condolences

I hope that the funeral on Friday wasn't too awful. I overheard
Liam mention that he saw you at Sound Republic on Saturday.
We all have to search for a personal way of expressing our grief
at times like these, and I am glad that you have found yours. If
you need a shoulder, you know where I am. All the best with
your new job.

Pinki Fallon – 10/1/00, 9.44am
to... Harriet Greenbaum; David Crutton
cc...
re... Coke

I think we are making good progress with Coke. The scripts are
in great shape and ready to brief out as storyboards the moment
you give the nod. Liam and I have done half a dozen posters,
which we're very pleased with. I also have three teams working
on press, radio, point-of-sale and guerrilla media ideas and I'll
be looking at their first thoughts at 12.30. So if it's cool with you
guys, I'd like to show you everything at 4.00. I know you were
talking about rewriting Dan's presentation, Harriet, so it would
be good if you had the work in your head before you make a
start. E me with your feelings . . . ☺

Nigel Godley – 10/1/00, 9.52am
to... All Departments
cc...
re... for sale

RONCO BUTTONEER
• Nearly new.
• So simple even a 'man' can use it!
• Use anywhere – on a train, on the loo, in a meeting.

- Never have that embarrassing 'I'm missing a button' feeling again.
- £9.00 o.n.o..
- First to see will buy.

Call x4667 – Nige

Harriet Greenbaum – 10/1/00, 9.59am
to...   Pinki Fallon
cc...
re...   Coke

You're making life easier already, Pinki. I'm free whenever you need me.

David Crutton – 10/1/00, 10.01am
to...   Pinki Fallon
cc...
re...   Coke

It sounds like you're on top of it, Pinki. I sincerely hope you're not just full of shit like your boss. I've got twenty-five minutes at 4.00. I guess that's when I'll find out.

debbie_wright@littlewoods/manchester.co.uk
10/1/00, 10.16am
to...   lorraine_pallister@millershanks-london.co.uk
cc...
re...   I'm back

Somehow I managed to get on a train home last night. Sorry I lost you but that guy Howie gave me the best E in the world. Ever. I was totally off my face. Liam's cute. I think. Can't honestly remember. Hit 'reply' if you're still talking to me . . . Debs

Zoë Clarke – 10/1/00, 10.21am
to...   Susi Judge-Davis
cc...
re...   my condolences

Thank you for your concern, Susi. It's good to know who your friends are. I feel quite strong. I learnt how to deal with death during my time working alongside you . . . Zxxx

simon_horne@millershanks-london.co.uk
10/1/00, 10.30am (2.30pm local)
to... susi_judgedavis@millershanks-london.co.uk
cc...
re... jobs II

1. When you parcel up those drugs, pop in a bottle of Laphroaig. It's proving quite impossible to find a decent drop of malt on this *île tragique*.
2. Inform Pinki that she *will* fax me all Coke material *now*. Remind her who saved her job last week when she lost her mind.
3. And tell her as well that *under no circumstances whatsoever* is she to use my office. She may have temporary possession of my title but there is no way I will tolerate her performing Feng Shui with my furniture.
4. Remind me to write to Michelin/World's Leading Hotels about le Touessrok. Its standards have plummeted since last I was here. It took room service six attempts to deliver a correctly prepared eggs Benedict.

lorraine_pallister@millershanks-london.co.uk
10/1/00, 10.33am
to... debbie_wright@littlewoods/manchester.co.uk
cc...
re... I'm back

Think I was worried about you? You're the girl who went AWOL for five days in Fuengirola. As long as you had fun in the bright lights it's OK by me. At my new desk now. If Liam leans over far enough he can just see me from his office. Actually he can just see the tempting flashes of gusset I'm giving him. Brain's telling him to work. Knob's got other plans. He's on his way over: BRAIN O, KNOB 1. See you later . . . Lolx

Susi Judge-Davis – 10/1/00, 10.38am
to...   Lorraine Pallister
cc...
re...   Liam

What is Liam doing under your desk? Did you not read my earlier note re fraternisation? Consider this a friendly warning.

Lorraine Pallister – 10/1/00, 10.40am
to...   Susi Judge-Davis
cc...
re...   Liam

Not what you think. He's reconnecting my PC to the printer. He'll be done in about . . . um . . . six minutes.

susi_judgedavis@millershanks-london.co.uk
10/1/00, 11.13am
to...   simon_horne@millershanks-london.co.uk
cc...
re...   jobs II

Don't worry, Si, darling, all requests in hand. Pinki is still being funny about sending you Coke stuff so maybe you should e her direct. By the way, I'm having terrible trouble with the new girl, Lorraine. I don't think she's going to be 'one of us'.

Lorraine Pallister – 10/1/00, 11.16am
to...   Zoë Clarke
cc...
re...   help!

Fancy lunch? Only been on this floor ten minutes and Susi is already getting right on my tits. Need to know how the fuck you handled her.

Zoë Clarke – 10/1/00, 11.19am
to... Lorraine Pallister
cc...
re... help!

Bar Zero, 1.00. I'll give you the full monty on the cow!!!!!! Zxxx

**harriet_greenbaum@millershanks-london.co.uk
10/1/00, 11.34am**
to... daniel_westbrooke@millershanks-london.co.uk
cc...
re... Coke

I hope this reaches you in Mauritius without getting chewed up and spat out in cyberspace. Everything is going well, I trust. I've just been going through your draft of the Coke presentation and I have to say that there are some bits that didn't make complete sense. I hope you don't mind but I'm going to have a bash at rewriting it. Of course I'll fax my attempt to you upon completion. I'd appreciate your input.

**simon_horne@millershanks-london.co.uk
10/1/00, 12.11 pm (4.11pm local)**
to... pinki_fallon@millershanks-london.co.uk
cc...
re... Coke

Susi tells me that you are reluctant to forward the Coke work to me.

You cannot have forgotten already that '*IT'S IN THE CAN*' is *my* idea.

Nor will you fail to remember that it was only my trust in you that enabled you to be promoted in my absence.

Bearing those two things in mind, you will fax the work to me forthwith.

Si

pinki_fallon@millershanks-london.co.uk
10/1/00, 12.14pm
to... simon_horne@millershanks-london.co.uk
cc...
re... Coke

Simon, it is honestly not my idea not to send you the Coke work. David is adamant that he see everything first. I'm sorry, but I can't go against him on this. Of course I'll get everything to you as soon as he approves it . . . ☺

simon_horne@millershanks-london.co.uk
10/1/00, 12.18pm (4.18pm local)
to... susi_judgedavis@millershanks-london.co.uk
cc...
re... migraine, migraine . . .

Add Migraleve to package.

Lorraine Pallister – 10/1/00, 12.26pm
to... Creative Department
cc...
re... reminder

Pinki has asked me to remind you that the creative gangbang starts in five in the boardroom. Enjoy.

brett_topowlski@millershanks-london.co.uk
10/1/00, 12.30pm (4.30pm local)
to... liam_okeefe@millershanks-london.co.uk
cc...
re... DATELINE MAURITIUS: DAY 1

Just read your e. Sure I've seen that Coke line somewhere before. It's bugging me now. I'll ask Vin when he gets out of the shower. Just got back from his recce. Says all the beaches were shite and Mel and Nathan both got stung by jellyfish. Vin reckoned his O'Neill wetsuit saved him (£200 well spent then). Horne still hasn't emerged from the honeymoon suite and he's got a room service waiter on permanent standby. You should see Westbrooke. He's one of those fashion tragedies who wears his socks on the beach. He's spent the day running after the client who's cruising the sands like a fat, sweaty David Hasselhoff. Got to go. Mandi has put my Deep Heat on her sunburn and she's squealing like a piglet. She's none too bright but she's got BJ lips (collagen is *A Good Thing*).

melinda_sheridan@millershanks-london.co.uk
10/1/00, 12.45pm (4.45pm local)
to... harriet_greenbaum@millershanks-london.co.uk;
pinki_fallon@millershanks-london.co.uk
cc...
re... Mako

I just wanted to catch up with you on Mako. I may be here in Paradise but I'd never forget my little petals back in dear old Blighty. Actually, Paradise it is not. My leg is doing a plausible impersonation of an inflatable salami after an encounter with a jellyfish. I take that as ominous. I asked a fisherman why all the boats had been hauled off the beach and he muttered darkly about a typhoon. Of course the local met office plead ignorance but I've been here before, darlings. My money is on the dusky señor mending his lobster pots.

But enough of me and my woes. Back to Mako! I understand the meeting went well last Friday so now we must hasten to production. Pinki, I have briefed my PA to get in a number of directors' reels for your perusal. You should inform her of your favourites. Harriet, perhaps you would let me have some info on timing and budgets and I can begin to prepare a schedule.

Now I must round up those lovable rascals, Vincent and Brett, before they wreak any more havoc. I have already had one of my talented cast drop out after a Vesuvian eruption of silicone. I should hate to lose any more to their sordid ministrations.

Wish you were here.

David Crutton – 10/1/00, 12.50pm
to... Zoë Clarke
cc...
re... lunch

I am working through lunch today. You can make up for your abysmal start this morning by getting me a sandwich (cheese, salad, mayo on white bap), family bag of cheese and onion crisps, Diet Coke, Fruit and Nut, and a king-size Mars Bar. And hurry up. I'm not nice when I'm hungry.

Lorraine Pallister – 10/1/00, 12.52pm
to... Zoë Clarke
cc...
re... lunch

Reception in two.

**brett_topowlski@millershanks-london.co.uk
10/1/00, 12.58pm (4.58pm local)**
to... liam_okeefe@millershanks-london.co.uk
cc...
re... bingo!

Knew I'd seen that Coke line before. Just asked Vin and it came to him straight off. A girl team from Watford left their book with Horne a few months back. He never bothered to look at it but we snuck a peek while it was under Susi's desk – they looked fit when they dropped it off so we thought we'd look inside for their number. Anyway, they'd done a campaign for 7UP. The line was 'IT'S IN THE CAN'. It was the best thing they had by a street. Is one of Horne's scripts about a beekeeper and a salesman? If it is, this ain't no coincidence. The cunning prick nicked it.

Topowlski of the Yard

pertti_vanhelden@millershanks-helsinki.co.fin
10/1/00, 1.19pm (3.19pm local)
to... david_crutton@millershanks-london.co.uk
cc...
re... FIZZY POP

I am worrying that your continuing indeciding on the Coke matter is holding us up too much at this end. So this morning I am taking the liberty of preparing presenting materials on your behalf. I am flying in top storyboard artists from Stockhölm. They will be making a super-dooper job, of that I am certain.

I also have news of a breakthrough of even more sizeability. I am nosing around my very good contacts in the pop record business and I believe I am making Aqua themselves interested in singing 'Fizzy Whizzy Pop' at the presenting meeting! Wowee, who would believe? Obviously, there will be fees and expendings for considering. But real pop legends in the blood and sweat!

Between you, me and the bed sheet I think the reason behind their interest is the fact that they are not having a top seller for some months. I know not if you are following the hit parade chart, but they are seeing tough competition from groups like Take This, the Space Girls (I am loving Baby Space!) and Kurly. It is difficult for them out there. But if it is bringing them into our Miller Shanks family, then who is caring?

I should be so lucky ... lucky, lucky, lucky – Pertti

liam-o'keefe@millershanks-london.co.uk
10/1/00, 1.33pm
to... brett_topowlski@millershanks-london.co.uk
cc...
re... bingo!

Shit, fuck and blimey o'riley. I've just come out of Pinki's first 'Community Creative Love-in' and that's some bit of news to greet me with. I knew Horne was an unprincipled motherfucker, but didn't think even he'd stoop to stealing ideas off a couple of

potless students. But what do we do with this bombshell? As I
see it there are two options:

1. We grass him up to Pinki, Crutton, Tarzan F. Weissmuller
and fucking *Campaign*. This plan has one distinct advantage. It
means the end of the low-life twat's career. Never eat lunch in
this town again? He'll be lucky to get egg and chips at a greasy
spoon on the Old Kent Road.
2. We don't do a sodding thing with this nugget of information.
This plan also happens to have a distinct advantage – Pinki and
I won't have to work through every single bloody night this week
coming up with a new campaign to replace the one Horne nicked.
(It's alright for you two, tucked up snug thousands of miles away
– you won't have to work on the brief.)

There we have it: a fascinating moral dilemma; an intriguing
conundrum; a fucking dog's dinner. What the hell do we do?

David Crutton – 10/1/00, 1.35pm
to... Zoë Clarke
cc...
re... lunch

Where the fuck are you? More to the point, where the fuck is
my sandwich? You're extremely lucky that you're not as plug-ugly
as the Craigie girl, otherwise you'd now be spending more time
at home with *TV Quick*.

Pinki Fallon – 10/1/00, 1.43pm
to... Creative Department
cc...
re... you're amazing

That was the most fantastic experience, guys! Not only were our
ideas mega but there was a real coming-together and sense
of common purpose. And we made progress on Coke. The two
new scripts were brilliant. Thanks, and let's do it again
tomorrow . . . ☺

David Crutton – 10/1/00, 1.49pm
to... Harriet Greenbaum
cc...
re... problem

I need your advice. There is a problem that I have been doing my best to ignore for a week. However, it refuses to go away and now threatens to get out of hand. Under normal circumstances I'd tell this particular thorn in my side to fuck off, but he's managed to get Weissmuller involved so that is not an option. In short it involves our colleagues in Finland and the Coke pitch. Come and see me the moment you return from lunch and I'll take you through it in detail.

daniel_westbrooke@millershanks-london.co.uk
10/1/00, 2.08pm (6.08pm local)
to... harriet_greenbaum@millershanks-london.co.uk
cc...
bcc...david_crutton@millershanks-london.co.uk
re... Coke

If you had immersed yourself as deeply in Coke as I have these past few weeks then my presentation would be clear as Waterford crystal. However, you are a newcomer to this pitch so I will make allowances and not put it down to stupidity. Feel free to make whatever changes you see fit. But in the final analysis, I will make the decision as to which version we go with. While I would normally hesitate to pull rank, I am Head of Client Services, and on an issue as crucial as this I will have no qualms. Incidentally, I am incredibly busy here trying to keep a tight rein on a very difficult client. I would appreciate it if the e-mails pleading for help were kept to a minimum.

Harriet Greenbaum – 10/1/00, 2.13pm
to... David Crutton
cc...
re... problem

I have a small misunderstanding to clear up with Dan, then I'll
be right up.

David Crutton – 10/1/00, 2.15pm
to... Harriet Greenbaum
cc...
re... problem

I know, I was blind copied on the 'misunderstanding'.

harriet_greenbaum@millershanks-london.co.uk
10/1/00, 2.21pm
to... daniel_westbrooke@millershanks-london.co.uk
cc...
re... Coke

Daniel, let's not start this week on the wrong foot. My earlier
e-mail was neither pleading for help nor trying to pull a fast one.
I was simply offering my input on the presentation document.
As my more experienced senior, you were always going to be
kept apprised and have the last word. Of course, if you'd rather
not be bothered during your arduous shoot, then I will keep you
out of the loop and deal directly with David.

Lorraine Pallister – 10/1/00, 2.27pm
to... Zoë Clarke
cc...
re... ta

Good to get together at lunch. Don't think your plan of coating
her with Shiphams crab paste and dipping her in a vat of piranhas
is feasible. Mind you, another few weeks of this and I might
feel differently. Can see her now and she's typing like a loony.
Something tells me another e is on its way.

Susi Judge-Davis – 10/1/00, 2.29pm
to... Lorraine Pallister
cc...
re... time keeping

I hate to be a nag, darling, but lunch is *one* hour only. It's another little thing that niggles Simon, and it's best if you know the ropes before he comes back.

Zoë Clarke – 10/1/00, 2.34pm
to... Lorraine Pallister
cc...
re... ta

Gotta keep this short. Forgot to get the Crettin his sodding lunch!!!! Had to go out and get his own. Don't think he knows what a sandwich bar looks like, so can't have been easy!!!! He nearly killed me when I got back!!!!!!!!!!!! Zxxx

Harriet Greenbaum – 10/1/00, 2.46pm
to... Pinki Fallon
cc...
re... prepare yourself

I've just been speaking to David and I should warn you that he's going to be more-than-usually rigorous when he judges your Coke work at 4.00. The reasons for this are complex. To cut a long story short, he's decided to give the kiss-off to another Coke campaign done by our office in Finland, and which apparently has the backing of Jim Weissmuller in NY. This being so, it is essential that we leave no chinks in our armour. 'IT'S IN THE CAN' must be as good as it possibly can be. I know you can do it. Think Girl Power!

Pinki Fallon – 10/1/00, 2.51pm
to... Harriet Greenbaum
cc...
re... prepare yourself

I think you just gave me my first taste of international office politics. Not sure that my life as a grubbing copywriter has prepared me for this. Anyway, I happen to think that Simon left us with the makings of an amazing campaign and the work we've done on it today is really exciting. See for yourself at 4.00 but I'm quietly confident . . . ☺

harriet_greenbaum@millershanks-london.co.uk
10/1/00, 3.09pm

to... pertti_vanhelden@millershanks-helsinki.co.fin
cc... james_f_weissmuller@millershanks-ny.co.usa
bcc...David Crutton
re... Coca-Cola

Dear Pertti,

David is terribly busy and he has asked me, as Senior Account Director on the Coke pitch, to write to you on his behalf. Firstly, to apologise that sheer weight of work has prevented him from getting back to you sooner. Secondly, to say thank you for all your efforts this past week.

It was very noble of you to throw your shoulder to the wheel on Coke, and all of us in London are bowled over both by your unselfishness and the brilliance of your idea. We thought 'Fizzy Whizzy Pop' amusing, off-the-wall and possessing some quite astute insights into the role of Coca-Cola in the millennial market place. Also the choice of Aqua as a vehicle for the product story is a delightful and charming piece of casting.

The bad news for you is that we have taken the difficult decision to go forward to the pitch with an idea that we have developed here in London. It was a close call but in the end we felt a locally derived concept would be more in tune with the very unique outlook of young, British consumers.

I am sorry to be the bearer of bad tidings. I must once again convey our sincere thanks for your hard work. Anyone who doubts the viability of inter-European co-operation need only look at your example to be proved hopelessly wrong!

Yours sincerely,

Harriet Greenbaum
Account Director

David Crutton – 10/1/00, 3.18pm
to... Harriet Greenbaum
cc...
re... Coca-Cola

Well put, Harriet. If you're ever stuck for a second career, stand for parliament. You've got the right line in bullshit.

james_f_weissmuller@millershanks-ny.co.usa
10/1/00, 3.31pm (10.31am local)
to... david_crutton@millershanks-london.co.uk
cc...
re... Coca-Cola

I've got to say that when Pertti hit me last week with his brilliant Coke idea I wondered how the heck you were going to beat it. I am very much looking forward to seeing the 'locally derived' idea that you have given the green light. Send me the work prior to my departure. There's nothing like a red-hot piece of creative to get the pre-pitch adrenaline flowing.

I'm very much looking forward to the pitch next Monday. Winning Coke in the UK is a foot in the door. Then we take it on around the world.

I'll be arriving early Sunday morning with Rick Korning, our senior VP in charge of global oversight and planning (I believe you met him at the get-together in Delhi last year). We'll head straight to the office so you can take us through your presentation.

By the way, who is Harriet Greenbaum? I understood Daniel was handling the pitch, but you seem to have found a wise and tactful deputy.

Best wishes,

Jim

Ken Perry – 10/1/00, 3.32pm
to... All Departments
cc...
re... a tidy office is an efficient office.

As part of the drive to have the office ship-shape for Monday's pitch, tomorrow has been designated Clutter Clearance Day. To ensure that the clear-up is expedited with the minimum loss in productivity I have arranged for the placement of colour-coded wheelie bins on each floor. These are strictly for the containment of rubbish and other surplus items.

RED: white paper (please ensure that all staples and clips are removed)
BLUE: used manila envelopes
GREEN: videotapes (VHS and U-matic)
PINK: overheads and other acetate materials
MAUVE: miscellaneous

Shanice will come round to appoint 'Rubbish Monitors' whose jobs it will be to see that the correct procedures are adhered to. If we all muck in and carry out this exercise properly it will not only be quicker, it will also be more fun.

Thank you for your co-operation.

Ken Perry
Office Administrator

Nigel Godley – 10/1/00, 3.33pm
to... Ken Perry; Shanice Duff
cc...
re... a tidy office is an efficient office

Brilliant initiative, chaps! Bags me be monitor on my floor. Do we get badges or caps?

Nige

pertti_vanhelden@millershanks-helsinki.co.fin
10/1/00, 3.38pm (5.38pm local)
to... david_crutton@millershanks-london.co.uk
cc... james_f_weissmuller@millershanks-ny.co.usa
re... I'm gutting

Dear David Crutton,

I feel I must write to you most frankly. I am very upsetting at your treating of me on the Coca-Cola snub. We are in Finland bending over to our backsides to be helpful. And we are spending time, money and perspiration to be making it happen.

In returning we are not asking for Nobel prizes, just a little respect. I can be accepting that you are not choosing our idea over your own. I am thinking you are wrong, but many years of the Eurovision Singing Contest are teaching me that the thrills of competition are not always resulting in triumph.

What is sticking in my craw fish is that you are asking a lady female subordinate to be giving me the information about your decision. This is rude and not respecting of me as a fellow Chief Executive Officer. I am believing that when you are including me on your e-mailings that you are valuing me for my friendly opinions and inputting. But about this I am wrong. I will not be so outcoming in the future.

Pertti van Helden

david_crutton@millershanks-london.co.uk
10/1/00, 3.44pm
to... pertti_vanhelden@millershanks-helsinki.co.fin
cc...
re... I'm gutting

Dear Pertti,

I am sorry that you are upset. Disrespect was not the intention. As we explained we have nothing but admiration for your endeavours on Coke. However, I have to say that the work you sent us was very wide of the mark strategically, and demonstrated a naïve misunderstanding of the British marketing landscape. As such it would risk being laughed off the TV screen. Perhaps I am being blunt, but I wish to demonstrate that our decision was reached objectively, without recourse to petty prejudice.

I hope that we can continue to work together in the future. Next time, however, your contribution might stand more chance of being useful if it were asked for.

Best wishes,

David Crutton

Zoë Clarke – 10/1/00, 3.47pm
to... Harriet Greenbaum; Pinki Fallon
cc...
re... Coke review

David has asked me to remind you to be on time for the 4.00 review. He is on a tight schedule and can't be delayed. Ta.

gabriella_delhoya@millershanks-sf.co.usa
10/1/00, 3.53pm (7.53am local)
to... david_crutton@millershanks-london.co.uk
cc...
re... I'm gutting

Dear David,

This is fantastic. For years we have been trying to build a true spirit of togetherness in the San Francisco office. Working with the proven principles of Primal Scream Therapy, our ultimate goal is 10,000 PEOPLE, 1 MIND. This can only be achieved once we break out of the confines of conventional corporate role-play and openly share our feelings with all of our co-workers. Your candid letter to Pertti, where you embrace your anger, is incredible. More importantly, your decision to share your private self with the entire network is a model of the methodology that we are reaching for on the West Coast.

Who is your teacher? I know that if we pool our knowledge we can lead Miller Shanks into the next dimension of spiritually energised business practice.

Your friend in enlightenment,

Gabriella del Hoya
Head of Human Development, Miller Shanks San Francisco

mike_appleton@millershanks-hk.co.hk
10/1/00, 3.55pm (11.55pm local)
to... david_crutton@millershanks-london.co.uk
cc...
re... I'm gutting

Hi, David. Terrific letter. I remember Pertti well from the CEOs' conference in Delhi and I, too, found him hard to shake off! I remember you as well from that shindig with great delight. Your presentation of the Bonio case history gave us all food for thought!

While I'm burning the midnight oil here I have a small favour to ask. I've been working the Asia/Pacific circuit for thirteen years now and feel I have achieved all I can. It is time for a switch back to Europe and I hear on the grapevine that there is a search for a new CEO in Bucharest. I've contacted Jim Weissmuller and though he promised to get back to me I guess he has been too busy with matters American. I know you have his ear, and I'd be forever indebted if you could make mention of me. I look forward to seeing you soon. Roll on Waikiki!

Mike Appleton
CEO, Miller Shanks Hong Kong

hans_vanderkok@millershanks-jo.co.rsa
10/1/00, 4.06pm (6.06pm local)
to... david_crutton@millershanks-london.co.uk
cc...
re... I'm gutting

There is a proverb on the veldt. 'The lion roars, the hyena laughs but the crocodile hunts in silence.' I think this says everything.

Hansi van der Kok
Account Executive, Miller Shanks Johannesburg

daniel_vargas@millershanks-san.co.chi
10/1/00, 4.10pm (12.10pm local)
to... david_crutton@millershanks-london.co.uk
cc...
re... I'm gutting

I am not one to beat my own trumpet, but as Head of Client
Services I was most instrumental in winning the Carmella soda
account, which is worth US$0.2 million. I think my experience in
this competitive market can help you with your pitch. Naturally, I
am so very busy with running the office here, but I will make
time to assist should you so desire. If you have any questions,
any questions at all, please do not hesitate to e-mail.

Daniel Vargas
Head of Client Services, Miller Shanks Chile

mohammed_fayed@millershanks-cai.co.egy
10/1/00, 4.12pm (6.12pm local)
to... david_crutton@millershanks-london.co.uk
cc...
re... I'm gutting

Is this a chain letter? How many friends and acquaintances do I
forward it to and will I be accursed if I do not do as requested?

Mohammed Fayed
Art Director, Miller Shanks Cairo

PS I am not relating to the Fayed who own Harrods and make
mischief with your Queen Majesty.

james_f_weissmuller@millershanks-ny.co.usa
10/1/00, 4.15pm (11.15am local)
to... david_crutton@millershanks-london.co.uk
cc...
re... I'm gutting

I am all for honest exchanges of views, and have no objection to your letter to Pertti. However, copying it to the entire network is unnecessarily cruel. It looks to me like you are showboating. I will not stand for my CEOs publicly upbraiding each other in an effort to score points. I am not impressed. In future leave matters of international diplomacy in the capable hands of your Harriet Greenbaum.

Jim

Pinki Fallon – 10/1/00, 4.33pm
to... Creative Department
cc...
re... you are so cool

I have just come out of a review of our Coke work with Harriet and David and they were blown away. It was a special experience and I wish you could all have been there to share it. Thank you, not just to those of you who did the work, but everyone else who gave support and created the atmosphere of positivity in which these ideas were made possible. I will visit each and every one of you to thank you personally . . . ☺

Harriet Greenbaum – 10/1/00, 4.35pm
to... Pinki Fallon
cc...
re... Coke

STUPENDOUS!

David Crutton – 10/1/00, 4.38pm
to... Rachel Stevenson
cc...
re... e-mail

I'd write direct to IT but they're so fucking inept, I suspect they don't actually exist. Now my e-mails are going not only to Finland but to every single employee in the Miller Shanks network. If my memory of the last annual report serves, there are over 15,000 of them. And every one of the keyboard-happy bastards seems to have decided to write me a reply. I am making it your mission to sort this out *NOW*, before I personally take a fucking sledge-hammer to every computer in the building and issue one and all with parchment, quill pens and carrier pigeons.

Katie Philpott – 10/1/00, 4.40pm
to... Liam O'Keefe
cc...
re... hiya!!

How was your weekend? Mine was brill! I got really, really, really drunk at Planet Hollywood. Tequila slammers! Such a hoot! I was useless on Sunday. Anyway, are we still OK for tomorrow? I went to Selfridges on Sat and spent a fortune on a fab outfit. Can't wait! Katie P

mike_appleton@millershanks-hk.co.hk
10/1/00, 4.42pm (12.42am local)
to... david_crutton@millershanks-london.co.uk
cc...
re... Bucharest

Did I mention in my e-mail that I'm learning Romanian? You could pass that on when you speak to Jim. Cheers, or, as they'd say in Bucharest, '*partile mici pot fi inghitite sau inhalate*'!

Mike

Rachel Stevenson – 10/1/00, 4.43pm
to... David Crutton
cc...
re... e-mail

I'll get on it now and report back as soon as there is progress.

David Crutton – 10/1/00, 4.45pm
to... Zoë Clarke
cc...
re... e-mail

I am about to walk out of my office. When I do, you will come in, sit at my PowerBook and trash every unread e-mail marked '*re: I'm gutting*'. You will find there are quite a few. Make sure this is done by the time I return.

brett_topowlski@millershanks-london.co.uk
10/10/00, 4.49pm (8.49pm local)
to... liam_okeefe@millershanks-london.co.uk
cc...
re... THE BIG SECRET

Just back from dinner and read your e. Here's what Vin and me think you should do. Nothing. Yet. Look at it this way. You don't want to make extra work for yourself. And if you want to throw maximum shit at the fan, the best time to do it would be Monday morning just before the pitch. That way it's too late to do anything about it, they still have to present the campaign, and Horne will actually be back in the country to take the rap. Better still, Me and Vin will be there to enjoy it as well.

Down to four LOVE birds now. Mandi's got sunstroke really bad. Even if she feels OK to get up for the shoot, she looks redder than a horse's knob. Mel is on the phone sorting out a casting session for tomorrow. The script would've worked with five but not four. We're going to look for a couple of local birds to stand in. Dearie me, another morning staring at tits. Will it never stop? Horne still hasn't left his suite. He might be dead in there, his corpse bloated and rotting in the silk sheets. Do I even care? I do actually. He borrowed my copy of *Performance Car* on the flight and I want it back.

pinki_fallon@millershanks-london.co.uk
10/1/00, 5.02pm
to... simon_horne@millershanks-london.co.uk
cc...
re... Coke

We had a very successful review with David this afternoon, and while there's still a lot to do, I think we're well on the way. I've left all the work with Susi to fax over to you. Let me know what you think . . . ☺

Susi Judge-Davis – 10/1/00, 5.05pm
to... Pinki Fallon
cc...
re... this takes the biscuit

Do you really think I'm going to spend half an hour on the fax machine sending this work to Mauritius? I thought I made it absolutely clear that I only work for Simon. You can come to my desk, take it all away and give it to Lorraine. It's her damn job.

Pinki Fallon – 10/1/00, 5.10pm
to... Susi Judge-Davis
cc...
re... this takes the biscuit

I've had just about enough of you. If you lifted your head from your magazine you'd notice that Simon isn't here this week. I haven't seen you do anything today apart from make trouble for Lorraine and read Italian, French and American *Vogue*. Why don't you actually do some work for once? I'm attempting to build an atmosphere of one-ness in the department. You are the only person not making an effort . . . ☺

mike_appleton@millershanks-hk.co.hk
10/1/00, 5.12pm (1.12am local)
to... david_crutton@millershanks-london.co.uk
cc...
re... Bucharest

Another thing – my wife, Noreen, is one eighth Hungarian on her mother's side so we feel a natural affinity for the region. It's one of those tiny things that would ease our assimilation into Romanian life – provided Jim thinks me to be the man, of course!

Mike

Zoë Clarke – 10/1/00, 5.13pm
to... Lorraine Pallister
cc...
re... sneaky slut!!!!

God, this is awful!!! Don't know how to tell you this, so I think
I'll just come straight out with it. You know that new girl, Katie
Philpott – the posh one in account management? She was up
here showing off this new dress. Looked stupid – who's wearing
lilac these days, and those pleats still couldn't hide her bum!!!
But that's not the point. She said she'd got it to wear to go
clubbing with Liam!!!!!! I know you'll be upset right now so meet
me in the ladies' on your floor and you can have a good cry. I'm
here for you – Zxxx

Pinki Fallon – 10/1/00, 5.17pm
to... Peter Renquist
cc...
re... EMERGENCY

I'm afraid there's been a bit of a disaster. Someone accidentally
spilt nail polish remover on Liam and quite a bit went on his
Mac. I switched it off at the mains straight away but it's taken
most of the letters off the keys. Can you replace it with a new
one as soon as poss? We've got tons of work on and he can't do
without it. Ta mucho ... ☺

susi_judgedavis@millershanks-london.co.uk
10/1/00, 5.21pm
to... simon_horne@millershanks-london.co.uk
cc...
re... Pinki

I don't know how much more of this I can take, Si. I'm drowning
in work and Pinki has just asked me to fax pages and pages of
Coke stuff to you. I explained as politely as I could that I only
work for you and she hit the roof. She said some horrid things,
not just about me but you as well. You know I hate it here and

I only stay because of you. I don't think I can last all week ...
Sx

Rachel Stevenson – 10/1/00, 5.27pm
to... David Crutton
cc...
re... e-mail

I have spoken to Peter Renquist and impressed upon him the
seriousness of the situation. They have called in some heavyweight
consultants. They will be here first thing in the morning and
promise not to leave until the problem is fixed once and for all.
It will necessitate e-mail being shut down for the duration.

David Crutton – 10/1/00, 5.30pm
to... Rachel Stevenson
cc...
re... e-mail

Whatever it takes.

Rachel Stevenson – 10/1/00, 5.34pm
to... All Departments
cc...
re... e-mail

Due to an ongoing software problem, e-mail will be shut down
from 7.00am tomorrow. The repairs should be finished by the
end of the day. IT apologises for the inconvenience. However,
there is always the telephone or you could even talk to each other
face to face. That would be nice.

Rachel Stevenson
Personnel

harriet_greenbaum@millershanks-london.co.uk
10/1/00, 5.36pm
to... melinda_sheridan@millershanks-london.co.uk
cc...
re... Mako

Sorry to be getting back to you so late in the day, but Coke is taking over. You're probably washing down your well-earned lobster with something chilled and sparkling right now. I'm just having the Mako timings typed and they'll be faxed to you straight away. As far as the money is concerned, if we can bring in all three commercials for under 750k to the client, I think I could sell that. He's notoriously tight but it's about time I taught him that the adage 'quality costs' applies just as much to advertising as it does to lunch. Every time I suggest a working meal he insists on le Gavroche.

Be good. And if you can't be good, etcetera . . .

Rachel Stevenson – 10/1/00, 5.39pm
to... Susi Judge-Davis
cc...
re... your resignation

Susi, if you are serious about resigning, I need to have it in writing. Doing it on voicemail is not strictly acceptable. I have tried you at your desk but perhaps you have gone home. I have looked at your file and this is the 6th resignation you have tendered. Are you absolutely sure this time or is this another 'cry for help'? Please come and see me in the morning when, hopefully, you will feel a little calmer.

simon_horne@millershanks-london.co.uk
10/1/00, 5.47pm (9.47pm local)
to... susi_judgedavis@millershanks-london.co.uk
cc...
re... GET IN TOUCH!

Where in heaven's name are you? I have been calling you for over fifteen minutes.

If you think that the moment I am out of the office you can clock-watch, think again.

I cannot get involved in your battles with Pinki.

You must learn to stand up for yourself.

If I have taught you one thing it must be that.

Besides, I need to speak to Pinki on far more important matters.

I have just received the fax and this work is all over the place.

The moment you return to your desk, find her and have her call me.

liam_okeefe@millershanks-london.co.uk
10/1/00, 6.02pm
to... brett_topowlski@millershanks-london.co.uk
cc...
re... THE BIG SECRET

Sorry about the delay in replying but I've had a fucking 'mare. Bit embarrassing actually. Lol got the idea I was screwing Katie Philpott. I mean, as if – you seen her? Any road, she came at me with the scorned woman's weapon of choice, nail-polish remover. Ruined my Ted Baker, but the good news is she completely fucked my keyboard. So now I'm typing this on my brand new 'cerise' iMac. It's got some tip-top games on it as well. Lol ain't speaking to me but reckon the offer of a full explanation over a min £60-a-head dinner might bring her round. Who says money can't buy me love? Fucking Beatles – tossers.

Your plan on THE BIG SECRET is a good one, though I don't know if I can keep my gob shut for a week. This is just too fucking good to keep schtum about.

E-mail is down tomorrow. Did you read the one Crutton accidentally copied to every Miller Shanks employee in the known universe? Wanker. The aftershock of his tantrum is still rattling the windows. Enjoy your fiesta of breasts tomorrow.

Liam O'Keefe – 10/1/00, 6.10pm
to... Lorraine Pallister
cc...
re... kiss, kiss

I know you're still mad, but would dinner make it better? I booked somewhere with 2 (two) Michelin stars.

Lorraine Pallister – 10/1/00, 6.13pm
to... Liam O'Keefe
cc...
re... kiss, kiss

See that big steel ruler on my desk? Go shove it up your arse and pray the bleeding doesn't prove fatal.

Ken Perry – 10/1/00, 6.15pm
to... All Departments
cc...
re... staff communications

Because we will be managing without e-mail tomorrow, I have arranged for extra photocopy paper to be available for memoranda. It would make most sense if we could revert to the pre-e-mail practice of colour coding all memos.

For those of you too young or too new to remember, this was pink paper for urgent all-staff, light green for non-urgent all-staff, and light blue for restricted circulation.

Thank you for your co-operation.

Ken Perry
Office Administrator

melinda_sheridan@millershanks-london.co.uk
10/1/00, 6.42pm (10.42pm local)
to... harriet_greenbaum@millershanks-london.co.uk
cc...
re... Mako

Lobster supper? I wish, my darling. I have spent my entire evening in the company of a club sandwich and a telephone, trying to sort out a casting call of local talent. Yes, we have lost another of our busty angels – this time to sunstroke despite repeated exhortations to keep her overpaid flesh in the shade. Anyway, it would appear that the bra size on this island stops at 34A. I am *so* at the end of my tether, I would seriously consider fishing my own tired bosoms from their cups if I thought it might help. After forty-five calls (I've been counting) I've rounded up nine girls. We will see them in the morning and I will go to bed praying that there are at least two whom the maestro Zapruder feels the camera will want to make torrid love to.

It would be fine if this were my only problem. It isn't. The crew arrives tomorrow and because Simon (who, incidentally, has not shown his face since we touched down) made me change the hotel booking so late in the day there's been the inevitable cock-up. Whichever way I turn my calculator, thirty-two people into thirteen rooms do not go. Now I must turn my attention to finding another hotel for the overflow.

But do you want to hear all this? Of course not. 750k sounds quite adequate for our needs on Mako – enough, for once, for full agency mark-up and a bit left over for lunch. I've looked at your timings and it's tight. But a little magic from Melinda and we should squeeze it all in. I'll look forward to shooting those with you if I ever get out of here. Oh, well, onwards and downwards.

simon_horne@millershanks-london.co.uk
10/1/00, 7.02pm (11.02pm local)
to... susi_judgedavis@millershanks-london.co.uk
cc...
re... I NEED YOU!

I despair of ever hearing from you again.

Have you any idea at all how isolated I feel out here?

simon_horne@millershanks-london.co.uk
10/1/00, 8.33pm (12.33am local)
to... pinki_fallon@millershanks-london.co.uk
cc... david_crutton@millershanks-london.co.uk;
harriet_greenbaum@millershanks-london.co.uk
re... Coke

I have taken some time out from preparations for the shoot to review the work you sent me, Pinki.

I would have preferred to speak to you on the phone.

It appears, however, that you left early. I did not realise that running my department would require so little of your time.

I commend you on managing so efficiently.

Here is what I think of the Coke work. It is wrong in a number of respects and I believe you haven't quite got a handle on my idea.

Allow me to be specific:

TV: You have committed the cardinal sin of beverage advertising by omitting the product-pouring shot from my scripts. For forty years no soft drink commercial has succeeded without a close-up of the fizzy goods cascading over copious rocks of clinking ice. Reinstate this immediately.

As for your new scripts, it is hard to put my finger on why they are not working. They just do not cut it with me. Work on this.

POSTERS: Dull, dull, dull. Do some more.

RADIO: I do not understand these at all. Who on earth is Ali G? Why can't he speak the Queen's English? I suggest a return to the drawing board.

I think you still have much to do.

I recommend a few late nights.

I think it would also do you a favour if you were to pin my core idea up on your wall and measure all your future efforts against it.

I am sorry to be so tough on you, but if it makes you realise that this job is not the breeze you imagined, then you will have learnt a hard but valuable lesson.

Si

pinki_fallon@millershanks-london.co.uk
10/1/00, 8.45pm
to... simon_horne@millershanks-london.co.uk
cc...
re... Coke

Just read your e – ta. I hadn't gone home. I was with Harriet
brainstorming a structure for the presentation. David wants me
to see him now to go through your comments in detail. I'll get
back to you ... ☺

david_crutton@millershanks-london.co.uk
10/1/00, 9.17pm
to... simon_horne@millershanks-london.co.uk
cc...
re... Coke

I have just discussed your thoughts with Harriet and Pinki. They
wanted to take some of them on board, but I overrode them. Do
you want to know why? I happen to think that Pinki and her
colleagues have turned your idea into a gem. For instance, the
product-pouring shots have gone precisely because we don't want
this to resemble every soft-drink ad of the last forty years. The
campaign is immeasurably better as a result.

By the way, my mother-in-law has heard of Ali G. She's seventy-
five, lives in Littlehampton and spends most of her time playing
rummy. You should take some time with her. You might learn
something about popular culture.

simon_horne@millershanks-london.co.uk
10/1/00, 9.24pm (1.20am local)
to... susi_judgedavis@millershanks-london.co.uk
cc...
re... Pinki

I know that e-mail is down tomorrow but on Wednesday morning
I expect a full report on Pinki's every movement to be on my
screen. Do not forget where your loyalties lie.

Nigel Godley – 10/1/00, 11.05pm
to... All Departments
cc...
re... calling all admen!

Anyone else still here, give me a shout. If not, byeeee! I'll miss
the e-mail 'banter' tomorrow. Talk to you again on Wed – Nige

Tuesday
11 January
2000

IT Help Desk – 11/1/00, 11.23am
to... All Departments
cc...
re... TEST

THIS IS A TEST MESSAGE. PLEASE DELETE. E-MAIL
WILL NOW CLOSE DOWN AGAIN.

Wednesday
12 January
2000

IT Help Desk – 12/1/00, 6.48am
to... All Departments
cc...
re... e-mail

E-mail is working again. Thank you for bearing with us.

Peter Renquist
Acting Head of IT

brett_topowlski@millershanks-london.co.uk
12/1/00, 7.11am (11.11am local)
to... liam_okeefe@millershanks-london.co.uk
cc...
re... DATELINE MAURITIUS, DAY 3

Greetings from the war zone. This is our first shooting day and it's looking grim. For a start, I'm sitting in my room staring at the worst rain I've ever seen. It wasn't like this in the brochure.

I'll bring you up to date.

Casting – they don't do tits in Mauritius. Didn't find anyone.

Leaves us with only four birds so Vin and me were up half the night on a rewrite.

Mel, Nathan and Vin disappeared again to look for the perfect powdery sand. Didn't find diddly so we decided to shoot the whole lot on the beach in front of the hotel. It looks pretty fucking soft and white to me so don't know why we didn't do that in the first place. Nathan keeps muttering 'should have gone to Zanzibar, should have gone to Zanzibar.' The hotel management weren't chuffed about a sweaty film crew driving their wrinkly punters from the sunbeds, but Mel's very persuasive when needs be.

Horne's had a crucial role in all these key decisions. He's been using his mighty powers of ESP to transmit his thoughts to us from his £1,800-a-night suite to make sure us useless tossers don't screw up. That's right, he still hasn't left his room. Suits me and Vin fine so we're keeping quiet. Desperate Dan's bothered, though. He's having a nightmare with the client and wants his chum Simon to help him out.

Fat Frank Sinton, the client – you'll like this. This guy looks like Jabba the Hut's bastard son but he must look in the mirror and see Ben Affleck because I've lost count of the amount of waitresses he's hit on. Anyway, first thing this morning there's Gloria Hunniford and a BBC crew out on the beach taping a piece for her pony holiday show. Why didn't we ever spot how much Mel looks like Gloria? Separated at birth or what? Bloody uncanny that of all the beaches in all the world they have to be shooting on the same one at the same time. To make it even spookier they're both wearing purple sarongs and black costumes. Hunniford's on a sunbed between takes and Fat Frank obviously thinks she's Mel basking in the rays. He bounces up to her and because he's a fat lech, whacks a freezing can of Pepsi slap in the middle of her mature cleavage. She jumps up and hollers for hotel security. Desperate Dan, who'd spent the morning drooling from afar at Hunniford (had a crush on her since he discovered Martina Navratilova was a dyke) wades in and takes her side – can't help himself. Fat Frank stalks off to his room threatening to fire the agency while Hunniford is thanking Dan for his chivalry. Torn? Ripped in bloody two, poor guy. He doesn't know whether to follow the client and save the business or follow his dick into the arms of Miss Hunni-Bunni.

In the end we got one shot set up before the rain. Looks like it might be stopping now so I'd better get back out there. We're shooting two birds duelling on jet skis. Speed, scary stunts, gorgeous birds with great big tits – it's art, mate. Did you sort things out with Lol? Normally, I wouldn't be worried for you, but don't balls this one up. She is sex on legs – and the legs are pretty good too.

Peter Renquist – 12/1/00, 7.34am
to... Rachel Stevenson
cc...
re... e-mail

We have finally got to the bottom of it. The consultants stayed through the night dismantling the server and re-installing the software. They couldn't find any faults. Then we thought that because David Crutton was the only one with a problem we should check Notes on his PC. This we did at 5.00 this morning. When we looked at his set-up it appeared that he has been mis-using his address book. It's complicated but when he sends he sometimes presses the wrong command key combination and automatically copies Finland. Yesterday he must have got it really wrong and copied all MS employees. We did some tests that tried to replicate his error and our theory proved correct.

He really needs to have a lesson or two in the basic skills. The question is, do you want to tell him or should I? Call me when you get in.

david_crutton@millershanks-london.co.uk
12/1/00, 7.51am
to... daniel_westbrooke@millershanks-london.co.uk
cc...
re... what the fuck is going on?

I was woken at 5.30 this morning by an hysterical Frank Sinton. He managed to blub that not only is the shoot proceeding like *Apocalypse Now* on a bad day, not only has he seen nothing of the creative director we sent out there to ensure a great film, not only is the director treating him like something on the sole of his Prada flip-flops, but on top of all that he claims you publicly accused him of sexually assaulting Gloria bloody Hunniford.

This is just too surreal.

Would you care to explain or shall we just say nothing and watch another piece of business slip out of the door?

David Crutton – 12/1/00, 8.06am
to... Zoë Clarke
cc...
re... have you seen the time?

Where are you? I'm going to a meeting now. By the time I return you will have written out 100 times in your best cursive hand: 'The next time I arrive later than eight o'clock, Mr Crutton will have my arse for a throw cushion.'

Rachel Stevenson – 12/1/00, 8.46am
to... David Crutton
cc...
re... e-mail

David, IT finally got to the root of the problem. I think it is best if Peter Renquist and I come to talk it through with you. Please do not use e-mail until we've spoken. I've booked 9.30 with Zoë. We'll see you then.

susi_judgedavis@millershanks-london.co.uk
12/1/00, 9.03am
to... simon_horne@millershanks-london.co.uk
cc...
re... Pinki Fallon

I kept track of her as best I could yesterday and I don't think she was suspicious. Here is my report.

08.35: P arrived at work. Made cup of tea (Typhoo). Read *Guardian* (Education Supplement).

08.46: LO'K arrived. Shut door. Possibly working.

10.30: HG went into P's office. Shut door.

10.46: HG came out with P. They hugged. HG got in lift. P went to loo (No 1s).

10.53: P came out of loo. Went walkabout round dept. Visited all teams briefly. Returned to own office with new Coke layouts. Smiling.

11.35: P informed SJ-D that she was going to recording of Coke demo track at Candle Music. SJ-D checked with TV dept. Two independent sources confirmed P's story.

13.59: P returned carrying Cranks takeaway bag. Impossible to verify contents. Presume non-meat lunch.

14.14: LO'K returned from lunch with LP. Caught SJ-D listening at door. Don't think he suspected.

14.33: P came out of office. Informed SJ-D she was going to see DC. Seemed agitated. SJ-D followed. P entered DC's office. Shut door.

15.00: P returned to floor. Calm. Entered office. Shut door.

15.16: P came out of office and went to loo (No 1s and 2s).

15.55: P came out of loo holding tissues. Stopped at waste bin on return to office. Removed copy of *Viz*. Relevance unclear.

16.22: DC came onto creative floor. Ignored SJ-D. Sat on LP's desk and spoke for six mins. Appeared friendly. DC then went into P's office.

16.40: DC came out of P's office with P. P informed SJ-D she would be at Bar Zero with DC. Not to be disturbed. SJ-D followed at distance and viewed subjects through window. DC ordered double espresso. P ordered tea. DC made joke with waitress. Subjects then spoke for thirty-four mins. P laughed twice.

17.14: DC paid bill (cash) and left with P. Encountered SJ-D upon exit. SJ-D explained she'd been shopping for confectionery

item. Don't believe subjects were suspicious. SJ-D walked with
P and DC to agency. Discussed HG's new hairdo.

17.17: P returned to office alone. Shut door.

17.43: P came out of office. Informed SJ-D she was going to tai
chi class. SJ-D followed P to YMCA.

19.07: P came out of YMCA. SJ-D followed P back to agency.
P joined LO'K in office. Shut door. Possibly working.

21.39: P came out of office. Informed SJ-D she was going home.
SJ-D followed P to tube. P bought single ticket to Belsize Park
and entered ticket barrier. Presume going home.

21.48: Surveillance ended. SJ-D returned to office to draft report

I'm sorry I couldn't hear what she was talking to David about in
Bar Zero, but I don't think it was the weather. Hope everything
is going well in Mauritius. Did the drugs arrive? E me soon. I'm
so lonely here without you, darling . . . Sx

melinda_sheridan@millershanks-london.co.uk
12/1/00, 9.19am (1.19pm local)
to...   harriet_greenbaum@millershanks-london.co.uk
cc...
re...   Mako

Did you get the timing plan I faxed to you yesterday? I haven't
heard, so I presume it's OK. Let me know.

If you're at all interested, it's going belly-up here. We're on our
lunch break now, but this morning, our first chance to shoot
anything, the weather closed in and we have nothing in the can.
Worse than that the client is threatening to fire us over a can of
pop, Gloria Hunniford and a sexual assault charge. Please don't
ask me to explain – way too bizarre. Danny Boy is with client
now doing his oily best to make the peace.

Yesterday was a bloody fiasco. First of all we had our little casting
session – let's just call it a *mis-casting* session and say no more.
Then I had to deal with the arrival of our crew. I spent the entire
afternoon in the lobby clutching my clipboard like a breastplate
to my bosom as miscellaneous gaffers, grips and clapper loaders

demanded their union-negotiated rights to sea views and four-posters. Do not become a holiday rep, my dear. It is a quite thankless job. After that it was a couple of Valium and go direct to the Land of Nod.

Incidentally, do you think I look like Gloria Hunniford? Everyone here is saying so but I can't see it. Darling, I thought I was more Michelle Pfeiffer (circa *The Fabulous Baker Boys*)!

Do write soon and assure me I'm not going completely doolally.

liam–okeefe@millershanks-london.co.uk
12/1/00, 9.30am
to... brett_topowlski@millershanks-london.co.uk
cc...
re... DATELINE MAURITIUS, DAY 3

You're dead fucking right about Mel – a double for Hunniford. (I could give that Caron Keating one, couldn't you?) Looks like you'll be coming home without a film *and* a client. I'm gonna do a department sweep on possible outcomes.

Lol's sweet again. Yesterday I did flowers, chocolates, silky girly things, a Nicky Clarke voucher and lunch. Think she bought my explanation that I've hardly spoken to Philpott and that she's been stalking me since she joined. I watched *Play Misty for Me* on cable on Sunday night and got the idea from that. Razor fucking sharp, me.

Pinki's playing a political blinder. Call me sexist but I never thought a bird could do the CD's job. The love child of Joan Baez and Tiny Tim is proving me well wrong. Crutton's falling for her big time. Been charming the Jesus sandals off her. Took her out for coffee yesterday afternoon. If she waxed her underarms and lost the henna body art she'd be in Horne's chair by Feb 1. You heard it here first.

Apparently Susi 'resigned' again on Monday but she still turned up yesterday. She was creeping around like Magnum PI. Caught her bending down outside our door trying to sneak a listen. Said she was clearing a paper jam in the copier (the one that's had the 'out of order' sign on it since November). Pinki's convinced she followed her and Crutton to BZ.

The word this morning is that they took the servers to bits yesterday looking for the e-mail fault, only to work out that Crutton doesn't know his laptop from an Etch-a-Sketch. We're being led into the 21st century by Cro-Magnon man. Nothing ever changes.

Rachel Stevenson – 12/1/00, 9.46am
to... All Departments
cc...
re... IT changes

Peter Renquist, the Acting Head of IT, is no longer with the company. He has decided to leave to pursue other interests. I hope you'll join me in wishing him well. Until a permanent replacement arrives Ravi Basnital will take over Peter's duties. Please give him all the support he needs.

Rachel Stevenson
Personnel

Zoë Clarke – 12/1/00, 9.49am
to... All Departments
cc...
re... David's schedule

All David's meetings for the rest of the morning are cancelled, as he has to attend an urgent IT training session. Sorry for the inconvenience – Zoë

simon_horne@millershanks-london.co.uk
12/1/00, 9.57am (1.57pm local)
to... susi_judgedavis@millershanks-london.co.uk
cc...
re... Pinki Fallon

....

thnks for rport . . . keep eye peeld . . . shhoot go welll . . . drrugss
arive . . . feeelin verry week...................................... mst sleeeeeeeep
.... nbahsqwygrshsbbtk

daniel_westbrooke@millershanks-london.co.uk
12/1/00, 10.05am (2.05pm local)
to... david_crutton@millershanks-london.co.uk
cc...
re... your concerns

I have just returned to my room and read your e-mail. I spent the
last few hours with Frank trying to calm him down. He did have a
bit of a turn earlier. I think it is a combination of sun, jet-lag and
stress from the fact that this is the poor lad's first location shoot. (I
remember mine – the Nimble balloon. I would not wish it on anyone!) Anyway, Gloria Hunniford did happen to be in the vicinity
but it did not involve her in the slightest. He is resting now and I
am sure that once he wakes he will be right as rain.

As for the shoot, it is going extremely well. There have been a couple
of teething troubles as there always are, but we have some very
exciting footage in the can. Nathan is eccentric but aren't all artists?
Simon has been ever present and is an enormous calming influence.

Hope all is well back at the Ponderosa. What developments on
Coke?

susi_judgedavis@millershanks-london.co.uk
12/1/00, 10.06am
to... simon_horne@millershanks-london.co.uk
cc...
re... rest, my sweet

Darling Simon, you really need to rest right now. You've been
working far too hard for far too long. You recharge those batteries
and let the others struggle on without you. It's time they learned
to stop taking you for granted. And remember, if there's anything
you need, I'm on the end of an e-mail . . . Sx

mike_appleton@millershanks-hk.co.hk
12/1/00, 10.10am (6.10pm local)
to... david_crutton@millershanks-london.co.uk
cc...
re... Bucharest

I hope all goes well with Coke. I'm sure it's keeping you terribly busy but have you found a moment yet to mention my interest in the Bucharest job to Jim? Do keep me posted.

Mike

daniel_westbrooke@millershanks-london.co.uk
12/1/00, 10.10am (2.10pm local)
to... simon_horne@millershanks-london.co.uk
cc...
re... what is going on in there?

I have knocked on your door, I have slipped notes under it, I have phoned you and I have stood in the gardens and thrown pebbles at your window. My last hope is that your laptop is on and you are reading your e-mails.

If you bothered to come out of your suite you would see mayhem. Frank Sinton is apoplectic and facing possible assault charges. The shoot is going appallingly. The cast are dropping like flies and we have yet to turn over. Melinda is coping manfully but Brett and Vince are treating the whole thing like a primary school trip to the zoo.

I need your help and support. I have just told David that you are doing a magnificent job. I suggest you emerge now and take some responsibility for this disaster. I will not cover your backside indefinitely.

Susi Judge-Davis – 12/1/00, 10.31am
to... Lorraine Pallister
cc...
bcc...Rachel Stevenson
re... you!!

What time do you call this? 10.30 is not acceptable. Do you think I can run this department on my own? You have not made an auspicious start this week. If you are unhappy I would be glad to speak to Rachel on your behalf about the alternatives.

Lorraine Pallister – 12/1/00, 10.36am
to... Susi Judge-Davis
cc...
re... you!!

Sorry I'm so late, Susi dear. I got shagged bandy last night, and took ages to get going this morning. You should try it sometime. It might loosen you up.

Susi Judge-Davis – 12/1/00, 10.39am
to... Rachel Stevenson
cc...
bcc...David Crutton;
simon_horne@millershanks-london.co.uk
re... Lorraine Pallister

Please find attached an e-mail I just received from Lorraine. I don't think I need add anything to explain why I will not tolerate her on my floor for a moment longer. Please arrange for her transfer. Thank you.

 Attachment . . .

Lorraine Pallister – 12/1/00, 10.36am
to... Susi Judge-Davis
cc...
re... you!!

Sorry I'm so late, Susi dear. I got shagged bandy last night, and took ages to get going this morning. You should try it sometime. It might loosen you up.

Lorraine Pallister – 12/1/00, 10.44am
to... Liam O'Keefe
cc...
re... busy?

On my way in I found out how to make the lift stop between floors. When are you free for elevator maintenance?

Liam O'Keefe – 12/1/00, 10.46am
to... Lorraine Pallister
cc...
re... busy?

I've got a snapper to brief, ten press ads to draw up and accounts are screaming for my time sheets ... see you in thirty seconds.

Rachel Stevenson – 12/1/00, 10.49am
to... Susi Judge-Davis
cc...
re... Lorraine Pallister

A variety of people, from David Crutton down, have informed me that Lorraine seems to be fitting in exceptionally well on *your* floor.

Perhaps *you* should come and speak to me about *your* alternatives. My door is always open.

susi_judgedavis@millershanks-london.co.uk
12/1/00, 10.55am
to... simon_horne@millershanks-london.co.uk
cc...
re... I need you

Darling, I know you're in 'Do-Not-Disturb' mode right now, but the moment you wake *please, please* call me. I can't go on.

Liam O'Keefe – 12/1/00, 11.05am
to... Lorraine Pallister
cc...
re... BIOLOGY EXPLAINED, PART I

before ...    after ...

Lorraine Pallister – 12/1/00, 11.11am
to... Liam O'Keefe
cc...
re... BIOLOGY EXPLAINED, PART II

before ...   after ...

(You weren't wearing a johnny, were you?)

brett_topowlski@millershanks-london.co.uk
12/1/00, 11.13am (3.13pm local)
to... liam_okeefe@millershanks-london.co.uk
cc...
re... DATELINE MAURITIUS, DAY 3

We're truly in the shit now. This morning we had four girls. Now we have two. A jet-ski disaster worthy of *The Boy's Own Bumper Video of Jet Ski Disasters*. Nathan got two of our birds to climb astride and shake their stuff. They did a few rehearsals and apart from the fact that Despina (your favourite on the casting tape) didn't know her left from her right, it was looking dandy. Our marine girls roared off for their first run. They crouched low like buxom panthers over their handlebars. Fearlessly they accelerated towards each other, preparing to turn at the very last second. We looked on from the beach, struck dumb by their power and beauty. Nathan yelled 'Turn!.' They turned. Nathan yelled, 'Left, Despina, left!' The dozy tart went right.

Nathan shouted, 'Cut!'

The two jet skis sank without trace. Despina had a broken femur and tibia (leg to you). Kerri (the other one) got two lungs full of the Indian Ocean and a vicious laceration (cut to you) above her eye. After that the weather turned lovely again. Cloudless. Sea like a mirror. But nobody was in the mood and Nathan wrapped. Anyway, we don't have a script to shoot anymore, being as we are four babes short of a full bevy.

It's not all bad news. Fat Frank is helping the local plod with their inquiries into the Hunniford Affair – the traumatised Queen of TV decided to make a complaint. He'd better mind what he says because the BBC crew got the whole thing on tape.

Mel is struggling to persuade the two remaining girls to stay with the movie. Vin and me are on our 2rd (3rd? 4th? 5th?) sodding rewrite. The last time I saw Desperate Dan he was sobbing into a Singapore Sling. Where the fuck is Horne? You tell me.

A word of advice from a mate to a mate: never, ever under any circumstances, even if a sixteen-stone psycho is pressing a seven-inch butcher's knife to your jugular, write a TV commercial that begins, 'Open on a palm fringed beach . . .'

Lorraine Pallister – 12/1/00, 11.27am
to... Katie Philpott
cc...
re... yellow card

Liam has been trying to convince me you're some kind of serious nutter. You're a fucking amateur, girl. I'll show you what mad is – just go within six feet of him again.

David Crutton – 12/1/00, 11.27am
to... Ravi Basnital
cc...
re... IT skills

Think of this as a test, both of my new found e-mail skills, and of your prospects of still having a job at the day's end:

PERTTI VAN HELDEN, YOU ARSEHOLE.

Katie Philpott – 12/1/00, 11.45am
to... Lorraine Pallister
cc...
re... yellow card

Golly, keep your hair on! I was just being friendly. I jolly well shan't bother in future.

Zoë Clarke – 12/1/00, 11.47am
to... All Departments
cc...
re... David's schedule

David's IT session is over and his diary is back to normal – Zoë.

David Crutton – 12/1/00, 12.03pm
to... Lorraine Pallister
cc...
re... well done

I have just read your e-mail to Susi, which she kindly forwarded to me. Good work.

Lorraine Pallister – 12/1/00, 12.05pm
to... Susi Judge-Davis
cc...
re... Fist meet Face

Ladies' bog. Now.

susi_judgedavis@millershanks-london.co.uk
12/1/00, 12.13pm
to... simon_horne@millershanks-london.co.uk
cc...
re... I really need you!

Have you woken up yet, darling? I've just had a ghastly row with Lorraine. She threatened me with a nail file. I tried so hard with her as well. As usual Rachel has taken her side. I don't know how David got involved but even he stuck up for her. Everyone's having a go at me and I don't know what to do . . . Sx

brett_topowlski@millershanks-london.co.uk
12/1/00, 12.21pm (4.21pm local)
to... liam_okeefe@millershanks-london.co.uk
cc...
re... STOP PRESS!

The Hunniford Affair has moved up a gear. Me and Vin were in the bar and got talking to this bloke. He was buying us drinks and asking us stuff about what we were doing here. Then he wanted to know what the score was with our Gloria. Turns out he's a *Sun* hack. He's here with a snapper trying to get shots of a topless McCutcheon but he's onto a much bigger scoop now. We clammed up when we found out who he was but I think we'd been quite mouthy up to then. You know what it's like – a few beers, and a bloke who's impressed that you're shooting with a bunch of soft-porn stars – well, you exaggerate a bit, don't you? Vin told him he was the creative director and I think we made the whole thing sound a bit juicier than it maybe was. He's doing the rounds now. Just saw Mel tell him to sling his hook. Fat Frank is back from the police. He and Desperate Dan are working on the grovelling apology in the hope it'll persuade Hunniford not to press charges. Got to admit, it's a crack. I remember getting my picture in the *Brighton Argus* when I was nine for catching a mutant three-eyed dab off the beach. Thought that was a buzz, but it had nothing on this. I'd buy all the red tops tomorrow. I smell Fat Frank's name in 140pt Franklin Gothic Bold Condensed.

david_crutton@millershanks-london.co.uk
12/1/00, 12.33pm
to... daniel_westbrooke@millershanks-london.co.uk
cc...
re... LOVE

I have just read your e-mail and feel wonderfully reassured. I am
sorry that I fretted at all – silly me. I won't worry one jot about
the call I just received from the *Sun* asking me if I'd like to
comment on 'the sexual assault' of Gloria Hunniford by one of
our clients. I am sure it is piffling, trivial, nothing at all to concern
me. If it was anything more than a silly storm in a teacup you
would be straight on the phone with a full and frank explanation.
Wouldn't you?

David Crutton – 12/1/00, 12.39pm
to... Harriet Greenbaum
cc...
re... LOVE

We have an impending crisis that threatens to engulf everything.
See me now.

james_f_weissmuller@millershanks-ny.co.usa
12/1/00, 12.40pm (7.40am local)
to... harriet_greenbaum@millershanks-london.co.uk
cc...
re... Coke

Harriet, I must say that I was impressed with your honest, yet
sensitive, handling of Pertti. David also tells me that in Daniel's
absence you are running Coke with aplomb.

Nothing gives me greater pleasure than to see a previously unsung
member of the Miller Shanks family rise and shine.

I spoke to David a couple of days ago about having an early sight
of the Coke strategy and creative. As yet he hasn't sent it through
– too busy running a top-twenty agency, I guess! I'd be obliged

if you could get the material to me as soon as possible. I have a wealth of experience on Pepsi from my days at BBDO so I might be able to make a modest contribution.

I look forward to hearing from you,

Jim Weissmuller

Harriet Greenbaum – 12/1/00, 12.42pm
to... David Crutton
cc...
re... LOVE

I've had something unexpected come up that I must deal with right away. I'll be with you in five minutes.

**harriet_greenbaum@millershanks-london.co.uk
12/1/00, 12.45pm**
to... james_f_weissmuller@millershanks-ny.co.usa
cc...
re... Coke

Dear Jim,

I'm honoured, but you are too kind. The handling of Pertti was very much down to David. I simply put my name to it.

I have instructed my PA to send you everything on Coca-Cola and it should be on your side of the Atlantic within the hour. Once you have had a chance to digest, perhaps we can discuss your thoughts over the phone. It goes without saying that I would value your opinion above anyone's.

Sincerely,

Harriet Greenbaum

**liam_okeefe@millershanks-london.co.uk
12/1/00, 1.13pm**
to... brett_topowlski@millershanks-london.co.uk
cc...
re... STOP PRESS!

Jesus Fucking Christ, I've just come back from a snapper and read your e. I'm gagging for more. I haven't been this eager for news since I camped outside the Portland waiting for word of Lady Di's first-born (A son, a son! Oh how I rejoiced).

brett_topowlski@millershanks-london.co.uk
12/1/00, 1.22pm (5.22pm local)
to... liam_okeefe@millershanks-london.co.uk
cc...
re... STOP PRESS!

No further developments. Mel ordered us to stay in our room and speak to nobody, not even room service. She found out we'd blabbed to the *Sun* and she went crazy-apeshit. She's scary as hell when she's mad. Did you really camp outside the Portland? Sad bastard.

liam_okeefe@millershanks-london.co.uk
12/1/00, 1.24pm
to... brett_topowlski@millershanks-london.co.uk
cc...
re... STOP PRESS!

Gullible twat.

Harriet Greenbaum – 12/1/00, 1.38pm
to... David Crutton
cc...
re... LOVE

I have had a chance to think about this now and here is my suggested plan of action:

Forget repeated attempts to raise Dan or Simon on the phone. I mean no disrespect to either of them but both are panickers and liable to be less than candid when the going gets tough.

Instead, locate Melinda at the earliest opportunity and demand a full report. We can't really proceed until we're armed with all the facts. Of everybody out there she is the most level-headed and is likely to give it to us straight. I'll call her if you like. We go back a long way and she won't give me any bullshit.

Tell her that whatever else happens, we must finish the shoot – with or without the client's co-operation. To pull the plug now would probably put us in breach of contract. Phone up the chief exec at LOVE and recommend a united front for now. It won't help our cause or theirs if we're chewing lumps out of each other.

Brief our lawyers at the earliest opportunity. I suspect that if this runs the course, the writs will fly so thick and fast we won't be able to duck quickly enough.

Impose an immediate blanket ban on all employees talking to the press about anything. All inquiries from Fleet St should be directed to you.

Finally, I went to uni with an assistant editor at Wapping. If you like I'll contact her, make some discreet inquiries as to what, if anything, they intend to run and see if I can put a Miller-Shanks-friendly spin on it.

Let me know what you think of the above and what further you would like me to do.

David Crutton – 12/1/00, 1.49pm
to... Harriet Greenbaum
cc...
re... LOVE

All good sense, Harriet. Thank you. Call Melinda now and report back as soon as you have spoken. Stress that the shoot must go on. Then phone your mate at the Scum and see what you can glean. While you're at it you might point out to her how much money we spend with her rag on behalf of our clients – biting the hand that feeds them and all that. In the meantime I'll take care of your other points. I suggest we aim to meet in an hour or so to re-assess.

David Crutton – 12/1/00, 1.53pm
to... All Departments
cc...
re... NO COMMENT

I am not at liberty to divulge why at the moment, but no-one must say anything to the press. I don't care whether it's *The Times*, the *Sun* or *Angler's Weekly*. Any approaches from any journalists will be referred to me. To go against me on this is to court instant dismissal.

David Crutton
CEO

David Crutton – 12/1/00, 1.56pm
to... Zoë Clarke
cc...
re... Max Gregory

Call him the minute you finish stuffing that disgusting baked potato into your face. His number's in the Rolodex under Hunter, McPhee & Partners. Tell him I need to see him immediately. That means this afternoon. I don't care where he is – in conference, court, Val d'Isère, it doesn't matter. If he tries to be elusive remind him not only of the hefty retainer we pay his practice of shysters, but also of the fact that his son has a blossoming career in advertising thanks to me.

brett_topowlski@millershanks-london.co.uk
12/1/00, 2.10pm (6.10pm local)
to... liam_okeefe@millershanks-london.co.uk
cc...
re... pants down

We've had the *Sun* snapper on our verandah taking shots of us through the window. Doesn't look too good – the contents of the mini-bar are scattered on the bed and Vin is comatose on the floor in nothing but a Fat Slags T-shirt. Worse still, I've got a bloody towel wrapped round my head and half a tub of Body Shop Mud Mask on my face – don't even go there. Mel just hammered on the door. Dawn call tomorrow. Can you believe we're gonna finish this shoot? I'd better rewrite this sodding script.

Harriet Greenbaum – 12/1/00, 2.11pm
to... David Crutton
cc...
re... LOVE

I've talked to Mel. The bullet points:
- Frank Sinton has spent the whole shoot on a pussy hunt and had goosed Mel, among others, on numerous occasions. Apparently the crew refer to him as Ol' Bug Eyes.
- Gloria Hunniford is in Mauritius shooting her holiday show.
- Mel is Gloria's doppelgänger – incontrovertible when you think about it.
- Frank saw Hunniford basking on a sun lounger, claims he mistook her for Mel and did something to her in the cleavage area – exactly what is in dispute. His version is that he playfully placed a cold can on her chest. She alleges he attempted to work his hand into the top of her costume. Auntie has it on tape so the truth will out.
- Hunniford is deciding whether to make a formal complaint.
- The police have interviewed Frank and seized the video.
- A *Sun* journalist was already out there keeping tabs on some ex-*EastEnders* star. Now he's onto this.
- Brett and Vince had inadvertently shot their mouths off to him before Mel could apply gags.
- Mel had no plans to can the shoot, but that, unfortunately, was already going disastrously.
- No film shot.
- Four cast down to injury/illness.
- There are two shooting days left and Mel promises to sweat blood to get something in the can.

- Simon has not been seen. He barricaded himself in his room upon arrival.

No good news at all, I'm afraid. The best-case scenario is that Hunniford decides not to press charges and we can present the whole thing as a silly misunderstanding. I've spoken to my *Sun* contact. It looks like this will be tomorrow's front page. She says she'll do what she can to mitigate the damage to us, but expect no favours. Frank Sinton is ex-*Sun* marketing dept and was none too popular (fired for touching up his secretary and taking kick-backs from his ad agency – good enough reasons for them to twist the knife). She says her editor would dearly like to talk to you. Let me know what else I can do.

David Crutton – 12/1/00, 2.15pm
to... Harriet Greenbaum
cc...
re... LOVE

Thanks. I've spoken to Sinton's boss. He agrees that we should circle the wagons on this. He's reading Sinton the riot act and asks us to keep him on a short leash. I'm going to see our lawyers soon. We'll speak when I return.

Zoë Clarke – 12/1/00, 2.18pm
to... Lorraine Pallister
cc...
re... the news!!!!

The Crettin swore me to secrecy but I'll explode if I don't tell someone!!!! All that stuff about not talking to the papers is 'cos of what's happening on the LOVE shoot. Apparently the client attacked Gloria Hunniford!!!!!!!!!!!!!!!!!!!!! Tried to give her one on the beach!!!!!!! It's gonna be in all the papers tomorrow!!!!!!!!!!!! The Crettin is going ballistic!!!!! Says he's gonna sue everyone!!!!!! He's going to see the lawyer in a mo. I'll come and see you as soon as he's left and tell you everything!!!!!! Zxxx

david_crutton@millershanks-london.co.uk
12/1/00, 2.22pm
to... melinda_sheridan@millershanks-london.co.uk;
daniel_westbrooke@millershanks-london.co.uk;
simon_horne@millershanks-london.co.uk
cc... Harriet Greenbaum
re... Hunni-Gate

Thank you, Melinda, for finally bringing Harriet up to date with your mess. Now that I am fully apprised here are your orders.

Melinda, you are in charge. Take no shit from anybody. Your first priority is to keep whatever lid you can on this fiasco. Do whatever you can to make the peace with Hunniford and persuade her it was an understandable case of mistaken identity. If necessary give her our client list and tell her to name her price for appearing in a high profile campaign for any one of them.

Then you must get the shoot back on the rails and finish the commercial. You will not come home without it.

None of you will speak to any journalists. That goes for production company and crew as well. Melinda, you will take Vince and Brett to one side and tell them that if I read anything in tomorrow's papers that suggests they have been dragging the good name of this agency into the sewer then they would be better off not boarding the return flight.

Daniel, you have one job. You will attach yourself at the hip to Frank Sinton. You will keep him out of any further trouble. You will not let him within two hundred yards of Gloria Hunniford, Vanessa Feltz, Tinky Winky or any other star of daytime television. In fact you will not let him within two hundred yards of anyone who possesses so much as a hint of breasts.

Simon, if you have left your room by now you will return there immediately, place the 'do not disturb' sign on the door and lock yourself in. You will not come out until Melinda knocks to inform you that it's time to come home. I have seen you in a crisis. You are not only a cringing embarrassment, you are a liability.

Melinda, I expect you to keep Harriet abreast of any developments, however minor. She will debrief me as necessary. None
of you have covered yourselves in glory so far. Spend the next
three days doing whatever you can to make amends.

Lorraine Pallister – 12/1/00, 2.24pm
to... Zoë Clarke
cc...
re... the news!!!!

I already know. I've seen the e's from Brett to Liam. In fact the
whole department knows now because Liam's opened a book on
tomorrow's *Sun* headline:

2/1: HUNNI'S HOL HELL
3/1: WISH YOU WEREN'T HERE
6/1: SUN, SEA, AND SEX
10/1: MAUL-ITIUS
500/1: DOW RISES 2 POINTS AS ASIAN ECONOMIES STABILISE

Come down and have a flutter. By the way, Judge-Dredd is sorted.
I took her aside before lunch and had a heart-to-heart. Told her
we had to try a little harder to get along and be friends. (I shoved
my nail file up her nostril and said that if she didn't lay off being
queen bitch I'd give her that nose job she'd always wanted but
could never afford.) It seems to be working. She just brought me
a coffee and asked if there was anything I needed a hand with.
Sent her off to get me some fags. Did I do good?

simon_horne@millershanks-london.co.uk
12/1/00, 2.33pm (6.33pm local)
to... susi_judgedavis@millershanks-london.co.uk
cc...
re... what is happening?

I have just awoken and read the oddest e-mail from David. I can
raise neither Daniel nor Mel to find out what on earth is going on.
Something to do with Gloria Hunniford? Could you forget your
trifling problems at the office for one moment and make a few *dis-*

creet inquiries your end to help me get to the bottom of this. I am going to look for my Migraleve now. My head is killing me.

susi_judgedavis@millershanks-london.co.uk
12/1/00, 2.41pm
to... simon_horne@millershanks-london.co.uk
cc...
re... what is happening?

There's a lot of gossip here, darling. I don't know how much of it is true but it sounds like your LOVE client molested Gloria Hunniford and has been arrested. David is ranting and raving and looking for people to blame. It sounds like the shoot isn't going very well either. If I were you I'd keep your head down, sweetheart. Don't look for trouble. I'm sorry I bothered you earlier with my Lorraine argument. I'm over it now. I know I just have to follow your usual advice and rise above her cattiness. E me if I can do anything . . . Sx

simon_horne@millershanks-london.co.uk
12/1/00, 2.48pm (6.48pm local)
to... susi_judgedavis@millershanks-london.co.uk
cc...
re... time for action

Tell David not to worry about a thing. I am taking charge of this *comedie d'erreurs*.

james_f_weissmuller@millershanks-ny.co.usa
12/1/00, 2.56pm (9.56am local)
to... harriet_greenbaum@millershanks-london.co.uk
cc...
re... Coke

I have received the work. Thank you very much for your prompt response. My initial reaction? Outstanding! The creative has the cutting edge we'll need to land this one. 'IT'S IN THE CAN' is a superb encapsulation of the brand promise. The whole campaign feels youthfully zesty. Some of the humour was a little 'alternative' for an old man like me, but I take that as a sign that it's spot on for the target.

I said to David that it would take something special to beat the exceptional campaign that Finland put up, and I believe this is it. I'd love to meet the party responsible. They have a very bright future.

Having skimmed the strategic presentation I think it backs up the ads well and I can see no glaring flaws in the logic. I do feel there are some unexplored avenues, however, and we should discuss these at your earliest convenience. Perhaps your PA could call my executive assistant to set up a video-conference. There is no substitute for dealing with these things face to face.

Jim

harriet_greenbaum@millershanks-london.co.uk
12/1/00, 3.02pm
to... james_f_weissmuller@millershanks-ny.co.usa
cc...
re... Coke

Jim, thank you for your endorsement. We had every confidence in the work but that isn't to say that your approval doesn't mean the world.

The campaign was originated by Simon Horne but has been embellished enormously by the whole creative department led by Pinki Fallon, our most senior copywriter. She will shy away from the limelight but a great deal of credit must go to her.

I would love to hear your full thoughts and my PA is setting up the call now. I am at your disposal.

Harriet Greenbaum

brett_topowlski@millershanks-london.co.uk
12/1/00, 3.11pm (7.11pm local)
to... liam_okeefe@millershanks-london.co.uk
cc...
re... just when you think you've hit rock bottom . . .

. . . things take a turn for the worse. Mel knocked for us. Simon
has come out of solitary and called us to a 'crisis meeting' in the
lobby. Oh dearie fucking me . . .

Harriet Greenbaum – 12/1/00, 3.20pm
to... Pinki Fallon
cc...
re... Coke

I am booked in for a video-conference with Jim Weissmuller at
4.00 to go through Coke. He was bowled over by the work and
I think you should join me to take a bow.

Pinki Fallon – 12/1/00, 3.27pm
to... Harriet Greenbaum
cc...
re... Coke

I'm supposed to be reviewing some new Freedom work at 4.00
but I can put that off. I've never done a video-conference. Is my
Kurt Cobain T-shirt OK or should I change? ☺

Harriet Greenbaum – 12/1/00, 3.30pm
to... Pinki Fallon
cc...
re... Coke

Come as you are.

Harriet Greenbaum – 12/1/00, 3.47pm
to... Zoë Clarke
cc...
re... Coke

I am about to step into the boardroom for a very important video-conference with Jim Weissmuller on Coke. I know David is with our lawyers at the moment, but when he's back could you ask him to join me? Thanks.

Liam O'Keefe – 12/1/00, 3.57pm
to... All Departments
cc...
re... gag

Got the first e-joke of the 21st century. True story apparently. Enjoy:

 Attachment . . .

Father Conor is walking by the Shannon when he sees one of his congregation fishing. He stops for a chat, and mentions that he's never fished before. 'It's a doddle,' says the angler. 'Take a rod and give it a go.'

'Well, I suppose the blessed Saint Peter himself was a fisherman. Perhaps I'll try my hand,' says the priest.

Father Conor sits down and casts his line. After a few minutes he gets a bite and reels in a fat ten-pounder. He's pleased as punch as his parishioner slaps him on the back and says, 'That's a great big fucker, Father!'

'Language!' replies Father Conor. 'I am a priest.'

'No, Father, this fish is called a fucker,' explains the angler, thinking on his feet.

Laughing at the misunderstanding, the proud priest takes his catch home and finds the bishop waiting in his front room.

'That's a splendid looking fish, Father,' exclaims the bishop.

'Aye,' replies the priest, 'it's a great fucker.'

'Please, Father! Such language,' says the bishop.

'No, no, Your Grace,' replies the priest, 'fucker is the name of the fish.'

It being Friday, the reassured bishop suggests they repair to his residence for a fine fish supper. Once there the bishop goes to the kitchen to clean and gut the fish. They are then joined by the mother superior of the local convent. Being no great cook himself, the bishop says, 'Reverend Mother, would you mind poaching this fucker for us?'

'Bishop, you cannot say that in the house of God,' gasps the horrified nun.

'You misunderstand, Reverend Mother,' explains the bishop, 'this fish is called a fucker.'

Calm again, the Mother Superior sets to cooking the fish. Shortly they are joined by the Pope, who is making a surprise visit (as he does). Delighted, the bishop invites him to supper.

They sit down at the table and the Pope says grace. Then the mother superior brings in the fish on the finest silver platter. Eagerly the three of them await the opinion of God's Mouthpiece on Earth.

'That is a fine fish,' remarks the impressed pontiff.

'That it is, Your Holiness. I caught the fucker,' says the beaming priest.

'I cleaned the fucker,' adds the bishop.

'And I cooked the fucker,' chips in the mother superior.

The Pope sits back and stares at them for a moment. Then he plants his feet on the table, lets out a mighty fart and says, 'Know what? You cunts are all right.'

David Crutton – 12/1/00, 4.03pm
to... Zoë Clarke
cc...
re... where is Harriet?

I've phoned her but she's not answering. As soon as you're back at your desk find her. Tell her there are pressing legal issues to discuss.

Nigel Godley – 12/1/00, 4.07pm
to... Liam O'Keefe
cc...
re... gag

I myself am a regular churchgoer and like many others I am highly offended by your tasteless and insensitive idea of a 'joke'.

And as for it being a true story, I know for a fact that the Pope's heavy schedule, as well as his need for a constant security presence would preclude him from making a 'surprise visit'. You don't have me fooled for a moment.

Nige

Zoë Clarke – 12/1/00, 4.10pm
to... David Crutton
cc...
re... where is Harriet?

She's in the boardroom doing some video-conference. I don't think she can be disturbed. I'll grab her as soon as she's out.

max_gregory@huntermcpheepartners.co.uk
12/1/00, 4.14pm
to... david_crutton@millershanks-london.co.uk
cc...
re... LOVE

David, it was good to see you even in troubled circumstances. Since you left I have had a chance to solidify my thoughts and it would help if I put them in writing.

As I said, I do not believe there is much you can do at the moment apart from wait and see. No judge would award an injunction against the *Sun* to withhold the story. Involving as it does potential criminal charges, it is unarguably in the public interest.

At this stage you are correct not to cut yourself loose from LOVE, yet neither should you tie your own fortunes too closely to theirs. When the story breaks the fallout may necessitate going to the mattresses.

Regarding any civil action that Ms Hunniford may pursue, the target of this would probably not be Miller Shanks, since none of your employees appear to have had direct involvement in the alleged offence.

In the meantime I suggest the wall of silence be strictly enforced and that we await the *Sun* and pore over every word, comma and colon of their report. Only then will we know how the land lies.

I will come to your offices immediately after the ballet tonight armed with the First Editions – ETA 11.00pm. If you have any questions or there are further developments before then, please feel free to contact me – you have all my numbers. I will risk the wrath of Darcy Bussell and leave my mobile on.

May I take this opportunity to thank you again for taking such good care of James. Every time I see him he has nothing but praise for you. He could not wish for a wiser or more benevolent teacher.

Best wishes, Max

melinda_sheridan@millershanks-london.co.uk
12/1/00, 4.24pm (8.24pm local)
to... harriet_greenbaum@millershanks-london.co.uk
cc...
re... LOVE update

So David has appointed you Crisis Monitor. You get all the best jobs, you lucky darling! Well, here is my first official report for you to digest, regurgitate and do with as you will. I apologise in advance for any tangents – you know what I'm like.

First, I made it my mission to seek out la Hunniford and make whatever reparations were necessary. I found her in the hot tub and approached with caution. She was understandably frosty so I made great play of the ridiculous resemblance that one and all think we share. This warmed her up a little, so I excused Frank Sinton's crass behaviour as mistaken identity, pure and simple. I told her that the man was mortified with guilt and even as we spoke was being talked down from the hotel parapet (a wicked lie, but needs must). She bought this and said she would drop charges in return for a written apology and the immediate repatriation of Frank.

Oh, I did mention to her entirely by the by that we were looking for a spokeswoman for our exciting new Freedom Catalogues TV campaign and that she was tailor-made for the role. Do we have an exciting new Freedom campaign? If not, I suggest we write one pronto and that it begins, 'Open on Gloria Hunniford . . .'. A 250k, one-year network buy-out may also have been alluded to.

She is a thoroughly charming and decent lady (a resemblance after all). After exchanging diet tips, I took my leave and had myself a well earned Scotch and American and my first fag since Dec 31st (you could probably omit that from your report to David) before informing Dan and Frank of the glad tidings. Relief was palpable.

I then set about rounding up Nathan, Vincent and Brett to see if we could find a way of finishing this shoot. I was rudely interrupted in my quest by the appearance of Simon. And, my dear, what a frightful appearance – death without so much as a cursory warm-up. Despite David's express order to the contrary he has decided to assume command. This is not good news. He called an immediate conference of war and launched an assault on all present. He screamed that while we partied in the sun he had been delirious with an unspecified tropical fever. It was, he claimed, only the attentions of the hotel doctor that had prevented death. I'm sure I heard Vincent mumble, 'More's the fucking pity', but I let it pass.

Horne subsided enough to allow Brett to present his and Vincent's revised script. This was a masterpiece of improvisation under pressure. They had pared it down to a simple and elegant two-hander between our remaining brace of LOVEbirds. Hilarious, clever and (music to the ears of an embattled producer) shootable in just one day. Nathan, who'd merely glowered until now, cheered up enormously. Simon, need I add, did not share our enthusiasm and pissed all over it. (Pardon my French, but my frustration is getting the better of me.) He flounced off saying that as usual he would have to write it himself. On his exit he spied la Hunniford at the bar and made a bee-line. Her new bodyguard (courtesy of hotel security) nearly ripped arm from shoulder.

As I said, Simon's re-emergence was not good news.

You may ask what our client thinks of the rewrite. With his press debut tomorrow and a marriage to save tonight he is way beyond worrying about his advertising. We could shoot the next Bond movie and I don't imagine he'd notice.

There is good news. It's Karaoke Night in the Lagoon Bar. After a pink-gin gargle my larynx will be primed for my duet with Simon – Donny and Marie's 'Morning Side of the Mountain'.

Yours resigned to her fate,

Mel

simon_horne@millershanks-london.co.uk
12/1/00, 4.53pm (8.53pm local)
to... susi_judgedavis@millershanks-london.co.uk
cc...
re... LOVE

Do me a favour and inform David that we are out of the mire apropos Gloria Hunniford. I mustered all my charm and did a number on her. She was eating out of my hand.

I ask no thanks – just tell him to worry no longer.

I would inform him myself only I am up to my neck in a mess of Brett, Vince and Nathan's making. Their incompetence means I now have to rewrite the script from scratch.

Thank Heaven I am here.

Have a root through the files for some scripts I penned for the abortive Tesco pitch. (Last June?) When you find them, fax them immediately.

I think with a little judicious tinkering one of them will fit the LOVE bill just perfectly.

Do not ask me to explain.

The mind of the lateral thinker is a complex beast!

Susi Judge-Davis, 12/1/00, 4.58pm
to... David Crutton
cc...
re... LOVE

Simon has just asked me to pass on the excellent news that he has smoothed over the Gloria Hunniford situation. He's sorry he couldn't tell you himself but as usual he's inundated with work – Susi

Harriet Greenbaum – 12/1/00, 5.10pm
to... David Crutton
cc...
re... LOVE

Sorry about the delay in getting back to you. I have stepped out of my video-conference with Jim and have only just found Zoë's Post-it telling me to see you. It was a useful meeting – it's a pity you couldn't join us. I'll be right up. I have a report from Mel. I've yet to read it but I'll print it out and we can go through it together.

harriet_greenbaum@millershanks-london.co.uk
12/1/00, 5.27pm
to... melinda_sheridan@millershanks-london.co.uk
cc...
re... LOVE

I've been through your report with David. Well done on at least getting the charges dropped. As far as I know Pinki is looking at Freedom ideas as I write. I will brief her immediately on the 'change of direction'. As for Simon strutting his stuff, I think David wants to take care of that one himself. It would be an idea if you faxed me Brett and Vince's revised script, so we can have an opinion at this end. And as for what will be in the papers tomorrow, there is little more you can do out there. Try not to worry and we'll handle the damage-limitation as best we can.

Focus on getting in a good shooting day tomorrow, though quite what you'll film is subject to conjecture at the moment. Keep your e-mail open, order cocoa and prepare for a long night. We will advise.

Keep smiling. It's only a job after all. And if it's any consolation, I've got my own problems here. David is being very touchy with me for having the temerity to hold a meeting with Weissmuller, the One True God, all by myself.

David Crutton – 12/1/00, 5.28pm
to... Zoë Clarke
cc...
re... are you totally fucking brain-dead?

Why didn't you tell me that Harriet's un-disturbable meeting earlier was with Jim Weissmuller? You will have the following tattooed on your forehead in reverse letters so that it is clearly legible every time you look in a mirror:

NOBODY EVER TALKS TO WEISSMULLER WITHOUT DAVID'S KNOWLEDGE.

This is what you might call a golden rule.

David Crutton – 12/1/00, 5.33pm
to... Susi Judge-Davis
cc...
re... LOVE

Fantastic news, Susi. Tell Simon he's a star and I don't know where I'd be without him. I know that his modesty prevented him from telling me himself of his coup with Hunniford. I'm glad you let me know, otherwise I'd have fallen for that devious old trout Melinda's line that it was all her own work. And tell him that I'm pleased he's rescuing the LOVE script. Ask him to fax me Brett and Vince's feeble effort, along with his own. I'm in need of light relief and it could provide useful ammo if and when we come to 'let them go'.

james_f_weissmuller@millershanks-ny.co.usa
12/1/00, 5.36pm (12.36pm local)
to... david_crutton@millershanks-london.co.uk;
daniel_westbrooke@millershanks-london.co.uk;
simon_horne@millershanks-london.co.uk
cc...
re... Coke

My unreserved respect and admiration to all three of you – not only for an outstanding Coca-Cola campaign that will surely put us in pole for the pitch, but also for finding two incredible talents in Harriet Greenbaum and Pinki Fallon to lead the agency's effort. I have spent a delightful and instructive hour in video-conference with them. I am sure that you are reassured to know that should the unthinkable happen and the three of you were to step under your notorious 'Clapham Omnibus', you have such worthy replacements in the wings.

Well done, gentlemen.

Jim

susi_judgedavis@millershanks-london.co.uk
12/1/00, 5.42pm
to... simon_horne@millershanks-london.co.uk
cc...
re... hoorah!

David's e'd me and he's so, so thrilled with you! He can't believe how well you handled Gloria Hunniford. And guess what! Melinda has been sneaking behind your back trying to steal the credit. The cow! I never wanted to say anything because it's not in my nature to judge, but I always had her down as two-faced. I should trust my instincts more often. And David says to send through Brett and Vince's stupid script. He wants to see for himself how rubbish they are! I knew that all you needed was a rest and you'd be able to turn everything around. Well done, my hero . . . Sx

Harriet Greenbaum – 12/1/00, 5.47pm
to... Pinki Fallon
cc...
re... Freedom

I know you're in the midst of reviewing this, but something has happened that necessitates tearing up the work and starting again. Call and I'll explain.

Rachel Stevenson – 12/1/00, 5.49pm
to... Zoë Clarke
cc...
re... pull your socks up

I've just talked David out of issuing you with a written warning as to your conduct. It was only your recent bereavement that saved you. He questioned your competence for the job and cited a number of instances where he felt you let him down. He is particularly angry that you failed to inform him of a conference call with James Weissmuller this afternoon. Commonsense alone should tell you that anything to do with the world-wide president must always take top priority.

I know that David can be a tricky boss but I don't think you are helping yourself. You must concentrate more.

It's not all bad. Normally, he skips the warnings and goes straight to firing, so he must have a soft spot for you. You've got a real chance to make amends now. Seize it with both hands.

daniel_westbrooke@millershanks-london.co.uk
12/1/00, 5.55pm (9.55pm local)
to... james_f_weissmuller@millershanks-ny.co.usa
cc...
re... Coke

I cannot tell you how gratifying it is to see Harriet receiving recognition at last. When she joined a couple of years ago, few people rated her but I saw the spark of something a little special. I must say that David had reservations about my protégée's ability to manage Coke in my unavoidable absence. I am glad I talked him round. Fostering talent is part and parcel of a head of client service's job, so thanks are not necessary. Inner satisfaction is its own reward.

My very warmest regards and I look forward to seeing you on Sunday, jetlag permitting.

Daniel

david_crutton@millershanks-london.co.uk
12/1/00, 6.09pm
to... james_f_weissmuller@millershanks-ny.co.usa
cc...
re... Coke

Thank you for your e-mail. I hope you don't mind if I take it as something of a personal endorsement.

As you know, I am a great believer in giving talent its head, however untried. I took the decision to award Harriet and Pinki the extra responsibility against the advice of some of my colleagues.

I am glad that for once I did not allow consensus to rule and trusted my judgement.

Roll on Sunday. I have taken the liberty of booking us into the Sugar Club for dinner. A certain Ms Ciccone is a regular on her sojourns in London, so it is New-Yorker friendly!

Best wishes,
David

simon_horne@millershanks-london.co.uk
12/1/00, 6.14pm (10.14pm local)
to... james_f_weissmuller@millershanks-ny.co.usa
cc...
re... Coke

Jim, your e-mail gave me an undeniable *frisson* of pleasure.

If I may be immodest for a moment, I have always prided myself on my ability to identify talent.

I found Pinki languishing in a dead-end agency and decided to give her a shot at the big time.

She has more than repaid my faith.

When I had the Coke idea last week I knew there was nobody else I could trust with it.

To the creative person, one's idea's are one's babies and it can be hard to let go.

Yet I knew she would seek my counsel at every stage of the campaign's gestation. While I have had to apply a few gentle nudges to the steering wheel she has never lost sight of the integrity of *my* idea.

I am so thrilled for her that I am no longer the only one to appreciate her flair and strength of purpose.

I look forward to introducing her to you personally when you fly in from *la Pomme Grande*.

Fond wishes,

Simon Horne

daniel_westbrooke@millershanks-london.co.uk
12/1/00, 6.20pm (10.20pm local)
to... simon_horne@millershanks-london.co.uk
cc...
re... NIGHT OF THE LONG KNIVES

Your phone is off the hook but we must talk. I am presuming
that you have read Jim's e-mail. I did not become Head of Client
Services by not being able to smell a plot. I am in my room
awaiting your immediate response.

Zoë Clarke – 12/1/00, 6.27pm
to... Lorraine Pallister
cc...
re... that fucking, fucking bastard!!!!!!!!!!!!!!!!!!!

I've spent the last god knows how long sobbing in the loo!!!!!!!
Rachel told me that David wants to fire me!!!!!!!!!!!!!!!!!!!!!!!! I've
bent over backwards all week trying to please him and I just
don't know what to do any more! I need a drink!!!!!! Take me
to Bar Zero!!!!!!

simon_horne@millershanks-london.co.uk
12/1/00, 6.33pm (10.33pm local)
to... daniel_westbrooke@millershanks-london.co.uk
cc...
re... NIGHT OF THE LONG KNIVES

I am applying a final coat of gloss to the new LOVE script.

Join me in my suite in fifteen minutes.

I will uncork the malt.

You are quite right, we need to talk.

Lorraine Pallister – 12/1/00, 6.36pm
to... Zoë Clarke
cc...
re... that fucking, fucking bastard!!!!!!!!!!!!!!!!!!!

I was supposed to be going to the flicks with Liam but he's blown me out. He's fucked off to Wapping to wait for the First Edition. Sad or what? Dry your eyes and call by my desk in five.

simon_horne@millershanks-london.co.uk
12/1/00, 6.43pm (10.43pm local)
to... susi_judgedavis@millershanks-london.co.uk
cc...
re... stand by

I am about to fax you the new LOVE script along with Brett and Vince's excuse for an idea. Rush both to David immediately and ask him to respond urgently with his blessing. It's late and I need to brief the director on what he will be shooting tomorrow.

david_crutton@millershanks-london.co.uk
12/1/00, 7.07pm
to... simon_horne@millershanks-london.co.uk
cc... melinda_sheridan@millershanks-london.co.uk
re... LOVE

I have read your new work. I know time is of the essence so I will come straight to the point.

Your script is crap.

It was crap six months ago when it was a Tesco idea.

Sadly, it has not aged like a good wine. It is still crap.

Besides, though I am neither copywriter nor producer, even I can tell you that what you have written is not achievable given the limited time and resources you have. Where, for instance, are you going to find a border collie versed in the art of sheep handling in the middle of the Indian Ocean? And do GI uniforms grow on the palm trees out there?

Shoot Brett and Vince's idea. It is simple, ingenious and on brief. More importantly, it made me laugh.

Who knows, if you give in gracefully and keep your trap shut, they might even make you look good.

By the way, if you're wondering why I have copied Mel on this, I'm simply ensuring that there are no 'breakdowns in communication', and that you don't return with *The Dirty Dozen* meets *One Man and his Dog*.

brett_topowlski@millershanks-london.co.uk
12/1/00, 7.32pm (11.32pm local)
to... liam_okeefe@millershanks-london.co.uk
cc...
re... praise be!!

God sayeth, 'I have sorely tested the scallywags Vincent and Brett with pestilence and plague, yet still they are not smited down.' And God was pleased with them.

✤

Then did God turn to His handmaiden Melinda and sayeth, 'Visit Vincent and Brett in the still of the night. Tell unto them that Horne is indeed the slime-oozing viper that crawls the earth on its belly and that he shall kisseth their arse. Bring unto them the glad tidings that they shall make their script into a film that shall be broadcast across the whole land.'

✤

And the film came to pass. And it was ripe with the quivering breast, the perky nipple and the saucy butt shot. And all the people of the land rejoiced and proclaimeth, 'That Brett and that Vincent – diamond geezers.'

✤

Yes, mate, we got a fucking result. We're gonna wake Nathan now and tell him to get his shooting pants on. We've got a movie to maketh.

David Crutton – 12/1/00, 7.38pm
to... Harriet Greenbaum
cc...
re... what the papers say

I'm going for a curry. If you are still here, you might like to join me and stay on to see Max Gregory and a copy of the *Sun*. At least that way I have you in my sights and know you are not sneaking off to confer with Weissmuller.

Harriet Greenbaum – 12/1/00, 7.42pm
to... David Crutton
cc...
re... what the papers say

I am with Pinki at the moment trying to shoehorn Gloria Hunniford into the Freedom creative strategy, so I'll sit out the vindaloo.

I'm afraid Gloria's mature profile is a less-than-perfect fit with the 18–24 target that Freedom are chasing. This afternoon Pinki approved a campaign featuring Richard Blackwood and a Busta Rymes track, which puts our problem into perspective.

I'll see you when you come back.

harriet_greenbaum@millershanks-london.co.uk
12/1/00, 11.59pm
to... melinda_sheridan@millershanks-london.co.uk
cc...
re... *Sun*

It's every bit as bad as we feared. They've made us all look shallow, conniving and driven by lust – in short, like we work in advertising. Brett and Vince come out especially badly. I'd suggest to them that they might like to seek the advice of counsel.

The worst thing was seeing Jeremy Paxman holding up the front page at the end of *Newsnight*. That supercilious smirk is all very well until he applies it to you.

There is nothing more you can do, save keeping lips zipped and getting on with the job in hand. I'll fax the story through to you first thing. Until then, sweet dreams.

Thursday
13 January
2000

liam_okeefe@millershanks-london.co.uk
13/1/00, 1.42am
to... brett_topowlski@millershanks-london.co.uk
cc...
re... READ ALL ABOUT IT!

I've cabbed like fuck back from Wapping to get this story to you but it's too big to fax and the scanner's down so can't e it. So I've reproduced the highlights using all the keyboard skills at my disposal. Enjoy your fifteen mins:

SCORCHING SUN EXCLUSIVE

LAND OF GROPE
AND GLORI

By HARRY SALTER in Mauritius
and KEENAN WILKIE in London

The paradise island of Mauritius was rocked yesterday when Gloria Hunniford, glamorous TV presenter and star of the BBC's _Wish You Were Here_, was the victim of an unprovoked sex attack.

The mature and buxom blonde was staying at the island's exclusive le Touessrok Hotel, filming the new series of her popular show when Frank Sinton, a top executive at the LOVE Channel, the cable porn station, made his move.

Boob

Billy Wardell, Hunniford's cameraman, said: "It was disgusting. Gloria was lying on the beach minding her own business when the slimeball just lunged. He tried to grab her boob, plain as day." As our exclusive pictures on pages 2,3,4 and 5 show, Wardell had filmed the whole sordid scene.

The balding Sinton said after the incident: "It was a harmless prank. I thought she was someone else and that's all there is to it. F*** off and leave me alone."

Lesbian

Sinton, 34, is in Mauritius to shoot a new TV ad for LOVE. It will feature busty **topless** models, simulated **lesbian** orgies and a 3ft **inflatable** fish. Vince Douglas, in Mauritius as creative supremo of Miller Shanks, the top London ad agency responsible for the commercial, said: "Basically it's a bunch of sexed-up dykes having a laugh on the beach. It will be dead tasteful." Brett Topowlski, Douglas's deputy, added: "It's just a bit of harmless fun. It's gagging with top totty though."

Fondle

Of the sex attack, Douglas, 21, who drives a Ferrari and earns in excess of £250,000 a year, said: "Frank runs a porn channel. That's bound to get the trousers twitching if you get my drift. It stands to reason that if he sees a chance of a quick fondle he's going to give it rock all. Especially if the bird's a celebrity. They're all perverts at LOVE."

In London David Crutton, Miller Shanks' Chief Executive, said: "Until we know all the facts we cannot comment. However, if an assault did take place then we would deplore it and would support the forces of law in any action they undertook."

Monty Sadler, Controller of LOVE TV, was not available for comment.

Fit

Anthony Burke-Johnson, Tory MP and Chairman of the Clean Our Screens campaign, said: "I have been trying to get filth like the LOVE Channel off the air for years. If its executives are rampaging around grabbing any poor woman that takes their fancy, then they are not fit to run a TV channel."

There's more:

THE SUN SAYS

Smut Peddlers, the game is up

It's one thing for the porn merchants at the LOVE Channel to fill our screens with filth. It's another when their employees act out their sordid fantasies on a public beach. They have ducked and dived to defend themselves in the past. Now they stand condemned by Vince Douglas of their own advertising agency: **"They're all perverts at LOVE."** We at the Sun say "Hear, hear." It is time that the broadcasting watchdogs showed their teeth. **Take this poisonous bile out of our living rooms**.

Glori, Glori, Hallelujah!

We are a family newspaper and would never condone the kind of sex attack suffered by Gloria Hunniford yesterday. But we are delighted that this glamorous gran is making a stand for the older woman and not hiding her charms under a twinset and pearls. **Good on yer, Gloria. We'd pinch your bum any day of the week!**

There are some great shots. My fave is you in your mud mask and Vin with his dick out for the lasses. They've done the decent thing and stuck a black bar across it – nearly went as far as his knee. Tell him it's one for his Mum's scrapbook. Hate to say it but I think you're in some serious shit here. Get a lawyer quick. You might be better off with Max Clifford though.

Great result on the script, by the way. Enjoy shooting it – could be the last one you ever do.

brett_topowlski@millershanks-london.co.uk
13/1/00, 3.01am (7.01am local)
to... liam_okeefe@millershanks-london.co.uk
cc...
re... READ ALL ABOUT IT!

Doesn't look good, does it? Vin is shitting himself. He can't remember what he said, but he has a horrible feeling they left out the worst bits. Haven't seen Horne yet, but I'm sure the smug twat will find us soon enough. Just showed Mel your e and all she could say was, 'Oh no, you didn't say that. Oh no . . .' I told Vin to look on the bright side – at least they made his knob look big.

The other bad news is that we've woken up to half a hurricane. We won't be shooting a bloody thing today. I want my mummy.

David Crutton – 13/1/00, 8.02am
to... Zoë Clarke
cc...
re... Rachel Stevenson

The moment she arrives have her come and see me. I'm in the mood for firing today.

Zoë Clarke – 13/1/00, 8.04am
to... Lorraine Pallister
cc...
re... fuck, fuck, fuck!!

David's just said he's firing people today!!!!!!!!! What shall I do!!!!!!!!! If I go home sick now he won't be able to do it, will he?

**max_gregory@huntermcpheepartners.co.uk
13/1/00, 8.48am**
to... david_crutton@millershanks-london.co.uk
cc...
re... LOVE

Top of the morning to you.

On my way in to the office I grabbed the *Sun*'s late edition, which thankfully contained no new revelations. Naturally, the other tabloids picked up on the story but none of them has anything lurid to add.

Having slept on it, I think this doesn't look too bad for you. You have some 'surgery' to do but once you have excised the 'diseased part' of your *body corporate* I think you will be home free. It will come as no surprise to you that I refer here to Mr Douglas. His mouth has got you into hot water. I recommend you do the following:

Check his contract where I am sure you will find a standard clause forbidding unauthorised utterances to the press. Assuming it is in there, you have all the grounds you need for summary dismissal.

Make your disassociation from him as public as possible. Make it absolutely clear to anyone who will listen that conduct like Mr Douglas's will not be tolerated at Miller Shanks.

Issue a written 'without prejudice' apology to the LOVE Channel and hope they decide not to sue for Mr Douglas's libel. My guess is that they will not. They will wish this story to die an early death.

As for Mr Topowlski, his short quote is far less incriminating. Unauthorised though it was, he did not expose Miller Shanks. I suggest you let him off with a formal caution.

I feel that this story will have an extremely short shelf-life. Unless Ms Hunniford decides to market her version (and if she wishes to maintain her dignity, she will not), I doubt that tomorrow's press will even follow it up.

When the fuss dies down in a day or two I would imagine that you will even be able to salvage your relationship with LOVE. With Mr Douglas and (presumably) Mr Sinton spending more time in their gardens, there is no reason why it cannot be business as usual.

As I said last night, things never look so bad the morning after.

Best wishes as ever,

Max Gregory

melinda_sheridan@millershanks-london.co.uk
13/1/00, 8.59am (12.59pm local)
to... harriet_greenbaum@millershanks-london.co.uk
cc...
re... LOVE update

The local met office was wrong. The Old Man of the Sea was right. This morning we are being pummelled by the raw force of a typhoon. We won't be shooting anything today. Gloriously simple though Brett's and Vincent's script is, it does require weather that doesn't rip roofs from houses.

Danny Boy blames the whole predicament on me – well, it must be someone's fault. 'Why on earth didn't you buy weather insurance?' he whimpered over his yoghurt and muesli. I reminded him that when I told him what the premiums would be a couple of months ago, he scoffed and said, 'Weather insurance? Don't be so silly – we're shooting in *Mauritius*.' Of course nobody surpasses Daniel when it comes to rewriting history, so I'm sure I've got it totally wrong.

Thanks for sending the story through this morning, though we had already seen much of it, courtesy of Liam. Poor Vincent and Brett are wearing the doomed looks of the puppies who have seen the sack with the bricks in it, and have realised the canal is but two minutes' brisk walkies away. I know they have been wicked little boys, but do you suppose there is any way they can be saved? They knew not what they did.

We were hoping to wave tutty-bye to Frank this morning, but the weather has shut down the airport. We're stuck with him for another twenty-four hours at least. I think he is relieved. He's smart enough to know that both P45 and divorce papers sit in his in-tray.

Don't worry about us though. The hotel staff are rallying round to keep the guests' spirits up. They've had us all in the lobby this morning playing bingo. I won a bottle of the local liqueur (pineapple), a souvenir ash tray and a box of le Touessrok Mint Thins (made in Bristol). This afternoon we have a traditional island dance class, where my booty will be well and truly shaken.

Lorraine Pallister – 13/1/00, 9.09am
to... Zoë Clarke
cc...
re... fuck, fuck, fuck!!

Don't panic. If you haven't seen the *Sun* yet, read it now. If he's going to fire anyone, my money's on Vince and Brett.

Harriet Greenbaum – 13/1/00, 9.15am
to... David Crutton
cc...
re... Freedom

I have spoken to Pinki again and she can see no obvious or

sensible way to write a youth-oriented campaign around Gloria
Hunniford. Can we discuss? Perhaps you can see a solution that
has eluded us.

David Crutton – 13/1/00, 9.23am
to... Rachel Stevenson
cc...
re... P45s

You are quite right. It would court disaster to fire Douglas while
he is on the other side of the world, and we have no control over
him. It will wait until Monday, 9.00. Prepare the letter and while
you're about it, a written warning for Topowlski – he can consider
himself a jammy bastard.

**david_crutton@millershanks-london.co.uk
13/1/00, 9.28am**
to... max_gregory@huntermcpheepartners.co.uk
cc...
re... LOVE

Thanks for your note. A letter of severance to Vince Douglas is
being drafted now. I have spoken to Monty Sadler at LOVE and
not surprisingly he is doing the same for Frank Sinton. Like us,
he wants to put the mess behind him.

Thanks, as always, for your help.

David

**brett_topowlski@millershanks-london.co.uk
13/1/00, 9.35am (1.35pm local)**
to... david_crutton@millershanks-london.co.uk
cc...
re... apology

Dear Mr Crutton,

We want to apologise for the comments that appeared in the *Sun*
today. We admit that we may have said these things but at the
time we didn't know we were talking to a journalist. Also, he

only wrote the bad stuff we said and he missed out all the bits about how we loved working for such an exciting agency and couldn't wish for more caring employers.

We know that's not much of an excuse and the way it came out in the paper wasn't very good. We understand now that we were wrong, and that it wasn't big or clever. All we can do now is say how sorry we are and promise that it will never happen again.

We hope everything is OK in London and good luck with the Coke pitch on Monday!

Yours truly,

Brett Topowlski
Vince Douglas

david_crutton@millershanks-london.co.uk
13/1/00, 9.42am
to... brett_topowlski@millershanks-london.co.uk
cc...
re... apology

You're dead right, boys, it won't happen again.

Zoë Clarke – 13/1/00, 9.47am
to... Lorraine Pallister
cc...
re... the goss

The Crettin's sworn me to secrecy, so don't tell this to a soul!!!! Vince is gonna get fired on Monday morning and Brett's gonna get off with a warning!!!!!!!!!! They just wrote him an apology and I've never heard him laugh so loud!!!!!!!

Lorraine Pallister – 13/1/00, 9.50am
to... Liam O'Keefe
cc...
re... bad news

Come and see me. Crutton's decided what to do with V&B.

Ken Perry – 13/1/00, 9.56am
to... All Departments
cc...
re... MSTV

I am proud to announce that today the brand new Miller Shanks in-house TV channel will make its first broadcast. All televisions in the corridors, reception and other public areas have been re-tuned and at 12.00 the programme will commence:

12.00: WELCOME TO MSTV – a short introduction by our CEO, David Crutton.
12.10: MY FAVOURITE ADS – an exciting journey through Simon Horne's illustrious advertising career from 'Do the Shake 'n' Vac' to Lombard Direct's zany animated phone.
12.25: GODLEY'S AD TRIVIA – a fun quiz with our own answer to Bob Holness.
12.45: BUILDING A SUCCESSFUL CAREER – a no-holds-barred interview with our Head of Client Services, Dan Westbrooke.
13.00: ON LOCATION – a behind-the-scenes glimpse at the glamour of a TV shoot. This month we visit Isleworth studios for the making of last year's Kimbelle Ultra Discreet spot starring Geri Halliwell.
13.15: YOU HUM IT, I'LL PLAY IT – a heartfelt plea by Simon Horne for the revival of the lost art of the advertising jingle.
13.20: CLOSE DOWN.

I hope you will join me in enjoying this televisual treat. Snacks will be provided.

Ken Perry
Office Administrator

David Crutton – 13/1/00, 10.03am
to... Harriet Greenbaum
cc...
re... Freedom

I'm already booked in for dinner with the senior Freedom people tonight. You should join us and I'll introduce you as our resident strategic guru. Dazzle them with some demographics – the power of the grey pound, longer life-expectancy, the usual bollocks. Tell them that after a considered re-think we believe it makes no sense to chase impoverished teenagers when there are old dears out there who'd much rather fritter their pensions on jeans and disco gear than stairlifts. Bring some laminated charts – they're not the brightest sparks, and some colourful diagrams will have them dribbling into their consommé.

When we present them with Gloria Hunniford, the new Freedom Babe, a week or so from now they'll lap it up.

liam_okeefe@millershanks-london.co.uk
13/1/00, 10.11am
to... brett_topowlski@millershanks-london.co.uk
cc...
re... bad news

You sitting down to read this? No nice way to put it, but Vin's fired the minute he sets foot in the office. No doubt Crutton will also want the keys to his Ferrari (sorry, couldn't resist). You get off light – a written warning. I had a word with Pinki and she doubts there's anything she can do but she'll say something to Crutton anyway. It's a bit delicate for her because we're not supposed to know about it. We only found out because Zoë blabbed to Lol. I'm really sorry, but I guess we saw it coming. Anything I can do, shout.

Nigel Godley – 13/1/00, 10.16am
to... All Departments
cc...
re... MSTV

Don't miss my small screen debut on MSTV (not counting the time I was on *Crackerjack*). I'm wearing a spinning bow tie! It'll be crazy!

Nige

brett_topowlski@millershanks-london.co.uk
13/1/00, 10.27am (2.27pm local)
to... liam_okeefe@millershanks-london.co.uk
cc...
re... bad news

Vin took it on the chin like a true geezer and went to the bar. Tell Pinki thanks, but not to worry about Crutton. Vin says it's a waste of time and he wanted to leave anyway. He's just glad that it's DC who's doing the business and not SH(it). I'll have to leave as well, you know. Me and Vin go all the way back to college and I can't desert him now. I've already put in the call to Letitia.

No break in the weather. It might have blown itself out by tomorrow, but the beach will look like Hiroshima, Ground Zero.

Le Touessrok Redcoats are coming round now to see who's up for native dancing in the lobby. There's a big bunch of jokes to be gleaned from that but I really can't be arsed.

mike_appleton@millershanks-hk.co.hk
13/1/00, 10.32am (6.32pm local)
to... david_crutton@millershanks-london.co.uk
cc...
re... Bucharest

Sorry to be a pest, but you haven't had a word with JFW yet, have you?

david_crutton@millershanks-london.co.uk
13/1/00, 10.36am
to... mike_appleton@millershanks-hk.co.hk
cc...
re... Bucharest

Mike, Jim flies in at the weekend. I will speak to him then. Goodbye.

Pinki Fallon – 13/1/00, 10.42am
to... Creative Department
cc...
re... today's review

The collective review will be a little later, at 2.00, owing to MSTV, which I'm sure none of you will want to miss . . . ☺

Pinki Fallon – 13/1/00, 10.45am
to... Susi Judge-Davis
cc...
re... today's review

Susi, I know you keep reminding me that you only work for Simon, but could you please help us out today? Lorraine is up to her neck, so I'd really appreciate it if you could do the necessary for the 2.00 review – pads, pens, drinks, etc. Ta . . . ☺

Letitia Hegg / letitia@tavistockhegg.aol.com.uk
13/1/00, 10.47am
to... simon_horne@millershanks-london.co.uk
cc...
re... catch-up

You'll be fascinated to hear that I've just had your lad Brett on the blower, simply desperate for a move. I didn't know you'd fired his chum Vince. You must keep me abreast, darling. I actually have a brief just in that would be right up their *strasse* – Campbell and Roalfe at Y&R are looking for a funky young team. But Brett had the beleaguered tone of the leper about him and it warned me off. Anyway, while I wouldn't normally pick it up with my mother's gardening gloves, I couldn't help but read the *Sun* this morning. I imagine two names beginning with V and B are being added to every creative director's blacklist this morning.

But I have some gossip for you that's so hot it should be served *flambé* by the *maître d'* at the Savoy Grill. Guess who I saw sharing a prime window table at l'Odeon yesterday lunchtime. Your very own Ms Harriet Greenbaum and none other than your old partner. You know I speak of Barry Clement. Of course, it could be true love, but I think not. He has been seen about town with a d-d-gorgeous producer from Stark Films – Jennifer Lopez with a clipboard. I don't like to be catty, but I doubt Harriet's child-bearing hips and stretch marks would light his fire. The fact is he has been restless at the Good Ship Abbott Mead for some time. He's run out of shelf space for his little gold lions and stubby black pencils. I believe he's open to offers of a creatively challenging bent. Isn't that how David C sold Miller Shanks to you – a creative challenge? What is going on there? If you know, do tell.

From what the papers and Brett tell me, it sounds like your Mauritius jaunt is not a dream holiday, you poor dear. Still, if I know you, you will be rallying the troops with stirring *cris de guerre* and saving the day with your usual *brio*! And you'll be able to tell me the full, riveting story when we do lunch. Soon!

By the way, are e's reaching you in Mauritius or will you be reading this when you return to your desk?

Keep the Union Jack aflutter!

Susi Judge-Davis – 13/1/00, 10.50am
to... Pinki Fallon
cc...
re... today's review

Sorry about the delay in replying, but I'm awfully busy preparing for Si's return. Love to help but couldn't possibly.

Pinki Fallon – 13/1/00, 10.55am
to... Susi Judge-Davis
cc...
re... today's review

I can see how busy you are. You have four pots of nail varnish laid out on your desk. It must be so hard to decide which colour Si would like the most. I'd go for the plum, but then again . . . Pardon the sarcasm, Susi, but I'm getting pissed off with this. I'll do it myself . . . ☺

Lorraine Pallister – 13/1/00, 10.56am
to... Zoë Clarke
cc...
re... lunch

I think Judge-Dredd is about to have another fit. She's at her desk looking red-eyed, and she's been in a typing frenzy – she only ever does that when she's sending poisonous e's. I don't fancy Multiple Sclerosis Television or whatever the fuck it is at lunchtime. How about Blakey's? I'm sick of paying £3 for a pissy Bud at Bar Zero. I can probably do half an hour at 1.00pm. Let me know.

susi_judgedavis@millershanks-london.co.uk
13/1/00, 10.59am
to... simon_horne@millershanks-london.co.uk
cc...
re... that does it

Darling, I hate to do this to you when you're under such ginormous pressure, but I cannot stand it any longer. As the Personal Assistant to the Executive Creative Director I expect to be treated with just a little respect. But this week I have had Lorraine Pallister threatening me with physical violence and Pinki Fallon bossing me around like she owns the place. You know that I'd do just about anything for you, but I've had all I can take. I've tried to phone you to discuss this but I can't get through. Now I feel I have no other option.

Please accept this as my formal resignation from Miller Shanks. I will of course work out the full month's notice – I would not wish to be accused of being less than professional.

I would like to take this opportunity to say thank you for giving me the chance to work for you. It has been a privilege to be part of the inner circle of one of British advertising's few creative legends. Perhaps if more people at Miller Shanks shared your vision and high personal standards, I would not be writing this e-mail.

I hope that even though we are parting, we can always, always remain close.

Your dear friend,

Susi Judge-Davis

simon_horne@millershanks-london.co.uk
13/1/00, 11.15am (3.15pm local)
to... susi_judgedavis@millershanks-london.co.uk
cc...
re... that does it

Do you think all I have got to worry about is your bloody welfare? If you weren't so self-obsessed you would perhaps have noticed that my career is in a crisis.

Pinki is trying to steal my job.

Harriet, probably with David's blessing, is wining and dining my talentless ex-art director as a potential replacement.

And David is taking every opportunity to scythe the legs from beneath me.

On top of that I am half-way round the world trying to tailor a silk purse from a porcine ear.

In fact, if anyone should be resigning, it should be me.

Now I have you fleeing like a rat on the *Lusitania*.

More than ever I need you to be strong.

Loyal.

Dedicated.

But all you can do is wallow in self pity and bleat about your own pathetic troubles.

Frankly, I despair. If you want to leave, then do so.

I am sure I can find another secretary who will stand by me when the going gets a little rigorous.

Zoë Clarke – 13/1/00, 11.17am
to... Lorraine Pallister
cc...
re... lunch

Can't do lunch. Crutton is insisting the whole management floor watch *MSTV* in his office. Yeuch!!!!!!! Sorry!

simon_horne@millershanks-london.co.uk
13/1/00, 11.25am (3.25pm local)
to... harriet_greenbaum@millershanks-london.co.uk
cc...
re... support

I just thought I would spend a few minutes catching up with you. As you will know, we are having a rare old time of it out here.

But with a little application I think I can wrestle the Miller Shanks Express back onto the rails.

We have some downtime due to the inclement weather and I have had a moment for calm reflection. You will be delighted to hear it has led to a burst of left-brain activity and I have the germ of some crazy ideas for Monday's pitch. As you must know, I have something of a track record at wacky stunts.

You may have heard of my dressing everyone at O&M, from the receptionists to the chairman, in cow suits for the Burger King pitch.

We came within a whisker of winning.

I was hardly to know that the BSE crisis would break that very week.

But I digress.

I will work up my ideas for you ASAP.

By the way, a little dickie bird tells me you were having lunch with my old mate, Barry Clement. I have not seen him since D&AD at the Grosvenor last year. He didn't win a thing and was not in the best of humour.

How is he at Abbott Mead? He hasn't been the same since our partnership split up. Well, he has not produced any decent work for over a year now, and you will not need to be told that campaigns are the creative person's lifeblood.

I do hope he manages to put his career back on track.

Inexplicable isn't it, how the frail candlelight of creative inspiration sometimes flickers and dies? Poor, poor Barry. It is so heartening that you are taking the time to comfort him.

Thank you.

Do let me know how Pinki is getting on with my Coke idea. I have had the raw smell of celluloid in my nostrils all week, but I do miss the adrenal rush of pitch preparation.

Best wishes,

Si

Pinki Fallon – 13/1/00, 11.41am
to... Ken Perry
cc...
re... EMERGENCY

KEN, CAN'T GET YOU OR SHANICE ON PHONE. NEED SECURITY UP HERE NOW!! SUSI LOCKED IN SIMON'S OFFICE. EMPTY BOTTLE OF SLEEPING PILLS ON HER DESK.

AMBULANCE CALLED BUT WE MUST BREAK IN RIGHT AWAY.

simon_horne@millershanks-london.co.uk
13/1/00, 11.48am (3.48pm local)
to... letitia@tavistockhegg.aol.com.uk
cc...
re... catch-up

Gorgeous as ever to hear from you, my dear. Of course e's reach me out here – how could I bear to cut my electronic umbilicus to civilisation?

It is a tricky old shoot, but you know how I leap salmon-like to a challenge.

I must say that it is rather stimulating to have one's intellectual biceps worked to the burn.

The *Sun* as ever blew a ridiculous non-story into a national issue. Even so, I was forced to charge Vince the ultimate price for his foolish remarks. Harsh, I know.

Such is *le monde de chien mange chien* in which we toil.

There are plenty more where he sprang from.

I am sorry to disappoint, but there is nothing at all salacious and/or Machiavellian in the Greenbaum/Clement connection. I myself asked Harriet to offer him moral support, so down has he been dump-wise.

And of course there is no call for fresh creative leadership here. We are on the proverbial roll.

Only this morning did David tell me that, in my absence, he feels the sense of loss of the amputee.

However, that is not to say that I myself am not musing about change. I was going to broach this with you when next we lunched, but since you brought it up . . .

I feel that I have fired the engines of revolution at Miller Shanks and now the challenge is diminishing. Perhaps it is time for a move.

Of course, David would fight tooth and nail to keep me.

But I believe he could be persuaded that the hard work is done and the task could be continued by a less colourful talent.

At the moment this is only the vaguest rumbling of *ennui*.

Of longing for the next creative Matterhorn.

But we should discuss soon – you know how much I depend on your sagacious counsel. I will be frantic with Coke when I return.

But call Susi and book yourself into my earliest slot.

Si

simon_horne@millershanks-london.co.uk
13/1/00, 11.58am (3.58pm local)
to... barry_clement@amv-bbdo.co.uk
cc...
re... long time, no see

My friend, I find myself encircled by the shimmering Indian Ocean.

Dusky waifs bear coconut and mango on rough-hewn wooden platters.

And the papaya!

What does that remind you of, my old mate? Our Iberian adventure I hear you cry, and you are right.

It *was* Seville, of course, and there was no ocean. We had oranges rather than coconut.

But I have that same raw scent in my nostrils. That mélange of honest film crew sweat, greasepaint, that *je ne sais quoi*.

That was some shoot, eh? To take an unassuming bag of salted nuts and give it ownership of the most magnificent of ancient Spanish conurbations was a stroke of genius.

That the client went into receivership before our advertising could weave its beguiling spell remains one of the late-20th-century's enduring tragedies.

What a partnership we had, Barry.

These days, it all seems a tad easy. Where are the challenges? The bravura displays of the mould-breakers?

Perhaps I am just in the wrong agency. Do not misunderstand me. Miller Shanks is a fine company. Just a little 'easy-going'.

I realise now that I still have too much of the muse coursing through me to settle for second best.

You too, I suspect.

If I ever sensed you being lured to a safe harbour such as that offered by Miller Shanks then I would leap aboard and pilot you clear.

No, the perilous, swirling waters of the creative maverick are still the habitat for you and me.

When I return I shall start a search for something with a little more danger – edge is what I yearn for.

I shall also be dialling your number.

After I have first booked the Ivy, where we can remember past glories and drink to those to come.

Si

Shanice Duff – 13/1/00, 11.59am
to... All Departments
cc...
re... MSTV

Ken Perry has asked me to let you know that because of a small medical emergency on the creative floor, the start of MSTV has been put back by half an hour. Sorry for the inconvenience.

Shanice

simon_horne@millershanks-london.co.uk
13/1/00, 12.10am (4.10pm local)
to... susi_judgedavis@millershanks-london.co.uk
cc...
re... there is work to be done

My apologies for the somewhat harsh e-mail earlier.

But it was for your own good, dear heart.

Sometimes a sharp slap to the cheek is the only way to bring the hysteric to her senses. I hope you have returned to your eminently rational old self, because there is important work to do.

As I mentioned earlier, my back is exposed.

The enemy is looking for the most tender spot into which to plunge the stiletto.

Here is what you must focus on: as well as the movements of the opportunist, Pinki, keep an eye on the machinations of Harriet.

And if Letitia Hegg does not call you within thirty minutes to arrange a tryst, then phone her and diarise a time.

Keep me informed, my darling.

And stay Gillette-sharp.

Our careers depend upon it.

Zoë Clarke – 13/1/00, 12.14pm
to... Lorraine Pallister
cc...
re... 999

What's going on?!!! David has chained me to the desk or else I'd have rushed down!!! I heard the ambulance!!!!!!! Is Susi dead?!!!!!!!!!!!!!!! You didn't, did you?!!!!!!!!!! Tell me, tell me, tell me!!!!!!!!!!!!!!!!!!!!!!!!!!!!!!

David Crutton – 13/1/00, 12.15pm
to... Pinki Fallon
cc...
re... can't you keep order?

What is going on? We can do without the building turning into the set of *ER*. It has thrown the whole day out. I thought you could run the department without resorting to Simon's melo-dramatics. Maybe I was wrong.

barry_clement@amv-bbdo.co.uk
13/1/00, 12.17pm
to... simon_horne@millershanks-london.co.uk
cc...
re... long time, no see

Surprise, surprise – a friendly letter after the last time we met. As I remember it, I was being dragged away as you hid under a table at the Grosvenor. Well, I was shit-faced, and what is D&AD without at least one punch-up?

You haven't changed a bit, have you?

You're still writing.

In those very.

Short.

Paras in the vague.

Hope.

That this will lend your.

Words more.

Profundity.

Than they actually.

Possess.

And if I read between your lines, you seem to be implying that
I would actually leave Abbott Mead Vickers for Miller Shanks –
swap an agency that's won more awards than you can shake a
fucking big stick at for one, erm, one that has you working for
it.

Fucking brilliant idea, mate. When can I start?

While you're reminiscing about our Spanish shoot, that was a
certifiable fiasco. Our bloody ad was the reason Happi Snax went
tits-up. A tiny company like that had no business spending 650k
on one thirty-second film.

Weird that we don't speak for months and you just happen to
write the day after I have lunch with one of your suits (sharp
cookie, that Harriet). If I told you Crutton was taking me to la
Mirabelle next week would you send me flowers?

Barry

PS I've just remembered your nickname at O&M. 'AS SEEN
ON TV'. Shagged any cute drag queens lately?

simon_horne@millershanks-london.co.uk
13/1/00, 12.21pm (4.21pm local)
to... susi_judgedavis@millershanks-london.co.uk
cc...
re... there is work to be done

Susi, where are you? Speak to me, darling.

brett_topowlski@millershanks-london.co.uk
13/1/00, 12.22pm (4.22pm local)
to... liam_okeefe@millershanks-london.co.uk
cc...
re... THE PLAN

Vin's back from the bar and he's steaming mad. He has a plan.
It's not subtle and it won't get us our jobs back. But it'll make

sure we leave with mile-wide grins. Sorry if it makes life a mite hairy for you over the next few days, but you'll enjoy it all the same.

brett_topowlski@millershanks-london.co.uk
13/1/00, 12.33pm (4.33pm local)
to... pinki_fallon@millershanks-london.co.uk
cc...
bcc...liam-okeefe@millershanks-london.co.uk
re... Coke

Hi, Pinki. Vince and me have thought a lot about what we're going to tell you, and it hasn't been an easy decision. We don't want to get anyone into bother, but we think you should know all the facts.

Liam told us about the Coke idea that Simon had and that you're working up for the pitch. As soon as he mentioned it, we had a feeling of *déjà vu*. After a bit we worked out why. Two girls called Jane Backer and Kitty Bates dropped their book off for Simon last year. We sneaked a look at it and they'd done a campaign for 7UP. The line was 'IT'S IN THE CAN'. We don't want to point the finger or anything, and it might just be coincidence. But we were talking to Letitia Hegg earlier. She mentioned that Simon was at her place last week looking at folios, and we know she's been punting Jane's and Kitty's around town.

Like we said, we don't want to make any wild accusations. But we think that for the sake of Miller Shanks you should check it out before you go too far down the road with things. You might reckon that because we're in the crap at the moment we're just doing this out of spite. We're not. We were students ourselves two years ago and we know what it's like to be exploited. Anyway, while it's no secret that we don't have a lot of time for Simon, we know that you have put a lot of hard work into the Coke campaign, and if it turns out to be someone else's idea, you know how shit sticks.

Sorry to do this – Brett and Vince

liam_okeefe@millershanks-london.co.uk
13/1/00, 12.44pm
to... brett_topowlski@millershanks-london.co.uk
cc...
re... Coke

Wicked bastards! You've probably lumbered me with a shit-load of extra work but I'll let you off since you're moments away from the job centre. There's going to be some spectacular displays of arse-covering now – I'll just sit back and enjoy. Pinki is doing a Coke review with Harriet so it'll be a short while before she reads your e.

You'll like this. An ambulance has just hauled Susi's arse off to hospital. Pinki found her locked in Horne's office and suspected an OD – empty pill bottle on her desk. She got security to smash down the door (the shiny new replacement for the one that was axed last week) and found her slumped over Horne's desk. After they'd stretchered her off, Lol was going through her bag to look for her mum's number. She found the contents of the bottle of tabs carefully wrapped in tissue. Should have known the skinny prima donna wouldn't have the balls to go through with it. Pinki called the hospital but it was too late – they'd already pumped her stomach (contents: half a Ryvita, two segments of Satsuma, a small cup of Earl Grey, a chewed finger nail?). Lol says it's done her a favour, saving her the trouble of doing the post-lunch fingers down the throat. Lol's sick like that – that's why I love her.

Did I just type the L word?

I'll let you know what occurs on The Great Coke Robbery.

Lorraine Pallister – 13/1/00, 12.54pm
to... Zoë Clarke
cc...
re... lunch

Sure you can't manage a quick one? I have to give you a full run-down on Judge-Dredd's totally useless attempt to take her own life. She can't do anything right.

Zoë Clarke – 13/1/00, 1.02pm
to... Lorraine Pallister
cc...
re... lunch

He'll kill me if I sneak off now, but gotta hear this!!!!!!!!!! See you in two mins.

pinki_fallon@millershanks-london.co.uk
13/1/00, 1.03pm
to... brett_topowlski@millershanks-london.co.uk
cc...
re... Coke

Brett and Vince, I'm sorry about the trouble you're in. However daft you've been, I don't think you deserve to be fired, Vince. I've thought about your e-mail and whatever motivated you to write it, this is a bloody serious allegation. I'll have to check it out and then work out how to play it. I don't want you to say anything to anybody about this. I don't think anyone should know until we have the truth. Please trust me to do the right thing. I'll keep you informed . . . ☺

pinki_fallon@millershanks-london.co.uk
13/1/00, 1.10pm
to... simon_horne@millershanks-london.co.uk
cc...
re... Susi

Bad news I'm afraid. Susi was rushed to UCH this morning following a suspected overdose. It turned out that she hadn't taken anything but obviously she is very upset about something. I've had a few difficulties with her this week but I didn't see this coming. I expect she'll be discharged later today – I'm sure a call from you would be appreciated. I imagine that this sounds terrible when you're miles away and can't do anything to help, but please don't worry. Susi has had troubles before and always comes through smiling. I'm sure this time will be no different.

By the way, do you remember seeing a book from two girls called Kitty Bates and Jane Backer from Watford College? It's not a big deal but they've been pestering me on the phone saying that you wanted to see it again. Do you want me to have a look for you or shall I leave it for your return?

Let me know. And I hope you don't mind, but I've sent Susi some flowers from the department . . . ☺

harriet_greenbaum@millershanks-london.co.uk
13/1/00, 1.15pm
to... simon_horne@millershanks-london.co.uk
cc...
re... support

Thanks for your e-mail. And thanks for the offer of stunt ideas. I mentioned this to David, but he wants to keep this pitch as minimal as possible. He's met Kelly Derringer at Coke a couple of times and thinks she's the sort of slightly puritanical Iowan who'd be deterred by excessive razzmatazz.

Lunch with Barry was excellent. He was far from depressed. In fact he couldn't stop bubbling about some new ads he's just shot for Guinness and Volvo. They sound fabulous. He told me to ask you to give his regards to Dick Chick – someone you both worked with I guess.

We're slowly recovering from the horror of the *Sun*'s front page this morning. I hope you can help put it behind us by returning with a fantastic film. Good luck!

simon_horne@millershanks-london.co.uk
13/1/00, 1.31pm (5.31pm local)
to... pinki_fallon@millershanks-london.co.uk
cc...
re... Susi

It seems that I have only to leave for five minutes before things fall apart. Susi was in fine fettle on Friday so I cannot begin to imagine the anarchy that has driven the poor girl to a suicide attempt.

I shudder to think what further damage I will find when I walk back in.

As for presuming to advise me on how to handle Susi, I know her better than anyone and I will not be lectured by the person who could well have driven her to such drastic action.

We shall say no more at present, but rest assured I will conduct a full inquiry.

As for these girls, Kitty and Jane, I cannot believe you are bothering me with them. I vaguely remember their work as dull and uninspired. I certainly made no promises to them.

Do not raise their hopes by looking at their book. The sooner they realise that their futures do not lie in advertising, the better.

I will not prejudge your handling of *my* department from this distance.

Suffice it to say that you had better tread with maximum caution in the day and a half you have left 'in charge'.

pinki_fallon@millershanks-london.co.uk
13/1/00, 1.35pm
to... letitia@tavistockhegg.aol.com.uk
cc...
re... Kitty Bates and Jane Backer

Hi Letty,

You're at lunch so hopefully you'll read this as soon as you get back. Simon mentioned he'd seen Kitty's and Jane's book last week and he's quite keen on them. He asked me to take a look and tell him what I think. Would you mind sending it over this afternoon? Time is of the essence as I think he wants to move quickly to get some new faces in.

Thanks and best wishes ... ☺

David Crutton – 13/1/00, 2.19pm
to... Zoë Clarke
cc...
re... MSTV

My express instructions were for you to sit in my office and watch the debut of our superb magazine show. I imagine then that you wouldn't have dared miss it, even though your arse wasn't glued to my sofa. So for your entertainment I have prepared a list of questions about the programme.

Zoë Clarke – 13/1/00, 2.22pm
to... Lorraine Pallister
cc...
re... shit!!!!!!!!!

David wants me to answer questions about MSTV!!!!!! Help!!!

Lorraine Pallister – 13/1/00, 2.25pm
to... Zoë Clarke
cc...
re... shit!!!!!!!!!

Why don't you go and see the walking anorak, Godley? Whoever he is, he seems to know bloody everything about this place.

Letitia Hegg / letitia@tavistockhegg.aol.com.uk
13/1/00, 2.36pm
to... pinki_fallon@millershanks-london.co.uk
cc...
re... Kitty Bates and Jane Backer

Pinki, darling, how perfectly delightful to receive an e from you. You are so touchingly redolent of the footloose sixties that I don't associate you with the digital revolution!

I must say that I am surprised. When dear Simon looked at Kitty and Jane's work he hardly spoke like a man who simply had to have them. Still, I am glad of his change of heart (especially when my own 15% is at stake!).

Of course I will have their book despatched to you post haste. It lies at TBWA as I write and I will have them send it direct. You can expect it before the close of play. Inform Si that if he does wish to make them an offer they can't refuse he will have to put his skates on. TBWA are mustard keen and the girls are poised to sign on the dotted.

Always glad to be of service,

Letty

Katie Philpott – 13/1/00, 2.45pm
to... David Crutton
cc...
re... MSTV

Wow, that was so inspiring!!!! An agency with its own TV show!! And it was brilliant – informative, professional and fun. Well done – Katie P

liam_okeefe@millershanks-london.co.uk
13/1/00, 2.53pm
to... brett_topowlski@millershanks-london.co.uk
cc...
re... you should have seen it

This might cheer you up, boys. We had MSTV today. How bad was it? Put it this way, if any clients see it, they'll never trust us again with their TV budgets. The best bit was Horne singing the old Sugar Puffs jingle ('there are two men in my life . . .'). Buy the fucking album.

harriet_greenbaum@millershanks-london.co.uk
13/1/00, 3.07pm
to... melinda_sheridan@millershanks-london.co.uk
cc...
re... LOVE

I have just had David tell me that he doesn't care what the weather is like over there, he wants you to come home with a commercial. At this stage he's not bothered about quality, he just wants to see exposed film. What are the probabilities so that I can get him off your case?

David Crutton – 13/1/00, 3.14pm
to... Ravi Basnital
cc...
re... silence is golden

It has been a glorious ninety-five hours and thirty-four minutes since I had an e-mail from Pertti van Helden. Well done. I am sparing in my praise so you might want to frame this note.

melinda_sheridan@millershanks-london.co.uk
13/1/00, 3.29pm (7.29pm local)
to... harriet_greenbaum@millershanks-london.co.uk
cc...
re... LOVE

You can tell David that in the course of my chequered career I have been on eighty-six location shoots and never once returned without a commercial. I have waited out seventeen days of monsoon rain in Indonesia with only 200 Silk Cut, three Harold Robbins novels and a local waiter with the stamina of a prize bull to keep me going. I have watched Amazonian leeches glue themselves to a model hired only for her matchless complexion. Still, I waltzed off with a gold at the British Television Awards. And I have witnessed my leading actress and her hairdresser plunge to their deaths in the Dolomites, all in the cause of ending flyaway frizz. I am not about to let a piffling typhoon ruin my track record.

Tomorrow the wind can blow away camera, focus puller and director (in fact, the petulant way the latter has been behaving, I rather hope it does). If I have to borrow a camcorder from a hotel guest and shoot this fucking script myself, then that is precisely what I will do.

Nigel Godley – 13/1/00, 3.34pm
to... Zoë Clarke
cc...
re... only me!

Chuffed to make the acquaintance of PA to the MD. I must be going up in the world! It was a shame you couldn't watch MSTV, but I'm glad I could bring you up to speed. Would you like to borrow my VHS copy for home-viewing purposes? Perhaps we could have a quick bite one lunchtime and I could fill you in some more on the fascinating history of Miller Shanks. I think you would find the knowledge a boon in developing your relationship with your lord and master. Nige

Zoë Clarke – 13/1/00, 3.50pm
to... Lorraine Pallister
cc...
re... Godley

Thanks a bloody million!!!!! Now the little creep wants to take me to lunch!!!!!!!!!!!!!!! I'd rather have got all the questions wrong and been fired!!!!!!!!!!!!!!

Letitia Hegg / letitia@tavistockhegg.aol.com.uk
13/1/00, 4.12pm
to... simon_horne@millershanks-london.co.uk
cc...
re... lunch

I called Susi but the little waif had gone home sick. I spoke to Lorraine – she sounds a friendly northern wench – and booked a slot in your busy, busy schedule. I've got you all to myself for lunch next Tuesday. Do you fancy the Greenhouse? I haven't been there for aeons and I hear tell they have a gifted new chef who can perform miracles with a loin chop.

By the way, I'm sending the two Watford girls' book to Pinki. She said you were distinctly interested. I'm thrilled at your change of mind after you damned them last week. I said this to your resident hippie and I'll say it to you: if you desire them, you will have to move like Linford Christie. Beattie wants them at TBWA and I'd be astonished if they turned down the Bubble-Permed God.

nigel_godley@millershanks-london.co.-uk
13/1/00, 4.19pm
to... brett_topowlski@millershanks-london.co.uk;
vince_douglas@millershanks-london.co.uk
cc...
re... timesheets

I have been checking my records and found that neither of you have completed any timesheets since W/C 7/9/98. Please could you let me have these straight away. I must stress the importance of the prompt return of timesheets for the efficient management of the company's accounts. I know it seems like a chore, but I find that if you make a game of it (for example, compile a simple league table to see which clients you spend most hours on), it can be fun.

Sorry to be a nag, but we all have a job to do.

Nige

PS Your cat can't get enough of the tripe I cooked him, Vince!

simon_horne@millershanks-london.co.uk
13/1/00, 4.22pm (8.22pm local)
to... letitia@tavistockhegg.aol.com.uk
cc...
re... READ THIS NOW!

IT IS IMPERATIVE THAT YOU RECALL THAT PORTFOLIO IMMEDIATELY. PINKI IS UNDER STRICT INSTRUCTIONS NOT TO LOOK AT POTENTIAL RECRUITS. I CANNOT OVERSTRESS THE IMPORTANCE OF THIS E-MAIL

!

simon_horne@millershanks-london.co.uk
13/1/00, 4.27pm (8.27pm local)
to... pinki_fallon@millershanks-london.co.uk
cc...
re... Kitty and Jane

Letitia informs me that, despite my express order to the contrary, you have gone ahead and requested their portfolio.

It stings me enough that you will not accept my word that they are mediocrities.

More than that, however, your disobedience has become a point of principle.

If on Monday I find that you have so much as fondled the zip on their book, then I will reverse my decision to take you back after your behaviour last week.

You have been warned.

Si

brett_topowlski@millershanks-london.co.uk
13/1/00, 4.42pm (8.42pm local)
to... liam_okeefe@millershanks-london.co.uk
cc...
re... Horne

All day long the arsehole's been looking smug as a bug on account of Vin's sorry plight, but we just bumped into him in the bar and he was white as a sheet (you know that blue whiteness you only get with Daz). Didn't realise he'd take the news of Susi's mock suicide so hard. Felt a bit sorry for him. Don't worry, it passed in under a second. Anyway, how could anyone seriously feel sympathy for a fat fifty-something in a Megadeth T-shirt and a Hilfiger cap? Tosser.

brett_topowlski@millershanks-london.co.uk
13/1/00, 4.52pm (8.52pm local)
to... nigel_godley@millershanks-london.co.uk
cc...
re... timesheets

There's a new system, Godders. Susi Judge-Davis does all the Creative Department timesheets now. She's much more efficient than any of us. Dump the lot on her desk and she'll have them back to you before you can say 'double-entry bookkeeping'.

Brett and Vince

liam_okeefe@millershanks-london.co.uk
13/1/00, 5.03pm
to... brett_topowlski@millershanks-london.co.uk
cc...
re... Horne

How wrong could you be? The death-row look is because he's just sussed that Pinki's about to see Kitty's and Jane's book. He must be evacuating breeze blocks. He e'd Pinki ordering her not to look at it on pain of dismissal. She's doing the decent thing and ignoring the sly cunt.

nigel_godley@millershanks-london.co.uk
13/1/00, 5.11pm
to... brett_topowlski@millershanks-london.co.uk
cc...
re... timesheets

Nobody tells me anything down in my cubby. Sounds like a topping plan though – maybe the creative department will at last catch up with the rest of the agency in this unglamorous but crucial activity. All outstanding timesheets will be with Susi first thing tomorrow. Thanks for the info, fellas!

Nige

Letitia Hegg / letitia@tavistockhegg.aol.com.uk
13/1/00, 5.22pm
to... simon_horne@millershanks-london.co.uk
cc...
re... READ THIS NOW!

Darling, I've this minute stepped out of an interview (a charming art director at Grey – I must send her your way) and I've read your screaming e-mail. I called TBWA but it was too late – the book was already *en route*. Never mind. I'm sure that if you call Pinki, she'll send it straight back to me unopened. I have to say though that I've never known you blow so hot and cold on one of my little teams – you're usually so firm and decisive. But Kitty and Jane seem to be having quite an effect on the CDs they encounter.

Letty

liam_okeefe@millershanks-london.co.uk
13/1/00, 5.32pm
to... brett_topowlski@millershanks-london.co.uk
cc...
re... *Cliffhanger*

The merchandise has arrived. Pinki wouldn't let me near it. She thumbed through it in total silence. Then she picked it up and swept out to see Crutton. Mood: fucking livid. Her close mates Love and Peace aren't getting a look in.

Pinki Fallon – 13/1/00, 6.21pm
to... Zoë Clarke
cc...
re... urgent

I've been looking everywhere for David, Harriet or you. I need

to see one or both of them on a matter of unbelievable importance. The second you return to your desk please let me know
where I can find them. Thanks.

Zoë Clarke – 13/1/00, 6.35pm
to... Pinki Fallon
cc...
re... urgent

Sorry, Pinki, but you've just missed them. They've both gone off
to a client dinner. Freedom I think. I'd suggest you call them on
David's mobile, but he's left it with me to charge up. Can it wait?

Pinki Fallon – 13/1/00, 6.36pm
to... Zoë Clarke
cc...
re... urgent

No it can't. Which restaurant are they in? I'll reach them there.

Zoë Clarke – 13/1/00, 6.40pm
to... Pinki Fallon
cc...
re... urgent

Can't remember. Sorry. I think it begins with P. Or is it V? I'm
not sure, to be honest.

**liam_okeefe@millershanks-london.co.uk
13/1/00, 7.16pm**
to... brett_topowlski@millershanks-london.co.uk
cc...
re... *Cliffhanger II*

She couldn't get Crutton. He's gone off to dinner with Harriet
and the dork Zoë can't remember which restaurant she booked
them into. So she showed me Kitty's and Jane's 7UP campaign
and asked me what I thought. The closet arse bandit is guilty as
charged. Now she's got Lol to round up whoever is still here so
she can brief them on a new Coke campaign. Looks like I won't
be tucked up at home tonight.

Sleep well, boys, content in the knowledge that you've just done a fucking superb day's work.

brett_topowlski@millershanks-london.co.uk
13/1/00, 7.21pm (11.21pm local)
to... liam_okeefe@millershanks-london.co.uk
cc...
re... *Cliffhanger II*

Sleep? You must be fucking joking. This is the best I've felt since I copped off with Delia Stubbs (year 2, Sacred Heart, Brighton). We're gonna hit the Swaying Palms disco before all the underage French minxes are dragged off to bed by their mums. I feel lucky.

Pinki Fallon – 13/1/00, 7.32pm
to... Harriet Greenbaum; David Crutton
cc...
re... Coke

I've done my best to find you because you need to know what I've just discovered. If I haven't managed to see you before you read this, I'm sorry, because it would have been better face-to-face.

Please don't ask who told me, but I heard that our Coke campaign isn't exactly original. 'IT'S IN THE CAN' was actually done for 7UP by a student team from Watford College. They're called Kitty Bates and Jane Backer. I did some checking this afternoon and apparently Simon was at Tavistock Hegg last week looking at books. One of them was theirs. That was the day he showed you 'his' idea. I had the book sent over so I could see any similarities for myself. The two campaigns are virtually identical. This couldn't possibly be put down to coincidence. The only differences are the things that we've added since Simon left.

I also have a couple of e-mails that I received from Simon this afternoon. Placed alongside the work, I think they are pretty self-incriminating.

I know you will want to see the evidence for yourselves before you decide what to do. Personally, my mind is made up. I couldn't possibly have anything more to do with this, and if it's the agency's decision to still present the work then I don't think I could work here any more. Young teams have had their ideas ripped off for no reward for too long and this practice is sickening.

I know you might think that I've got an axe to grind and want to steal Simon's job or something, but that isn't the case. I feel gutted about this. I believed that Simon had a brilliant idea with 'IT'S IN THE CAN' and it has been exciting to be part of its development this week.

For your information I am briefing the department to work through the night on a fall-back. Given the hour, few people are around, so I'm not that hopeful of cracking it by the morning.

I'm sorry to be giving you such bad news. For the life of me, I wish I could spot a silver lining ... ☹

pinki_fallon@millershanks-london.co.uk
13/1/00, 7.35pm
to... brett_topowlski@millershanks-london.co.uk
cc...
re... Coke

I've looked at Kitty's and Jane's 7UP campaign and you were right. I've told David but he's out and probably won't respond until the morning. Whatever happens now, I want you to know that I wouldn't be prepared to work for an agency that presented stolen work. If Simon keeps his job after this, I wouldn't be prepared to work for a thief. Given how unscrupulous advertising is, I'll probably be joining you at the DSS next week. Good luck with the shoot tomorrow ... ☺

brett_topowlski@millershanks-london.co.uk
13/1/00, 10.20pm (2.20am local)
to... liam_okeefe@millershanks-london.co.uk
cc...
re... night, night

Just back from getting jiggy with it. On the way we stopped by the Horne Suite for a quick round of knock-down ginger. All we could hear through the door were the muffled wails of a man watching his career flush down the Royal Doulton. There was a lobster salad under a silver dome outside his door – obviously not taking deliveries from room service. Vin is tucking into it now – consolation for choosing not to bring the gorgeous Françoise back from the discotheque. Well, she was eleven and even Vin draws the line at twelve.

Pinki sent us a sweet e. Tell her she can play her Leonard Cohen CDs as loud as she likes and we'll never take the piss again.

Time for bed, said Zebedee.

liam_okeefe@millershanks-london.co.uk
13/1/00, 10.31pm
to... brett_topowlski@millershanks-london.co.uk
cc...
re... night, night

Gratified to hear SH is taking it like a big girl's blouse. No rest for us. Trying to do Coke and Pinki is encountering a thirty-storey writer's block. We're doomed I tell you, doomed.

Friday
14 January
2000

---

brett_topowlski@millershanks-london.co.uk
14/1/00, 1.31am (5.31am local)
to... liam_okeefe@millershanks-london.co.uk
cc...
re... rise and shine

Horne is still sobbing. The typhoon has stopped and the sun is shining. The idyllic Mauritian sands look like Omaha Beach, 6 June 1944, but what the fuck, this is a great day to shoot an ad.

David Crutton – 14/1/00, 7.47am
to... Pinki Fallon
cc...
re... Coke

If you're here, my office immediately. Bring all the work – everything that Simon, you and your department have done, as well as the 7UP campaign. I'll make a side-by-side comparison.

Harriet Greenbaum – 14/1/00, 7.52am
to... Pinki Fallon
cc...
re... Coke

This is a disaster, Pinki. As soon as you get in, call me. I'd like to take a calm look before David sees it and any chance of a rational appraisal flies out the window.

Pinki Fallon – 14/1/00, 7.56am
to... Harriet Greenbaum
cc...
re... Coke

I'm here now. We didn't go home last night. We've got a few ideas, but nothing that could be a pitch-winning campaign by high noon on Monday. Come and see me now and then we'll do David. He's already e'd me ... ☺

Zoë Clarke – 14/1/00, 8.35am
to... Lorraine Pallister
cc...
re... screaming fits

David is in his office with Pinki and Harriet and he's going fucking spare!!!!!!!! He's chucking stuff at the walls!!!!!!!!!!!!!!! It's something to do with Coke!!!!!!!!!!! I can't work it out, but he's going to kill Simon when he sees him!!!!!! I'm not kidding – he is going to *KILL* him!!!!!!!!!!!!!!! Knew there must be a bonus to getting in this early!!!!!!!

David Crutton – 14/1/00, 8.49am
to... Pinki Fallon; Harriet Greenbaum
cc...
re... Coke

I'm sorry I went off the deep end. I appreciate that you are only the messenger, Pinki. But if you reckon that was angry, just watch me when I get hold of Horne.

I've thought about this now. There is an obvious and simple solution. Hire these two girls. Have them start immediately and give them full credit. It's the only way we'll get to present what is a very good campaign and keep from besmirching your precious conscience, Pinki. What do first-jobbers get these days – 15k? Offer them twenty and they'll chew your hand off at the elbow.

Pinki, you have my permission to call Letitia Hegg and get their signatures on a contract.

Even if they don't take the bait, my inclination is to present anyway. We can argue that the elements that have been added to their idea make it different. If it gets out and we have a PR disaster to deal with, hopefully we'll have the Coca-Cola business to mitigate the embarrassment.

And if this course of action brands me a common thief and leads to the resignation of a senior female member of the Creative Department, well, I can live with that.

By the way, if Horne or Westbrooke try to contact either of you, do not talk to them. I don't want the former to get wind of his fate and 'accidentally' board a return flight to a country that has no extradition treaty with the UK.

Pinki Fallon – 14/1/00, 9.03am
to... David Crutton; Harriet Greenbaum
cc...
re... Coke

I will try my best to hire Kitty and Jane. They have an excellent book anyway, and if you are genuine about owning up to them and crediting them with the Coke work, I believe this is a fair solution. Letitia isn't at work yet so I'll e-mail her next. Hopefully it will be the first thing she deals with.

If for some reason we can't get them to come here and you still decide to go ahead with 'IT'S IN THE CAN', I will have consider my position. The theft of ideas is too big an issue to ignore . . . ☺

David Crutton – 14/1/00, 9.07am
to... Pinki Fallon
cc...
re... Coke

Are you trying to threaten me? That is funny.

pinki_fallon@millershanks-london.co.uk
14/1/00, 9.13am
to... letitia@tavistockhegg.aol.com.uk
cc...
re... Kitty Bates and Jane Backer

Hi Letitia,

We want to offer Kitty and Jane a job at Miller Shanks. There is a gap in our resources that we need to fill urgently and we think they have the flair that we're looking for. We would like to offer them £20,000 each. I know this is slightly above average, but we do think they are a bit special.

Could you convey the news to them as soon as possible and let me know their reaction?

Ta . . . ☺

liam_okeefe@millershanks-london.co.uk
14/1/00, 9.26am
to... brett_topowlski@millershanks-london.co.uk
cc...
re... *Cliffhanger III*

I know you'll be sunning yourselves on the beach now watching cameras roll and tits jiggle, but got to bring you up to date. Pinki hit Crutton first thing with the case against Horne. Apparently he turned purpler than Barney the purple dinosaur's big, purple knob and threw his lava lamp at the wall. When he calmed down he told Pinki to hire the Watford birds. Even if they won't come he wants to present the campaign anyway – guess it was too much to hope that he'd actually have a conscience under that £1,500 suit. Makes no odds though, because he's definitely going to waste Horne.

More news as it comes in.

Lorraine Pallister – 14/1/00, 9.49am
to... Liam O'Keefe
cc...
re... you will not believe this

If you stick your head out your door and peer down the corridor
you'll see Susi-cide dressed tit to toe in pastel pink (pink tights?!).
She gave me this really weird smile as she sat down. What the
fuck is she doing here? I'm frightened.

Letitia Hegg / letitia@tavistockhegg.aol.com.uk
14/1/00, 10.00am
to... pinki_fallon@millershanks-london.co.uk
cc...
re... Kitty Bates and Jane Backer

Pinki, darling, nothing thrills me more than when my babies are
the objects of lustful desire. But are you absolutely sure? One
minute you are gasping 'yes, yes, yes', the next Simon is yelling
'over my dead body'. What is a girl to think?

Anyhow, this is academic now. The little winkles were buying
drinks for all and sundry at the Dog & Duck last night to celebrate
their acquisition of a job at TBWA. Beattie has put them on 18k
so I don't think a couple of grand will change their minds.

I'm sorry you missed the boat, but I have dozens of other teams
for you to fall head-over-heels in love with. Give the word and
I will drown you in a sea of black, zip-up portfolios.

Letty

Pinki Fallon – 14/1/00, 10.03am
to... Zoë Clarke
cc...
re... urgent

I know David is in a meeting, but tell him I'm coming to see
him right away . . . ☺

Susi Judge-Davis – 14/1/00, 10.11am
to... Rachel Stevenson; Pinki Fallon
cc... Simon Horne; David Crutton
re... an apology

My breakdown yesterday has given me a chance to reflect upon certain things. I now realise that I may have over-reacted to events lately, and I would like to apologise if I have given anybody unnecessary cause for concern. I have been under a great deal of strain but I know that we are all under similar pressures and that it is wrong to rise to provocation. I would be grateful if you would give me the opportunity to remind you that I do have the qualities required of a member of Team Miller Shanks.

Yours truly,

Susi Judge-Davis

daniel_westbrooke@millershanks-london.co.uk
14/1/00, 10.16am (2.16pm local)
to... harriet_greenbaum@millershanks-london.co.uk
cc...
re... Coke

Would anyone like to tell me what is going on with the Coke pitch? I need not remind you that it was I who attended the original briefing with the client. Neither should I have to remind you that I am Head of Client Services. It should be common courtesy to keep me informed of developments. Or is that too much to ask?

pinki_fallon@millershanks-london.co.uk
14/1/00, 10.23am
to... letitia@tavistockhegg.aol.com.uk
cc...
re... Kitty Bates and Jane Backer

I have spoken to David and he has authorised me to go to £45,000 each. They would also be entitled to full benefits – company cars, parking spaces, mobile phones and BUPA.

I know this is an unusually generous package, but it's an indication that we think they are unique talents who would have a great future here.

Please let me know their response.

Ta . . . ☺

Letitia Hegg / letitia@tavistockhegg.aol.com.uk
14/1/00, 10.26am
to... pinki_fallon@millershanks-london.co.uk
cc...
re... Kitty Bates and Jane Backer

For once I am lost for words. I shall tell them immediately.

David Crutton – 14/1/00, 10.33am
to... Rachel Stevenson
cc...
re... Judge-Davis

I've just read that strange e-mail from Susi. That girl spooks me. Some events will probably transpire early next week where it would be opportune to lose her – we can put it down to collateral damage. Please make sure that I don't forget.

Susi Judge-Davis – 14/1/00, 10.39am
to... Rachel Stevenson
cc... Simon Horne
re... the final straw

A few moments ago Nigel Godley brought up a huge stack of timesheets and literally dumped them on my desk (which, by the way, I had only just tidied). He then informed me that it is now *my* job to fill these in for the *entire department*. I pointed out that I am a senior *personal* assistant who only works for the Executive Creative Director, but he simply stalked off saying that this was the new system and if I didn't like it I should take it up with David Crutton.

I am making a real effort to get on, but I should not have to deal with rude and ignorant people like him. Rachel, I demand that you deal with this immediately.

Rachel Stevenson – 14/1/00, 10.48am
to... David Crutton
cc...
re... Judge-Davis

Don't worry, I won't for a minute let you forget.

Letitia Hegg / letitia@tavistockhegg.aol.com.uk
14/1/00, 10.55am
to... pinki_fallon@millershanks-london.co.uk
cc...
re... Kitty Bates and Jane Backer

I told them. I stressed that an offer of this magnitude is virtually unheard of for a first job. I even made Miller Shanks sound like Shangri-La. Well, a little embroidery is *de rigeur* if one wishes to make the grade as a headhunter.

Quite astonishingly they said no thank you. They feel that they have made a commitment to TBWA and couldn't possibly let down the curly-haired Brummie. Besides, they had some words to say about your own employers. How should I put this – they feel the choice of one's first agency is crucial and believe their prospects would be better served in 'a more creative environment'.

I'm so sorry, my dear. But as I said, plenty more fishies in the deep blue sea.

Letty

Pinki Fallon – 14/1/00, 11.01am
to... David Crutton; Harriet Greenbaum
cc...
re... Coke

Can I see you both straight away?

David Crutton – 14/1/00, 11.03am
to... Pinki Fallon
cc...
re... Coke

Harriet is with me now. Stroll on up.

**Letitia Hegg / letitia@tavistockhegg.aol.com.uk
14/1/00, 11.21am**
to... simon_horne@millershanks-london.co.uk
cc...
re... truly bizarre

Perhaps I am telling you something of which you are already
aware, but reading between the lines suggests that you have been
excluded from this particular loop, my darling. Despite your clear
disinterest in them, Pinki started an outlandish auction for the
services of Kitty Bates and Jane Backer this morning. The price
went up to 45k. Well, I wasn't about to complain, given my cut.
But I have to say that while they are good, they are not Evelyn
Waugh and Pablo Picasso. She claimed to have David's full backing. In the end she didn't get them. They are now the bought-and-
paid-for property of Trevor Beattie.

What in heaven's name is going on, sweetie? You simply must
tell your favourite headhunter.

Letty

Pinki Fallon – 14/1/00, 11.30am
to... David Crutton
cc...
re... resignation

Dear David,

I regret that I must tender my resignation. I do not want to leave
but under the circumstances I feel I have no other option.

The decision to present Coca-Cola with a campaign idea that is not original, and that we know to be the property of a creative team who do not work at Miller Shanks is one that I cannot support. I feel that this betrayal of principle lets the company down, and it has ceased to be the place that I joined with such high hopes last year.

I would prefer to leave immediately, but if you wish I am prepared to work out my three-month notice period.

Yours truly,

Pinki Fallon

Nigel Godley – 14/1/00, 11.38am
to... All Departments
cc...
re... Sale, Sale, Sale!

FOR SALE

Mahogany-style CD rack
- Holds 65 CDs.
- Durable polyurethane construction.
- Authentic mahogany effect.
- Mint condition, apart from one slight scratch.
- £14 o.n.o.
- First to see will buy!

Call x4667 – Nige

David Crutton – 14/1/00, 11.43am
to... Pinki Fallon
cc...
re... resignation

Your resignation is accepted. You can leave at the end of the day. Would you ask Liam to see me?

Liam O'Keefe – 14/1/00, 11.45am
to... Lorraine Pallister
cc...
re... 'bye

Pinki's walked. Crutton wants me. I'm 5'10", 42" chest, 32" inside leg. Order coffin.

**liam_okeefe@millershanks-london.co.uk
14/1/00, 12.08pm**
to... brett_topowlski@millershanks-london.co.uk
cc...
re... meet your new boss

Pinki resigned. Crutton called me up for what I'd have bet both your bikes on being my P45, but he put me in charge. Well, not as such – he said that as the most senior remaining member of the Creative Department, would I be prepared to present Coke on Monday. I thought about the stolen work, the ruthless exploitation of defenceless students and the point of principle that had driven my partner to make the ultimate sacrifice.

Then I said yes.

Look, I know Pinki's done the decent thing, shown rare integrity, nobility, heroism, blah, blah, blah . . . but there's glory, pay rises and free lunches to be had. And as 'the most senior remaining member of the Creative Department', maybe I can get you your job back, Vin – at least until the next cunt they make creative director sweeps in with his new broom (they all have new brooms) and fires your arse.

David Crutton – 14/1/00, 12.10pm
to... Harriet Greenbaum
cc...
re... Coke

Unsurprisingly, Saint Pinki of Glastonbury has resigned. So be it. I hope that you won't be infected by her outbreak of ethic-itis and will show the required resolve to see the job through. 99% of the pitch work is done, so it's down to dotting the i's. Do you think the hooligan Liam is capable of sprucing himself up to present on Monday?

In the longer term, we need to search for a new creative director. Simon is beyond redemption and while I entertained mild hopes of Pinki replacing him she is clearly out of the frame. You are something of a creative groupie. Any ideas?

Harriet Greenbaum – 14/1/00, 12.23pm
to... David Crutton
cc...
re... Coke

You know my feelings on this. I empathise with Pinki, but my resignation at this point would be irresponsible. You are the CEO, and it is incumbent on me to abide by your decisions.

As for a new CD, I do have some ideas, and there is one name in particular I'd like to canvas. Perhaps when the dust has settled next week we can have a chat.

harriet_greenbaum@millershanks-london.co.uk
14/1/00, 12.33pm
to... james_f_weissmuller@millershanks-ny.co.usa
cc...
re... concerns

Jim, I apologise for bothering you first thing in your day, but I have some serious worries that I need to share with you. I would appreciate your advice on how we should handle it. A crisis has developed on Coca-Cola, and in his understandable eagerness to win the pitch, I believe that David has made the wrong call.

This morning we discovered that the campaign we showed you a couple of days ago is not an original concept. Pinki was informed that Simon Horne had seen it as a 7UP idea in a student portfolio and had adapted it for our purposes. It is David's opinion, given that it is undeniably a good idea, and given the lateness of the hour, we should present anyway. Unfortunately, this decision has led to Pinki's resignation.

While I would not do anything so precipitate, I do think David is mistaken. Besides principle, I believe that common sense should prevent us from taking this course. Assume we win the pitch with 'IT'S IN THE CAN' and run it as a campaign. The evidence of our theft will be there for all to see, not least the two girls who originated the idea. The plot is further complicated by the fact that they now have a job at TBWA, who, as you know, are competing against us for Coke. I have put this argument to David but he remains intransigent.

We have little time to come up with a viable alternative. But even if we have to make a late withdrawal rather than risk exposure, to my mind that would be a preferable option.

I have thought long and hard before writing to you with this. I have no desire at all to land David in trouble. As I said, he has only the best interests of Miller Shanks at heart, but I believe that his admirable zeal has clouded his judgement.

I await your view, and will follow whatever course you recommend.

Harriet

David Crutton – 14/1/00, 12.39pm
to... Harriet Greenbaum
cc...
re... Coke

Thank you for sticking with it, however reluctantly. Loyalty, you will find, pays dividends. Why don't we have lunch? We can talk about Barry Clement. It is him isn't it? Ironically Simon was only my second choice for the creative director's job. Guess who my first choice was.

Lorraine Pallister – 14/1/00, 12.42pm
to... Zoë Clarke
cc...
re... lunch

Susi's on Panadol and Prozac, and Liam's on a power trip. See
you in ten in reception and I'll tell you about it.

Harriet Greenbaum – 14/1/00, 12.44pm
to... David Crutton
cc...
re... Coke

I'd love to have lunch but I have to wait in for some important
news. Incidentally, your intelligence is good.

David Crutton – 14/1/00, 12.49pm
to... Zoë Clarke
cc...
re... lunch

I appear to be at a loose end. I suppose I could take you for
lunch as a welcome to my outer office. Get your coat on.

Zoë Clarke – 14/1/00, 12.51pm
to... David Crutton
cc...
re... lunch

I can't, I've got plans. Sorry! How about Monday?

David Crutton – 14/1/00, 12.54pm
to... Zoë Clarke
cc...
re... lunch

What?

susi_judgedavis@millershanks-london.co.uk
14/1/00, 12.58pm
to... simon_horne@millershanks-london.co.uk
cc...
re... your homecoming

I'm trying to make everything perfectly lovely for your return (can't wait, darling!) and I thought I'd pop out to Liberty for some new silk flowers. I know we only got the lilies a couple of months ago, but they're awfully dusty. I thought I'd look for a sort of autumn bouquet, but would you rather soft pinks and yellows? Also, I'm restocking the fridge. Would you prefer Charles Heidseck or Mumm Cordon Rouge – the kitchen has both?

Love you/miss you . . . Sx

james_f_weissmuller@millershanks-ny.co.usa
14/1/00, 1.15pm (8.15am local)
to... harriet_greenbaum@millershanks-london.co.uk
cc...
re... concerns

You are quite right to share your concerns. David can be an obstinate so-and-so. I will deal with this from here. And thank you for the information. Your loyalty to the greater good of Miller Shanks will not be forgotten.

Jim

james_f_weissmuller@millershanks-ny.co.usa
14/1/00, 1.34pm (8.34am local)
to... david_crutton@millershanks-london.co.uk
cc...
re... Coke

David, a matter has been brought to my attention that troubles me enormously. I understand that 'IT'S IN THE CAN' is second-hand goods. I also understand that, despite knowing this, you intend to present it regardless.

This is not acceptable. It is shabby, dishonest and un-American. As CEO you surely know that when they set up shop in 1929 with just $50 and the Crabtree Cookies account, the founding principle of Donald K. Miller and Cyrus Shanks was 'To sell through integrity'. It has served us well these past seventy years, and your action is a scurrilous betrayal of our forebears.

It hurts me more than you could know to think that you are prepared to implicate Miller Shanks in the crime of handling stolen property.

You will now do the right thing. If you are in any doubt as to what this might be, I will lay it out for you.

Kill 'IT'S IN THE CAN' – no ifs, no buts.

Make immediate contact with Pertti van Helden. Beg, grovel, do whatever you have to do to get him and his campaign in London by Monday. As I said all along, his is excellent work. It recalls the heyday of great Coke advertising. I can only think that your negativity towards it was a result of envy.

And I recommend also that you use all your powers of persuasion to make Pinki Fallon retract her resignation. Given your own lamentable lack of integrity, you need hers very badly.

I do not need to tell you how disappointed I am.

Jim

david_crutton@millershanks-london.co.uk
14/1/00, 1.44pm
to... james_f_weissmuller@millershanks-ny.co.usa
cc...
re... Coke

Jim, you read my mind. Naturally as soon as I uncovered Simon Horne's despicable deception I knew straight away that we must purge ourselves of him and his work. The only reason for my delay was that I wished to test the ethical standards of my staff.

I am afraid that Pinki Fallon is the only one who emerged with any credit.

And while you know I do not share your enthusiasm for 'Fizzy Pop', I am already on the case with Pertti. I will keep you fully informed of developments.

David

David Crutton – 14/1/00, 1.52pm
to... Harriet Greenbaum
cc...
re... fucking disaster

A fucking rat has told Weissmuller about Simon's theft. I can only presume it was Pinki's warped idea of a leaving present. He is demanding we fly in van Helden. This is about as bad as things can get. No, it could be worse – he could bring Aqua with him. See me.

david_crutton@millershanks-london.co.uk
14/1/00, 2.13pm
to... pertti_vanhelden@millershanks-helsinki.co.fin
cc...
re... Coca-Cola

Long time, no hear, Pertti! I may have been a little brusque with you the other day. My humble apologies. My only excuse is that I have been under heavy pressure with the upcoming Coke pitch.

Speaking of which, I have been thinking deeply about our creative approach. I have come to the conclusion that the radical route that we developed in London is perhaps a little too risky and 'cutting-edge' for a company as conservative as Coke. My team and I took a second look at your campaign. As Harriet Greenbaum wrote in her e-mail to you, we were always greatly impressed by the Aqua campaign – we love the refreshing absence of irony and the childish sense of fun.

We are now of the opinion that your excellent creative work is precisely what we need to win this huge piece of business. It recalls the heyday of great Coke advertising and taps into the emotions evinced by, 'I'd like to teach the world to sing'. I don't need to tell a gifted adman such as yourself that nostalgia is perhaps the most powerful weapon in our armoury.

I am hugely sorry to put you to this trouble so late in the day, but I would very much like you to join our team for the presentation on Monday. I appreciate that it is far too eleventh hour to mobilise Aqua to attend. However, if we could have yourself and the work, I am sure we can put on a show that will have the ladies and gentlemen from Atlanta dancing in the aisles! I have informed Jim Weissmuller of my decision and he is looking forward immensely to seeing you.

My PA is looking into flights now. Please let me know as soon as possible how this last-minute request sits with your own schedule.

Yours sincerely,

David Crutton

David Crutton – 14/1/00, 2.15pm
to... Harriet Greenbaum
cc...
re... a job for you

I have just written to van Helden. Now I want to be sick. I think I am incapable of eating a second slice of humble pie and crawling past Pinki's sphincter. Please do it for me. Anyway, she is far more likely to listen to you.

David Crutton – 14/1/00, 2.19pm
to... Zoë Clarke
cc...
re... you

Where the hell are you? I need you to look into flight availability, Helsinki/London. And I need something to eat. Get me a bap. Any bap.

susi_judgedavis@millershanks-london.co.uk
14/1/00, 2.26pm
to... simon_horne@millershanks-london.co.uk
cc...
re... your homecoming

I got some divinely gorgeous silk roses – pinks, violets and fiery
yellows – and I found something else you'll love: aromatherapy
cushions for your sofas! I bought three. They're called 'Inspire',
'Revive' and 'Sensuous' and they were only £49.99 each. The lady
in Aroma Amour said they really help the creative mind find its
balance! Hope you don't mind but I moved the furniture round
a bit. I put the sofas in an 'L' under the windows and your desk
facing the door. I think it will make you look much more forceful
and commanding when people walk in. Write soon – can't wait
for Monday!! Sx

Harriet Greenbaum – 14/1/00, 2.33pm
to... David Crutton
cc...
re... Pinki

I have spoken to her and she was moved by your change of heart.
She's on her way in to help in whatever way she can with the
pitch. I'm sure it wasn't her who told Jim by the way – she hasn't
a political bone in her body.

I've blocked out most of the afternoon to adapt the pitch document to the Finnish campaign but if you need any help to smooth
Pertti's passage over, give me a shout.

pertti_vanhelden@millershanks-helsinki.co.fin
14/1/00, 2.57pm (4.57pm local)
to... david_crutton@millershanks-london.co.uk
cc...
re... Coca-Cola

My dear David,

All apologisings accepted. As fellow Chief I am familiarised with the gale-force pressures at the top. Jim is also phoning to beg me to be at your disposing. I am only too happy to be placing myself in your service and be 'pitching in'! I was making an earmark this weekend to teach my oldest boy the pleasure of the ice fishing, but not to matter. He is understanding since a small age that for the Warrior of Advertising, the battle is always coming first.

You are in good luck that the storyboards are already completing and we are ready to rock 'n' roll. And the excellent news is that as soon as I am reading your message I get onto the phone like quick lightning to the manager of Aqua. Can you believe that they are free and are very delighted to join our merry band? I am now confessing that I was foreseeing this outcoming so I am maintaining them on standby the whole week. Do not be worrying about booking tickets. This we are doing at our end of things. I am arriving in Luton International Airport on tomorrow at 1.00. Aqua are flying in their own pop-star executive plane charter on Sunday.

There is much to be discussing and planning but perhaps you are joining me for dinner tomorrow and we can chew the fats.

Tora, tora, tora!

Pertti

David Crutton – 14/1/00, 3.01pm
to... Harriet Greenbaum
cc...
re... it just got worse . . .

. . . he's bringing Aqua.

james_f_weissmuller@millershanks-ny.co.usa
14/1/00, 3.12pm (10.12am local)
to... harriet_greenbaum@millershanks-london.co.uk;
david_crutton@millershanks-london.co.uk
cc...
re... arrival

In light of today's events I have changed my travel plans. Rick Korning and I will fly in tomorrow morning at 8.30am. We will travel directly to the office, but would you let the Marriott know of our earlier arrival. David, I know that Rick is keen to take you through the two-year growth plan tomorrow evening. If Pertti has arrived it would be useful if he joined you. Harriet, if you are free, perhaps you could join me for dinner.

I look forward to seeing you both,

Jim

David Crutton – 14/1/00, 3.17pm
to... Harriet Greenbaum
cc...
re... dinner

Am I missing something here?

**david_crutton@millershanks-london.co.uk
14/1/00, 3.22pm**
to... james_f_weissmuller@millershanks-ny.co.usa
cc...
re... arrival

We're delighted that you're arriving sooner rather than later. Harriet would love to join you in the evening. Her inexperience can only be diminished by sitting at the feet of the Gods! It will also give her an opportunity to take you through my own new Five-point New Business Strategy. Until then, best wishes.

David

David Crutton – 14/1/00, 3.26pm
to... Zoë Clarke
cc...
re... job

Look in the new business files for a document called 'Five-point

Strategy, '95'. I think it has Westbrooke's name on the cover.
Bring it straight in. Don't make plans for this evening – once I
have amended it, you have some typing to do.

Pinki Fallon – 14/1/00, 3.35pm
to... Harriet Greenbaum
cc...
re... I'm back

Just got in. Anything I can do on Coke? ☺

Harriet Greenbaum – 14/1/00, 3.44pm
to... Pinki Fallon
cc...
re... I'm back

Thank heaven for that. Come and see me with Liam. The Finnish
campaign is diabolical. It's also TV only – perhaps the pair of
you can lend it some credibility with a few posters.

liam_okeefe@millershanks-london.co.uk
14/1/00, 4.12pm
to... brett_topowlski@millershanks-london.co.uk
cc...
re... *Carry On Advertising*

You will not believe the pure fucking farce that is playing out.
Someone told Tarzan F. Weissmuller that we were presenting hot
work and he turned moral majority. So Crutton's canned 'IT'S
IN THE CAN' and we're going with a piece of tosh they came
up with in Finland. I was in Harriet's gaff just now having a
look at a fax of the storyboards and it's ten times worse than
embarrassing. It has sunshine, dazzling smiles and teenagers that
make the Brady Bunch look like mother-fucking crackheads. And,
get this, it has Aqua singing a version of fucking 'Barbie Girl'.
Harriet asked us to do some posters for it to, you know, give it
an edge. Where the fuck do we begin?

Pinki's back. Apparently Tarzan F. made Crutton persuade her to return. She floated in on a perfect cloud of righteousness. That changed the moment she clapped eyes on the Scanda-bollocks. She's sitting at her desk now with her pen frozen over her pad – totally lost, poor cow.

If we win this pitch, I swear on the life of my mother I will hang up my Magic Markers and get a McJob.

melinda_sheridan@millershanks-london.co.uk
14/1/00, 4.22pm (8.22pm local)
to... harriet_greenbaum@millershanks-london.co.uk
cc...
re... LOVE update

We have had a day that can only be done justice to in the poetic words of Vincent – 'Bollock-bloating brilliant, pet.'

It started like all the others – appallingly. Having mislaid four LOVE girls we took carelessness to new heights by losing the last two. Sharon and Winona (Rides, would you credit?) succumbed to vicious attacks of botulism. I've lost count of the times I told them to steer clear of anything that looked as if it crawled along the seabed. As we gathered at breakfast you could have measured the long faces with a metre rule. But Brett and Vincent did me proud. After a couple of bacon rolls they sprang into action and plucked a new script from the ether. Let me describe it because it is their finest yet.

We open close up on the filthy tailgate of a truck. Bloke One (Vincent) walks into shot and with index finger writes in the grime: I WISH MY WIFE WAS AS DIRTY AS THIS VAN.

Exit Bloke One and we pause on his scribbling for a moment.

Enter Bloke Two (Brett, you guessed right) who reads the graffito before adding a postscript: SHE IS, MATE.

We then fade to black and a title:

THE LOVE CHANNEL
BUY HER A SUBSCRIPTION

BEFORE SOMEONE ELSE DOES.

We headed for the car park and commandeered a van (curiously, a Coke truck) and shot. It went like a dream, my darling. The hapless Frank Sinton joined us and said 'You could've shot this in Dalston bloody High Road.' But he was missing the point entirely – that point being awards, precious heart. Besides, he is Mr Yesterday and are we concerned for his opinion? Don't be so silly.

Danny Boy was flapping that we had not had this script approved by a living soul, but my two lads cared not a jot. To be honest I am beginning to acquire their taste for the dangerous life.

So our film is in the can at last. I am going to pack my bags and then we will party like it's 1999 – well, bless my silk socks, we just did that! I have my eye on a waiter who looks like Omar Sharif in *Dr Zhivago* – you know my weakness for a lush moustache.

Simon has gone to ground again. Not a whisper from the old gasbag. Is something afoot? Brett and Vincent have been wearing the expressions of the cats that inherited the St Ivel Creamery, and I think there's more to it than their cinematic triumph.

brett_topowlski@millershanks-london.co.uk
14/1/00, 4.30pm (8.30pm local)
to... liam_okeefe@millershanks-london.co.uk
cc...
re... *Carry On Advertising*

Are we brilliant or what, mate? We have shot the best film ever today. Remember the dirty van script – the first one we did on LOVE that Horne trashed? It starred yours truly and my lovely assistant, Vin. Apart from the fact that it took him twelve takes to spell DIRTY right, he was Bobby sodding de Niro.

Sounds like you're having a barrel of laughs over there. How the fuck did Finland get in on the act? Don't expect us to dig you out. As of Monday we're selling our butts to the highest bidder. This time I'm not getting out of my Slumberland for less than fifty grand and a 325i with a fuck-off sound system.

It's our wrap party now. We're going to watch Nathan and Mel fight over this waiter they've both been gagging for all week. See you Monday, or Sunday night. Assuming we're not too jetlagged and/or you're not impaling Lol on the shag pile.

David Crutton – 14/1/00, 4.43pm
to... All Departments
cc...
re... Coke

Everybody who has worked on Coke, or has even drunk one these past two weeks, will be at their desks tomorrow. I'm sure I can find plenty for you to do. Besides, James Weissmuller will be in the office and it is in all of our interests that he thinks none of us have lives beyond these four walls.

As for the rest of you, you will spend the next two days picking your most client-friendly outfits and working out how you will spend Monday showing more bustle than you have ever done. The pitch is at 12.00 and when the Coke people arrive this agency will not only shine like a new pin, it will crackle with activity.

Enjoy the weekend.

David Crutton
CEO

David Crutton – 14/1/00, 4.50pm
to... Rachel Stevenson
cc...
re... Coke

Further to my all-staffer, I would like you to calculate the empty secretarial desks we will have on Monday and fill them with temps. If they want something to do, hand them Bibles, and tell them to start typing at Genesis, Chapter 1, Verse 1.

daniel_westbrooke@millershanks-london.co.uk
14/1/00, 4.57pm (8.57pm local)
to... harriet_greenbaum@millershanks-london.co.uk
cc...

re... Coke

I have had no response to my earlier e-mail. If I am to play a leading role in Monday's meeting as my status dictates, I do not see how you can expect me to do so if I have not seen the work. Your six-monthly assessment is due shortly, Harriet, and you would do well to bear in mind that I am not always forgiving.

While I am writing, I should inform you that today Melinda, Brett and Vince shot a commercial that bore no resemblance to any script that had previously been approved. I made it quite clear to them that never in my time as Head of Client Services had I allowed anything like this to happen and that I wanted no part of it. I have tried to talk to David about it but he has not returned my calls. Please convey to him my profound misgivings about what has occurred here.

Zoë Clarke – 14/1/00, 5.05pm
to... Lorraine Pallister
cc...
re... tonight

Crutton has given me a five-point plan to retype for the morning!!! Seventy fucking pages to make five poxy points!!!!! Can't believe I'm losing my Friday night and my weekend as well!!!!!!!!!!!!!!

Harriet Greenbaum – 14/1/00, 5.11pm
to... David Crutton
cc...
re... Dan

He has been nagging all day for word on Coke. What, if anything, shall I tell him?

He is also bothered that the film they shot for LOVE today wasn't what was agreed. On the other hand, Mel e-mailed me to say they'd made excellent progress. She described the script and it sounds superb. Going by your criterion of 'just make sure they return with any film', they have more than met the brief.

Incidentally, I have no political agenda regarding Jim Weiss-muller. I had plans tomorrow night and I'm disappointed to have to break them. If you want to stand me down from dinner with him, I'd be delighted.

pertti_vanhelden@millershanks-helsinki.co.fin
14/1/00, 5.21pm (7.21pm local)
to... david_crutton@millershanks-london.co.uk
cc...
re... Coke

I am having last-minute brainstorms with my teams and we have some crazy-mad ideas that maybe we can incorporate.
• Coke baseball caps and bombing jackets to give a youthful, 'rock band' look.
• Decorating of the pitching room in an ocean theme to be reflecting the underwater world of Aqua. (I can supply Finnish herring artefacts for this purpose.)
• A musical poster lorry that is singing the song as the clients are leaving.
Let me know which of these are bowling your socks off. I will be at my workstation a few more hours yet and I am at your disposing – **Pertti**.

Nigel Godley – 14/1/00, 5.26pm
to... David Crutton
cc...
re... Coke

I have processed a number of purchase orders on the Coca-Cola pitch, so does that qualify me to work at the weekend? I do pop in most Saturdays and/or Sundays but tomorrow I am due to take part in a sponsored Hymn-a-thon for the St Mary's of Balham Steeple Fund. I would hate to let Father Clive down.

Nige

David Crutton – 14/1/00, 5.33pm
to... Nigel Godley
cc...
re... Coke

Use your own judgement.

David Crutton – 14/1/00, 5.42pm
to... Harriet Greenbaum
cc...
re... Dan

Tell him no more than he needs to know. Given that he will not
be attending the pitch, that means nothing.

Lorraine Pallister – 14/1/00, 5.59pm
to... Liam O'Keefe
cc...
re... get a bloody move on

When are you going to take me away from all this?

Liam O'Keefe – 14/1/00, 6.04pm
to... Lorraine Pallister
cc...
re... get a bloody move on

Not tonight. Me and Lily the Pink are trying to do Coke posters.
We're stuffed. I don't think I'll be going anywhere till Monday
PM.

Susi Judge-Davis – 14/1/00, 6.16pm
to... Creative Department
cc...
re... Simon's return

As you know Simon is back on Monday. You know he dislikes

people drifting in, so can we all make an extra-special effort to arrive on time? Also, could whoever put the life-size cut-out of Charlotte Church with the obscene speech bubble by the coffee machine please remove it? Just one other thing – please observe Simon's ban on smoking in the corridor. I notice that this has been ignored over the last few days.

Since Simon will be busy sorting out Coke I imagine he will want to delay the Monday morning progress meeting. I have pencilled it in for 8.45 on Tuesday. Please make sure that it is in your diaries.

Thx – Susi

daniel_westbrooke@millershanks-london.co.uk
14/1/00, 6.36pm (10.36pm local)
to... david_crutton@millershanks-london.co.uk
cc...
re... Harriet

I have been attempting to raise her all day so that she can bring me up to speed on Coke. I wish only to help. Perhaps my experience could afford some insights that may make the difference between defeat and victory. Would you have a quiet word and ask her to get in touch? You know that I hate to tattle, but I suspect she is avoiding me deliberately.

david_crutton@millershanks-london.co.uk
14/1/00, 6.42pm
to... daniel_westbrooke@millershanks-london.co.uk
cc...
re... Harriet

You may be thousands of miles and four time zones away, but even from there your powers of perception are staggering.

susi_judgedavis@millershanks-london.co.uk
14/1/00, 6.50pm
to... simon_horne@millershanks-london.co.uk

cc...
re... home news

Darling, I have finally got everything just how you like it. I can't wait for life to return to normal. I have briefed the department on your expectations. Pinki has let standards slide this week, so they needed to be reminded. I hope everything is well with you. I'm a little worried that I haven't heard from you all day. You're probably just unwinding after a hard shoot – I'm being silly aren't I? You relax and enjoy yourself. You deserve it . . . Sx

Nigel Godley – 14/1/00, 6.55pm
to... David Crutton
cc...
re... Coke

Father Clive was disappointed but he understands the importance of my career. He thinks he can find a replacement tenor. I'll see you tomorrow – Nige

Harriet Greenbaum – 14/1/00, 7.09pm
to... Pinki Fallon
cc...
re... Coke

Any joy on posters?

Pinki Fallon – 14/1/00, 7.14pm
to... Harriet Greenbaum
cc...
re... Coke

You're kidding aren't you? Ask us tomorrow morning . . . ☺

david_crutton@millershanks-london.co.uk
14/1/00, 7.22pm
to... pertti_vanhelden@millershanks-helsinki.co.fin
cc...
re... Coke

Thank you for your thoughts, Pertti. Like the Energiser Bunny, you just go on and on. You have some astonishing ideas, but I believe the secret of a successful pitch is to not have too much of a good thing. Until tomorrow.

Saturday
15 January
2000

David Crutton – 15/1/00, 11.23am
to... All Departments
cc...
re... meeting

Would everybody who is in to work on Coke (excluding Nigel Godley) assemble in the boardroom. James Weissmuller has arrived. He would like to meet you and make a brief announcement.

David Crutton
CEO

Zoë Clarke – 15/1/00, 11.59pm
to... Lorraine Pallister
cc...
re... yuck!

Crutton has just given me their lunch order. Big Jim wants sushi! Raw fish!!!! Disgusting!!!!!!!!!!!!!

Lorraine Pallister – 15/1/00, 12.02pm
to... Zoë Clarke
cc...
re... stars and tripe

Think of the speech he just made. When that much shit comes out of your mouth, you've got to replace it with something.

Pinki Fallon – 15/1/00, 12.58pm
to... Harriet Greenbaum
cc...
re... posters

We've got some ideas. Can't tell whether they're brilliant or crap. You'd better come and see them ... ☺

Harriet Greenbaum – 15/1/00, 1.22pm
to... David Crutton
cc...
re... Coke

Pinki and Liam have just shown me some posters, which we all agree are well below par. If you can free yourself from Jim and Rick for a few moments you should take a look.

David Crutton – 15/1/00, 1.27pm
to... Harriet Greenbaum
cc...
re... Coke

They're about to leave for their hotel. I'll be with you in ten minutes.

David Crutton – 15/1/00, 1.54pm
to... Harriet Greenbaum
cc...
re... Coke

You're right. Those posters are shit, but frankly I'm past caring.

Let's go with them. It wasn't my idea to present this campaign and when we lose the pitch I'm not going to carry the can.

Zoë Clarke – 15/1/00, 2.48pm
to...   David Crutton
cc...
re...   someone's here

Security called to say there's a man called Perry Van Halen in reception to see you. Shall I go and get him?

David Crutton – 15/1/00, 2.54pm
to...   Zoë Clarke
cc...
re...   someone's here

He's called Pertti van Helden. He's the CEO in Finland. Bring him up and be extremely nice to him.

David Crutton – 15/1/00, 2.58pm
to...   Harriet Greenbaum
cc...
re...   Pertti

Noggin the Nog is in the building. Why don't you come and be introduced?

lorraine_pallister@millershanks-london.co.uk
15/1/00, 3.34pm
to...   debbie_wright@littlewoods/manchester.co.uk
cc...
re...   what am I doing here?

We all had to come into work today because there's a massive presentation to Coke on Monday. Don't know why the fuck I am in. I haven't got any work to do, but I think it's about looking busy. The whole place is going more stupid than usual. The American President of Everything has arrived for it. He's wearing a blue striped shirt with a white collar and yellow braces. He's got a sidekick with him who's wearing the same gear, only with slightly narrower stripes and braces. It must be a sign of rank. Mr President gave us a speech. Remember the 'greed is good' number that Michael Douglas did in *Wall Street*? It wasn't anything like it – this one was bollocks. They must be spending a fortune. They're flying Aqua in for the meeting on Monday to sing a bloody thirty-second jingle. No sense, no taste, just too much fucking money. Get in touch soon and say something to keep me sane – Lolx

Lorraine Pallister – 15/1/00, 3.38pm
to... Liam O'Keefe
cc...
re... jump

You look like you need some executive stress relief. I've found a spare key to Daniel Westbrooke's office. He has a big sofa and a bottle of vodka in his fridge. See you there.

David Crutton – 15/1/00, 3.55pm
to... Harriet Greenbaum
cc...
re... posters

I have shown Van Halen (Zoë's slip of the keyboard but I rather like it) the posters and he loves them, especially the one with the musical notes coming out of the can. What the fuck do *we* know, eh? If you need to take him through the presentation I have put him up in Desperate Dan's office. Zoë is taking him down there now.

David Crutton – 15/1/00, 4.14pm
to... Liam O'Keefe
cc...
re... warning

You are very lucky that the man who just walked in on you with your spotty arse humping away comes from the Land of Mixed

Saunas and found the episode wholesomely touching. It could easily have been the other foreigner we have in our midst – the one who would be exercising his constitutional right to bear arms were it not for the airport x-ray machines. If you insist on shagging in the office, learn some discretion and lock the door from the inside. Or find a broom cupboard.

Sunday
16 January
2000

David Crutton – 16/1/00, 10.19am
to... Harriet Greenbaum
cc...
re... dinner

Last night I spent three hours at the Savoy Grill in the crashingly
dull company of Van Halen, Korning and Korning's stultifying
flow charts.

How was it for you and Jim? Did the earth move? I trust you
made me sound excellent.

Harriet Greenbaum – 16/1/00, 10.28am
to... David Crutton
cc...
re... dinner

It was very good, thank you. Jim is entertaining, if a little gung-ho.
I now know all there is to know about Florida big-game fishing,
his fifty-room house in the Hamptons and Mark McGwire's seventy home runs in a season. I'm afraid I wasn't able to present
your new business plan. Jim wanted to steer clear of shop talk.

Liam O'Keefe – 16/1/00, 11.43am
to… All Departments
cc…
re… marker pens

Having drawn my 5,000[th] Coke can I've finally run out of blood red Magic Markers (A313). Anyone got some?

Nigel Godley – 16/1/00, 11.52am
to… Liam O'Keefe
cc…
re… marker pens

I have a box of red biros. Any use? Nige

David Crutton – 16/1/00, 12.13pm
to… All Departments
cc…
re… pitch rehearsal

There will be a full-scale run-through at 1.00 in the boardroom. Everyone who needs to be in it, don't be late. The rest of you, some peace and quiet please.

David Crutton
CEO

Lorraine Pallister – 16/1/00, 1.58pm
to… Zoë Clarke
cc…
re… laugh? I pissed myself.

I just walked by the boardroom and heard DC and that Scandinavian weirdo doing a duet of 'Barbie Girl'. When they finished the Yanks were yelling 'Whoo! Way to Go! Whoo!' I think people here must get dumber as their salaries get bigger.

David Crutton – 16/1/00, 3.06pm
to… Harriet Greenbaum
cc…
re… what are we doing?

Being obliged to stand up and sing that ridiculous song with Van Halen as if it was the CEOs' karaoke night is about as humiliating as it can get. Whatever sins I have committed in my life, I have more than atoned for them now. Remind me when this is all over that my first priority is to rip out the Finn's liver while he is awake to enjoy it.

Zoë Clarke – 16/1/00, 3.35pm
to... David Crutton
cc...
re... someone else is here

Aqua are in reception. What do you want me to do with them?

David Crutton – 16/1/00, 3.38pm
to... Zoë Clarke
cc...
re... someone else is here

Get their fucking autographs. How should I know what to do with them, you dozy cow? Find Van Halen and get him to look after them. They were his imbecilic idea.

David Crutton – 16/1/00, 4.03pm
to... Harriet Greenbaum
cc...
re... tonight

Van Halen is insistent that I join him, Jim and Aqua at the sodding Fashion Café tonight – his fucking treat. I'm going to cry off with a migraine or something. Go for me. Please.

Harriet Greenbaum – 16/1/00, 4.09pm
to... David Crutton
cc...
re... tonight

Jim has already asked me. It's a shame you're not up to it. I actually think Pertti is about as far as you can get from being a

typical CEO, and all the more fun for it. If you're not there, I'll
see you tomorrow.

brett_topowlski@demon.co.uk – 16/1/00, 4.49pm
to... liam_okeefe@millershanks-london.co.uk
cc...
re... home sweet home

We're home. Pitcher and Piano on Upper St at seven. Vin will
whinge about Bruno. Apparently after a week with Godley he
gets jammed in the cat flap. Humour him.

Liam O'Keefe – 16/1/00, 5.06pm
to... Lorraine Pallister
cc...
re... the boys are back

I've got about another hour of this shit to do then I'm meeting
them in Islington. You on for it?

Monday
17 January
2000

David Crutton – 17/1/00, 7.57am
to... Susi Judge-Davis
cc...
re... Simon

The minute he gets in ask him to come and see me. We have much catching up to do and I am sure he would like to see what we have done to his Coke idea. After that I'd like to see Vince Douglas.

Daniel Westbrooke – 17/1/00, 8.02am
to... David Crutton
cc...
re... good day!

In my excitement to view the Coke work I broke all records getting here. When can I get together with yourself and Jim? I spent a good deal of the flight home making notes for my introductory speech to the client and I would appreciate your wise input.

Have you caught up yet with Simon? I believe he took an earlier plane on Friday, so I presume he was in at the weekend.

Let me know when is a good time.

David Crutton – 17/1/00, 8.15am
to... Daniel Westbrooke
cc...
re... good day

You're not good at hints, are you? Let me be blunt. I feel it would be unfair reward to the enormous efforts that Harriet and others have made over the last week to give you the starring, or indeed any, role in this pitch. You have no idea of the difficulties we have faced while you were topping up your Air Miles. Before you run to Jim, he agrees that we shouldn't overload the meeting with superfluous bodies. Besides, he is making puppy dog eyes at Harriet – I don't think your Tuscany timeshare will cut it any more.

As for Simon, no I haven't seen him, but he'll be dog meat the moment I do.

Susi Judge-Davis – 17/1/00, 8.31am
to... David Crutton
cc...
re... Simon

No sign of Simon yet – probably stuck in traffic. I'm sure he'll be straight up the second he arrives. I'll pass the message on to Vince.

Daniel Westbrooke – 17/1/00, 8.44am
to... Rachel Stevenson
cc...
re... PA

It is almost 9.00 and I hope that when the clock strikes I will witness the arrival of the highly qualified new PA you promised

me over a week ago. If this is not the case, then be warned that
I am in no mood to be messed about today.

Melinda Sheridan – 17/1/00, 8.49am
to... Harriet Greenbaum
cc...
re... Simon

I don't know quite who to tell this, but I have a horrible feeling
that Simon has gone AWOL. I told you that we didn't see him
at all on Friday, and when we asked at the desk on Saturday
morning they said he'd already checked out. Dan assumed he'd
merely rushed back in his eagerness to flex his biceps on Coke,
but something about the smirks on the faces of Brett and Vincent
told a different story. I called him at home yesterday but Celine
had neither seen nor heard a thing. I think I might have spread
panic in the Horne *ménage*.

Between you and me, I fear the worst. I know that he's a big boy
and can look after himself, but as the producer on the shoot I
do feel responsible for not accounting for all my little ducklings.
What do you suggest I do now? Won't David be livid when he
finds he's not here to do his duty at the pitch?

Harriet Greenbaum – 17/1/00, 9.02am
to... Melinda Sheridan
cc...
re... AWOL

If you forgot to pack Simon in your suitcase you've most likely
done us all a favour. David will only be livid because he'll have
to delay satisfying his bloodlust. See Pinki and tell her she has
my permission to give you the story.

Oh, and welcome home.

Susi Judge-Davis – 17/1/00, 9.04am
to... Brett Topowlski
cc...
re... welcome back

David Crutton would like to see Vince immediately. I know he doesn't use e, so could you tell him?

Brett Topowlski – 17/1/00, 9.07am
to... Liam O'Keefe
cc...
re... dead man walking

Susi told me that DC wants to see Vin. I could feel her e-mail gloating. Vin wonders if he can sue Crutton for racial discrimination?

Liam O'Keefe – 17/1/00, 9.12am
to... Brett Topowlski
cc...
re... dead man walking

For being a scally? Just tell him to take his punishment like a man. And can I have his Anglepoise, rubber plant, set square, pen pot . . .

David Crutton – 17/1/00, 9.17am
to... Zoë Clarke
cc...
re... shape up

Where is the blue suit you promised to have back from the dry cleaner first thing? I'll feel enough of a pillock at this pitch without having to do it in my underpants.

Liam O'Keefe – 17/1/00, 9.20am
to... Brett Topowlski
cc...
re... dead man walking

. . . steel ruler, ashtray, marker rack . . .

Harriet Greebaum – 17/1/00, 9.25am
to... David Crutton
cc...
re... the *Sun* never shines

Bad news I'm afraid. When Jim's taxi driver realised he was heading here this morning he went into a cabby's rant about the depravity of the LOVE Channel and their ad agency, regurgitating, with a little embellishment, last week's *Sun* scoop. Jim is none too thrilled. He made me dig out the paper and he's reading it on my sofa now. I'm sure he'll be up when he's through. I thought you were going to tell him.

David Crutton – 17/1/00, 9.32am
to... Harriet Greenbaum
cc...
re... the *Sun* never shines

I thought *you* were. At least I can inform him that I've fired Vince. I knew this was going to be a piss-poor day the moment I saw Van Halen arrive. He's sitting on Zoë's desk trying to tempt her with some dried reindeer meat.

Brett Topowlski – 17/1/00, 9.39am
to... Liam O'Keefe
cc...
re... dot cum

Vin is clearing his desk and I've just written my resignation. With Horne MIA, who the fuck do I give it to? Want some top news though? Remember I sent a copy of that little film you shot to Glenn and Toni at Grey? Remember I told you ages ago that Toni had his own home page? Click on **http//www.antonio.com**. Horne has joined Pammy and Tommy in the land of cyber-erotica. Tommy's dick is bigger, but I'd say the ladyboy has better implants than Pammy.

David Crutton – 17/1/00, 9.56am
to... All Departments
cc...
re... Vince Douglas

This morning I have had to take the unpleasant step of sacking Vince Douglas of the creative department. This is solely because of the comments he made to a journalist last week regarding not only the agency, but also one of our clients. These remarks were wholly unauthorised and led to some extremely negative PR.

As you know, I would not usually make someone's humiliation so public. But the action taken against Vince Douglas serves as an example of what will happen to anybody who breaks their contract and speaks to the press without prior permission.

I did not wish to start such an auspicious day in our history on a low note. Perhaps now we can put this distasteful episode behind us and move onward to greatness.

Let's win Coke!

David Crutton
CEO

Susi Judge-Davis – 17/1/00, 10.12am
to... Melinda Sheridan
cc...
re... Simon

It's not like Simon to be so late, especially on such a big day. Did he say anything about his plans on the way back?

Melinda Sheridan – 17/1/00, 10.20am
to... Susi Judge-Davis
cc...
re... Simon

My dear Susi, has nobody said a thing? I suspect that Simon may not be back for a little while, and when he does appear, it will probably be only a flying visit. If you want my advice, darling, I'd call Alfred Marks, Kelly Girl or whoever it is that you use these days and investigate your options.

Rachel Stevenson – 17/1/00, 10.22am
to... David Crutton
cc...
re... Brett

I'm sorry to bother you this morning of all mornings but I have Brett Topowlski with me. He has just tendered his resignation. In Simon's absence would you like me to accept it?

David Crutton – 17/1/00, 10.25am
to... Rachel Stevenson
cc...
re... Brett

I'd say he's lucky he didn't get fired with his mate. Get him out of here.

Harriet Greenbaum – 17/1/00, 10.29am
to... Pinki Fallon; Liam O'Keefe
cc...
re... Coke

I have just spoken to Jim Weissmuller who now feels that although you didn't do the work, it would be a mistake not to have a British creative presence in the pitch. Would you both be free?

Pinki Fallon – 17/1/00, 10.38am
to... Harriet Greenbaum
cc...
re... Coke

Liam is wearing the T-shirt he had on all weekend – it's covered in red marker and pizza – and I'm not exactly dressed for the Oscars, but we'd be glad to come. Do we have to pretend to like the work? ☺

Harriet Greenbaum – 17/1/00, 10.43am
to... Pinki Fallon
cc...
re... Coke

Yes, I'm afraid you do – that's normally how it works. And don't worry about how you look. It's called being creative.

Nigel Godley – 17/1/00, 10.50am
to... Rachel Stevenson
cc...
re... David Crutton

Dear Rachel,

You will have read the all-staff e-mail that David Crutton sent where he publicly excluded me from a meeting on Saturday. Now he is treating Vince Douglas like a criminal just because he exercised his right in a so-called 'free society' to speak his mind to the press. I feel that I must now make a stand and resign. I cannot work in a company that constantly gags its employees as if we were in Russia.

Yours sincerely,

Nigel Godley

Susi Judge-Davis – 17/1/00, 10.51am
to... Rachel Stevenson
cc...
re... Simon

Will someone please tell me what is going on. Simon has disappeared and all I get are sniggers when I ask anyone where he is. Does nobody realise that Simon is one of the most important people in this place, and that I am his Executive Personal Assistant? Will you at least treat me with some respect and inform me of what is happening?

Daniel Westbrooke – 17/1/00, 10.52am
to... Rachel Stevenson
cc...
re... I'm waiting

There is no sign of my new PA and no word from you as to when she will arrive. Do you really expect the Head of Client Services to fetch his own coffee and make his own telephone calls? If you do not deal with this in a prompt and satisfactory manner, Rachel, I will have no hesitation in taking it up with David and, if necessary, James Weissmuller while he is here.

Rachel Stevenson – 17/1/00, 11.04am
to... Daniel Westbrooke; Nigel Godley; Susi Judge-Davis
cc...
re... enough is enough

Daniel, believe it or not, finding you a new PA isn't the most important job on my list. Until I get round to it, please try to cope like the rest of us. I didn't rise to become Head of Personnel by being rude, so I will stop myself there.

Nigel, nobody is gagging you. If you really want to leave, then do so, but please do not make it a point of principle.

Susi, I don't know where Simon is either. Unlike you, I don't really care. Maybe people would stop sniggering and treat you with respect if you didn't stamp your foot like a two-year-old and learned some manners.

I apologise for writing to the three of you together, but I, for one, have work to do and it saves time.

Liam O'Keefe – 17/1/00, 11.24am
to... Brett Topowlski
cc...
re... don't leave me this way

Harriet's told us we're needed in the pitch. I'm worried – I don't think I'll be able to stop pissing myself when Aqua take the stage. Have you seen them setting up in the boardroom? They look like a Hanna Barbera cartoon. You guys better not leave without saying goodbye. If you hang on till I'm through we can go out and get well and truly lashed.

I just got Simon's quivering arse up onto the net for Pinki. If you listen out, you can hear her shrieks of disgust. Who'd have thought hardcore could be so damn amusing?

David Crutton – 17/1/00, 11.47am
to... All Departments
cc...
re... our finest hour

In little over ten minutes we embark on a journey that could set us fair for a glorious future. James Weissmuller is with me now and he joins me in thanking every one of you for your enormous efforts, whatever the outcome.

Wish us well.

David Crutton
CEO

Lorraine Pallister – 17/1/00, 12.16pm
to... Zoë Clarke
cc...
re... in Miller Shanks, no-one can hear you scream

Hasn't it gone quiet? Even Susi has stopped whinging. Is it always like this when there's a pitch?

Zoë Clarke – 17/1/00, 12.23pm
to... Lorraine Pallister
cc...
re... in Miller Shanks no-one can hear you scream

Only the ones where half the agency's jobs rest on the outcome. It was nice knowing you!!!!!!!!!

Brett Topowlski – 17/1/00, 12.36pm
to... Liam O'Keefe
cc...
re... brace yourself

Vin is about to break the habit of a lifetime. He's asked me to boot up his Mac. He's going to send an e.

Vince Douglas – 17/1/00, 12.54pm
to... All Departments
cc...
re... my first e-male

right you twats heres somthing to make you hard/moyst (deleet as apliable) **http//www.antonio.com**

enjoy

luv you

vin

Zoë Clarke – 17/1/00, 1.06pm
to... Lorraine Pallister
cc...
re... OH, MY GOD!!!!!!!!!!!!!!!!!!!!!!!!!!!!!!

That's truly gross!!!

Lorraine Pallister – 17/1/00, 1.13pm
to... Zoë Clarke
cc...
re... OH, MY GOD!!!!!!!!!!!!!!!!!!!!!!!!!!!!!!

I told you it was disgusting. I think Judge Dredd has just clocked it. I can hear her struggling with the child-proof cap on her Valium. Going for beers with V&B later?

Brett Topowlski – 17/1/00, 2.15pm
to... All Departments
cc...
re... and now the end is near

It's time for us to go. Those of you that we like (you know who you are) can join us in Bar Zero where we'll be available for premium beers, wines and spirits for the remainder of the day. The rest of you can piss off – Brett + Vin

PS: if you're doing a whip-round, Vin wants a Dreamcast and I want cash to pay my bike insurance.

Zoë Clarke – 17/1/00, 2.49pm
to... All Departments
cc...
re... Coke

The presentation is over and David has told me to ask you all to be at your desks as he's taking the clients on a short tour of the agency. Smile please! Zoë x

David Crutton – 17/1/00, 3.32pm
to... Harriet Greenbaum
cc...
re... pitch

That was an excruciating embarrassment. I had Weissmuller and Korning on either side of me in a frenzy of toe-tapping. If Van Halen had got out a lighter and held it aloft, I wouldn't have been surprised. And do you think the clients actually liked the work? I have a creepy feeling they did.

Anyway, you'd better come up to my office. Pertti, Jim and Aqua are on their way and the back slapping is about to begin.

And what's this website that everyone is referring to?

David Crutton – 17/1/00, 3.47pm
to... All Departments
cc...
re... Coke

I am sure you are all eager to know how it went. I don't believe a stronger strategic or creative case for Coca-Cola to come to Miller Shanks could have been made. Our performance made me proud to be your Chief Executive.

TBWA, WCRS, McCann Erickson and O&M have also made

their bids, and now we must wait. I understand it will be a couple of days. Fingers crossed.

David Crutton
CEO

Daniel Westbrooke – 17/1/00, 3.53pm
to... Harriet Greenbaum
cc...
re... thoughts

I'm sorry I haven't been able to speak to you today, but I've been terribly busy catching up. Congratulations on your handling of Coke. It is a shame that, from what I can gather, we do not stand a realistic chance of winning. However the experience will stand you in good stead for the future.

While I was away I had an opportunity to mull over some ideas for a restructuring of the account management function. I foresee a redefined role for you: less hands-on client responsibility, more getting stuck into the graduate intake and taking a firm grasp of the staff training nettle.

As you know, I am a confirmed believer in nurturing tomorrow's little Cruttons and Westbrookes, and I think you have a gift for teaching as opposed to doing. Of course, I have to run these thoughts past David, but perhaps the two of us could get together and chew the unsaturated.

Ken Perry – 17/1/00, 3.58pm
to... All Departments
cc...
re... pop groups

The reception area is presently being overrun by young girls who are here to see the pop group Aqua. The furnishings and carpeting of the frontal lobby zone were not designed to cope with the stresses imposed by large numbers of children of school age unaccompanied by responsible adults.

This incident serves as a good example of why myself or a member of my department must be informed prior to the arrival of members of the showbusiness fraternity, so that we can ensure that adequate security is in place.

Thank you for your co-operation.

Ken Perry
Office Administrator

Harriet Greenbaum – 17/1/00, 4.14pm
to... Daniel Westbrooke
cc...
re... thoughts

Thanks for your e-mail. By the strangest coincidence, I have just a few moments ago been talking to Jim Weissmuller about my own ideas on a more efficient structure for account management. We must get together and pool our thinking. Let me know when you would like to do it.

David Crutton – 17/1/00, 4.33pm
to... Susi Judge-Davis
cc...
re... Liam

If he is around tell him I would like a chat. I have a suspicion he can tell me much about this website upon which your erstwhile boss's buttocks figure so prominently. If I'd known he was that hairy, believe me, I would never have hired him.

Susi Judge-Davis – 17/1/00, 4.41pm
to... David Crutton
cc...
re... Liam

He, like the rest of the department, is in Bar Zero getting disgustingly drunk with Brett and Vince. I will leave a Post-it on his desk. Now, if you don't mind, I would like to go home. This has been a very difficult day.

Kelly Derringer / k_derringer@cokeGB.com
17/1/00, 5.12pm
to... david_crutton@millershanks-london.co.uk
cc...
re... your presentation to Coca-Cola

Dear David,

Thank you for a quite outstanding presentation. There was so much to be impressed by, not least the strong evidence of international co-operation with your Helsinki office. This is something we are looking for in our search for a more homogenous approach across our European markets.

We also loved the creative. It is bright and cheerful, and in Aqua you have found the elusive vehicle that appeals to a multiplicity of age groups. Not only am I a fan, but so, too, are my twelve-year-old son and six-year-old daughter!

Allow me to cut to the chase. When we left TBWA on Friday we had them in first place. My team and I felt that it would take a superlative pitch from you to remove them from that position.

On the return journey to our offices we were unanimous in agreeing you delivered just that. We further agreed that it would serve no purpose to delay our verdict. It therefore gives me great pleasure to say that we would very much like to award our advertising account to Miller Shanks.

There only remains the issue of agreeing remuneration levels. However, I anticipate no major hurdles in this regard. I would be grateful if you could call my office to arrange a time in the next day or two to discuss. I would also be grateful if you could keep the news within the confines of your offices until we have had the opportunity to formally tell the other four competing agencies of our decision.

Congratulations, David. I am very much looking forward to getting down to work with you and your excellent team. There is much to do!

Yours truly,

Kelly Derringer,
Senior Vice President, Marketing and Promotion, Coca-Cola GB

David Crutton – 17/1/00, 5.20pm
to... All Departments
cc...
re... Coke

WE WON! CHAMPAGNE AND COKE IN THE BOARDROOM NOW!

David Crutton – 17/1/00, 6.58pm
to... Harriet Greenbaum
cc...
re... dinner

My apologies, but I won't be able to join you and the Coke team for dinner tonight. Jim wants a private chat before he flies out. After this afternoon's triumph, it seems he has plans for me. Don't worry, I won't forget you from my throne at the right hand of JFW.

Tuesday
18 January
2000

Harriet Greenbaum – 18/1/00, 8.47am
to... David Crutton
cc...
re... Coke

Since Kelly is in at 4.30, I thought it would be sensible to present her with a management structure for our handling of the account. I've drawn up an outline. Can I have some time this morning to talk it through?

You'll be pleased to know that Pertti missed you last night. He climbed onto the table and sang 'I Need a Hero' in your honour. It was very funny, but I guess you had to be there.

Zoë Clarke – 18/1/00, 9.10am
to... Harriet Greenbaum
cc...
re... Coke

I got your voicemail about putting a time in with David. Is 11.15 OK? He's not here yet but I'll tell him when he arrives.

Zoë Clarke – 18/1/00, 9.19am

to... Lorraine Pallister

cc...

re... my fucking head!!!!!!

I can hardly see for this headache and I threw up on the platform at Baker Street!!!!!!! I'll never, ever, ever, ever drink again, I swear!!!!!!!!! Anyway, I bloody rushed in, didn't I, and David's only decided to have his first late start for a million, zillion years!!!!!!!!!! He's just phoned me from his car. He'll be another half hour!!!!!! What happened to you? The last time I saw you, Liam had his head up your skirt!!!!!! Good time then?!!!!

Zoë Clarke – 18/1/00, 9.43am

to... Lorraine Pallister

cc...

re... Crettin

He's just got here. Told me to cancel all his meetings and not put any calls through!!!!!!!!!!! I told him Harriet needed to see him and he threw his mobile at me!!!!!!!!!!!!!! Then he went into his office and slammed the door!!!!!! He's really pissed off!!!!!!!!!!!!!!

David Crutton – 18/1/00, 9.48am

to... Harriet Greenbaum

cc...

re... you

My conversation with Weissmuller contained some unanticipated twists. He is not entirely happy. It follows then that neither am I. See me now.

Daniel Westbrooke – 18/1/00, 10.29am

to... David Crutton

cc...

re... Coke

I am sorry that I did not have the chance to congratulate you personally. This is a staggering win. There are plenty of moaning minnies both inside and outside the agency who questioned our ability to pull it off, but I said all along that with you at the helm we'd prove them wrong. I had a good feeling about it right at the very start when I met with Coke to take the brief.

Now the real work begins. I stayed late last night to draft a structure for our administration of the business, and I would like to talk it over with you. When would you be free?

David Crutton – 18/1/00, 10.37am
to... Daniel Westbrooke
cc...
re... Coke

fuck off

**liam_okeefe@millershanks-london.co.uk
18/1/00, 10.51am**
to... brett_topowlski@demon.co.uk
cc...
re... very weird

You up yet or did you choke on your own vomit and die in your sleep? There's some strange things going on here. Harriet had a closed-doors session with Crutton and according to the Zoë grapevine there was some serious shouting and chucking of hard objects. Harriet came down a few minutes ago and dragged Pinki off to the ladies. I sent Lol in to earwig and it turns out Tarzan F. has put Crutton on a yellow card – the *Sun*, the Great Coke Robbery, Carla Browne's drug allegations, Kimbelle, you name it. His failure to spend four hours a day doing Tarzan-style ab crunches probably got chucked in as well. Crutton's job description obliges him to pass the blame on, so he's sticking it to Harriet – claims she's stitching him up. If you ask me, Weissmuller's being a tad ungrateful. Doesn't winning Coke count for something? Don't get me wrong, I'm not feeling sorry for Crutton, I just hate those fucking Yanks. Tossers.

Anyway, get out of bed and get a job. I'm sick of paying my taxes and watching idle spongers like you sit around watching Jerry Springer. I read the *Mail*, you know.

Kelly Derringer / k_derringer@cokeGB.com
18/1/00, 11.13am
to... david_crutton@millershanks-london.co.uk
cc... james_f_weissmuller@millershanks-ny.co.usa
re... change of circumstances

Dear David,

It is with the deepest regret that I am writing this, but I feel I have no other choice.

Last night I arrived home to find my son on his PC. Ordinarily the private activities of my family would be no concern of yours, but this situation is very different. I told him about our new advertising agency and to show off his computer skills he keyed in Miller Shanks and executed an internet search.

The result of this was a short video clip. It featured your Executive Creative Director and a transvestite performing an act of unspeakable depravity in the very office I was given a tour of yesterday afternoon.

You will appreciate that I had no option other than to break the news of this distressing discovery to my colleagues this morning. After a short discussion we were of one mind.

A brand like Coca-Cola, with its proud history of clean living and family values, could never be placed into the trust of those who maintain such libertine standards.

It is therefore with sadness that I inform you we have decided not to award our advertising account to Miller Shanks after all. As you will read in the trade press, we have handed TBWA the challenge of representing us.

Once again I would like to thank you for a highly professional presentation. I am only sorry that it gave a less than candid picture of the full breadth of your agency's abilities.

If I may close on a personal note, it sickens me to the marrow that I have been exposed to the perverted antics that you allow to go on in your offices. However, there are not the words to describe how angry I feel that my two young children have also been scarred by them.

Yours sincerely,

Kelly Derringer
Senior Vice President, Marketing and Promotion, Coca-Cola GB

Zoë Clarke – 18/1/00, 11.19am
to... Ken Perry
cc...
re... emergency

A window has been accidentally broken in David's office! Could we have a couple of your lads to clean it up please? Ta!!

liam_okeefe@millershanks-london.co.uk
18/1/00, 11.31am
to... brett_topowlski@demon.co.uk
cc...
re... your leaving present

You know you and Vin were too arse-holed to ride your bikes home last night and left them parked out front? Your R1 now has an accessory that Yamaha never dreamed of – Crutton's laptop is buried in the petrol tank. I think we just lost Coke.

Monday
7 February
2000

liam_okeefe@millershanks-london.co.uk
7/2/00, 10.31am
to... brett-topowlski@tbwa.co.uk;
vince-douglas@tbwa.co.uk
cc...
re... welcome back

So, how was Tenerife? You got pissed, shagged and tanned, yes? You surprise me. Anyway, hope you're nicely rested up for your first day at TBWA. What are you working on? Don't tell me. Coke. By the way, when you see Beattie, tell him from me, if he wants to call himself a copywriter he should use his sodding spellchecker – 'fcuk', I ask you.

You missed the first airing of your LOVE ad. I caught it in the *South Park* break on Friday. Stonking effort, boys. Except Lol says you should've got your hair cut, Vin.

You also missed a top leaving do for Crutton last week. As our longest serving senior arsehole, Desperate Dan made a sincere and moving speech. It featured the words 'major', 'contribution', 'advertising' and 'history'. You get the drift. The whip-round had raised all of forty-seven quid, but Crutton only stayed half an hour and wasn't there for the presentation of six Dartington tumblers in a hand-tooled leatherette presentation casket – ungrateful tosser.

Miller Shanks Bucharest won't know what's hit them. Give the poor bastards a couple of weeks and they'll be dreaming of the carefree days of Communism.

Judge Dredd has taken to working for Dan like a dream. She's already sounding off that she's PA to one of the most senior figures in advertising and she should be shown a little more respect – Dateline couldn't have made a better match.

Lol looks a treat in her power suit outside Barry Clement's office. He hasn't arrived yet, but I hope he doesn't give the future Mrs O'Keefe (look, she's met my mum and that's as good as a ring in my book) the notion that she's too important for me. Mind you, her saucy mate, Debbie, started this morning so there's always Plan B.

All the changes haven't affected Pinki a bit. She's the same fruitbat as ever. Her hypnotherapist told her she's the reincarnation of Ernest Hemingway. That would explain both her writing abilities and the fact that she's started smoking cheroots.

Still no sign of Horne, and they can't fire him until they find him. He's a slippery cunt alright, but Ronnie Biggs he ain't. He'll turn up sooner or later. There's gossip that the CEO of MS Manila spotted him outside a drag bar. There's also a rumour he's getting a prime-time slot on LOVE presenting 'Live from Madam Jo-jo's' – no, I just made that up.

That's all the news that's fit to print. Give me a bell as soon as they plug in your phones. I've got work to do now – casting for a bloke to play opposite Gloria Hunniford in the new Freedom ad. Has to be young enough to look like her toy boy but not young enough to be her son. It's a fine fucking line we tread.

I'll close on an item from *The Twilight Zone*. Lol just took a call from Quentin Tarantino's agent who was wondering when the Kimbelle shoot was so they could work it into QT's hectic schedule. You figure that out.

Harriet Greenbaum – 7/2/00, 11.11am
to... Zoë Clarke
cc...
re... I'm parched

If you could take your nose out of *Cosmo* for one moment, a fresh pot of coffee would be nice.

Harriet Greenbaum – 7/2/00, 11.25am
to... All Departments
cc... james-f-weissmuller@millershanks-ny.co.usa
re... A NEW DAWN

It has been a turbulent start to the year, but I am certain the changes that have resulted are both exciting and positive.

Firstly, I would like to say an enormous thank you to David Crutton. His Herculean efforts have given us a solid foundation upon which to build a bright future. His forceful personality and ceaseless dynamism are our loss and Romania's gain.

Secondly, I would like you to join me in congratulating Dan Westbrooke as he takes up his important new role. As Director of Resource and Training, the graduate intake programme is in excellent hands.

And finally I would like you to offer your full support to our new creative directors.

Over the last six months Pinki Fallon has demonstrated both her dedication and flair on countless occasions. She deserves this opportunity to lead Miller Shanks in the quest for creative excellence.

In Barry Clement, who joins us today from Abbott Mead Vickers, she has a charming, experienced and incredibly talented deputy.

Pinki's promotion and Barry's arrival stand as a symbol of our determination to rise to a position of pre-eminence in British advertising.

Let's help them get off to a flying start by winning the Barbie pitch!

Harriet Greenbaum
CEO

Pinki Fallon – 7/2/00, 11.34am
to... Harriet Greenbaum
cc...
re... Barbie

Harriet, you know my reservations. I find it hard to condone a product that cynically exploits girls at a vulnerable age and presents them with oppressive stereotypes. I'd feel more comfortable with it if we proposed a fundamental repositioning of their entire product range. Think of the positive role models we could give children. Imagine Lesbian Trucker Barbie, Single-Mum Barbie or Size-16 Barbie. Perhaps Barry and myself should get together with a couple of teams and brainstorm this ... ☺